Databyte

Cat Connor

I0661313

9mm Press
New Zealand

Databyte © 2014 by Cat Connor

ISBN ePub: 978-0-6159833-5-6
ISBN: 978-1-311290410
ISBN Draft2Digital: 978-1-0670072-2-5
Cover design by 9mm Press
Interior design by 9mm Press

Acknowledgements

This is the second of two books I wrote while cancer consumed my mother.

Mum would say to me, "You should be working."

And every time I'd reply, "I am."

Thanks, Mum.

There are some people I need to acknowledge, people who hung in there and never faltered when it got rough. So to Anna, Carolyn, Dave, Megan, Murray, and Rosanne, thank you for being remarkable and for showing up when I needed you. Words can't express how much that means to me.

Right, now that's out of the way ...

Special thanks to Mark Valley for taking the time to talk to me about acting. Would've been a helluva lot harder coming up with Mike Davenport without you. So, thanks, Mark, you rock.

Thanks to Jayne Southern, my fabulous editor at Rebel ePublishers, who believes in me even when I don't ... we didn't even argue this time!

And for the wonders of wine and coffee ...

I say, Thank you God for Pinot Noir and Italian roast espresso.

For Dad.

There is a crack in everything,
that's how the light gets in.

Leonard Cohen (Anthem)

Chapter One
Poker Face

"Special Agent Ellie Conway?" said the suit standing in my office doorway. He wore a visitor's badge clipped to his lapel.

"Yes, and you are?"

He held up identification. Looked like a gold shield. Every man, dog, and parrot in D.C. has a shield.

"Aaron Keller, can I come in?"

"Please and show me that again." I moved my mouse pointer to hide the work on my desktop. Just in case. "Have a seat, Mr. Keller."

He showed me his shield again. He was a Metro cop, a detective.

"I'd like to ask you a few questions, if I may."

It sounded like a request but it really wasn't.

"What can I help you with?"

"This morning we found a hand ..." He paused, gauging my reaction.

A hand? He didn't get sent boxes of ass then, or have pizza delivered by a torso? A solitary hand won't impress me much.

"A hand? Do you have any more information than that?"

"Yes, ma'am. Fingerprints tell us the hand belongs to Edward Connelly."

What now?

"Hang on, you're saying it is Eddie Connelly's hand?"

"Yes, ma'am."

I chewed my lip. I knew a smirk would tweak my lips as the news set in. It's very hard to explain to people who haven't met Eddie how awful a person he is and how much I wouldn't miss him, should he die a horrible slow death. I dared not hope that that had happened.

"That's pretty damn careless of Eddie." People don't usually lose their hands. They're not the sort of thing anyone puts down and leaves without. "Where is the rest of him and do his parents know?"

"We don't know where the rest of him is. I was hoping you'd be able to help us locate the rest of Mr. Connelly."

"I haven't seen him in two years. There's an ongoing protection restraining order against him to safeguard my daughter."

"We know, ma'am. We also understand you threatened to kill him numerous times prior to taking out the restraining order."

How would they know that? The times when I threatened Eddie, we were alone, or at his parents' home. Oh, of course. Beatrice Connelly, the ex-mother-in-law from hell. Bet she couldn't wait to drop that on the cop. The restraining order also included her.

"What can you tell me about the hand?"

"I can't tell you anything. You're a potential suspect."

Well, that was honest of him.

I sighed. "I didn't kill Eddie. Nor did I chop off his

hand."

If I'd lopped off a body part, it would've been his poisonous tongue in preference to his fat hand.

He looked a little uncomfortable.

Oh. Yuck.

"He wasn't dead when the hand was removed?"

"I can't talk to you about the case."

I moved my mouse pointer. Work filled my screen. At the bottom corner sat the icon for our intranet chat program. I double-clicked Delta A. The window opened. I typed one word – *trouble* – and closed the window.

"Do you have any leads or any suspects, you know, real ones, not me?" I said, rocking back in my chair. Kurt appeared in my open doorway. "Come in, Kurt."

He walked into the room followed by Sam and Lee. The feel of the room changed, it tipped more in my favor.

Keller turned his head and faced with a wall of men, he scrambled to his feet and stuttered, "Aaron Keller, Metro PD, Detective Aaron Keller."

Lee shook his hand. "What are you detecting?" he asked with a good-natured smile.

"Not much," I interjected. "Seems Metro found Eddie Connelly's hand and think I chopped it off."

Detective Keller sat back down. I think he was trying to pretend the room wasn't stuffed with large men. Good luck.

Kurt suppressed a smile. "That's not likely."

Keller honed in on Kurt. "Why do you say that?"

"Because Agent Conway would be more likely to shoot

him. She doesn't like being close to Mr. Connelly."

Eddie Connelly was the epitome of the bottom of an ashtray filled with bourbon, enhanced by body odor. Yeah, attractive.

Sam stepped forward. "So where is the rest of dear Eddie?"

Keller swiveled his head in the other direction to see Sam. "We don't know. We only have a hand."

"Is he dead or alive?" Kurt asked.

"We think he was alive when the hand was removed."

Possibly by someone wearing a level-A Hazmat suit. I thought about the hand removal for a moment. Bet someone lopping off his hand stung. I knew there was a stupid grin on my face.

I looked up to see Kurt run his thumb under his chin and point to his mouth. I worked harder on trying to dislodge the smile. Sam was doing a great job of keeping Detective Keller's attention off me.

"Where and when was the hand discovered?" Sam asked.

"I can't discuss the case in front of Agent Conway, she's a suspect."

Sam smiled. It wasn't pleasant. "When was the hand discovered and when was it removed from the body? If Agent Conway is a suspect then she should be allowed the opportunity to refute the claims and provide an alibi."

Keller looked uncomfortable. I think he realized he wasn't going to get anywhere with Delta A sucking all the air in my office.

"Where were you last night, Agent Conway?" he said.

"I was at home, Detective Keller."

"Can anyone confirm you were at home?"

I smiled. "My house."

He looked confused.

I could have told him that the house monitors all comings and goings using a sophisticated computerized security system and stores data on an off-site server. I could have.

"You're not being very cooperative."

"I was at home. I didn't anticipate having to provide an alibi, so I was at home, alone."

Keller leveled his eyes at me and made a last ditch attempt. "I'm asking you to accompany me to the police station to continue this conversation."

"You know, Detective Keller, I think I'll give that a miss."

"Do I have to arrest you?"

That was ballsy.

"If you want to arrest me, go ahead. I'd like to see your evidence and also, you might like to share your findings with SAC Grafton and Director O'Hare."

"I ... ah ... just need to ask you some questions to rule you out of the investigation."

"You did and I answered them. You won't tell me anything ... I'm done." I swung in my chair. "Just a heads up – Eddie has more enemies than anyone I've ever met. The list includes his ex-wife and his children."

"I hope you have another line of inquiry because this

one just dried up," Lee said, leaning over Keller just a little.

Keller blathered, "Don't leave town."

"You don't get to say that to me," I replied. "If you'd like help with your case, you can give us a call." I handed him my card.

As if on cue, my desk phone rang. The display indicated it was the Connelly's home phone number calling. No way was I going to take that call with a Metro cop in my office.

I stood up and offered him my hand. "Goodbye."

He shook my hand and nodded. "I'll be in touch."

"I'm sure you will."

My phone continued ringing then abruptly stopped. Dammit, there'd be a message. Kurt ushered Keller from my office. Sam and Lee sat down.

"This is not good," Sam said.

"No, it really isn't," I replied. "For the record, I didn't do anything to Eddie the 'tard, but I'm having trouble feeling sorry that karma has finally caught up with him."

"Us all. Wonder where the rest of him is and where they found that hand ..." Sam said.

"Not on his arm," I muttered. "Typical freaking Eddie, he's always been trouble."

The phone sat on my desk taunting me. I knew I had to listen to the message.

I lifted the handset from the cradle and pressed four numbers, accessing my voice mail. As soon as I heard Beatrice Connelly's voice, I hit the speaker button.

"What did you do to my Eddie? Wasn't it enough that you killed my youngest son, now you have to take my Eddie? And as for our poor granddaughter ... you gave her access to the drugs that killed her. I'm sure you are in jail by now. The police were here. I told them all about you and how you hate my family and are killing us off one by one and how you killed your daughter." She disconnected.

The grins Lee and Sam wore at the start of the rant slid off their faces, replaced by unadulterated anger.

There was no way I could acknowledge the horror of Beatrice saying I'd killed my child, so I ignored it.

"It's nice that we can always count on my ex-mother-in-law to be level-headed and sane," I said. "I'm sure Detective Keller enjoyed her ranting and earnest declarations about how I'm killing them all off one by one."

Maybe I should.

"As senseless as she sounds, he was just doing his job. She pointed her fat finger at you, he's obliged to investigate," Lee said, the struggle to keep rampaging anger from his voice obvious. "He didn't have to go about it the way he did, though."

"I'm sure he'll be back ... Beatrice won't let this go."

She's found a way to be annoying and lash out at me at the same time and she'll make the most of it.

"That's as sure as bears shit in the woods," Lee drawled.

"We can poke around," Sam said. "See if we can find

any more of Eddie."

"Or we could let it go and move on. Detective Keller will be back. Until then, we've been asked to look into a stalking case," I said.

"Stalking?" Kurt said. "A serial stalker?"

A smile erupted into laughter as a mental image took hold. I pictured a crazy but pretty woman stalking the Frosty Flakes in Safeway. Maybe she liked tigers or maybe she just liked sugar. I suspected it was a package deal. Cereal stalker, indeed.

"No, not a serial stalker, at least not as far as we know," I replied, sending the Frosty Flakes image packing.

"Who's being stalked?" Kurt asked, taking his pen and notebook from his jacket pocket.

"A celebrity," I replied. "LAPD have asked for our help."

That made everyone focus.

"We're going to Los Angeles?" Sam sounded hopeful.

"Not at the moment. Our guy is flying out east for some public appearances and also to vacation."

"Why us and not Metro?"

"The threat assessment turned up something interesting." I turned my gaze to Lee. "Want to hazard a guess what that might be?"

He shook his head.

I continued, "If I said his name was Michael Davenport would that ring any bells, Agent Davenport?"

Lee smiled, just a little.

8

Kurt and Sam both frowned.

"I don't know any celebrities called Michael Davenport," Sam said. He turned to Lee, "You have a brother named Michael, don't you?"

Lee nodded. "Mike is my little brother."

Not that much littler. or younger. My information said they were born in the same year. Irish twins. Lee was almost ten months older than his little brother.

"Celebrity? Does he look like a rocker, too?" Kurt said. "Because I could understand that."

"No, he looks like an action hero," I replied. "He looks a lot like someone from a very popular series currently on television."

"He's an actor?" Kurt said.

"Yep. Michael Fisher, aka Michael Davenport, aka Lee's baby brother."

Sam and Kurt digested the information.

Sam was first to speak. "You never mentioned Michael was an actor."

"No one ever asked," Lee replied with a grin. "So when does the kid arrive?"

"I thought you would know the answer to that," I said.

"Nope. He never mentioned he was coming out. I knew he was going away but I figured he was off climbing another mountain somewhere."

"You're close then?" I muttered.

Lee laughed. "We're brothers. I'm sure he'd arrive on my doorstep at some point, and then I'd know he was in town."

I pulled up the information we had on Michael and his situation. "Michael's management and studio apprised LAPD of a threat situation two days ago." Scanning the rest of the information on the screen, I said, "Security at the studio worked with a liaison officer from the LAPD to tighten up weak areas after both the studio and Michael received threatening letters, via his management."

"Sounds fairly standard so far," Sam said.

"Yes, it does. And this is where it gets a little messy," I said. "LAPD saw the letters but were not permitted to copy them or keep the originals. It is unknown who is sending the threats. We do know the studio and his manager received a series of letters, stating that he would not leave Washington D.C. alive."

"LAPD haven't taken the letters into evidence?" Sam queried, his brow furrowed.

"No."

"No forensic examination of the letters?" Kurt asked.

"No."

"That's highly unusual," Kurt added. "A written death threat and these people won't hand over the evidence … makes no sense."

My thoughts exactly.

"Did you know about this?" I asked Lee.

"Not about the trip to D.C. and no, I didn't know about those letters. I knew he'd picked up a few stalkers on and off over the years and I gave him advice on how to deal with them," Lee said. "Does Michael know about the latest letters?"

That was where it all got a little bit tricky.

"I can only go on this request in front of me. He's barely mentioned in the police report. He didn't make the complaint. It was made on his behalf. Does he know? I have no idea." I leaned back and looked at Lee. "If he knew, would he come to you?"

"Yes. He has done before. If this was a serious situation, yeah, he would." Lee said. "How the hell is he supposed to protect himself if he's not given the facts?"

He took the words out of my mind.

"There is a final note at the bottom of this email from the officer who requested assistance. He notes Michael Fisher's management decided the best course of action was to limit his knowledge, and put extra security in place."

It was all so familiar. I'd heard Rowan's management state dumber things in the interest of protecting their client. "We have been asked to step in, because LAPD believe this is a credible threat situation and they're not getting anywhere with the management. Also, Michael will be under the biggest threat while in D.C." I reached for the phone on my desk and found the phone number for Michael Davenport's manager from the LAPD file.

"This is SSA Ellie Conway, FBI. Can I talk to Sara Rosen, please?"

"Speaking."

She sounded like a twelve-year-old. "We've been asked to protect a client of yours, Michael Fisher. I'd like you to forward me the threat letters."

"I'm not happy about releasing the letters, Agent."

"You're not releasing them. We require the letters to conduct our investigation, they are evidence. Without them this is all hearsay."

"I don't think that's right."

Of course you don't, you're twelve.

"The letters corroborate your story that there is a threat," I said with mustered patience. "Without seeing them, we cannot determine the nature or seriousness of the threat to your client. Or even if there is one. A report from LAPD isn't evidence. We need forensic testing on the documents."

Silence.

"Ms. Rosen, we need those letters. I'll give you an address of the nearest field office and you can take them there yourself."

"When do you need them?"

"Preferably before your client arrives in Washington," I said.

Really, she should have handed them over to police. It was only because the officer in charge of the case felt concerned about the level of threat that he bothered to let us know. With no evidence on file, he could have easily dismissed it.

She agreed to take the letters in herself. After divulging the address and the name of an agent she should take them to, I hung up.

"Mike needs to wake up and smell the coffee," Lee muttered. "That woman is not filling me with confidence.

How good a manager can she be? Notifying police, not letting them have the evidence, or give them enough information to do their jobs, and not telling the client just how bad it is ... sheer stupidity."

We were definitely on the same page regarding Mike's management.

"I don't know your brother, how will he react to this news?" I said. He's an actor. I knew nothing about actors. If he was highly-strung, telling him could cause more issues. If he freaked out and handled things like a diva it would make protecting him a pain in the ass.

"Like you or I would," Lee replied. "He's my brother."

Ah, wonderful. He'll arm himself with knowledge and maybe a weapon and carry on as normal. I smiled. Very familiar. On hearing that, I wondered how much of him was in the character he played on television.

This would be fun with a capital F. As long as he didn't get dead on our watch.

"Right, Lee, get onto your brother for the travel details. You don't have to tell him over the phone what's going on. In fact, we don't know how tech savvy the stalker is, so probably say nothing." I stopped in my tracks. "Scratch that whole idea. Do you two have a way of communicating that no one else knows about?"

My cell phone buzzed. I glanced at the text but it didn't register.

Lee nodded. "Yeah, we leave messages for one another through a veterans' website."

I didn't ask why: I have a brother. He and I leave

messages for each other on a website using aliases. It's one of those things. You never know when it will prove handy.

"Get on it, tell him you need to know when to pick him up. He needs to be vigilant and looking for tails, et cetera. He will have an LAPD escort, they have him under surveillance but probably not a marked car. Tell him not to ditch the LAPD."

Lee pulled his phone out of his pocket.

"Don't call him," I cautioned. "You don't know who is listening on his end."

"Not calling," Lee replied with a smile. "Texting a pre-arranged message so he knows to log in."

"Nice."

"Can I?" Lee pointed at my laptop.

"Go for it," I said and stood up, picked up my cell phone and stepped away from my desk. Lee passed me and sat down.

"It's not right," he muttered.

"What's not?"

"Sitting in a warm chair."

I left him to it. Kurt, Sam, and I joined Sandra in the bullpen.

"This could be fun," Sam said, giving me a nudge.

"Yep, or a total pain in the ass."

Sandra poured me a coffee. "What'd the cop want?"

"He thinks I chopped off my ex-brother-in-law's hand," I replied.

"You want to find out what's going in that case?"

14

"Hell, yes."

"One moment, what was his name again?"

"Aaron Keller."

Sandra typed fast while the three of us waited for her to work her magic.

"I'm not asking if you just hacked into the Metro computer system, but did you just hack into the Metro computer system?" I said in a hushed whisper.

"Would I? Really?" She almost looked innocent for a nanosecond. "I so hacked their asses," she whispered. "They found the hand on the south side of the Washington monument, displayed. There are photos."

I slipped around to her side of the desk to see the photos. It was displayed. Eddie's armless hand was flying the bird. I couldn't help but smile. Even unattached, his body parts were offensive. Kurt and Sam peered over our shoulders. Sam chuckled. Kurt grinned.

"You think maybe he annoyed someone and they chopped off the offending appendage?" I asked. "God knows I've been tempted over the years."

Kurt tapped me on the shoulder and asked me to move a little. He wanted a closer look at the stumpy hand.

"Sandra can you download these photos without anyone knowing?" he asked.

"I am a magician. It is within my realm of expertise."

"If you wouldn't mind forwarding them to me," Kurt said.

"Not at all, consider it done."

"What else have they got? Fingerprints or anything

substantial?" I asked.

"The hand, nothing left at the crime scene. That's it." She typed some more. "And a transcribed conversation with Beatrice Connelly where she accuses you of killing her sons. Also, Mac's dad, on record saying his wife is insane and that he is certain you have nothing to do with any of this."

"Good to know."

"I can check back, and poke around a little as the investigation goes on."

"That would be handy."

My cell phone went again; another text message from Assistant Director Owen.

Instead of reading it, I ignored it. She is not my favorite person. The only reason she texts me is to harass me about something, probably the Connelly situation, without my team knowing she was trying to contact me. She's sneaky like that.

Because I knew what she was like, I forwarded her texts to the entire team and to Caine, our SAC. Caine called me within minutes.

"She's on the warpath," he said. "Hold off replying to her today."

"I have no intention of replying to her at all."

"You'll have to sooner or later, just don't do it today. Leave the building. Be hard to reach."

"Why am I in her sights, after all these years?"

"She's one for holding grudges. You dressed her down in front of others once ... she's heard about Eddie and is running with it. I know her. She's looking for a way to crucify you."

"Good luck. I didn't do anything."

"That will make no difference to her," Caine growled. "In her mind, this has been a long time coming."

"Awesome. I can end this now and go to O'Hare."

"I know ..."

"But?"

"But I think you should give Owen some rope and let her hang herself."

"I like how you think."

"Keep your head down and get out of the office for the rest of the day."

"Yes, sir."

I hung up and grinned at Kurt. "Caine wants me out of Dodge for the rest of the day."

"I'm up for a road trip. We could accidentally happen by the Metro crime scene."

"Yeah, nah, they'll figure out we've been snooping, or worse, think I actually did it!"

"We don't want that."

I hurried back to my office and checked on Lee.

"He gets in tomorrow morning. I'll pick him up."

"Great. I need to get out of here for a bit." I also needed to outline my plan for Mike Davenport's protection while he was in D.C. "Before I go – as long as your brother is in our care, so to speak – he is to be accompanied by one of us at all times. I don't want him checking into hotels using his own name or announcing his presence using any form of social media sites. Let's not make it easy for anyone to get near him. I know he has public engagements while in the city but until he fronts up to the venues, I don't want his whereabouts known. We'll need details of security at the venues and will supplement as required ourselves. Can you and Sam get on that, please?"

"Sounds good. Sam and I will handle the venue security."

"We'll revise once we have those letters, if necessary. I'll see you and your brother here tomorrow."

"We'll be here."

My cell phone buzzed as it dropped a text message. Mitch: Grab a coffee?

I paused before pulling on my jacket and texted him to say I'd be at his office in ten. Kurt wouldn't mind and I felt like being around a friend, not a colleague-slash-friend-slash-minder.

Chapter Two
Have A Nice Day

"Fuck you and the horse you rode in on!"

Time to leave.

I stormed from the building before doing something that would land me in jail for murder one. My hand strayed dangerously close to the grip on my Glock several times during the ten minutes I spent in Owen's company.

What just happened?

A tantrum. One any two-year-old would be proud to own. I couldn't stay around for the rest of the dispute because I had no idea what was going to happen next. I berated myself for my lack of control and put some distance between me, the building, and the crazy bitch inside. I needed to be better than that. Never fight fire with fire, always use water. Owen pushed all my buttons and I'd let her.

I hurried down an alleyway trying to figure out what the hell was going on. The world spun off its axis and nothing made sense. There was a good chance I had just shot my career in the foot. Unless I got to Deputy Director Thomas and told him what happened before Assistant Director Owen filed her report, or maybe even took my badge. I still had a piece of paper crumpled in my hand.

The cool air on my face soothed the raging furnace of

anger. The whole thing was beyond stupid.

I wrestled my phone from my pocket and called Deputy Director Thomas's direct line. There was an away message on his phone.

Dammit.

My next call was to Director O'Hare's direct line. Another away message.

Damn.

I called Caine.

"It's me. I'm trying to get hold of Thomas but there is an away message. So I tried O'Hare and got another away message. What's going on?"

"O'Hare is in hospital. The memo came through early this morning," Caine replied. He sounded cranky but that was his norm.

More bad news I didn't need.

"I'll be in the office soon. Is it serious?" I said.

"I don't know but it doesn't sound good. O'Hare is on indefinite sick leave."

"Where is the Deputy Director?"

"Deputy Director Thomas is on leave. I believe he's out of the country."

"The chief?"

I watched straws slip through my fingers leaving a sense of futility. Caine can't be the only person capable of talking sense to Owen.

"Taking a law enforcement seminar down in Georgia."

"Who is acting Deputy Director?"

"No one at this point. Assistant directors can handle

their various divisions according to the memo."

Oh, crap-a-doodle-doo. I'd just got my answer as to why Owen was being Owen.

I'd reached the end of the alleyway.

Time I confessed. "I think I pissed Owen off this morning. There'll be trouble."

"Thanks for the heads up. I'll see you when you get in and you can brief me."

I hung up and shoved my phone back into my pocket. This was not good.

Not good was the biggest understatement yet. I paced back and forth across the alleyway for about ten minutes then stopped and thumped my palm flat against a cold brick wall, trapping the creased paper between my hand and the wall. Probably should've been my head against the wall. It might knock some sense into it.

My phone rang.

Mitch. "Having a good day?" he asked, his smile evident in his voice.

"Been better," I replied, staring at the brick wall in front of me.

"You okay?"

"Yeah, work issues, is all."

"Is this about your ex-brother-in-law?"

"Yes."

"You can't talk?"

"Just trying to make sense of something. Call you later?"

"You sure you're okay?"

I injected a smile into my voice before replying, "Of course."

"Want to go for a run later?"

"Yes, great idea."

Mitch hung up.

A run might be what I need. Mom's voice exploded in my head, "Run, Ellie, run."

Not funny, Mom.

My phone rang again. I looked at the screen, trying to decide whether to answer it or not. Caine.

"Do *not* come to the office," he said quietly.

"Why?"

"Owen has issued a warrant for your arrest."

"She's done *what?*" A warrant seemed like an extreme response to me yelling at her.

"Don't come in. Don't use your car. Keep your head down."

"I'll be in touch."

"Be careful. I'll try to talk sense into Owen."

I hung up and shoved my phone into my pocket. My next thought made me take my phone back out and remove the battery. I put the battery in one pocket and my phone in another – couldn't have Owen tracking me via my phone's GPS. I wanted Caine to have a shot at calming her down.

This was going brilliantly. Not.

Another few minutes of pacing followed before I gave smacking my head into the wall some serious consideration.

A light cough alerted me to company. My right hand dropped to the grip of the Glock on my hip and rested there.

My eyes flicked left and glowered at the interloper.

He leaned on a doorjamb sporting what I'm sure he thought was a charming smile, with his right hand jammed in his jeans pocket and his sunglasses reflecting my incredulousness back at me. If I ever needed any proof that I was losing it, he was it. Not a ghost, thank God, but most definitely an interesting hallucination. The interest was clinical, as in I bet a shrink would find it fascinating that I hallucinated someone I was going to meet anyway. I wanted to punch him. Hard.

Yep, I was losing it.

I hit the wall with my open palm. Seemed safer. The paper fell to the ground. A small gust of wind blew it onto his shoe. He bent down and picked it up but didn't look at it. Instead he pushed his sunglasses on top of his head and asked, "You all right?"

"Yeah. I'm awesome."

His smile became a grin, dimples, and all. "You are," he said slowly, his eyes crinkling as his smile traveled upward. "But I asked if you were all right?"

"Shut up." A wise-assed hallucination I did not need.

"You look like something upset you."

"Aren't you observant?" I clenched my teeth. "I'm perfectly fine. Thanks for the concern."

His light blue eyes never left mine. "Want to try that again?" He moved closer, leaving the doorway and leaning his left shoulder on the wall not far from my hand.

He was within striking distance.

What the hell was wrong with me that I thought that? The paper in his hand rustled. I didn't look at it. I never wanted to see it again. His eyes flicked downward. I knew he was looking at the paper. So, he saw it. Changes nothing. Doesn't make him or the image in his hand real.

I shook my head. "It doesn't matter."

"You sure about that?"

Again the paper rustled. When I looked, I saw him fold it into his pocket.

"Of course," I said, taking a deep breath. "It's an illusion. It never happened." Or maybe a delusion. Rational thought came back in leaps and bounds. This made the presence of the man leaning on the wall peculiar, to say the least. I knew who he was. I didn't know *why* he was.

"I might be able to help," he offered.

I wanted to know what was really going on, and curious as to why he stood in front of me.

"How'd you know something happened and why are you here?"

"I'm here because I flew in this morning. I knew where to find you because my brother told me about fifteen minutes ago. Someone needed to come for you and it had to be someone who wasn't FBI."

I let his words sink in. How could anyone know I'd choose the alleyway as my thinking place? I'm not fond of them. The smell of urine has never been something I seek out. Hence I prefer D.C. to New York.

My phone. If Lee tracked me using my phone before I took my battery out then someone else could have, too. Who would Owen send after me? Not Delta. They'd be warned off and threatened with disciplinary action to dissuade their involvement. If Lee could find me, why hadn't someone working for Owen found me? We needed to leave before someone did.

"Where is your brother?"

"He's waiting for us."

"There is a whole lot of very weird stuff going on here."

He smiled. "No kidding."

My left hand reached out and touched his arm. Soft leather felt like butter under my fingers. I squeezed solid arm underneath his jacket. He was real. Good to know. This wouldn't have been the first time that my dead husband Mac had *appeared* to me as someone else. It wasn't so long ago that he appeared as another hunky blond actor who had his own action-packed television show. It was even more disturbing because it was a recurring thing throughout a case. With my history of odd occurrences, it pays to check. A dead man with a warped sense of humor: exactly what I needed. Not.

"We need to talk," I said, my hand still wrapped around his forearm, powerless to move it. "And not about what happened over there." I waved a hand toward the street. "My car is ... somewhere," I said looking back to the road bathed in light behind me and shivered as the shadows around me deepened. I couldn't take my car, Caine told me to leave it. There would already be a BOLO out on that and me. Grey fog fizzed on the edges of my vision. "Gimme a minute."

I fumbled in my pocket for a small vial, unscrewed the top, and breathed in the vapors. No way did I want to risk a migraine. Since Gillian at *Le'Esscience* started making the synergy for me, heavy duty migraine vanquishing drugs were a thing of my past.

And it was a safer option than keeping drugs in the house. Bit late on the zero drug front. I set that thought aside. I screwed the top back on the tiny bottle and pushed it into my pocket.

"All right?"

"Sure."

"My car is this way," he said pointing. "We're leaving yours behind."

My lack of contrariness both shocked and disturbed me as I walked without so much as a comment, through a door, down a corridor, out onto E Street, and climbed into the waiting silver Camaro. I assumed it was a rental. It's a long drive from California to Washington, D.C. and I knew his brother was picking him up from Dulles. Part of my brain curled itself into a dark corner, that part knew he was real, but it wasn't communicating well with the rest of my brain. I fumbled for the vial and breathed in more soothing vapors.

Maybe he hadn't stepped out of a television series, maybe I had stepped into one?

None of it seemed real. I was on the run from the FBI – of course none of it seemed real; it was however typical of the weird shit that happens in my life.

I knew he was flying in, but having him turn up in the exact alleyway I was in, right when the shit hit the fan – that was odd.

My reality has never been like other people's. Never. You'd think I'd be used to it. On the grounds that nothing is what it seems to be, I convinced myself it was perfectly okay to be sitting in a Camaro while someone I'd never met before and who shouldn't be there, was driving me through the streets of Washington, D.C.

This called for another deep breath of synergy, its magic working overtime to keep the migraine at bay.

As I watched the streets merge into a blur, I wondered where I really was.

In a coma? In a secure psychiatric facility? In some serious trouble and obviously unconscious. A voice in my head gave me two options. One, go with it and see what comes of this. Two, fight it and try to find the way back to reality. What was reality? Wasn't it different for everyone? Mine is more colorful than most. Yeah, colorful. That's a good description.

Another voice reminded me I still had a Glock on my hip. I'm armed. Even if I wasn't, I consoled myself with being able to take out an actor: I once dropped an angry marine on his ass when he wanted to kill me.

"You all right?" he asked again, glancing at me. "You're not thinking of shooting me, are you?"

"Eyes on the road. I'm okay." A smile flickered across my lips. "I've thought about it a few times and yet you are lead-free and not leaking."

Lee might have an issue with me shooting his brother. Best not to test that.

He laughed, as if he wasn't entirely sure of the situation. "I'm hoping to stay lead-free."

"We haven't formally met."

He smiled, flicked the turn signal, and made a left turn. "You're right, we haven't." The smile never left his lips. "Pleased to meet you. I'm Michael Fisher or Michael Davenport or just plain Mike."

"Pleased to meet you, just plain Mike. I'm Gabrielle Conway. As we don't use the G word, you may call me Ellie."

"Delighted to make your acquaintance, Ellie."

"Sure, that's what they all say, in the beginning."

Mike laughed.

"Remember that laugh and how it feels. They might be few and far between from here on in."

"I'm a pretty imaginative guy but I can't imagine that being true."

Oh, but it is.

"So, what's happening here? Did you escape from a DVD? Am I having a psychotic break?"

If so, not surprising; I knew it would happen one day.

"You're not psychotic," he replied. A heavy undercurrent of humor rippled in his voice. "I didn't escape from a DVD."

He flicked the turn signal again. The driver of a car behind us leaned on the horn. Mike frowned. "Impatient."

I shrugged. "It's D.C, you get used to the honking." It's not a patient city and it suits me well. "Drivers give you all of a split second before they start tapping their horns around here."

"I noticed."

Another driver honked. Mike mumbled unflattering things about the driver who zoomed by us.

"So if you didn't escape from a DVD, where did you escape from?" It was all going so well until those words fell out of my mouth. I didn't mean to say them aloud. And with that, I found myself tossed into a scene from *Escape from L.A.* Maybe I needed to talk to "Map to the Stars" Eddie. Maybe Snake Plissken was the guy who hacked off Eddie Connelly's missing hand. There were way too many Eddies floating around in my head and Plissken looked unwell.

Mike's voice filled with amusement. "I didn't escape. Lee picked me up from Dulles about two hours ago." He stole a glance in my direction. "You sure you're all right?"

Plissken jumped into a car with "Map to the Stars" Eddie and drove off.

Oh, yeah. We've had this conversation already. I took the vial from my pocket and inhaled the vapor again, successfully pushing the encroaching migraine farther away.

I chose not to answer his question. I couldn't. All right

and I parted company when I started hollering at Owen. And for a new spin on crazy, we were supposed to be protecting Mike and yet here he was driving me through D.C. It made about as much sense as an arrest warrant out for me. No wonder there was a migraine determined to disrupt my mind.

"So where is Lee?"

"Waiting for us."

Chapter Three
You Gotta Move

He parked by the curb and smiled at me. For the life of me, I couldn't figure out why his smile made everything okay. Total irrationality. Oh well, rolling with it looked like the only choice as I doubted the insanity would improve anytime soon.

"And we are where?"

"A safe house."

I looked around and recognized the area. It was one of Delta A's safe houses. Owen didn't know about our safe houses. No one outside Delta A did, not even Caine. The safe house thing just twisted the warp factor another notch.

An actor took *me,* the special agent, to a safe house.

Ridiculous.

"I don't need a safe house." My finger pointed to him by itself. "But you need protection. What the hell was Lee thinking sending you after me?"

"He asked me if I would pick you up. He didn't know who else to trust. I was happy to."

I'd rather like to just go home, drink some tequila and drown it all out until Assistant Director Owen gets over herself, or pulls her head out of her ass. It wasn't the first time I'd yelled at her over the course of my career and I doubted it would be the last. This time though, she'd tried to make out I'd killed my ex-brother-in-law. This time shouting at her wasn't going to do it.

He climbed out the car. I sat there and watched him walk around to my door and open it for me. An actor and a gentleman. I groaned internally. As much as I didn't want to admit it, part of me enjoyed the madness.

He wasn't hard on the eyes. There was something about him. Maybe it was the confidence with which he carried himself.

I looked up at him. "Asked?"

"Trust me."

"Sure, why the hell not." It's not as if I haven't survived some very weird situations in the past.

A smile eased over my lips. Delta A is a good-looking team. This rendered me immune to hot men, so Mike's movie star qualities were wasted on me. At least that's what I told myself. Mike guided me up the path toward the house with his hand resting on the small of my back, the warmth from his palm permeating through my jacket.

He knocked twice. The door swung open a few seconds later. Lee stood in the hallway.

I shook my head. "This is ludicrous."

"Come in, Chicky. We'll explain."

"I can hardly wait." I walked through the door still feeling the pressure of Mike's hand on my back, remembering that I'd felt solid flesh under his jacket. Seemed like something I should hang onto.

Solid muscle.

Don't go there.

My mind pushed the outer limits. Thinking about muscle under a leather jacket could topple it right off the cliff. We stood in the hallway. Lee rested on the wall; I turned to face Mike and waited for the explanation as to why it was Mike who fetched me from the alleyway.

A noise from outside grabbed my attention. I craned my neck to see around Mike.

"Chicky?" Lee turned to follow my line of sight.

A dark colored car slowed outside.

"Get down!" I said.

A series of rapid popping sounds followed. Mike fell, pushing me to the floor. He landed with his elbows on either side of my shoulders, pinning me underneath him. How gallant. He became a human shield with his body crushing me. I struggled to see beyond him. I heard bullets hitting the doorframe. I heard Lee moving and firing. I had no hope of getting my weapon out: Mike was a dead weight.

"Mike." One of my arms was pinned down, the other stuck; I wriggled the trapped one free. He didn't move. "Mike?" I touched his carotid artery with two fingers and felt a pulse. Not a dead weight then.

"You in there?"

A pale blue eye flickered open. He grimaced.

"Can you talk?"

He groaned on an exhale and said, "Yeah."

"Are you hit?"

"Yeah."

"Bad?"

"No. Vest."

Lee kept firing and there were no more returning volleys. He slammed the door. An eerie quiet blanketed the hallway. Mike didn't move.

"Get off me," I whispered.

He struggled to his feet and groaned as he straightened up.

Lee reached down and pulled me to my feet. "Everyone okay?" he asked.

"Winded that's all," Mike replied, his voice catching in his throat as he tried to get his breath.

"You'll have some bruises," Lee commented but he didn't seem overly concerned. "Ellie, you okay?"

"Yeah. He's not light."

Mike smiled and unbuttoned his shirt to reveal a bulletproof vest. He took off his shirt, then ripped open the Velcro and pulled the vest over his head. In the back were three rounds.

"Turn around," I said. Corresponding bruises had already appeared on his skin. "That's gotta hurt."

"Only when I breathe," Mike replied, pulling his shirt back on after sticking his fingers through the three holes in the back. "I liked this shirt."

"It doesn't pay to be too attached to clothing in this line of work," I said with a smile. "At least you're all right."

Lee took the vest. "I'll get ballistics onto this, see if we can't narrow down the weapon."

I looked at the men in front of me.

Tall, blond, chiseled strong jaw and good cheekbones; either one of them would make a good superman. There were a few differences. Mike's eyes were light blue while Lee sported pale golden brown eyes. Lee was taller and his hair darker but not by much. They could do a double act, superman and batman.

Holy bat shit, superman.

"All right, can someone, either of you, I don't care who – but someone needs to tell me what the hell is going on and why an actor with bullet proof vest just saved my ass." I glanced from one to the other. Mike beamed in my direction and rocked on his heels. Lee raised an eyebrow. "You can start with why I'm not on my way home. I get that the office would be risky."

"Owen," Lee said.

I looked over my shoulder and crossed myself at the same time. Thankfully she wasn't there.

"She's been an issue this morning. But what does Mike picking me up have to do with Owen?"

"She's put out a warrant for your arrest."

"I know. But I don't know the charges."

"Insubordination, wanted for questioning in a murder investigation. The BOLO went out as 'Dangerous Do Not Approach.'"

"Wanted for questioning in a murder investigation?" At least they got the dangerous bit correct. I wanted to smile but it seemed inappropriate given the circumstances. "Who the hell did I murder?"

"Owen said she has evidence that you are implicit in

the murder of Eddie Connelly."

"Oh, fucking Eddie strikes again." I sighed; I should've taken him out years ago. It's not as if I hadn't had many opportunities. Apart from Mac and his dad, the rest of the Connelly family seemed determined to ruin my life; it was tiresome. They ruined everything they touched. Ideas, people, even plant life rotted under the gaze of the Connelly clan.

Mike pulled the photo out of his pocket and handed it to Lee.

A grimace crossed my face as Lee studied the picture. "Can you say Photoshop? Because I sure as hell did not kill Eddie," I said, flicking the underside of the picture.

"I know you didn't. We just have to keep you out of federal prison until we can prove it."

A federal holding facility was not somewhere an agent ever wanted to end up. Not even solitary could protect you from the inmates. Mostly, people we put in prison weren't too happy to see us again on the outside, but inside, now that's their territory and anything goes. I'd be another incarcerated death statistic within days.

"Meanwhile, I'm looking at an actor who knew how to find me this morning. Not even I knew where I was going to end up."

Mike smiled and shrugged. "I'm part of the solution, not the problem."

"Jesus!" I rolled my eyes. "You're an actor. Don't take this the wrong way but there are no second, third, or fourth takes in what we do. No script involved and no stunt doubles, either." That'd be kinda cool. On second thoughts, a stunt double would be awesome cool.

"Which is why he wore a vest," Lee said. "He can handle himself."

"Good to know." So he can handle himself; he carries himself well and he's physically fit. Yeah. Nah. "I'm not comfortable with a civilian involved in whatever the fuck this is. And I still want an answer as to how you found me."

"We were worried about Owen, she's been trying to get you away from Delta A since yesterday, so ..."

So, it wasn't my phone that told him where to find me.

"You GPSd me. Where is the bug?"

"Inside your wallet."

"Thank you." It seemed appropriate.

"Let's get out of here, before whoever was shooting at us comes back," Lee said. He opened the front door again and peered out. There was no one in the street at all.

"Could the shooting be stalker related?" Mike asked.

Lee shrugged. "Wouldn't expect that level of violence from a stalker. Stalkers tend to be more personal in their attacks, less drive-by. I dunno who they are," Lee said. He rocked from foot to foot. "But I think we need to find out. If it is the stalker then that's some impressive tracking skills they have going."

"Owen wouldn't have anyone shooting at me. She wants to humiliate me and make my life hell, not kill me," I said. I didn't think the shooting was about me. If it was, it wasn't coming from the FBI. We don't do drive-by shootings. Maybe I can't say the same for the CIA.

Bob Connelly lurched into my mind. I had to tell him it wasn't me who chopped up his son. I had to.

"I need your phone," I said to Lee holding my hand out.

He handed it to me and I made a call.

"It's me," I said. "Are you alone?"

"Yes, Ellie," Bob Connelly replied, his voice rumbling into my ear.

"I didn't do anything to Eddie, Bob. I didn't do what they're saying."

"I know, I know."

"I'll find out who did."

"Keep your head down. That assistant director of yours is not a nice woman."

No kidding.

"Has something else happened?"

"The Foundation lawyers are circling the wagons kiddo, you better do the same."

"Why?"

"Because someone posted a photo of you holding a dismembered hand on The Foundation Forum."

Crap!

"I'll be in touch when I can."

"You be careful out there, Ellie."

I hung up and gave Lee his phone back. At least Bob believed I didn't chop his son into pieces.

My dad. I needed to talk to him.

"Can I have your phone back, please?"

Lee handed it back. I walked to the other end of the hallway and made the call, willing my voice to stay strong. "Dad, I'm in trouble."

"I know, Ellie. I also know it wasn't you."

"I called Bob. Let Aidan know I'm okay, please," I said, staring at the swirls in the wallpaper in front of me, as if they held some magical clue to the situation.

"You talk to Mitch?"

"Yeah, but not really. He knows a bit but not about today ..."

Dad interrupted me. "I'll go over and see him at work."

"Thanks, Dad. I gotta go. I dunno ..."

"Hang in there, Ellie. You'll find a way to fix this. We'll see you when we see you. It'll be fine." Dad displayed more confidence in my ability than I had.

"Love you, Dad."

I hung up before he could reply, walked back to Lee and handed him his phone.

Lee frowned. "Where were you really last night?" he asked.

"Around, why?"

Personal. I was with a friend.

"There was a security breach at your place."

"Excuse me?" My turn to frown. "I thought you said there was as security breach at my place?"

That didn't make sense.

"You haven't been home?"

"No."

"We'll talk more about this later." Lee's brow

furrowed. He checked his phone. "Time is not on our side. We need to get you somewhere safer."

Mick Jagger's voice filled the hallway and my voice followed before I could check it, "Really, Mick? He said time is *not* on our side, not time *is* on our side."

"Ellie? Rolling Stones?" Lee asked. "Anything I need to know?"

I shook my head.

"Let's get out of here before someone comes running back ..." Lee nudged me and grinned.

"Not even funny."

"If they knock on the door," Mike added, "we'll know who they are."

"You two are about as funny as it gets."

The song came back with a vengeance with Jagger strutting up and down the hallway.

Mike was humming along to "Time Is on My Side" as he pulled car keys from his pocket.

"Where's your car, Lee?" Mike asked.

"Out back. Take Ellie, I'll meet you at Rock Creek Cemetery visitor's center."

"That doesn't sound like a random meeting place and why am I traveling with an actor?" I struggled to vocalize my thoughts but now they were running free. "I can see merit in me being with Mike. Someone just shot at us; he's not armed, and I am. And there is a warrant out for my arrest, which means being with you, Lee, would make me more obvious. Not to mention you should technically arrest me and could lose your job by helping me."

"No one is going to arrest you," Lee said.

"Where is that cemetery?" Mike asked. "I haven't had much time to look around."

"Got GPS?" Lee asked, watching the road for signs of anything.

"Doesn't matter. I know," I said.

Lee and I ran our palms together, catching fingertips. "Alert and safe."

Chapter Four
It's A Game

Mike held the passenger door open for me. I climbed in, shut the door, and clicked my seat belt into place.

"The car is remarkably unscathed. You were lucky. It could've looked like Swiss cheese. Rental companies get pissy over bullet holes in their cars."

"Speaking from experience?"

"A little bit."

Mike drove and hummed.

"Enough with the Rolling Stones," I muttered.

"Catchy tune," he replied.

"A little too catchy."

I gave him directions. A sigh of relief escaped as the song ended. We took the scenic route. So scenic that I had him ditch the car at the nearest metro that green- or red-line trains ran through. We took the green line to Fort Totten then walked along Galloway Street to the Keene Recreation Center and cut through the path that ran down one side and up to Gallatin Street, which would lead us to North Capitol Street.

Plenty of time for talking.

As we walked up a slight rise and along the path adjacent to the rec center, I glanced around. This was not the best part of town to be walking through, but hey, I'm armed. It's North West D.C., it's not like its Anacostia. It did occur to me that the difference between the North West D.C. and Anacostia was all semantics. Chances were we wouldn't see anyone anyway.

We walked side by side and in silence for a while. A small red butterfly flew up from the grass under our feet. Then Mike spoke, "What you're doing with The Butterfly Foundation is really good."

"Thanks. It's a shared effort. I have some great people working with me."

"I saw Rowan Grange's name as a supporter. Heard you were dating him?"

Fishing? Really?

"*Was* dating him." Past tense. He's all about making things awkward now. "Grange remains a big supporter of the Foundation."

I stopped walking for a minute and looked back down the hill. There was no one around. I didn't want to talk about Grange or the Foundation. A bird swooped across my line of vision and settled on a branch. Hovering on the ground under the tree were silvery wings. A small dragonfly flitted from grass blade to grass blade.

Mike wasn't done with his questions.

"Must've been quite difficult dating a rock star?"

"Too much publicity for my liking." With one last look down the hill, the dragonfly flew away chased by the bird, and I walked on. Mike caught up in two strides.

"Your husband started the Foundation with you?"

"Yes."

So many topics I'd rather not discuss.

"And your daughter?"

"I'd rather not ..."

"I'm sorry. I'll shut up."

"I'd appreciate it if you did," I replied, my voice just breaking a whisper. My eyes followed a sound near the community center buildings we were passing. "We've got company."

"Company?" His voice matched mine.

"Someone who doesn't want us to know they're there."

"No one knows where we are right now," Mike said, as he glanced toward the building.

"That's what I thought too. So this person *could* be unrelated to the other situations." I successfully reminded myself that there were situations – the Owen thing and someone shot at us or possibly just me at a supposed safe house, plus the arrest warrant. I lead an interesting life.

There was a high likelihood that whoever was watching us was indeed involved. My luck tends to go like that. I am blessed in the nut job attraction department.

Mike's voice mirrored some of my thoughts. "Someone shot at us at a *safe house.*"

"Let's get out of here," I said. I nodded toward some large dumpsters. A battered wire gate stood partially open in front of us. There was enough room to slip through without having to shove the gate and make more noise. "That way, behind the dumpsters, they'll give us some cover."

Just in case.

The feeling of being watched made me hurry faster than I intended. Maybe I wasn't in the best space to deal with any of these surprise events. Mike reached out, his hand clamped around my arm. He pulled me behind the first dumpster. A metallic ping resounded. Something hit the edge of the dumpster.

Jesus! An actor heard something I didn't and saved my ass, again. A wave of useless crashed over me.

Another round ricocheted off the dumpster.

"We need to get out of here before we get killed," Mike said, moving to the far end of the dumpster.

"Death might be a relief," I murmured, following him. I tapped his shoulder. "Stay put."

A look of horror stuck to his face as he turned his head toward me.

"Why?"

"Because fuck this shit."

He said nothing else. I pulled my Glock free of its holster and crept back to the other end of the dumpster. I glanced back at Mike, the horror gone. Outwardly, he appeared calm.

"Stay down," I said in a hushed whisper. "If this goes pear-shaped you need to head for the road up there," I pointed past him. "Gallatin Street, stay on Gallatin until the first main intersection, then left onto North Capitol. Stay on that until you reach the cemetery. Main route, public. Got it?"

"Yes."

Another shot ricocheted off the dumpster, and

sounded like it hit about the middle. I scanned the area behind us. Nothing but scrubby plants and a high wire fence, with a building on the other side of the dumpsters. The recreation center. I pictured it in my mind. Where was the shooter? On the right. He was on the right.

Another shot rang out and pinged off the dumpster ahead of us. At that point, it occurred to me there could be more than one shooter. Not if I'm lucky. Did I feel lucky? I took a breath and exhaled slowly, ridding myself of the Clint Eastwood moment curling around me. Did I want to get into a firefight that could go on until someone ran out of ammunition?

Not especially.

Maybe bravado was the way to go.

"Federal Agent! Put down the weapon!" I hollered across the open space in front of the dumpster.

A shot rang out.

I yelled out again, "Federal Agent. Put down the weapon!"

A quick tally told me he was five bullets down which wasn't helpful. Depending on his gun of choice, he could have zero to twelve rounds left. Hell, if he were using something with an extended magazine we could be here all day.

"I like 'em stupid," I hollered.

Another shot hit the dumpster. Six.

"You couldn't hit the side of a barn from the inside," I replied.

Another shot, this time closer to me. Seven.

Mike hollered at the shooter, "Yo, moron."

Another shot. Eight.

Mike yelled again. Another shot fired. Nine. He kept yelling insults. I had my window and took it. While Mike engaged the shooter with witty banter, I broke cover. The shooter stepped out to fire again. My finger closed on the trigger. Surprise registered as he thumped to the ground.

I ran over and kicked his weapon away. He lay clutching his shoulder and groaning.

"Are we having fun yet?" I asked, toeing him with my boot.

"What did you do that for?" he snarled, his voice laden with accusation. "I'm bleeding. You shot me."

"That's what happens when you act like a moron." I showed him my badge. "Care to explain?"

He moved a little. I saw a wire going to his ear. I pulled out his earpiece and followed the wire to inside his shirt. A radio, taped to his body. Weird.

Weird.

Oh, crap. I took a few steps back. I had no desire to end up as red mist and didn't want to attempt to disconnect what I believed was an IED.

"Who hired you?"

"Some guy."

"What'd he look like?"

"Never met him face to face," he said.

"Did he give you that?" I pointed at the radio.

"Yeah, told me it was part of the deal."

"He listening now?"

"I guess so."

I guessed so, too.

"What do you call him?"

"Colonel Mustard."

I walked back to the dumpsters, willing my legs not to run, not yet. I ducked behind the dumpsters and hurried to Mike.

"We gotta go – now. Same route as I explained before."

He took a deep breath and grimaced. I'd forgotten about the bruises on his back. He sucked it up.

"Why?"

"Because Colonel Mustard did it outside the rec room with an IED."

"What?" Mike asked.

I still had my Glock in my hand; seemed wiser to keep it there. I grabbed his right hand with my left.

"Stick close and move fast."

"The shooter?" he asked.

"He's the bomb. Don't think he knows."

"Whoa. Blast range?"

I smiled at him. "We'll be fine."

"You lie well," he commented.

"*Tick-tick*. Let's go," I replied. We ran. There was no looking back. As we ran, I holstered my gun. Twenty seconds after we hit the street running I heard an explosion.

"Was that him?" Mike asked, keeping pace with me.

"Yeah."

Colonel Mustard did do it outside the rec room with an

48

IED. I needed to call emergency services and also had a certain amount of guilt about letting the guy blow up.

We didn't stop running until we got to North Capitol and traffic. Slowing to a fast walk I tugged his hand, encouraging him to follow me left on North Capitol. Walking was nicer than running. Mike breathed as deeply as he could, allowing for the bruising, but didn't struggle. I was right about him being fit. I let go his hand.

"Can I borrow your phone?" I asked.

He handed it to me without question. I called 9-1-1, gave a false name and told them I'd heard gunfire and an explosion from Keene rec center. Then hung up and handed Mike his phone.

Chapter Five
Why Am I The One?

"Whose idea was Rock Creek?" I asked, watching the traffic.

"Lee's," Mike said. "

"And the safe house?"

The pause told me he didn't like where my questions were heading. I didn't like it either, but we'd sprung a big leak and I needed it plugged.

"Lee's."

"Houston, we have a problem." I looked around and saw a bus stop nearby. "We're not going to the church," I said, pointing to the bus stop. "We're taking the bus back into town."

Damn D.C. and its cameras. For the first time ever, I cursed the city for having such good surveillance coverage. Usually it worked for me, but not when running from Owen. If she thought I'd taken the metro she could find us via the metro cameras. Buses had cameras onboard, too. I settled the jumpy feeling in my gut with some truths. Owen is not that smart and with five metro lines, it'd take a while to locate me.

"It's not Lee," Mike stated.

"I really fuc'n hope not. From my point of view, he put a GPS in my wallet and bad things have happened ever since."

I pulled my phone from my jacket pocket, plugged the battery back in and looked at the list of recent messages flooding my screen. Four from Lee asking where we were. He could find us using the GPS. Why text me? I felt sick. It couldn't be what it looked like, surely to God. Not Lee.

I texted him and said we were on our way and had stopped for coffee. He'd know there was no coffee place near us if he was using the GPS to keep an eye on our movements.

"How close are we?" Mike asked, looking at gravestones inside the fence next to us.

"Not far, it's inside that fence but the gate is bit of a walk from here, fifteen minutes to the gate, maybe."

My phone buzzed. Lee. I ignored it.

"Cross the road," I told Mike.

We crossed and waited at the bus stop.

"Okay, someone found us or someone found me, which is it?" I said, watching traffic for a bus. "We know I'm carrying a GPS tracker but the only person who should be able to use that to find me, is Lee."

Something else bothered me. I had the battery back in my phone and if Owen used some of her brain cells for something other than choosing nail varnish, then she could use my phone to find me.

Mike looked slightly horrified then gathered himself together. "You're sure this isn't television?" he asked.

"If it isn't Lee, then he's only in danger when we turn up. If it is …" I'd just said he was the only one who could track the GPS, that was enough. "Then, well, we're in danger no matter what, but we can prevent Lee from becoming a target by staying away from him."

"How would anyone else track us? The shooter ..." he pointed back where we'd come from, "... at that place was there before we were."

"Yep, but it's the logical route from Fort Totten metro to St. Paul's. It's where I'd be if I knew someone took the metro and was heading to St Paul's." And no one would know we were heading to St Paul's unless someone overheard our conversation.

My mind ran every possible scenario trying to exclude Lee. It ended with if we were being tracked, then it would get real ugly here, real quick.

"I don't know if that's comforting or scary," Mike replied.

"Don't suppose you're armed?"

He shook his head.

I made a call. My mind flashed a red flag to remind me that every time I used my phone I left an electronic footprint.

"Sam, I need you. I'm heading to a Firehouse and I need you to come get me and a civilian. Engine Company 14, North Capitol Street NE."

"Chicky Babe – Lee is over that way."

I tapped Mike's shoulder and indicated we should walk. The Firehouse was close and I wanted to get inside and out of sight.

"There is a *situation*. Tell no one. No one."

"Tell me about it. You shouldn't be using your phone."

He exhaled, I imagined his teeth clenched. "You think Lee is involved?"

A sigh escaped as I paused before answering a trust question about someone on my team. Never before had I felt the need to pause before answering such a question.

"I don't know. You might wanna hurry."

Something made me turn around as I pocketed my phone, a car slowed, a window rolled down.

I grabbed Mike's elbow. "Run!"

We were fifteen feet from safety. We barreled through the open doors of Engine Company 14. I shoved Mike to the left behind the cover provided by a brick wall between the large pump bay doors. A barrage of gunfire hit the brick exterior of the building. Sparks flew across the floor as bullets hit the concrete. Glass showered down from the second set of closed doors. I held Mike's arm and pulled him hard against the thick brick. Tires squealed as a car accelerated away.

Two fire fighters jumped to their feet in the office at the back, scraping chairs across the floor. I pulled my badge from my pocket and held it up so they could see it, then hung it around my neck.

"Special Agent Ellie Conway," I called to the firefighter who walked towards us. "We need a safe place." I shook hands with Station Officer Greg Cabot. "Sorry about your doors. Seems someone doesn't like me very much."

Greg nodded. "Who can I call for you?"

"No one, thanks. I already have someone from my team on the way over here."

A paramedic came out of the office with a pack slung over one shoulder.

"You okay?" he called, walking toward us. "Anyone hurt?"

They both seemed a little casual for having just had bullets spray across their pump bay. Maybe it wasn't the first time.

"Yeah, we're okay," I replied. "I'm Ellie Conway, this is a ... friend of mine, Mike."

I'd said my name without even thinking, twice. Until the Owen situation was under control I needed to be more careful. I shook hands with the paramedic as he told me his name. George Papadopoulos.

"You want police?" he asked. "A call went out a few minutes ago about an explosion at a rec center not far from here. We're on standby and police are en route."

I shook my head. I didn't fancy being arrested. "FBI problem. My people will handle it. Probably best if we let police work on that explosion call out. Can we hang here?"

"Sure, it's a safe place."

I smiled. I remembered seeing the sign outside above the park bench that sat between the bay doors. The bench and sign probably had a few bullet holes now though.

"Make yourselves at home. You sure neither of you are hurt?"

"Thanks. We're good." I glanced at Mike. He nodded. I watched him slide down the wall until he was sitting on the concrete floor with his knees bent and feet flat on the ground.

"You sure?" George asked Mike.

Mike nodded. "I'm fine."

Greg grabbed a broom and began sweeping up the glass.

I grinned at Mike. "Okay, let's say it's not Lee because Lee doing this makes no sense, especially when we know you have a stalker and I have an arrest warrant. We must be carrying another tracker." But how did they know that we were heading to St Paul's? To track means to follow, not bounce ahead and be waiting. GPS tracker and something else. A bug maybe.

My phone rang. Lee.

Before I could speak he said, "There was gunfire – you okay?"

"Yep. We have a problem. Do you have your RT toy with you?"

"Yeah, always. That's a bad problem to have, Chicky. Where are you? Do you need Kurt?"

"Close. Engine Company 14. Sam is on his way," I replied. "We're not bleeding – let's not bother Kurt at this point."

SSA Doctor Kurt Henderson would be here in a heartbeat if we needed him. I knew he was on another assignment and wasn't prepared to pull him off it for nothing.

I hung up. Mike leaned against the wall, looking a little pained.

"Mike?"

"I'm fine." He rested his arms on his knees and watched his hands shake just a little.

"That's normal, you'll be okay. Just … just breathe."

George smiled. "I'll get you a glass of water."

"Is this what life is like for you?" Mike asked. He seemed paler than before.

"Sometimes but less often than you'd think." Lies, all lies. It's so normal I don't know why it ever surprises me. "You sure you're okay? You're not going to puke or pass out or anything?"

"I'm fine." He threw me a wry grin. "Are you all right?"

I grinned at him and nodded.

A car pulled up outside. I lifted my weapon smoothly from the holster on my hip and peered around the wall. That was when I spotted a cable above the door that ran down the wall. I saw Lee climb out of his car.

"Hey, Lee, in here," I called out. I turned to Greg who was still sweeping up glass. "Is this cable for a camera?"

"Yes. It is."

"Do you store the data?"

"We do. You want me to make you a copy of the half hour before and after the event?"

"I sure do, thanks."

"I'll finish up here then get that done for you, Agent."

Lee hurried in with a backpack.

"Hey, Michael, you all right?" Lee said, setting the pack on the floor and removing a black box from it.

"Yeah, I'm fine." He lowered his voice to whisper, "Not used to you calling me Michael."

"It sure goes against the grain," Lee whispered back. "Would it be easier if I called you Sleepy?"

Mike grinned. "Been a while since you called me that, Sneezy."

"You're dwarfs now? Really, you two? I bet there is a fun explanation but time is short, just like dwarfs and not like you two," I said. "And I'm not feeling much like Snow White."

Both men grinned and I heard a low whisper from Mike and tried hard not to smile. "Mirror mirror on the wall. Who is the most dangerous of them all?"

There could be some truth in that.

Lee opened the box and took out a small device. After some fiddling with the settings he announced he was ready.

"How many wireless devices are there in a Firehouse?" Lee asked Greg as his toy made high pitched squeals.

"Radios, GPS in the trucks, and phones. I'm afraid we can't turn any of it off, it remains on standby."

"That's okay – I can adjust the range. If you head back down to the office over there, your gear won't affect the machine." He glanced at the fire engine in the pump bay. "That should be far enough away not to cause an issue."

Greg took his broom and disappeared.

"Let's start with us and what we're carrying," I said. I pulled my wallet out of my pocket and found the little GPS unit. I handed it to Lee, who promptly crushed it under his foot. "Mike, phone? Take it out and turn it off."

I took mine from my pocket and turned it off, too. Lee

did the same with his. The squeal stopped.

Lee moved closer to me. Nothing. He moved over to Mike and the device buzzed, squealed and almost had heart failure.

"Take everything out of your pockets," he instructed.

Mike dropped his wallet, car keys, pack of gum, small notebook and a pen on the ground. We eliminated them one by one, pretty sure it was the pen.

Lee flicked off the RT detector and sat down in front of Mike.

"Where did this come from?" He held up the pen.

"The airport."

Lee unscrewed the barrel.

"It's the same, isn't it?" I said.

"Looks very similar."

A bang outside drew our attention. Greg called out from the back office. "Big black guy just arrived."

"God, I hope it's Sam," I mumbled, creeping around the wall between the doors, with my Glock firmly in my hand.

"Me, too," Lee muttered, tipping out everything inside the pen over the open notebook. "Is it Sam?"

"Yeah," I replied as Sam walked in.

"Someone shot up those doors pretty good. I take it you've resolved the problem?" Sam's eyes flicked from me to Lee.

I nodded. "Some of it."

Mike hadn't moved. He watched Lee. "It's the same as what?" he asked.

"Pardon?" Lee asked.

"Before Sam arrived, Ellie said it was the same."

"A few years ago we came up against a terrorist who bugged Ellie, the pen was similar. What's inside is the same."

I looked at the contents: a microphone and a transmitter. That explained how the person knew where we were going.

"The same person?"

I interjected, "No, that's not possible."

As much as everyone would like to blame all bad things on the Abbasi brothers, they're not reaching out from their graves and meddling with our lives.

"And now the big question, where did this pen come from?" Lee asked, gathering the components that shouldn't be inside a pen. He held the tiny transmitter between his fingers. "This little thing has been sending your location to whoever is monitoring the signal."

"And that other thing?"

I handed Lee the glass of water that one of the firefighters had given Mike. He dropped the transmitter into it. There was a tiny plop as it sank to the bottom of the glass. Lee picked up the very small microphone.

"This is the microphone, everyone say 'hi.'" He dropped that into the glass of water, too. "So where did this pen originate?"

Mike scratched his head. "Dulles Airport this morning."

"Dulles ..."

"I signed an autograph but the woman left without her pen."

"Any chance you can remember what she looks like?" I asked. So how did someone know Mike would be at Dulles? "Was she on the plane?"

My eyes drifted to Lee then back to Mike.

"I was a little tired but I think she was. I signed the autograph on my way to the shuttle to collect my luggage." Mike thought for a bit. "Yeah, I can remember what she looks like."

"Good, we'll sit you down and get a proper description back at the office," I said and immediately changed my mind. The office wasn't happening. "No, we won't. I can't go back to the office. Let's pack this up, we'll find a hotel."

Sam bumped me with his arm. "A word, Chicky Babe."

I raised an eyebrow and followed him behind a fire truck. "Sam, the shooter at the rec center was wearing an IED. He said the guy who hired him called himself Colonel Mustard – pretty sure he was in communication with the shooter/bomber the whole time."

"That puts a more sinister twist on everything."

"It sure does."

"Speaking of sinister, I had a call from Lee earlier. He said you had an issue with Owen today, before she put out the BOLO."

News travels fast.

"An issue ..." I suppose that's one way of looking at it.

"Chicky, I saw the photo."

I didn't even ask how. Lee had it; he probably snapped

a picture with his phone and sent it to him.

"Okay, Sam, you saw it. It's nothing."

He pulled out his phone and showed me the black and white photograph.

"Doesn't look like nothing," he said. "Looks like you holding a severed hand."

"Photoshop. I didn't do it."

"Your home security was breached last night."

"I heard that, what kind?"

"We think a hacker got into the security system and blocked it, sending out alerts, also took out the cameras. They were clever, Ellie. It was at least fifteen minutes before the security company noticed something was off with the cameras and internal audio. While the system was down, someone broke into the house."

Slow breaths. Slow steady breaths.

"How did anyone find my house to start with?" Unless they had access to FBI personnel files. Someone had a can of worms and a can opener.

"We're dealing with a hacker. Even though you have your address withheld from property tax records and so forth, a hacker could get into the closed records by hacking into the government servers."

"Is that what happened?"

"We don't know. Sean is working on it. He mentioned something about a specific type of worm or virus that could allow a third party access to everything. Five days ago someone got through the firewalls at the Fairfax County Government site with a worm. It was picked up and isolated by the system's anti-virus software on its scheduled run but that may have been too late."

I sensed he was holding something back. "And?"

"The Butterfly Foundation reported a worm or virus attack the same day."

"The same program that attacked the government site and my house?"

"I don't know, Sean is doing the techy thing. He'll let us know when he figures it out."

"How did this worm get into the systems? Email? Or did some idiot click a link?" I keep nothing on the Foundation site that would lead to me. But the directors would have my email addresses and probably my Post Office box details. And yet it all smelled like a cover up and Owen. But everything to do with her smelled like that to my mind. Well, that and burning flesh. Owen the witch hunter. Owen the evil freaking queen. Owen my nemesis.

"We don't know how it got into the computer systems."

"Was the UPS system challenged?"

"Yes."

"Well, fuck. This is too complicated for Owen. She's not into getting her hands dirty." She might break a nail. I doubted any of her henchmen were capable. "Someone has gone to a lot of trouble to set me up. That's a lot of hate and a lot of patience ... might be considerably easier to take me out en route to work or home. Or set me up on the road." The usual tried and true methods work best.

"That kind of comment worries me," Sam said.

I puzzled over this for a moment. "What worries you?"

"That you can provide easier ways for people to kill you."

I moved on. "Have you received the report from my security company about all this?"

"Sean is writing it himself. Let him work his cyber geek magic, Chicky."

"Okay. Now what's missing?"

Sam leaned on the truck. His brow creased. It was bad. I could tell.

"Your office was turned over and Carla's room, too."

I stood next to him. "What's missing, Sam?"

"Her laptop."

"Why would anyone want a kid's laptop?"

"We don't know yet."

Crap there was more.

"Spit it out, Sam."

"Photos are missing from the frames in your office.

"Photos?" I mulled that over for a second. "That's a helluva lot of effort to go to for photos. They must've taken something else."

"Chances are they did but only you would know," Sam replied.

Chances are.

Fuck.

I wanted to curl up into a ball and hide. Carla's laptop. I ran through my memory of the office and the photos on the walls and my desk.

"All the photos?"

"Yes."

Family pictures. My wedding photos. Pictures of me, Carla, Dad, my brother. A few group pictures of all of us, including Delta. Nothing worth so much effort.

I felt sick again.

"So to recap, an actor needs our protection while we locate his stalker. Owen puts out a BOLO on me and would like nothing more than to arrest me and throw me in federal prison just because I piss her off. And back to Mike ... someone leaves him with a bugged pen at Dulles airport. Lee adds a GPS tracker to my wallet and sends Mike to pick me up. Someone shoots at us entering a safe house. I encourage the actor to ditch his car. Someone shoots at us on the way from Fort Totten metro to St. Paul's – then explodes. Someone shoots at us entering the Firehouse. Government sites and The Butterfly Foundation have reported some kind of viral attacks. And my house was broken into. Oh yeah, and there is a photograph of me holding Eddie's severed hand and someone posted the photo on The Butterfly Foundation forum where the kids could see it."

"That's some heavy stuff right there." Sam regarded me for a second or two. "Whoever hacked The Foundation site could have posted that photo?"

"That's what I am leaning toward."

Because that's better than thinking someone from within the Foundation did it.

"It's a mess, Chicky."

"Yeah, it is. But wait, there's more, one of us has been bugged, above and beyond the GPS and the pen. There is another listening device somewhere. I just know it."

"Where do you think it is?"

"Until you told me of the firewall breaches, the only the common denominator was—"

"Lee," Sam whispered. "No fucking way, Chicky."

"Who else knew when Mike was coming?"

"Thinking Lee could be involved is like me thinking you *did* chop Eddie's hand off."

"I'm not suggesting Lee did anything on purpose. I trust *him*."

"Who don't you trust?"

It's a long list. We don't have that much time.

"He was in the office and using my laptop when he messaged Mike to find out when to pick him up, so it wasn't a leak there. Who would he tell about his kid brother coming to town?"

"Tara?"

I nodded. "Yeah, his girlfriend. Tara met Mike when Lee was shot." Maybe she's a total whack job. Who knows with people? "If she had something to do with this, she could've bugged Lee at any time and used someone else to meet Mike at Dulles and bug him."

Did I really believe that theory? Maybe.

"Jesus."

"Where's that fucking photo I had with me this morning?" I said.

"Lee has it."

Lee's voice rang out across the pump bay. "We need to get out of here so these fire fighters and paramedics can get on with their jobs."

"Coming," Sam called back.

I hurried across the pump bay with Sam and spoke to Lee and Mike. "We're going dark. Batteries out of cell phones until I say otherwise."

We all removed our batteries. The logical listening device would be software installed on Lee's phone. With the phones off, the sharing would stop.

"I'll go thank our hosts," I said.

Chapter Six

Baby Come Home

Mike checked into a reasonable hotel in Fairfax with a guest – me – using a false name and a false ID, provided by his brother. Sam and Lee escorted us up to the room.

The room was a fairly large open-plan room with a small kitchenette adjacent to a large bathroom, dining area, two double beds and two armchairs by the window. Across from the stairs and next to the elevator, the room overlooked the main entrance to the hotel, part of the Lee Highway, and the Seers car park at Fair Oaks mall. The four of us made the room feel small.

Lee produced my laptop which he'd managed to get out before my office was locked down. The thought of agents going through my stuff made me queasy. Mentally I did a recon, hoping there was nothing else in my office that they could snoop into and use to cause trouble. Messages from anyone saying where I was last night, for starters. My business, no one else's. The voice message from Beatrice Connelly provided the potential for them to make a mountain out of it. Nothing I could do about that. My brain switched to work mode.

"So explody guy was hired by someone calling himself Colonel Mustard to shoot at us, then go bang. I don't think he knew he would go bang though. He looked like a thug, muscle for hire, not trained, not very intelligent," I said, thinking aloud. "He was probably pliable and easily swayed by cash. The drive-bys weren't professional."

"Caps," Sam said. "If someone is hiring thugs in D.C, he'll have heard something."

"Find him, Sam."

Sam made notes in his notebook and I turned my attention back to the photograph and the Eddie situation.

"Lee, can I see the photograph, please?" I said, sitting at the small table with my laptop open in front of me.

He passed me the photo. I heard him ask Mike to make coffee. Good thinking. The photo was me. It was a real photo of me.

It lay there on the table.

"Cover the severed hand," I said.

Sam covered it with his finger.

"Look at the rest of the picture – anything familiar?"

Sam nodded. Lee closed in for a look.

"You were holding ... you were holding, a bunch of flowers in your left hand," Sam said.

"Flowers, not a disembodied hand by the bloody wrist stump."

"Any chance anyone else has a copy of the original photo?" Sam asked.

I shook my head. "No idea. I can't remember much of that week. Who took the photo?"

"I don't know. How'd you get it?"

"Email probably."

I thought about it some more. I wasn't just holding flowers. I was about to place them on a coffin. The look on my face was not a happy one. What did I do with the picture? I sighed.

"You might still have the email. We need that photo, Ellie. Then we can prove that this," Sam tapped the black and white on the desk, "is a fake."

"Can't the Questioned Documents lab prove it was photoshopped without the original?"

"Probably. But with the original there will be no doubt."

"Everything pertaining to that week was in my desk drawer at home. I printed all the emails and attachments I received and put them in my top drawer."

"What about on your laptop?"

I nodded and opened my email program. I searched by date. Nothing for that week or the week after.

Deleted.

But that's not like me. I don't delete important stuff before copying it. If I was a normal person I could just run an undelete program and get everything back. I use Department of Defense and NSA approved data deletion software – there is no way to restore my destroyed files. That meant I had to find the copies. Flash drives.

I slipped the yellow flash band off my wrist, plugged it into the USB port on my laptop, and searched for email. Nothing. Where else would I keep it? It was important.

"The bank," I said.

"What about a bank?" Lee asked, passing me a cup of coffee.

"When I transferred Mac's stuff to this flash band, I

took the original flash drives to my bank, they're in a safety deposit box." Bits and pieces from the weeks after Carla's death surfaced. "I downloaded everything I wanted to keep regarding Carla, photos, emails, stuff she'd sent me, and scanned a whole bunch of her stories and school things. I put it all on a new flash drive and left it with Mac's stuff in the bank."

I pushed the flash band over my hand and back under my cuff.

"We need to get into the bank," Lee said.

"That's easier said than done," Sam replied.

I smiled. "There is a CVS over in the mall, you two need to go shopping for me." On second thoughts, that wouldn't work either. If anyone saw them buying what I needed, they'd probably remember. I couldn't put them in jeopardy. "Never mind, I'll think of something else."

I had nothing with me but my laptop. My go-bag was a hostage in my office, my house now under constant surveillance, along with my dad's house and my brother Aidan's home.

Time to find an unrelated person. Someone everyone knew would not compromise himself, or more aptly whose management would not allow him to compromise himself. Silencing the scoff that tried to escape was difficult. Our history proved that I was the one compromised by the relationship, not him.

I walked across the room and picked up the handset of the room phone. Dialing the number I knew by heart seemed to take an extraordinarily long time; waiting while the phone rang was killer. My heart rate climbed.

"Hello."

"Hey," I replied, unsure of the reaction my voice would garner. We were so low-key these days, we were sliding into the "barely friends" category.

"Ellie, good to hear your voice," Rowan said. I heard his smile and I knew he meant it, which made the phone call worse.

It was good to hear his voice, too, and I could never tell him that. "Do you still have a bag of mine at your place?"

"Yes. Do you want to come get it?"

"Can you tell me what's in it?" I couldn't remember if I left a useful bag there or if I'd taken it back.

"All right, you want to tell me what's going on?"

I heard his footsteps and doors opening and closing as he looked for my bag.

"Better if you don't know."

He sighed. I heard a zipper open. "In the bag there are two pair of jeans, three tailored short-sleeved shirts, a jacket, underwear, makeup bag, girl stuff, hairbrush, toothbrush."

He paused. I sensed a question. "What?"

"Short-sleeved shirts, since when?"

"That's really got nothing to do with you."

When I'm not me is the answer, but I wasn't about to tell him that.

He carried on. "A box of 9mm shells." He took a breath. "Seriously? You brought a spare box of ammunition to my house?"

"Seems that way." My gun and my job were always an issue. "Anything else?"

"Yes, a document wallet."

"What's in it?"

Papers moved. "Looks like it's a complete identity, driver's license, credit cards included." He paused. "They belong to someone called Laura Graham."

I stuck the blade of the imaginary can opener into the can and gave one twist.

"Thanks, that's helpful."

"Who is she?"

"Take a closer look."

There was silence for a beat. "Wow, doesn't even look like you on the driver's license picture." I listened as he put everything away and zipped up the bag. "You stashed a new life at my house?"

No, it's an old life.

"I did."

"You want to explain why?"

Not really. No. I don't. But I knew I had to if he was going to help me.

"There was always a chance that my life would implode and I'd need a new one ... you used to figure in that plan."

It was not easy keeping up this banter. Break ups are never fun. Ours was splashed about the newspapers and glossy magazines, and appeared way more exciting than the truth. I received so many requests for interviews that it was ridiculous. I ignored all of them.

"What do you want me to do with the bag?"

"Courier it to me."

"Give me the address."

Before I did I said, "You can't tell anyone that you've spoken to me, no one in the FBI. That includes Delta."

"How bad is this?"

"It can't get any worse."

"I have resources. Tell me what you need."

"I need that bag, Rowan." I also needed access to my closet at home. That was difficult.

"Check the bag again, is there a wig in there?" Hoping I was that clever.

I heard another zipper.

"No, there isn't. I can get you hair dye, will that help?"

"Don't worry, not your concern." Hair dye wouldn't turn my straight hair curly like Laura's. I needed the wigs.

"I'm bringing the bag myself."

I closed my eyes for a second. "No, Rowan, no. You being in D.C. will be like red flag to a bull." Owen's the bull. "Keep away from the city."

"I'm bringing the bag."

I blew air out trying to halt the rising irritation. "Forget the bag then. I don't need it."

"Some things don't change."

"What the hell is that supposed to mean?"

"You're still contrary. I'm bringing the bag. Where will you meet me?"

"Leave the bag with Gracey in Merrifield, someone will pick it up."

Lee lives out that way and he's been there before.

"I want to see you."

No, you don't. We've been down this road before. You want to be a hero but it's just an old tattoo.

"Seeing me is dangerous."

"We have foundation business. There is a fundraiser coming up. Grange will be playing."

"Nice try. For that, you need to talk to my father." And he knew that.

"I miss you."

"Julia not what you thought?" The words bounced around the room. The hum of voices that had surrounded me until then stopped. Dammit. I didn't need to say that. "I'm sorry, that was uncalled for."

Julia was the one he turned to when Carla died. He told me I was distant and shut him out, after I found out he'd slept with her.

"I'll drop the bag at Gracey's and talk to your father," Rowan snapped and hung up.

The hum in the room returned.

Chapter Seven
Who Are You?

An hour later, Mike looked back at me, his eyes brimming with curiosity.

"It's just us then, while Lee and Sam go back to work. They'll turn their phones back on once they get to Key Bridge and also the GPS on the cars," I said. I knew Sam would warn Lee that his phone may be a roving bug, so once the phones went on they would not discuss me or Mike at all.

He nodded.

My life is one weird place. How fast I went from being the SSA of Delta A to being holed up in a hotel with an actor, made my head spin. Time didn't stand still despite me thinking it might and wondering how on earth I'd stave off inevitable boredom.

It was so quiet in the room that I heard the footsteps approaching the door despite the thick carpet. I checked my watch. It'd been almost two hours since Sam left. We weren't expecting visitors.

I motioned to Mike to go into the bathroom and peered quickly through the peephole. Kurt stood outside the door with a bag hooked over his shoulder.

I smiled and opened the door. When he was inside I closed it and flipped the security lock.

"Everything all right here?" he asked.

"Yes." I knocked on the bathroom door. "It's okay to come out."

Mike emerged. He and Kurt shook hands while I did the introductions. Mike flopped down on the bed closest to the window. Kurt and I sat at the table.

"You spoke to Sam?" I said.

"Saw him and Lee. I've been looking for you all afternoon."

"You and the rest of the FBI."

"Not too many agents want to bring you in. Owen is making a lot of noise, but people are slow moving."

"Good to know."

"Just don't go walking up to anyone and putting them in the position where they have no choice."

"I won't." Commonsense reared its pretty head. "Surely we could end this by telling Owen my house was broken into and photos stolen?"

"Owen knows. I briefed her myself."

"She knows about the possibility of a hacker?"

"Yes."

"And she still released the warrant?"

"She's not the only one. Metro has a warrant out for you."

"On what grounds?"

"Owen turned over more photographs to Metro. You are wanted for questioning."

I leaned back in the chair. That's better than being wanted for murder.

"Hold on, there are more photographs?" I said, sitting

forward again.

"Yes. Same hand, same clothes on you, different angle."

"Dammit, that's not good." I took a breath. "Everyone's after me and I didn't do anything to fucking Eddie, but I wish I had." Someone had an ax to grind. "Any luck finding the hacker?"

"Not yet."

"Is Owen behind this?"

Kurt grinned. "I wish. But it doesn't look like it. She's a bitch, no doubt about it. She's cashing in on a situation instead of trying to resolve it, but I doubt she has the guts to plan this."

I took a deep breath. "For now, we're okay. Mike is safe and no one knows I'm here or with him, except Delta."

Kurt nodded. "You need to keep a very low profile. Do not ... I repeat, *do not try* investigating this yourself."

"Okay, I won't." I didn't cross my fingers: this time I would let Delta figure it out and stay out of trouble. I glanced toward the window, half expecting a lightning bolt to zap me. Nothing.

The phone on the nightstand rang. Mike answered it and handed it to Kurt while making eye contact with me.

"Who is it?" I whispered.

"Lee," he replied, matching my tone.

I knew by the furrowed brow that whatever Lee said to Kurt did not please him. He walked over and hung up the phone.

"An email arrived at your work account," he said

sitting back at the table. "It's got Owen very excited."

Dread filled my stomach. "What email?"

"I'm sure you'll see it soon. It says, 'Sleepy isn't safe with Snow White and Sneezy can't save them.'"

Mike and I locked eyes. "I suppose you want an explanation?" I asked Kurt.

"Please. Owen thinks it's a code."

I laughed. "Excellent that should keep her busy for a while then."

"It's not code?"

"No. It does mean someone was monitoring the feed from the pen the mystery woman at Dulles gave Mike."

Kurt still looked perplexed. "Sleepy, Sneezy, and Snow White? And this isn't a code?"

I pointed to Mike. "He's Sleepy, Lee is Sneezy. Something from their childhood I believe. I made a smartassed comment about not being Snow White or something while we were in the firehouse."

Kurt smiled. "Let's hope it does keep Owen busy and she doesn't figure it out."

"Can I work on Mike's stalker issue?"

"As long as that means you stay put and don't send any red signal flags."

I smiled. Sure. I can do that. "Sure."

"Ellie, I'm serious. This is bad."

I nodded. "I know." Very aware of how bad it was and how much the situation sucked, I changed the subject. "What's in the bag?"

He dropped his voice to a soft whisper, "Just some

things you left at my place."

"Thank you."

"Thank you for last night." Kurt kept his voice low.

I smiled. "No problem. It was fun." They weren't words anyone would ever expect me to say about babysitting a three-year-old. Olivia was Kurt's girlfriend's child. She was adorable. "Anytime you and Rachel want a night off, I'm only too happy to watch Olivia."

Okay, that took me by surprise. Sometimes my mouth writes checks that shock my brain.

"I'll remember that."

Kurt took a cell phone from his pocket and passed it to me. "It's one of the burn phones from the first-aid kit in my car. Never been used. We each have one. Think it's safer if we stick to these phones to communicate. I put the other numbers in it for you. Only contact us on our work cell phones in an emergency, Conway. Owen will eventually have our work and home phones monitored."

"Eventually. She's not a field agent so having her run the case is probably going to slow things down somewhat, especially if other agents are reluctant to help her. It also depends on how long this goes on." I tapped my fingernails on the tabletop. "So far she's lacking any real evidence against me so getting the wiretap warrants wouldn't be that easy."

"I don't get it either. I don't understand how she got a warrant at all," Kurt said.

"Guess someone owed her a favor. I'm sure we'll be dealing with that in the fullness of time."

Kurt nodded.

She could easily put out a BOLO but to back that with a warrant to arrest, she'd need actual evidence or a very friendly district attorney. I put the phone on the kitchenette counter behind me.

Kurt stood up.

"You leaving?"

"Yes. Sam and Lee are back on the grid now. Time I joined them."

"Won't the bitch get a bit suspicious if y'all go off grid then back on?"

"Yes. Thought of that. All the Delta teams are going on and off the grid until this is resolved. Her screens will be full of darkness then sudden reactivation, it will drive her insane."

That I liked. Always thinking.

Kurt paused at the door.

"You two take care," he said, then disappeared into the hallway. I closed the door and flipped the security lock into position.

Being off duty because of the shitty circumstances left a strange and hollow feeling in my stomach. With a sigh, I decided to make the most of the downtime and settled on the bed by the window with the bag and went through the contents. Clothes, girl stuff, chocolate bars. Chocolate bars. He'd put four 3 Musketeers bars in the bag. My favorite candy bar. One had even saved my life once.

"Catch." I threw a bar to Mike.

"Thanks," he said with a grin and caught it midair.

"Chocolate always works."

Mike picked up the phone and walked into the kitchen area with it. No doubt he had a girlfriend to check in with.

Scrabbling through the bag turned up some DVDs. A small selection of television programs and a few movies that I liked. I chose my favorite television program to watch even though it was probably a little odd considering the company I now kept. A glance at the kitchenette told me Mike was talking on the phone and taking no notice of me. I put the chosen DVD into the player then piled up the pillows on the bed.

Comfortable and ready to enjoy the entertainment, I had a plan, kind of. My plan was to see how much information I could get from Mike regarding his current situation in a more relaxed setting and hoping my DVD choice would help break the ice. Also maybe get an answer to a burning question: do actors watch their own shows?

Mesmerized by the action and engrossed in the television, I jumped when Mike's voice cut through the action on screen. "What are you watching?"

He placed the phone back in the cradle on the nightstand and I hit pause. A smile curled the edges of his lips. His hand squeezed my shoulder. "Sorry, didn't mean to startle you. What are you watching, that's so absorbing?"

My heart rate slowed and returned to normal. "I'm fine. You didn't startle me much."

Who knew he was so freaking light on his feet?

"What did you say you were watching?"

"I didn't."

He shrugged. "Thought I heard my voice."

"That's a little vain don't you think?"

Mike grinned. "You might want to rethink your answer." He pointed to the screen. Brilliant place to pause. There he was front and center. "Looks familiar, like an episode of a series I'm in?"

I nodded like a retard. "It's a good episode, it's a good series."

"You watch it much?"

He indicated the pile of pillows and I moved over a little. Mike sat next to me and got comfortable.

"Hardly ever," I replied, crossing my fingers; my DVD set of the first two seasons was in danger of wearing out. It's not like I knew every episode of the series word for word or anything. It's not like that.

"You going to leave me hanging like that?" He pointed to the television where he was suspended in midair over a river.

"I was going to turn it off."

"Don't do that on my account." He nudged me, reached for the remote and pressed play.

"This isn't strange for you?" I said.

"Not really."

"Does anything faze you?"

"Sure. I'm human."

Not superhuman then? Because so far he was coming

off as quite extraordinary.

"Do you get nervous?"

"I get nervous when I don't have my lines fully memorized, when I haven't had enough rest, when I am distracted and not focused, when I start comparing myself to other people. Mostly it's lack of preparation. Which is to say, I get nervous when I think I have something to hide."

Good answer.

"But watching yourself on TV is okay?"

He laughed. "Yes. But sitting next to a real-life FBI legend makes my heart race a bit."

"They do that to me, too."

He beamed at me and the penny dropped. "I'm not ..."

I shook my head. "I'm not a legend. I'm just an SSA with Delta."

"Really? I have heard some stories about you. From what I've heard you fit the legend mold."

"Legend makes me sound old. I'm nowhere near old enough to be a legend."

I tried to focus on the action on the screen. He was distracting. I wanted to lose myself in the program and forget the world, but I knew getting him to talk was vital. Lee's voice kept popping into my head. I recalled how he once questioned my preference in men. Blond men. In particular, he drew my attention to how I was dating Rowan Grange at the time and had mentioned a certain actor, also blond with blue eyes. No one likes a smart ass.

I glanced at Mike. "By the way, your brother telling

stories about me doesn't count."

The program paused in a quarry.

"It's not just Lee. I did some research of my own." He smiled. "You have a fan base. You have to be the first special agent with a fan base."

Oh dear God. That I did not need. I'd hoped that once Rowan was publically gone from my life that the large amount of attention he brought to me would also go. Topic change time.

"So, Mike, tell me about you?"

"I'd sooner watch this episode," he said.

For the first time since I'd met him, he seemed guarded. Interesting. His closed posture prompted me to poke around.

"Nothing weird going on in your life?"

A tentative smile graced his lips. "I wouldn't say weird."

"I presume Lee told you about the LAPD request to monitor you and the threats that were brought to our attention ... that's not weird?"

He shrugged. "I was on a daytime soap once, now that opened my eyes to how much weirdness there is in the world of television. In comparison there hasn't been a lot of weirdness that I've noticed recently."

"Okay, fair enough, walk me through the day before you left to come out here ... what time did you wake up?"

"Out of bed at five, coffee, showered, shaved, and drove to work. Arrived about six-thirty. Went into the make-up trailer, smiled, and was nice to everyone. Then it was a wait for rehearsal, then back to get into wardrobe while they did the lighting. Head to the set, do the scenes. It was a twelve-hour day of this with an hour for lunch."

"Did you speak to anyone you don't usually talk to?"

"No."

"Let me try something. Close your eyes. You arrived at work, passed through the ..."

"The entrance and parked my car in the parking lot."

"Were there a lot of cars in the lot?"

"It was about half full."

"Is that normal?"

"Yes."

"Get out of your car, who do you see?"

"There is a woman putting something in the trunk of a car and a man walking toward studio two."

"The woman is ..."

"About thirty, slim, dark hair past her shoulders. She's wearing tight jeans with heels and a red short-sleeved dress, or long top thing that came maybe half way down her thighs."

"Anything else?"

"She looked over and smiled, then closed the trunk and got in the car."

"And the man?"

"Wearing a dark suit, short brown hair, carrying a laptop case."

"Do you know him?"

"I don't think so."

"Carry on, do exactly what you did that morning. Do

you see anyone hanging around the set you haven't seen before?"

"Outside the makeup trailer there's a man I don't recognize, he walks away when I go up the steps."

"What was he wearing?"

"Dark blue jeans, a white button-down shirt. He has hair darker than mine but not dark enough to be brown. I saw him again when I went to rehearsals and again when we were doing the scenes."

"Where was he when you broke for lunch?"

"In the parking lot. I went to get a jacket out of my car. I saw him in the parking lot walking toward the studio door."

"Anything moved or different inside your car?"

He was quiet for a few seconds. "I took out my jacket from the back seat. When I went to shut the door there was a receipt on the ground. I picked it up, it was one I thought it was in the glove compartment."

It probably was until the mystery man went through the car and it blew out.

"How many more times did you see the man?"

"I didn't. That was the last time." He opened his eyes.

Job done. I suspected the man planted a GPS tracker in Mike's car.

"You didn't see him near your house or anywhere else after that?"

He shook his head.

"I need to make a call to a colleague in LA, where's your car?"

"At home in my garage."

"Okay, good. Pass me the phone, please." I pointed to the hotel phone on the nightstand. Time to make another long distance call. I listened to the phone ringing and hoped it didn't go to voice mail. Eventually I heard the voice I wanted to hear.

"Special Agent Joe Harris, how can I help?"

"It's SSA Ellie Conway in D.C.," cringing as I said my name. I sucked it up and carried on as if my people weren't hunting me. "Can you go to an address for me and check out a car?"

"Hey, El. Sure, give me the address." It sounded as though today's fun hadn't reached anyone in Los Angeles. Without the benefit of the row of clocks on my office wall, I had to do some quick math. Minus three hours meant that Joe would've been on his way or just arriving at work when all hell broke loose here with Owen.

I handed the phone to Mike. "Tell the nice man your address." I took the phone from him. "Joe, this is classified. Anything you find, contact Lee Davenport at Delta A, no one else."

"Will do. I can head out to that address now. Beachwood is on my way home ... be nice to get home at a reasonable hour."

I checked my watch. It was three-thirty in the afternoon for Joe.

"I appreciate it, love to Carol and the kids."

"I'll be in touch," and hung up.

Mike watched me as I sat back down on the bed.

"What's he looking for?"

"A GPS tracker, maybe a listening device, too. Do you make phone calls from your car?"

He nodded. "Sometimes. But before you ask – hands free."

"Good to know."

Yeah, like I really care at this point.

"Lee said you'd figure this out." Mike looked quickly around the room. "I don't hear music. How'd you do it?"

His brother talks altogether too much.

"I do what I do, it doesn't pay to question how." Only this time it was just old-fashioned police work, no music involved. "Usually the music I hear isn't audible to others. You know, like the Rolling Stones thing at the safe house."

Nuggets of candor like that never failed to make me sound bat shit crazy. Gotta love it.

Mike shook his head then changed his mind and nodded. "Do you like your job?" he asked.

"Yes." Most of the time. "Now, back to you. Can you describe the woman from the airport? The one who asked for your autograph."

He appeared thoughtful then said, "Not as tall as you, what are you five-nine?" I nodded. "She'd be five-four tops. She probably weighed about one-ten. Short blonde hair, not a natural blonde. Quite pretty. Brown eyes."

I typed the description into my laptop. In the back of my mind, someone whispered Tara's name. I shushed the whisper. Mike would recognize her straight out. Also, I had no reason to suspect Tara apart from my trust issues. I couldn't push them aside. Tara was an FBI diver with USERT operating out of D.C. and even that didn't alleviate my concerns.

"Any distinguishing marks?"

"Pierced ears but wasn't wearing earrings." He closed his eyes. "A tattoo, on the inside of her wrist. I saw it when she handed me the pen. She had long sleeves on and I never got another look at it." Mike's eyes opened. Cool blue met my dark blue.

"Any idea what the tattoo was?"

"A rose or bird, it was colored and quite small – reds and pinks."

"How small?"

"Just over an inch and a half."

I made a note to check if federal employees were included in the new biometric tattoo and scar database; if not, that was one hell of an oversight and we should be. An image of a hand and an arm passed across my internal field of vision. I followed it to a face, recognized Tara then let my eyes slide back down the arm, stopping on a tattoo on her inner wrist. It was a blue dolphin.

"Anything else?"

He shook his head.

"What are you doing?" he asked.

"Hang on." I moved the laptop a little so he could clearly see the screen.

"Your brother installed some pretty cool software onto this thing for me a while ago," I said.

"What's it do?"

"Hopefully, it will help us create an identikit picture of the woman from the plane." I carried on filling in the fields I could, asking Mike more questions and getting him to choose eye shape, nose, ears, cheekbones, et cetera. After about an hour we had an image that Mike declared was accurate according to his memory, which I suspected was true. I imagined part of what made him so good as an actor was his attention to detail. He was also ex-military and that, too, came with good observational skills.

I breathed a sigh of relief. Even though I knew it wasn't Tara, the confirmation was welcome. Not only did Tara have a different tattoo but the on screen image did not look like her.

The next step was to run the facial recognition software, and get Mike to help me draw the tattoo. Once we had something he was happy with, I ran it through the biometric database.

"And now we wait," I said.

"Finish watching this episode?" he said with a smile, the remote poised in his hand.

I really didn't want to watch it. I took the remote back. It was too bizarre watching him on the television while he sat next to me.

Instead of television, I slid the laptop onto the chair in the corner by the bed, walked across the room, and turned on the radio. Static filled the air. No matter what I did, I couldn't tune into a station. I clicked it off. No sense listening to white noise.

"I don't know that much about you," Mike said. I could feel his eyes watching me. I didn't know much about him either. I knew a fair bit about his public self but not who he really was.

A familiar yet disconcerting song cranked across the room. "Who Are You?" The Who. I spun around, a frown forming on my face.

Serves me right for missing the songs.

"Freaky," I murmured crossing to the window and lifting an edge of the curtain.

"The Who?" Mike replied smiling.

He could hear it? It's not just me? I stared at the radio from the window. No lights.

I nodded and shut my mouth before I made some comment about him being able to hear the song. I let the curtain fall back into place then walked across the room and checked the door lock.

"Anything?" he asked.

"Nope, just us. Same cars as half an hour ago."

"You think the stalker will find us?"

"Yes."

"You think the FBI or police will find us?"

"Yes."

"You're not one for sugar coating anything are you?"

"No. It's always best to be prepared."

Think worst case then nothing is a surprise.

"Do you ever relax? Have fun?"

I checked the door for a second time then sat down on

the bottom of the bed, then stood up to look out the window again. "I'm always having fun, or haven't you noticed?"

"Must've missed it."

"I'll relax when Delta find the freak who killed Eddie and is trying to frame me, and when whoever it is who wants you shows their hand." I lifted my Glock from the holster on my hip and checked the magazine, then slid the gun back into my holster. "I'll relax when we find whoever broke into my house and whoever the hell Colonel Mustard is."

I unclipped my duty holster from my belt and set it on the nightstand, within arm's reach. Then I unclipped my handcuff case and unbuckled my belt, pulling it free of the belt loops. I dropped my belt and handcuff case onto the chair by the bed.

"You can be quite intense, you know that?"

"Me?"

I'm not seeing it.

"Movie?" he asked, changing the subject.

Maybe he was quite bright.

"Sure, what are the choices?"

He picked up the remote and started flicking channels. "Titanic, Knight and Day, Salt, Zombieland, Defiance, Snow White and the Huntsman."

Okay. I dislike Tom Cruise, can't stand Titanic, Defiance was awesome but intense, Salt was okay but was probably a tad dark. Snow White tended toward deep grey; it's definitely on the dark side and after the email about Sleepy and Sneezy an extra layer of creepy blanketed the title. That was out. Didn't want to watch an intense movie, so the best two movies of those on offer, Salt and Defiance, were out. I was determined to be all about having fun.

"Zombieland."

Look at me being all relaxed and fun.

"Yeah, Zombieland, even though zombies that can run, climb, and turn door handles are fuc'n scary."

"Agreed. We could watch Knight and Day ..."

"No, not Tom Cruise. He's short and he annoys me."

Mike tossed me a lopsided smile. "I don't want you annoyed by anything, so, Zombieland it is then." He paused. "Defiance is excellent."

"It is, but it's not a fun movie."

"Agreed."

I checked outside one more time. No change. I checked the programs running on the laptop. Still running. Forcing myself to sit and stay seated wasn't easy. The pillows seemed all wrong. I stacked them again to support my back. Convincing myself it was okay to have a few laughs didn't go so well.

I can be fun. I am fun, dammit.

Mostly I just didn't want to talk or think. Bring on the mindless zombie gore and comedy.

Just relax. Everything will be fine.

We were screwed.

Chapter Eight
Memory Motel

Holed up in a nondescript hotel room wasn't exactly a hardship. It could've been much worse and that needed to be my focus.

I felt myself slide down on the bed. The movie played on, every now and then Mike chuckled next to me. My mind rolled over everything that had happened, trying to make some sense out of the situation.

Hiding didn't sit well.

I wanted to wave a flag and paint a fresh target on Mike's back. I was pretty sure I could protect him.

Fuc'n bring it on and get this over.

Intense? Not me.

The movie played on. I slid down a little more on the pillows and let my cognition wander free. It was a dangerous maneuver but being still and doing nothing did not work for me, so freeing my mind seemed like a good idea. I must have done it wrong. All I got was a blank inner screen. No amount of twisting knobs and pushing buttons worked. It was blank and stayed blank.

A nudge got my attention.

"Movie. Watching," I murmured.

"Okay," he replied. "What just happened?"

Crap. I stared at a big hole where the middle of the screen should've been. My head tilted to the right, as I tried to see around the grey shroud. I could just make out a fancy looking room. In a house, maybe. Hard to know when I could only see the edges. I searched my pockets without seeming obvious. The synergy bottle had gone. Not good news.

"They're in someone's house," I said.

"They're in Bill Murray's house."

"See, in a house."

"You're not watching," he remarked. "You want a drink of something?"

"That would be nice."

Be much better than trying to see the disappearing television.

"Preferences?"

Without thinking about the giant hole, I tried to check my watch. There was nothing there. But he didn't know that. If I wanted to sleep, coffee was not a good choice. For a moment I considered tea. Kurt made me tea when he was trying to calm me down. I wasn't un-calm. Is that a word? It is now. My brain refused to give me anything to replace it. What I really wanted was tequila. That wasn't going to happen. I could not think where the bottle of migraine synergy had gone.

"Hot chocolate," I replied. "Unless you have a bottle of tequila stashed somewhere?"

"I could do with a scotch and you want tequila ... Didn't we pass a bar just down the road?"

"Yes, we did, and before you suggest it ... no, we can't."

"That's a shame."

"Yeah, it is. There's also a Champps over at the mall and they make wicked blackberry margarita. Can't go there either."

"Hot chocolate it is then. Not sure how good this powdered stuff is," Mike said.

"It's usually not too bad."

The kettle boiled. Water poured. A spoon stirred.

"Mike, can you do something for me?"

"Sure, name it."

"Have a look and make sure there aren't any cameras hidden anywhere in this room."

"Cameras?"

"Humor me."

Yeah, I'm fun. Look at me being fun. I tried scanning possible camera hiding places from the bed but my dodgy vision wasn't conducive to much of anything.

There weren't many places to hide a camera. The smoke detector was about the only viable place.

"Smoke detector?" Mike said.

A frown crept across my forehead, I felt it hiding under my bangs. That's twice now. Twice. First he knew what song I heard, and now he knew about the smoke detector. What the hell? Get out of my head.

"Yes, anything?"

He unclipped the casing and inspected the interior. "Looks normal, nothing extra."

"Good, thanks."

I heard him put the cover back on the smoke detector and then lift the cups off the counter.

It tested the limits of my peripheral vision to watch him approach the bed and take the proffered cup. Holding my hand steady took some effort; the last thing I wanted to do was dump hot chocolate all over the bed or myself. That would be whole new level of humiliation.

"Smells good," I said, blowing across the surface. Ripples bounced off the sides of the cup. "Thanks, Mike."

Manners hurt no one. In hindsight, that was a whopping great big red flag. I'm just not that polite.

"You're welcome." He took a silent sip. "Why the paranoia regarding cameras?"

Just jump right in and call me paranoid, why don't ya? That's so endearing.

"Long boring story," I said.

"I doubt that. You can't tell me?"

"I can tell you."

Maybe talking would push the encroaching dark clouds away. Worth a try.

"Delta stayed in a hotel while on a job some time ago and I attracted another nutjob. Her victims, always women, charged restaurant meals to their room, always women. While the victim finished the meal she hid cameras in the victim's room. She usually drugged their coffee or some similar. Ketamine was her drug of choice. She watched via the room cameras and men went in at the appropriate time. The women were raped. She made a fortune on the live viewing and these women never knew."

I sipped the hot chocolate.

"You weren't ...?"

"No. She chose badly. I wasn't alone. Kurt and I were sharing a room."

"That's what Lee means when he refers to you as Delta's very own Christopher Chance?"

"I make a good target."

"So I've witnessed."

Mike's tone change, I couldn't explain it exactly, but it changed just enough that I noticed. "You and Kurt often share rooms?"

"Depends on the situation. There have been times when we've all been in the same room." It's a special kind of hell sharing a crappy motel room with the entire team. Snoring. Farting. Sleep talking. Hell.

Silence descended but not in an awkward way. It became clear after a few minutes that Mike wasn't done with his questions.

"Tell me, while you were pretending to watch the movie, what were you really doing?" He sipped his drink. "This is probably a dangerous question, but what was happening in your head?"

"I thought only women asked that question."

"Women ask it of men, knowing full well nothing is happening. I'm asking because you're definitely not a guy and therefore you were thinking about something."

Let's not start messing about in my head.

"Maybe nothing was? Perhaps I was in stand-by mode."

"You do realize I'm not buying bullshit tonight?"

I finished my hot chocolate.

"I'm not serving any ..."

He cleared his throat. "I think you might be."

The hole grew, wobbled, and lightning flashed through the center, the storm moving in. A new weather forecast emerged, one with thunder, torrential rain, and hail. If I was a betting person I'd put money on at least one tornado and it might even be an F-4.

I gathered my wandering wits and shuffled them until they sat quietly in my hand. From the deck, I choose four cards and lay them in front of me. An owl, a scythe, a coffin, and a key. Now that was dark. I kept the images to myself.

"Hey, you still with me?" Mike's words scattered the cards.

The images faded but the sense of doom remained.

"Maybe I was trying to figure out the best way to draw out your threat, while not getting myself arrested?"

He coughed and muttered, "Intense."

"I heard that."

"Did you come up with anything?"

Well, no, because I wasn't really thinking about anything constructive. I knew that the images I'd seen pointed to a death but it seemed smart to keep that to myself. Good chance it would be my death, anyway.

And then I was saved by the bell. Not really a bell more a beep from the laptop. Something had finished.

We looked at each other for a second. To be more accurate I looked where I thought he was. Crap. It was now too late for any sort of preventative treatment.

"Ellie?"

"Mike?"

"You going to check the computer?"

"In a second."

I'm just trying to clear my vision and push through the intensifying pain. It's all good.

"Do stalkers usually employ drive-by shooting?"

Oh, okay, he's worried.

"Hmm, see, that's where it all falls over. Stalkers tend to be more personal in their contact and murder attempts."

No one will forget John Lennon's shooting.

"So they weren't after me?"

"I wouldn't go that far. But I don't think that was about you."

Everything was swimming in and out of focus. I was about to show him what intense was, inadvertently. He was obviously not as fine about this stalker thing as Lee thought he would be.

"Lee said something about you being tracked and bugged before ... how'd you handle it?"

Nerves? I wanted to nod but knew better. The white walls and beige curtains could end up decorated with the contents of my skull.

"It's happened a couple of times. The first time was messy and very ugly. He almost had me. But I caught him. The second time, I was an annoyance who thwarted the plans of a couple of terrorists. They took offence. I shot one in the head. The other died in a desert."

I may have smiled when I said that. Some memories are worth holding close, some remind us of all we were and still can be, and some simply bring pleasure. The deaths of the Abbasi brothers brought me more pleasure than maybe they should have.

"You're very intense."

"So you said earlier."

"It still stands." He stretched and then relaxed. "Do you always get them?"

"No, not always ... but mostly." Lightning flashed across my internal screen. I flinched. I really hate the thought of a criminal winning.

"Lee said once you never give up."

"Bet he didn't say it that nicely."

"He did."

Good to know.

"Why do you think someone has made those photos of you with the hand?"

Interesting subject change. It didn't seem to be a cover for anything. I suspected he just didn't want to think about someone so actively trying to end his life. Fair enough.

"I have no idea."

"No demands, right? Isn't that strange? Don't people who create or use things like that usually have a purpose in mind, like extortion?"

"You ask a lot of questions."

"Good? Bad?"

I shrugged. I didn't feel like answering his question aloud. Subject change coming right up.

"Is that TV working okay?"

"Yeah, why?"

That smacked of more trouble.

"Nothing. Must be tired I guess." Without warning, the cup I held fell from my hand, bounced off my leg, and onto the floor.

Here comes that trouble now.

"I'll get it," Mike said. He stood up and walked around the bed to find the cup. I knew where he was, but I couldn't see him. He moved away. Each footstep vibrated through my body, yet I knew he was light on his feet. Every nerve on edge, I waited to see what would happen next. Feeling started to return to my arm.

The television blared. Louder and louder. Flashing lights sent sharp barbs into my eyeballs. I felt around the bed until my fingers connected with the remote.

Red button. Power. I pressed it, plunging the area in front of the bed into a dark silence.

"We're done with the movie?" Mike asked, sitting back down.

"Done," I replied, hoping I sounded normal. I needed the medicine in my bag. But my bag was all the way across the room by the television. It may as well be in Timbuktu. There was a horrible thing happening inside my head. Worse even than the hellish spikes driving into my head courtesy of a sledgehammer: an unwillingness to ask for help.

"Ellie, you okay?"

"Sure," I replied, as a huge railroad cleat impaled the left side of my brain just above my eyeball. Instinctively my hand locked onto the source of the pain and clamped over my left eye.

"You should check the laptop. We might have some answers."

"I can't."

"Headache?" And there he was, in front of me, blue eyes searching mine. I could see him if I moved my head from side to side – but that also made me feel sick.

"You don't look so good."

"But I feel so awesome."

"We've had the bullshit discussion already," Mike said. He hadn't moved. He was still giving me one helluva scrutinizing look. And I'm intense. Uh huh.

Another stake drove into my head.

"Migraine, it's nothing unusual. My bag ..." I pointed toward the beds. Kurt wouldn't have brought me a bag without adding necessary medication to it.

"Okay." He jumped off the bed.

His sudden movement confused my brain. Vomit rose. I struggled to keep the hot chocolate inside my stomach.

When Mike was in front of me again, he had my overnight bag.

"Do you want to do this?"

"No." I leaned back and closed my eyes.

"What am I looking for?"

"Demerol and, I can't remember the name, but ... antinausea pills. Check the packages for dosage."

"Didn't you have a bottle in your pocket earlier?"

"Yes."

He searched through my bag and found what I needed. He also searched my jacket pockets and came up empty.

"I don't know where it is," he said.

"It must've fallen out of my pocket."

Three white pills placed in my hand. In the other hand, a glass of water.

Someone whispered. I swallowed. Pain exploded. Sudden cold landed on my head. Cold. It almost felt good.

Pain. Ice. Cold. Less pain.

I heard whispered words that made no sense. The joy was I knew they'd make even less sense in about twenty minutes. I wanted to speak. Maybe I did. Mac moved closer. Mac?

"You're not here."

"Babe, neither are you. Tell him to call Kurt."

"I'm okay."

"Babe, you and okay parted company when the movie started. You need help. This hasn't happened in months."

"I'm fine. Got drugs on board. Fine."

The ice started to soothe my ravaged brain. Soothing, but still Mac filled the darkness.

Another voice came in.

"Ellie, you still with me?"

Mike.

"I'm here," I whispered. "I'll be okay in a few minutes."

As soon as the words left my lips Mac started to fade. He shrugged and shook his head as he melted into the ceiling.

"What can I do?"

Unless magician was part of his skill set, I didn't think he'd be able to do much.

"I need sleep, silence, and dark."

Perhaps not in that order.

"Then sleep," he said, pulling a blanket up over me.

Darkness crawled across the room. One by one the lights went out and all noise stopped. The dark pulled crazy thoughts together and made a collage of stupidity for me to view. Focusing on one dark square finally halted the images and the spinning.

Sometime later, a buzzing sound jolted me awake. My eyes pinged open but took some time to adjust to the shadows and strange surroundings. I rolled over trying to locate the source of the buzz. A groan escaped before I could stop it.

"Ellie," Mike sounded sleepy.

"What buzzed?" I replied. He was close but I didn't know where.

"I didn't hear anything. What do you need?"

"More drugs," I replied. "Ketamine if you have it." I was half-joking.

"I have to turn on a light. Cover your eyes."

I heard water running into a glass.

"Put your hand out."

Four pills dropped into it.

"What are they?" I muttered.

"Two Advil and two Tylenol."

"No Demerol?"

"Nope, it's too soon."

A flash of anger exploded within me. I threw the pills across the room.

"These won't fuc'n work!"

"You can't have Demerol. I'll get you more ice." He sounded calm, firm, and reasonable.

So goddamn reasonable.

Mike handed me a plastic bag of ice. "Here."

I lay back down and put the ice on my head. The lights went out. A bed creaked. Mike must've lain down.

The cold seeped in, pushing the pain away. The next time consciousness taunted me I heard another voice and no buzzing. Mike, talking to someone, quietly, over by the table. I listened to the conversation and the new voice. He'd called Kurt.

Guess Lee gave him the phone numbers before he left us here. "What are you doing here?" I asked, propping myself up on one elbow, pretending I could see perfectly well without squinting against the light.

"You're sick," he replied.

"You broke protocol," I responded. "I'll live."

Kurt strode across the room to the end of my bed. "This time," he said. "I'm staying."

"That's unnecessary."

"I stay or I leave with all your pain medication."

"What?"

"If I go ..."

"Yeah, I heard. 'Why' is what I meant to say."

"Because you woke after an hour and a half and wanted more Demerol."

"I didn't know it was only an hour and a half ..."

"My point exactly, if Mike hadn't woken up you might have taken more ..."

We stared at each other. No one willing to look away and neither of us wanted to finish his sentence.

Then all of a sudden my mouth kicked in. "It was a legitimate mistake. Nothing more."

"Same result."

True.

"Now what?"

"Now I think we should all get some sleep," Kurt replied. "Mike, bed. I'll wake you in two hours. We'll sleep in shifts. One of us needs to be awake at all times."

A horrible thought entered my head and swam around before exploding from my mouth. "Am I on suicide watch?"

"No, you are not," Kurt said with slow deliberation. "My being here has potentially compromised your location. Sleeping in shifts is for Mike's security." He left the bit about my security out.

I didn't respond, instead I lay down, closed my eyes, and wished those words back. I knew it was too late. The idea was out, they both heard it. Now they'd both be thinking it. Or at least Kurt would. He was there when Carla ...

He was there.

Intense. Maybe I have good reasons to be intense. Pretty sure I used to be fun.

Chapter Nine
Lady In Red

The room phone rang twice then stopped. It rang once and stopped. Then again twice.

Lee.

"Hey, what's up?"

"I have the bag. You ready to adopt a new identity?"

"Hell, yes." And all of a sudden, everything looked brighter. One night trapped in a hotel and I'm climbing the walls. That did not bode well for a low key off-the-radar existence. "I have another request. It might not be easy."

"Shoot."

"I need you to go to my house and bring me a wig from the closet in my room. There are four human hair curly auburn wigs on the shelf, and they're dated. Get the most recent one, that's the one I wore last time I was Laura." They were different lengths but all the same color and a similar hair style.

"Okay. Cross your fingers that Owen hasn't got agents outside your house."

"I need that wig."

"I'll be there soon."

I hung up. Kurt opened an eye and looked at me from the chair next to the bed.

"Who was it?"

"Lee. He's running an errand for me then coming over."

"I heard. Hope he brings breakfast, too."

"Didn't say."

"How you feeling?"

"Okay," I said.

"Let's keep it that way. Where's your synergy?"

"I don't know. It was in my pocket yesterday."

"Spare bottles?"

"Of course." But they weren't so helpful now. "One in my desk drawer at work and one in my nightstand at home."

"How long does it take to get here from Le'Esscience?"

"Five days."

"I'll order more and have it sent to my place," Kurt said.

"This isn't going to go on for another five days ..."

He didn't reply.

"Kurt, call Lee. Ask him to bring the bottle of synergy from my nightstand." Five days was too long to wait.

Kurt made the call and Mike rolled over in his bed and stretched.

"Morning," he said, yawning.

"Morning," I replied. "Sleep well?" My eyes watered as I yawned.

"Yeah, every few hours."

"Go back to sleep, there's nothing happening here."

Kurt lifted the laptop off the floor.

"Did you check this last night?" he asked.

"No, we got sidetracked," I said.

Mike headed for the bathroom while Kurt and I peered at the screen.

"You got six matches on that tattoo," Kurt said.

I would have asked him to print the list but there was no printer in the hotel room. Mike came back and sat on his bed. He looked tired. I figured that was my fault.

"What about the identikit picture?" I asked.

"That narrowed it down some, three matches," Kurt replied.

"Let me guess, those three all have the same or a similar tattoo on their inner wrist?"

"Yes. Current addresses put one in Oregon, one in New York and one in Pasadena," Kurt said.

"Read out their names. You listening, Mike?"

"Uh huh," he replied.

"Kim Smith, China Caldwell, Nancy Trevgard," Kurt said. "Any of them familiar?"

Mike shook his head. "Sorry, no. Can I see pictures?"

Kurt walked over to Mike's bed with the laptop. He showed him each photo.

"That one, she asked for the autograph," he said pointing to the picture of China Caldwell. "I feel like we might have met before?"

Kurt and I smiled at each other. She was the one who looked the most like Tara, Lee's girlfriend. It definitely wasn't Tara. I figured Mike would have recognized his brother's girlfriend. Did I really think Tara could be involved or did that theory manifest because I'd spent too many years with "trust no one" as my battle cry?

"Clarify that, Mike. Have you met the woman before?" I asked.

He studied the picture. "No, I haven't. I thought she looked familiar in that photograph but in person she wasn't."

"How well do you know Tara Sutherland?"

"Lee's girlfriend? We've only met once and that was in the hospital when Lee was wounded," Mike said.

A stressful time all round.

"Did you get on?" I asked.

"Didn't have time to find out. Haven't seen her since. Lee talks about her sometimes. He seems happy." Mike shrugged. "We lead busy lives on different coasts."

"This China Caldwell woman bears a resemblance to Tara," Kurt told him. "It's definitely not her but there is a similarity."

Mike smiled. "Ah, I see."

"So, we have an ID on the mystery airport woman. Let's find out if she was on the plane," I said to Kurt. He was already at the table and typing on the laptop.

"There was a China Caldwell on the same flight as Mike from L.A," he said.

"We need a background on that woman and current address and travel plans."

I heard my email alert.

"Ellie, you might want to see this ..." Kurt said. He did not look happy.

I scrambled off my bed and joined him, as did Mike.

We peered over Kurt's shoulder at an email and a new color picture of me holding a foot. A severed foot, wearing a sneaker. It was time and date stamped. Today's date, 3 a.m. Two photos now. A definite increase in activity.

"That's a nice shot," I commented. "Shame it never happened."

"What were you holding in the original photograph?" Mike asked. "It looks very convincing."

It did look convincing, right down to the smile on my face.

"I'm not sure what I was holding."

"A microphone," Kurt said. "I think this was one of the photographs from a fundraiser for The Butterfly Foundation. I could be wrong."

I looked at myself in the picture. A really nice red long-sleeved shirt and jeans, my hair loose, and about two inches shorter than now. Maybe it was a fundraiser but I had a feeling it was taken at Oakton High school. I'd talked to Carla's class about life as a Special Agent. He was right about the microphone then.

"Can I?"

I motioned to the laptop. Kurt stood up and let me sit. I opened the email header and copied the contents into a little program I use that tracks back to the sender's Internet Service Provider. Within about two seconds, I stared at a very familiar set of ISP numbers. I used a fixed ISP at home. There was no way around what I saw on the screen; the email had been generated from my home.

"Holy shit," I said.

"What?" Kurt asked.

"Whoever sent it, sent it from my ISP. Mine. Even Owen on her worst day will be able to extract that information from the email." That was a stretch; she wouldn't but one of her henchmen would. "She'll use that to hang me."

My fingers typed on the keyboard. Moving on, there was nothing I could do about the email and its origin. What I needed was the real photo. I found the school website and went searching. Sure enough there was one of me with a bunch of kids from Carla's class. Same red shirt and my hair was the right length for it to be a photo from that day.

I emailed the school and asked them to send me copies of any photos taken that day. At least I could get those without going to the bank.

"Who sent the picture to you?" Mike asked.

A frown formed as I thought about his question. "Sam forwarded it from his personal account." Scrolling through the source information I found the code that told me where he got it from. "This email was sent to Owen and Metro."

So how did Sam get it? Sandra.

"Knowing Sandra like I do, I'd say she's activated a little something inside Sentinel that's capturing copies of emails going to Owen's account."

"This is bad, right? I mean another photo of you with a body part?"

"It isn't good," I said. I'm a bit screwed. "Owen is going to use it to push her cause and Metro will, too."

The difference being Metro are investigating the photos and Owen is on a witch hunt.

"Kurt can you check with Sandra and see how the Metro investigation is going?"

He nodded. "I'll do it in person. Meanwhile, it's time I got going."

"I'll see you later," I said, flopping back onto my bed. "Lee will be here soon."

I waved a hand in Kurt's general direction. Mike walked Kurt to the door. I heard them say their goodbyes. The door opened and closed, followed by a metallic sound as Mike flipped the security lock.

"I'll take a shower," Mike said.

I closed my eyes for a moment as images and thoughts about that day at Carla's school swirled around in my mind. Not really the day, but the night that followed. That night I wore a red dress and Rowan sang 'Lady in Red' to me at The Butterfly Foundation fundraiser that Kurt spoke of earlier. Rowan enjoyed how it made me cringe to have everyone's attention on me. That was not one of his more endearing qualities.

The red dress memories disappeared as more pressing things took over.

I had a plan. It was awesome.

Chapter Ten
When We Were Beautiful

"Let the transformation begin," I said. I turned on the bathroom light and the fan started. Clever. I left the door open.

Lee appeared in the bathroom doorway. "Couldn't find the synergy."

"I'll live," I replied and taped a photo of Laura to the mirror. That was who I was about to become – complete with long curly auburn hair and green eyes.

I took off my wedding rings and removed the necklace I wore, giving them to Lee for safekeeping. The tan line on my ring finger might be tricky. Laura was not married and she wore a small gold cross around her neck, not a silver Saint Michael.

I looked at him in the mirror. "I'm going to be a while. There's a staff bathroom near the laundry room on the ground floor."

He grinned. "I'm good. Just wanted to see if you needed help."

"I'm questioning the wisdom of letting my hair grow so long," I replied. "Makes it harder to put on the wig."

My eyes met Lee's.

"No, Chicky, I'm not cutting your hair." He backed away.

"Not all of it. To just below my shoulders so there isn't

so much of it."

"What's the plan once you've transformed," Lee asked, changing the subject. I clipped my bangs back off my face. It was odd seeing my forehead again.

From the sponge bag next to the basin I took a small box containing green disposable contact lenses. I had another nine boxes just the same, and lens solution – with care, nine months' supply. It'd been a long time since I'd worn contacts and my eyes watered.

"I'm going out," I replied, blinking. My eyes were not happy.

"Is that wise?"

"Hell, no," I said with a grin. "I'll be fine. I'll be with your brother."

"You'll be what?"

"Potentially you and I could be related one day," I said, with a wink.

Lee laughed. "I was right about the blond thing."

I ignored his comment. He was, but he wasn't right about this particular blond.

"Mike has been careful to keep his girlfriends out of the media ... or he's just not that famous. Either way, that's going to work in our favor."

"You're planning to accompany Mike on his public appearances and establish yourself as his girlfriend, so you can move around and investigate Eddie's missing limbs?"

"Sort of. I'll pose as Mike's girlfriend but I don't give a rat's ass about Eddie. I want the hacker and whoever broke into my home." And Carla's laptop. "Plus, there is a good chance the stalker will target me, not him."

"Because stalkers often target anyone who stands between them and the object of their misguided affection," Lee said.

"I'm counting on it."

"Does Mike get a say in any of this?" Mike said.

I stuck my head out of the bathroom and saw him in the chair by the window.

I met his gaze. "Sure, what say you, good sir?"

"I say ... this sounds like fun."

It really did.

"Are you sure about Laura?" Lee asked.

"It'll be okay. It's not like I dug up Demelza." Another redhead, another lifetime.

"True."

"We could create a new cover but Laura exists and has legitimate paperwork. One phone call and she can walk back into her job." As much as I hated to think it, if this doesn't get resolved I may have to become her permanently.

"She also has baggage."

"Everyone does, it makes the cover more believable." I was spinning shit hard and fast, hoping some would stick and be less smelly. I was really hoping for sparkly rainbow unicorn poop to come from the sticky brown mess.

"It makes this dangerous."

And that makes it fun.

In my head I heard Mike telling me how intense I am. I shook it off.

My newly green partially bloodshot eyes stared at me from the mirror. I glanced at the wig sitting on the counter. My hair needed cutting.

I poked my head out the bathroom door. "Mike, you got scissors?"

Mike nodded and scrabbled through his luggage. He brought them to me. Nail scissors. Lee shook his head. "Not me," he said, exiting the bathroom.

"Mike, I almost don't want to ask this but can you cut my hair with those?"

"It's not going to be a great cut ..." he said.

"That's okay, I just need to get some of the length off, so I can wear the wig more comfortably."

"Sure, how much?"

He stood behind me and pulled all my hair to the back. "How much do you want off your hair?" he asked.

"About eight inches. Take it as close to my shoulder blades as possible with those teeny tiny scissors."

Mike laughed.

I watched in the mirror as Mike snipped, taking small sections at a time. Masses of blonde strands covered the bathroom. My head felt lighter than it had in years. A weird kind of freedom flowed over me. "You did a pretty good job, Mike. What's it looking like from the back?"

"Better than I thought it would," he said.

That was comforting.

The men went back to the main room leaving me to

enjoy the new freer me for a few minutes before tucking up my hair and pulling on the wig. I gave my head a shake. Long auburn curls fell down my back. One more shake and curls tumbled over my forehead. Laura had no scars to hide but I did. She also swept her long bangs across her face, exposing just some of her forehead. My eyes took some time to settle so I made coffee for us all and went through the bag Lee had brought. Clothes.

Ellie Conway wore long-sleeved shirts, always. She wore cowboy boots, always. Laura wore short-sleeved tee shirts, cute jackets, and regular black boots with a lower heel. I chose clothes and disappeared back into the bathroom with them and coffee.

I pulled the tee shirt over my head. The low v-neck looked fabulous with my suddenly perky bosom. I had the girls padded a little and trapped in a push-up bra. That I could deal with but it felt so strange seeing my right arm exposed. I inspected the scars. They didn't look as bad anymore. Time does heal most things.

Opening the door. I stepped out and said, "What do you think?"

"Cute," Lee said without missing a beat. "The hair color suits you. Curly hair always makes you look different."

Mike smiled showing off his dimples. "What Lee said. How do you feel?"

"Not good," I replied. "Self-conscious. It'll take me a while to get used to being her again."

"Welcome to my life," he said.

"I'm not as used to it as you."

"I can help," he said. "It's kinda my thing."

Who better to give me acting lesson?

"All right."

"Don't be offended but are you concealing the scars or does Laura have them, too?"

"Concealing."

It's what I do best.

He pointed to the bathroom and followed me in. I took concealer from the sponge bag on the door and a makeup sponge.

Mike took the tube from my hand. "Same stuff they use in the makeup trailer on set. Do you have any primer in that bag?"

"Yes." I fished it out for him. It didn't seem odd that a guy knew about primer.

He squeezed a little primer onto his fingertip. "I've learned a thing or two in my years on television. Turn your arm over." He carefully smoothed the primer over the scars and surrounding skin. "What are they from?"

"The big one running down my inner forearm was an argument with a marine," I replied.

Mike's eyes met mine. "And this one?" he asked, applying more primer to the second scar.

"I can't even remember," I lied.

It was the same fight. We really went at it.

"And the ones on your upper left arm?"

He was very observant. I supposed being an actor made you aware of detail.

"Glass," I said. "And a graze from a nine millimeter."

"Your forehead?"

"That's an old one. It was a graze from a bullet." Mike took the makeup sponge and dampened it. He started working on the scars on my forearm "Corrective makeup. It's the reason no one knows I have a tattoo unless I play a character requiring a tattoo."

"I saw it, on your arm."

"Yes, you did."

"Is it a dragon?"

"It is."

I watched in the mirror as he rendered the scars on my right arm invisible. He was good; guess he'd had a lot of practice. "That looks good."

"I'm going to cover them all, even though your sleeve covers the two on your upper arm, someone could catch a glimpse, and you don't want anyone coming back for a second look."

Cover them *all* sounds bad.

"Okay."

He carried on. Before long I stood scar free in front of the mirror.

I turned to Mike. "Pleased to meet you, I'm Laura Graham." I shook his hand firmly.

"I'm Michael Fisher and you now have dinner plans."

I smiled.

Together we packed away the makeup and scooped up all the hair into a plastic bag, ready to drop it in the trash room on our way out.

I took an over-the-shoulder handbag out of Laura's overnight bag and put her wallet in it. She had a permit to carry concealed. I took her Glock from the compartment hidden under a false bottom in the bag, finding it hard not to smile about Rowan's reaction to the rounds.

No one said a word as I sat at the table with a Glock cleaning kit and dismantled the weapon, cleaned and reassembled it. There was a paddle holster with the gun. Perfect. I slid the paddle and gun inside the back of my waistband. Lee handed me a lightweight Nike jacket.

I plugged Laura's phone into a wall charger. From the bag I found a jewelry case and fastened a small gold cross around my neck on its fine chain. I searched for a ring that would pass for an engagement ring to cover the tan line on my finger but had nothing suitable.

"Hey Mike, can you cover this for me?" I held up my hand and pointed to the white line.

"Sure, but it won't last. Better to find a ring to wear."

I raised an eyebrow as the next thought rallied. "If I'm going to be seen with you and I'm seen wearing a ring ..."

"The rumor mill will churn, but so be it."

Lee stood up and looked out the window, obviously thinking.

I carried on with my immersion into Laura's world. From the hotel phone I called her office. It was something I did periodically anyway. Just to keep the staff on their toes and to remind everyone Laura existed. She took long jobs offshore, which was why she wasn't seen in the city very often. A few times a year, I donned one of the wigs, green contacts and appeared in the office as Laura.

The only people who knew who she really was were the members of Delta A. We'd used Laura a few times. She was a private investigator which meant she could occasionally do things we couldn't. Well, we could, but we had to be able to justify our actions to a select committee if needed, and Laura didn't have any such restraints.

"Good morning, it's Laura Graham."

"Good morning, Miss Graham. Would you like to speak to Simone?"

"Yes, please," I said. Moments later I heard Simone's voice.

"Simone Dubois."

"Simone, it's Laura. I'm in town."

"*Magnifique*! We will of course do lunch," Simone said, her French accent punctuated her words and made a simple sentence sound exciting.

I launched into French and asked if she'd like to meet for a late lunch and that'd I'd bring a friend. Simone decided on the Hard Rock Café. Perfect. I asked her to book a table overlooking E Street.

"See you there," Simone said and hung up.

I knew I was smiling. Lee wasn't. He still stood by the window but now he faced me, frowning. Mike sat in the chair by him. He was smiling.

"Problem?" I mustered innocence to go with the query.

Mike's right hand gestured toward Lee. "*Mon frère se*

préoccupe de nous savoir si proches de l'immeuble Hoover."
My brother is concerned about you being in such close
proximity to the Hoover Building.

"I didn't know you spoke French," I said with a wink.

"Votre frère n'a rien à craindre. Nous sommes en train de
déjeuner. Qu'est-ce qui pourrait mal tourner?" Your brother
has nothing to worry about. We are having lunch. What
could possibly go wrong?

"You can both start speaking English, thanks," Lee
growled. He did a pretty good impersonation of Caine
when he felt the need.

"Who is Simone?" Mike asked.

"She runs my business for me," I replied. He needed to
know some things if we were playing at being a couple. "I
am the owner of a business called L'Agence."

"The agency," Mike said with a small laugh. "And it
is?"

"A private investigation business."

"Do they know who you are?"

"Absolutely, Simone is well aware that I am Laura
Graham from Richmond, Virginia."

"How do you keep a cover intact like that?"

"It's not easy. I keep a special phone for Laura which is
usually set to voice mail only. I clear the voice mail once a
week and deal with whatever the issue is that has cropped
up."

"Doesn't she ask questions?"

"No, why would she? I hired her to manage the
business." I ran my hands through my hair, untangling

some of the curls. "Simone takes care of the day to day running of L'Agence. I just float in and out when it suits me."

Lee rested on the window sill and shook his head.

"Mike," he said, "keep her away from the Hoover Building. Do whatever it takes."

"We need to stop by a jeweler to get a ring," I said. "Across the road in Fair Oaks mall is a perfectly suitable jewelry store."

Yes, I was ignoring Lee's comment.

"Refresh my memory, where is your public appearance this morning?" Lee asked Mike.

"Museum of Natural History in the mall."

Lee directed his next remark to me, "Gimme the gun."

I had a deal of reluctance about handing over my weapon, but he was right. I could not walk into the museum armed. Not only were bags checked but there was a metal detector to walk through. Undue interest would be aroused by the alarms going off. Even with Laura's permit to carry and a Private Investigators license it was best to try to keep a low profile.

Low. I heard the word in my head but it failed as a caution.

"What time?" I asked.

"Midday," Mike replied.

I checked my watch. "Let's order a town car," I said.

Lee made a call using the hotel phone and booked one for the rest of the day. It was due to pick us up out front in thirty minutes. So much easier than driving ourselves and more secure. Tinted windows and a driver.

"Am I dressed okay for this museum thing?"

Mike smiled. "Totally."

"Casual then?"

"Yes."

"And what's it for exactly?"

"It's a promo event for the next series. The new season starts with the theft of the Hope Diamond."

I swallowed. The last time I saw the Hope Diamond was when a new exhibit was installed at the museum. A new diamond exhibit, courtesy of Zachary Bleich. He'd bequeathed The Heathcote Diamonds to the museum. Seemed the best place to keep the diamonds after the death of his family. They were displayed along with the history of the diamonds and the more recent story of their theft to fund a terror cell. The thing about that was there was a photo of me and the rest of Delta giving the recovered diamonds back to Zachary.

A photo of Ellie.

I am Laura.

"If you want to get that ring you better get going," Lee said. "The car will be here soon."

"Let's go," Mike said. "Will you be at the museum?"

"No, I'll hand off to another Delta agent. It's better that way."

Lee walked across the room to the door. I went with him.

"Alert and safe, Chicky."

"Alert and safe," I replied as our hands ran along each

other catching at the finger tips. "He'll be okay."

"I know, you're with him."

Nice to get the vote of confidence.

Chapter Eleven
Shine On, You Crazy Diamond

The front steps of the Museum of Natural History rose in front of me. Children dotted the steps in groups as adults milled around the food cart at the bottom, getting coffees and snacks. Not too many in the crowd noticed Mike as we walked up the wide steps, where visitors filed through the side doors. The main doors were closed.

Mike placed his hand lightly on the small of my back as we walked.

"I'm not going to run away," I whispered.

"I'm the attentive boyfriend," he replied with a grin.

My eyes worked on focusing on the darker museum interior as we approached the doorway. "You first," I said in a whisper.

"No, you're my girlfriend. You go first."

"We don't have time to debate this. If I go in, you're exposed."

"Honey, you made yourself the target. Go first."

I smiled and kissed his cheek. Hoping it would throw off anyone who was watching our exchange. I walked ahead of him and through the door. I handed my bag to the guard and walked through one of the metal detectors.

I couldn't help but hold my breath. No alarms.

Sam stepped out from behind the security guard holding my bag. It was hard not to acknowledge him as a close friend and colleague. Mike was right behind me and the three of us moved off to the side. Being overlooked by a huge elephant in the middle of the room was slightly disconcerting; large stuffed animals are creepy in a *Night at the Museum* way.

Introduction time.

Sam shook Mike's hand. "Agent Sam Jackson, call me Sam."

"Michael Fisher and this is Laura Graham."

"Shall we?" Sam said, ushering us through a large doorway toward some well-worn marble steps. In the dim hallway, Sam handed back my bag.

"I think this is yours," he said.

It felt heavier. I slung the strap over my head and casually peered inside and there was my gun and holster.

Yes!

"Thank you."

"We are going up the stairs and along the corridor to the room that holds gemstones. The Hope Diamond is in the middle of the room," Sam said.

"You've already been up?" Mike asked, as we walked slowly up the stairs, keeping to the right.

"Yes," Sam replied.

"How is it?"

"Plenty of media present."

"So hard to tell the scum from the stalkers then?" I said.

"Very, be careful," Sam said. We neared the top of the stairs. "Follow me, stay close."

We did as we were told. After all, I was Laura, Michael's girlfriend. No telling what we were walking into. That's when Mike took my hand as if reminding me he was Mike the TV star now, just like I was Laura.

He whispered into my ear, "Do you know what to expect in there?"

"Yes, no, sort of. I try to avoid large gatherings of vultures. Haven't always been successful though. Remind me."

"Lots of flashes, noise, people asking you to look in a certain direction. Ring a bell does it?" he said.

"Makes me antsy and my trigger finger itchy … is that what you mean?" I smiled.

Mike laughed. "I can imagine you reacting like that. Can you do this today without shooting anyone? Will the flashes be an issue?"

"I don't know to both questions."

"You've been around strobe lighting? Does that set off your migraines?"

"Yes."

Another reason I don't like rock concerts.

"Okay, I'll deal with the media."

Sam walked into the room first. People who obviously had something to do with the TV channel and promoting the series met us at the door. Mike spoke to someone and seconds later that person walked to a podium and addressed the flashbulb-crazy crowd.

"I'm going to ask that you refrain from taking photographs using flashes, for medical reasons. Anyone who doesn't comply will be removed."

There was a low murmur then nothing. A moment later someone from the press crowd spoke, "Can we get some more lighting in here?"

A conference ensued.

"The museum will bring in some extra lighting."

While the staff set up extra lights, we had time to meander around the edges of the throng and check out some of the other exhibits. So many diamonds and precious stones. Mostly people left us alone to look; I'm guessing Sam following us had a lot to do with that. No one usually wants to mess with him. The same man who had addressed the crowd came to get us.

"Michael, they're going to introduce you in a minute. You ready?"

"Sure, I'm good."

"We'll let the Q and A go for half an hour, I know it goes without saying but don't give too much away. We want people to watch the new season." He patted Mike on the back. Friendly, like his tone. I didn't think he was our stalker.

While Mike was out front, I had time to study everyone in the room. Sam took one half and I the other. Then we swapped, meeting by a ginormous topaz exhibit.

"Anything?" I asked.

"A woman has been watching you and Mike, she took photos, tried to do it covertly."

"Describe her," I said.

"Can do better," he replied and produced his phone.

"Her."

I matched the picture to a woman in the room. She focused on Mike, right up until he saw me and did some weird-assed eye-lock thing, that without a word of a lie felt like a tractor beam. I couldn't look away. What the hell?

I nudged Sam.

"What's she doing now?" I whispered.

"She followed his line of sight," he said, and angled his body toward me a little more. "She is looking right at you."

Mike, still answering questions, broke his gaze and I felt as though I'd plummeted to the ground. With a shake of my head, I carried on. That was weird.

"And now?"

"She's staring at Mike again."

"And so is that guy on the edge there." I pointed subtly.

"Got a picture of him, too, he was a little too interested in you for my liking."

Mike had a new question fired at him and suddenly I was involved in his Q and A. The tractor beam gaze was back. He smiled and then he grinned.

I struggled to remember the question. Then it was fired at him again.

Guess his grin wasn't an answer.

"Michael, you arrived with a very attractive redhead, is it serious?" someone said.

"Michael, she's wearing a ring, anything you want to

tell us?" another journalist said.

"Laura is my girlfriend," Mike said, disarming at least four questioners with a killer smile.

One regained enough composure to throw another round of questions at him. "And the ring? Is there an announcement pending? Where does Laura live? You've kept her under wraps, is there a reason why you're showing her off now, here by The Hope Diamond?"

Showing me off?

Oh, I don't think so. I stepped forward.

Sam's hand clamped down on my arm. "Stay with me."

Mike's eyes never left mine. I tried to figure out how he did it – something I intended asking him.

With the finesse that comes with experience, he turned the questions back to the show and it was nearly ten minutes before anyone else piped up with personal questions. I relaxed, feeling okay about being Laura. I trotted out a little bit of French while speaking with Sam, just to get back into her fully. It's not that she's French, but she does spend a lot of time in France. I heard someone new speaking from the podium, followed by a round of applause, then a photo opportunity. Michael Fisher with the Hope Diamond.

Two armed guards stood close by as the curator of the gem exhibit opened the display case and let Mike hold the diamond and its sculpted diamond ribbon setting, a newish setting, designed in 2009 by Harry Winston to celebrate the fiftieth anniversary of his donation of the Hope Diamond to the museum. Photographers asked

Mike to look this way and that way and over here. They seemed to have a lot of instructions.

Mike's eyes found me again. He drew me in. His mouth opened, words came out. I pretended not to hear him. He smiled and repeated, "Laura, come over here."

"Suck a duck," I hissed at Sam under my breath.

"Yeah," he breathed back. "Go on, Laura."

I strode over and joined Mike in front of the cameras. This would test our ability to keep my real identity secret.

He whispered, "The curator said you can wear this for a few photos."

Before I could react he passed the diamond ribbon around my neck and fastened the clasp.

I was wearing the Hope Diamond. Its other names circled in my mind. Le Bleu de France – the Blue of France. Le Bijou du Roi – The King's Jewel.

It was stunning.

"Matches your real eye color," he whispered. "Shame you hid your beautiful blue eyes from the world with those green lenses. Now smile and let the media have their moment."

I plastered a smile on my face. I was wearing the Hope Diamond. They could photograph me all day. I was wearing the Hope Diamond.

Memories of the last time I held a diamond that size, caught in my throat. I didn't even want to think about the Heathcote Diamonds. I'd avoided the display cabinet containing them, managing only a passing glance before moving onto less impressive stones and ones that held no memory for me.

After about five minutes of photographers asking me to turn this way or that way, and look over here or there, the curator politely said it was time to put away the diamond.

Mike thanked everyone for coming and reminded them what night and time the new season of his show started.

I smiled and hung on his arm.

See? I can be a dutiful girlfriend as long as I'm being someone else, and it's a job.

We were done. Sam escorted us from the room and back down the stairs away from the media and interested people. I could feel eyes on us as we walked. I knew that the woman and the man were both watching.

At the bottom of the stairs, I steered Mike toward the glass cabinets lining the walls.

"The birds are lovely," I crooned.

"Sure are," he said. "Look at this one."

He played along perfectly, pointing out a bird.

Sam stayed with us. I maneuvered to be able to talk to him while we walked along the hallway looking at birds.

"Did you get usable photos?"

"I think so," he said. "I've sent the images to Sandra, she'll run them through the facial recognition database."

"Let me know. I'm not getting a good vibe from the male. The woman is giving off an air of desperation."

"Duly noted."

I smiled and pointed out another bird to Mike, who in

turn found a funnier looking one.

"Did you find Caps?" I asked.

"I did. He said if anyone's recruiting, then they are doing so quietly. He hadn't heard anything," Sam replied. "He might be recruiting from Maryland or Virginia."

"I guess I hoped Caps would've heard something."

"If he had he would've come to us. Don't worry, he'll ask around. You never know what he'll turn up."

"Keep in touch with him."

"Are we done?" Mike asked. "You good to go? There'll be media outside."

"We're done. Let's go for a walk and grab a coffee before we meet Simone."

"You want to dismiss the car?"

I looked at Sam who shook his head. "No, she does not."

I kinda do.

The idea of walking through the mall with Mike had a certain appeal. I let an image of Michael Fisher fill my mind. He wasn't invisible. I would not be invisible walking through the National Mall with him.

The little voice in my head that sounded like the voice of reason told me to take the car and go somewhere safer for coffee.

I overrode the voice. "I want to go to the Castle for coffee."

Sometimes it's safer to hide in plain sight.

Sam sighed. "I'll come with you."

"The Castle?" Mike queried.

"Yeah, come on, Mike, you gotta see the Castle."

"Where is it?"

"Right across the National Mall from here," I said.

"Sam?"

"I'll tell your driver to meet you on Independence, outside the Haupt Gardens," Sam replied. "We'll walk across the grass, you can have coffee and then go right through the Castle and out the Independence Ave side, walk through the garden, get in the damn car and go to your lunch."

"Good plan," I said. I could see the same woman from upstairs walking toward us, trying to appear nonchalant but failing. I whispered to Sam, "Now, why is that woman pretending to look at birds, but really checking out Mike in the reflection of the cabinets?"

"You two go that way," he said, pointing to a large hall and a gift shop. There were a lot of people in the store. I spotted a restroom sign.

"Restroom," I said. "Meet you in the gift shop."

Mike walked me into the hall. Sam waited for the woman.

Chapter Twelve
Make You Feel My Love

I hurried into the bathroom. Two women with small children were washing the kids' hands and generally doing motherly things. No one took any notice of me.

I walked into a stall just as someone I recognized walked out of the one next door.

Taking note of the media pass around her neck, I quickly shut the door behind me.

Dammit.

Three minutes later I went to the basin and washed my hands. There she was. Waiting.

"You're Laura Graham. Can I have a few moments of your time?"

Ellie would have snapped back, I know who I am and no, fuck off. Laura was by far a nicer person.

"Yes, I am Laura Graham, How can I help you?"

"I'm curious about you and Michael Fisher. No one has seen you before."

I smiled. Hoping it was sweetly. "I'm sure that's not true."

From the corner of my eye I saw a shadow, move across the room. Odd.

It grew as it came closer. A shadow with a long pointy finger.

No.

I shoved the journalist out of the way as a blade cut the air.

"Ouch," she squawked as she hit the floor.

The knife-wielding loon struck out again. I didn't move fast enough. She hit the top of my shoulder with the blade. I stepped back as she swung again.

Words tumbled across the chaos.

"Why are you with him? He's mine."

I ducked and blocked the blade with my bag. The knife hit the gun, causing the arm holding it to jolt back. The reporter screamed. I moved sideways drawing the attacker away from her. Wasn't hard. The psycho bitch seemed quite focused on me.

"Who?" I said.

She lashed out with the knife again and I bobbed out of the way. "Michael should have put the diamond around my neck!"

Something should be around her neck all right, a collar and leash or maybe a noose.

She stumbled forward, trying to slash at me again. I slipped to the side and kicked her thigh. She groaned but came back with another attempted stab.

Good try.

I kicked again. The side of my foot connected with soft stomach tissue. She doubled over and fell forward. The knife clattered across the marble floor. I scrambled after it.

Every bone in my body wanted to grab the bitch, cuff her, and tell her she was under arrest. And I couldn't.

I had the knife in my hand. Still doubled over, her strangled sobs were building in momentum.

"You okay?" the reporter asked from the floor under the basins.

"Yeah. Hey, what's your name?" I said to the reporter.

"Rosanne," she said, standing up and coming closer.

"Do me a favor, outside in the hall with Michael is a big black dude. Go get him, please."

"Are you sure you are all right?"

"Of course, but hurry," I said. "I'm not feeling very friendly toward this heap of bubbling snot." I pointed to the woman on the floor with my foot.

Rosanne walked behind me to the door. Avoiding the sobbing woman. When she was gone I turned my full attention to the woman.

"Who are you?" I asked. It wasn't the woman Sam and I had flagged from the media event. This one had mousy brown hair, watery blue eyes, and wore less than elegant clothing.

She didn't reply, cold hatred filling her eyes. The tears were nothing but show. I knew she'd been at the Q and A or she wouldn't have seen Mike put the Hope Diamond on me.

Heavy footsteps ran in. Sam. He held his finger to his lips. There was no need – I saw Rosanne behind him. "What happened, Miss Graham?"

"This woman attacked me," I said. "Here." I handed him the knife. It was a decent sized blade. She had help. There is no way she walked into the museum with a knife.

"Are you hurt?" His eyes never left the woman on the floor but his tone meant the question was for me.

"I'm okay," I said.

He looked up and gave me a once over. To be honest I was a bit shaky. I hadn't expected a restroom ambush.

"You're not. Hang in there for a few," he said.

I stumbled to the paper towel dispenser and grabbed a handful of towels. Blood dripped down my left hand and onto the floor. I threw a few towels on the bloodied floor and folded up the rest. I shoved the wadded towels inside my tee shirt from the neck and held them against the wound on my shoulder.

He grabbed the woman by the arm and pulled her to her feet. "And you are?"

"Her worst nightmare," she jeered.

"I don't think so," Sam said, pulling both arms behind her back and cuffing her. He called the office. "I need transport for a woman who attacked the lady with Michael Fisher."

I couldn't hear the other side of the conversation. But I knew how it went. Experience told me it would be at least ten minutes before someone arrived to remove the woman. Blood soaked the shoulder of my tee shirt and seeped through my thin jacket. I had no option but to go out to Mike covered in blood. Sam would drag the woman out but I needed to go to Mike. He was alone. Alone.

She hadn't worked alone.

Horrible things ran through my mind. I slipped behind Sam and the woman.

"Where are you going?" he asked.

"Michael," I said.

Rosanne followed me out.

"You're not all right," she said as she stepped up beside me.

"I'm fine." I used my most dismissive tone, keeping pressure on my shoulder while trying not to look injured or stand out in anyway.

Mike was in the gift shop, a small open store selling mostly stuffed animals, unlike the large one at the end of the hall. I scanned the entire area but no faces stood out, none from the press conference. This didn't fill me with confidence – I didn't recognize the nut in the toilet either, and she was obviously there.

I crossed the stone floor.

"Michael?" I called as I neared him, not wanting to attract too much attention. "Mike?"

"Laura," he said turning to face me. His brow creased. "You okay?"

"I'm fine," I said. "You all need to play a different song."

Rosanne spoke, "She's bleeding."

"I can see," Mike replied.

"It's a scratch, it's nothing. I'm fine."

Even I knew that didn't sound right. I saw the size of the blade. I felt it hit the top my shoulder.

"I suppose now isn't a good time to ask why no one's seen Laura until today and what she does for a living?" Rosanne said.

"Not really," Mike replied. His arm circled my waist and he whispered into my ear, "You're dripping."

I pressed harder on the wad of towels. "It's a flesh wound, it's nothing," I whispered back. "Don't suppose you have a first aid kit?"

"Not on me. We need to leave before someone starts taking photographs."

Two more of the media people I'd seen upstairs were walking toward us. It was too late. Rosanne saw them too and had heard our whispered conversation.

"We're screwed," I said.

"No, you're not," Rosanne said. "Go."

She pressed a card into my hand and hurried into the path of the approaching journalists.

I pushed the card into my pocket. "I'll call you."

And I would. Because Laura was a nice person.

I looked around for an exit. Sam waited by the entrance to the women's restroom with the crazy chick and her knife. He pointed back toward the corridor with the birds. I nodded.

Mike took off his jacket and slung it around my shoulders to hide the blood and my hand pressing on my shoulder.

"Thank you," I said.

"Don't mention it."

"We're going out the front," I said.

"I'll get the car back," Mike said. He pulled out his phone and called the car service.

I had to let go of my shoulder to find my phone in my

bag. Hoping blood wouldn't drip off my hand – leaving drips across the floor wasn't cool – I fumbled for the phone. My fingers hit the gun before scooping up my phone. I noticed on the way in that they were using scanners on the designated exit door. Security had closed the main doors and they were using one side door as an entrance and one as an exit, scanners on both. Maybe it was something to do with the attention bestowed on the Hope diamond during the press conference.

Whatever the reason, security was tighter than I remembered and that made things tricky for me. The gun would set off the alarms.

Crap.

I called Kurt. "It's me. I need you."

"The three magic words," he said. "Where will you be?"

"In a town car outside the Castle on Jefferson Drive."

"See you soon."

I dropped the phone back into my bag and with a clunk it hit my gun.

I couldn't leave with my gun. Pressing hard on my shoulder I thought about what I should do.

Sam was still with the woman. I needed to go back to him.

"Mike, I need to see Sam."

"We need to leave."

"Hug me," I whispered.

He wrapped his arms around me in a bear hug.

"What's up?"

"I have my gun. I can't go through the scanner ..."

"Distraction?"

"Too many people."

"Sam," he said. "Let's go."

We turned back toward Sam but media people blocked our way. I didn't want to ditch the gun and risk someone finding it.

"Mike, we have to go," I said, my hand growing tired of holding my shoulder and I wasn't sure how bad the cut was.

We hurried back toward the door. From beside the large elephant we checked the doors. Two guards on each side door: main doors still locked. No way out except through the scanners. From where we stood the exit was the right side of the room and the guards faced the entrance. No one approached the exit.

"Either I drop this gun or I can run it." Maybe. Pretty sure I could run, stab wound or not. "I can get down the steps before they turn around, and well before they make a call."

"Alternate plan," he said. "Gift store, change of clothes. Go tourist."

That was pretty good but tourists don't carry weapons.

"We can't go back through the hall," I replied.

"I saw a map upstairs. I think there is another gift store down here somewhere."

It's the Museum of Natural History, there are gift stores all over.

We slipped around the other side of the elephant, watching as journalists headed for the door. Guess they thought we'd gone. Awesome.

Mike pointed to a directory map, and a gift store nearby. In the store, we bought Smithsonian caps and tee shirts and changed in a more secluded location. Mike pulled a light blue tee shirt with the Smithsonian symbol on top of the tan tee shirt he already wore. He lifted his jacket off my shoulders, and helped me with mine, now bloody. I struggled into my new dark blue tee shirt.

I needed both hands to twist my auburn hair under my new cap and the blood-soaked wad of towels fell onto the floor with a wet *splat*. Not ideal. We stared at it for a moment.

"That's a lot of blood," Mike said.

I felt blood running down my arm again. Crap. I rifled through my jacket pocket for a pack of tissues. I put all of them inside both tee shirts over the wound, and tucked them under my bra strap, hoping that would apply the necessary pressure.

"Nah, it looks worse than it is," I said with my best dismissive tone. I picked up the saturated paper with my bloodied left-hand, scanned for a garbage bin and disposed of the mess.

A smear of blood decorated the marble floor. My calling card.

Mike took my bright blue jacket and folded it inside out and small, hiding the blood completely. He dropped it into the bag that had held our tee shirts, then slung his black leather jacket around me again.

"All right, now. You go first," I said. "I'll meet you

where we're meeting Kurt."

"Be careful," he said.

"You, too. I will give you three minutes to get down the steps and into the car, and then I'm coming out."

I hoped the driver would get him away from the front of the building quickly. I also hoped I could tag along with a group of people as they left. A little bit of confusion would be a good thing.

Mike left as I watched him from beside the elephant. From the corner of my eye I saw Sam and the woman walking toward the door. He must be meeting agents by the door. That could either be good or very bad for me.

When I looked at the entrance I saw Lee and Kurt walk in. All good.

I changed my plan; I could palm the gun off to either of them. Mike's jacket hid my hands, so I just needed to accidentally walk into their path. I pulled my gun still in its holster from my bag and switched it to my left hand. My right hand clamped back onto my shoulder as I felt blood seep, my bra strap not holding the tissues firmly enough. When Kurt and Lee were almost at Sam, I slipped between them, slid the holster inside Kurt's waistband, and kept moving to the exit without looking back.

No alarms. No problem.

Walking fast, I crossed the full width of the mall. I stuck to the path and avoided eye contact with anyone. As I approached Jefferson and the Castle I saw the town car waiting. We couldn't leave yet, Kurt would be on his way and wouldn't be far behind.

Opening the back door of the car, I scrambled in. My heart thumped at an alarming rate, as I took a few deep breaths.

"Everything okay, Laura?" Mike said.

"Yes, was kinda fun." I didn't elaborate, not with the driver in the car.

"How long before Kurt meets us?"

"He probably isn't far behind me ..."

The front passenger door opened and Kurt climbed in. He looked at the driver.

"Park somewhere then go get yourself a coffee. Be gone fifteen minutes," he said showing his credentials to the driver.

The driver nodded.

No one said anything until we'd parked and the driver walked away.

Kurt twisted in his seat and looked at me.

"Mike swap places with me," he said.

Doors opened and closed and Kurt was in the back with me. That was when I noticed he had his bag with him.

"What did you do?" he asked.

I dropped Mike's jacket from my shoulders. Kurt handed the jacket over the seat to Mike. My shoulder felt uncomfortable but I managed to struggle out of both tee-shirts without help.

"I resent that," I said. "I was attacked by some nut job who thought Mike should have put the Hope Diamond around her neck."

Mike turned his head to look at me. "You never told me that."

"Eyes forward!" I replied. I saw his mouth turn up in a smile, as he obliged.

Kurt held a wound pad against my shoulder. "You're lucky, it's not as bad as this wad of soaked tissues looks."

"As I said, it's a scratch."

"I wouldn't go that far, it's a little more than a scratch. I can't glue this."

Great – glue stings like a bastard.

"If you're going to stitch, hurry up," I said and prepared for the local anesthetic. Needles don't bother me half as much as glue.

I closed my eyes and forced my mind to a happy place while Kurt wiped my arm with alcohol wipes and stuck a needle around the cut on my shoulder.

"Okay?" he asked.

"Yeah."

A few minutes later Kurt had sewed the cut, covered it with a sticky dressing and wiped all the blood off my arm and hand with some medicated wipes from his bag. "There you go, as good as new."

I smiled. "Thanks. I need clean clothes before we go to lunch."

"Yes, you do," Kurt said holding up the bloodstained tee shirts I'd been wearing. "I saw a street vendor back a bit. I'll get you a tee shirt."

I glanced at my arm. The blood was gone and so was

the concealer covering the scars. At least it wasn't my right arm. The scars on my left were higher and easier to hide with clothes. "I don't have concealer with me. Need a longer sleeve than I was wearing."

He screwed the shirts in his hand and got out of the car. "I'll see what I can do."

"Where's my jacket?" I asked Mike. "Don't turn around."

"In the bag on the seat. Do you want mine?"

"It's okay, mine will be fine."

I rummaged in the bag until I found it and draped the bloody jacket over myself. Sitting in the back of a town car wearing a bra and jeans wasn't exactly comfortable, especially with Mike there.

Especially with Mike there.

Kurt came back and threw me a tee shirt, then dropped two more on the back seat.

"Three for ten bucks. Long sleeves," he said with a smile.

I looked at the one he'd thrown me once I had it on. A million dollar bill. Awesome.

Mike turned around. "You look like a million bucks. Ready for lunch?"

It was so lame I laughed.

Chapter Thirteen
You Had Me From Hello

Our driver, Raj, dropped us off outside the Hard Rock Café where Mike gave him instructions about when to pick us up, and also asked him if he'd consider being our driver for our entire stay in Washington. He agreed.

Mike tipped him handsomely.

At the front desk I asked for Simone's table and a friendly server led us to where she sat, with the view of the Hoover building from the windows behind us.

I couldn't help but smile. "Simone!" I said, leaning in to kiss her cheeks.

"Laura, you look *magnifique!*"

"So do you. This is Michael," I introduced Mike. He shook Simone's hand then pressed it to his lips.

"A pleasure," Simone said.

"*Tout le plaisir est pour moi,*" Mike replied. The pleasure is all mine.

And Simone was instantly won over. She always had been easy. "*Je l'aime bien,*" she said to me. I like him.

"Me, too," I replied.

Mike pulled out a chair for me beside Simone, facing the Hoover Building. The server came back with menus.

"How long are you in town?" Simone asked.

"Maybe a few weeks. Mike has some engagements he must attend and I would like to spend some time with friends."

"When does your show start back on the television?" Simone said, directing her question to Mike.

So she did know who he was.

"Two weeks today."

She nodded. "I never miss it."

Me neither, but I decided to keep that to myself.

From my vantage point I watched Kurt and Lee enter our office building. Lee stood in the window of the bullpen and stared out. I could see him but I didn't know if he could see me.

Cars came and went from the under the building. I spotted Owen hurrying across the road toward the Hard Rock Café. I crossed my fingers under the table and hoped she was coming in for lunch. I'd love to run across her in the restroom.

From memory the woman's restroom closest to us was a single toilet inside a large room. It wasn't likely that I'd run into anybody unless they'd just ducked in to wash their hands and hadn't locked the door.

Hope evaporated.

Owen wasn't the sharpest tool in the shed but even she might smell a rat if someone accosted her in a bathroom. Unless I only spoke French. A smile played upon my lips.

"Penny for them?" Mike said.

"Having improper thoughts about someone," I replied, and then realized what I'd said.

Simone laughed.

Mike grinned. "*J'espère que les pensées coquines étaient à propos de moi.*" I hope the improper thoughts were about me.

"Who else?"

Simone laughed louder. "You two are incorrigible."

Mike did that thing with his eyes again and all my power melted away.

What the hell?

Simone was talking and I couldn't hear her words. How he stopped me from hearing words by locking his eyes with mine, I did not know.

He blinked and smiled, the spell broken.

"We're going to talk about that little move of yours later," I said in a hushed tone.

"It's a trade secret," he said with a smile that made his eyes sparkle.

Simone interrupted us. "You two are in your own world, it must be love."

"Must be," I said.

Mike's hand covered mine on the table.

"You are so sweet together. Where did you find this one, Laura?"

Where did I find him? He found me. Sometimes the truth doesn't need too much tweaking.

"In an alleyway," I said.

She laughed.

Mike nodded. "It's true. And I did the finding."

"It must be fate," Simone said. "You are *parfait.*" Perfect.

"We are and now I'm afraid we must go. We have

another engagement," Mike said as he stood.

"Oh, so soon," Simone said. "We will do this again before you leave town."

"*Tout à fait,*" I said. Absolutely.

"You will come into the office?"

"Of course. I'll call you."

We all left together. Nothing says class like a waiting town car and a million dollar tee shirt. Raj, held the car door.

Simone waved us off.

Mike told Raj to take us to our hotel. He reached over and hooked an arm around my shoulders; keeping his hand low and away from the wound, he pressed me closer to him.

"I think, Laura, we should be in D.C, we're too far away at our current hotel."

"I would like that, but I think my people might have reservations about such a move."

"We'll talk about it later," he said.

He hadn't let me go and I rested on his shoulder. I'd been in worse situations.

The loving couple behaved like a loving couple all the way back to Fairfax.

Mike gave our driver instructions for the morning. He also warned him we would require him for tomorrow night, the first I'd heard of his plans.

Apparently, we had a meeting in the morning and then a cocktail party in the evening.

That would require shopping. I wasn't sure how I felt

about that, but everything I could possibly need was available over the road from the hotel at Fair Oaks Mall. I wasn't feeling too naked without my weapon, so shopping unarmed should be okay.

For now, getting into our room and seeing what fresh hell Owen had unleashed was a priority. Also on the list was finding out how the crazy woman got into the museum with a knife.

Those thoughts consumed me as we rode the elevator and walked the ten feet to our room.

Mike stuck the keycard in the door, opened it and let me in. I flopped down on my bed. It was nice to relax. My head itched. It was hot. I sat up and took off the wig, shook out my hair and rubbed my scalp. I took the wig into the bathroom and set it carefully on the counter, wishing Lee had managed to sneak the polystyrene head out with the wig. Back in the main room I saw a light flashing on the phone urging us to check the messages.

"You want coffee?" Mike asked, as he pressed the flashing button.

"Please," I said.

The first message was long-winded and from Lee, wanting to check on his brother and organize dinner. He could've said it so much quicker than he did which told me there was something else in his message, something for me. That would make sense: if anyone overheard him, it was just one brother calling another.

Clever. I wrote everything he said down in my notebook. With the words in front of me, I could see a pattern, a message within a message.

I heard a beep and looked up. Mike was checking voice mail on his phone and put the phone on the countertop to listen. I could hear a woman's voice, annoyed. I figured it was Mike's agent or publicist or someone like that. She wanted to know how today went and confirmed the engagement tomorrow. She also asked who had accompanied him.

He picked up the phone and called her while I played with Lee's message. Lee's message answered a question I had. One he knew I'd be asking. The knife wielding loon got the knife from the kitchen. She was a chef in the museum cafeteria. I called Lee on his safe phone.

"Is she the one we're after?"

"No, we went through her apartment. She's definitely over-the-top obsessed with Mike but hasn't flown recently, never been to L.A. and doesn't have anything connecting her to anyone else."

"I was thinking … you know when we first came across Grange and discovered those chat rooms with people pretending to be members of the band?"

"Yes."

"And how there was a whole online community of insanity ticking like a time bomb, and they all believed they were talking to Rowan or Tony, and would do anything to protect them …"

"You think we might come across something similar for my kid brother?"

"I'm thinking there could be a network of loons

working together."

"Definitely something to look into. It's a shame she's not the one we were after."

"I can do some research into any online Michael Fisher sites, it'll give me something to do."

"Tell Mike I'm taking him out tonight."

"Will do," and hung up.

When Mike finished his call, I said, "Lee is coming over tonight to take you out, some sort of brother bonding thing."

"Fun," he replied with a raised eyebrow. "My publicist wants to know who you are and why she's had so many calls from the media about the ring on your finger. She's unhappy. Said I made her look like an idiot by getting engaged without telling her."

"Will this make things difficult for you?" I asked.

"Might do. I'm sure my publicist will get over it, one day."

"Sorry," I said. I wasn't – worse things could happen. Hell, it's only fair that Laura has some fun with her actor. God knows I had a blast with my rock star. As badly as I knew it would end, it was fun while it lasted.

"Don't be, I'm having fun."

"Thought I was intense?"

"Ellie is intense. Laura is more relaxed."

I left that alone.

"Where's that coffee you promised?"

I jumped off the bed and went to help him make coffee. Intense, my ass.

I'm fun dammit.
No matter who I am.

Chapter Fourteen

Who Says You Can't Go Home?

Lee knocked on the door just before eight.

I opened it and he handed me my gun. "Kurt said you might need this."

"Thanks."

Mike grabbed his jacket off the back of a chair then kissed me on the cheek. "Don't wait up, honey."

"Don't wake me up!" I countered, smacking him on the backside as he left the room.

Lee laughed. "I'll bring him back safely."

"I'm sure you will."

I closed the door, flipped the security lock, and then flipped it back, otherwise Mike wouldn't be able to get in later.

I had a night to myself. I was four miles from home. I had the keys to Mike's rental.

Without a lot of thought I changed into black clothes, put the wig back on and pushed my paddle holster comfortably into my waistband. My Glock slid into place just in front of my hip. I slung a black messenger bag over my head. Inside the bag I put my wallet, the hotel keycard, camera, and phone. I picked up a plastic bag and shoved a few items in it that needed washing. Laundry time. Car keys in my hand, I left the room. The stairs were adjacent to our room and running down four flights of stairs was preferable to taking the elevator.

The stairwell opened into a corridor opposite the hotel lobby. It was straight ahead to the front desk or right to the laundry room. There was no one around. I detoured to the front desk, found a manager, and changed two singles into quarters for the washing machine. In the deserted laundry room, I tossed the clothes into a washing machine, fed in the quarters, and turned it on. I'd be back by the time the machine finished.

Instead of going out the main doors and risking the night manager or anyone else seeing me leave, I walked along the corridor to the very end, and out a side exit into the parking lot. Mike's car was around the corner.

As far as anyone was concerned, I was doing laundry. I left with a smile on my face.

Ten minutes later I drove past my house. There were no guards posted. Even so, I parked down the street and walked back to the closed front gate. Punching my code into the panel by the pedestrian gate could send up a red flag. If I could've just called Sean to find out how compromised the system was, it would've been much easier, but the burn-phone only had the numbers Kurt pre-installed for me.

So I used Carla's code hoping that anyone watching would only be checking for activity on my login. Surely there would be no point flagging a dead person's code, not like resurrection was a possibility. The gate buzzed. I opened it far enough for me to slip in, pressed it closed behind me and followed the glow of solar-powered lights up the path.

The difference between Carla's code and mine was that hers triggered the cameras, so if someone slipped through behind her before the gate closed, video footage would be available. That worked to my advantage. This was one of those times when I really wanted video of anyone on my property.

If someone had hacked the system, they could be watching now. If it was the same person who created the photographs of me with Eddie's body parts, they could be watching me walk up the path. Seemed smart to expect trouble, or the FBI, which amounted to the same thing.

I used Carla's code again to open the front door and disable the interior alarm. It wasn't until I was inside with the door shut that I breathed out. No alarm. No flashing on the alarm panel to suggest a silent alarm ringing elsewhere. No little blue light indicating I'd activated the house audio recording system. I ran up the stairs and into my room without turning on the lights.

From the top drawer of my bureau I took a small flashlight. The red glow was enough to see by but harder for anyone looking in to see. Red light doesn't travel like white light.

Using the light, I found my spare vial of migraine synergy – I did not want a repeat of the migraine incident. Intense? No, just embarrassing. Almost as cringe-worthy as realizing what Lee saw in my nightstand. Bet he shut the drawer in a big hurry when he saw my toy. A girl's gotta do what a girl's gotta do, and I do me rather well.

My next move was to search Carla's room, where the only thing that appeared to be missing was her laptop.

From a box in the bottom of her closet I took a flash drive, a cute little pink pig. Cute, but it also contained the contents of her laptop. She'd backed up the whole thing only days before her death. I hadn't yet looked at the contents of the flash drive and I don't know why I left it there and didn't take it to the bank with all the things I'd scanned of hers and all Mac's stuff.

I dropped the pig into my bag and went downstairs. I walked along my hallway and through the kitchen into my office. It seemed ridiculous for someone to go to all this trouble and take only photographs and a laptop. A regular burglar could've made quite a haul with the amount of electronic equipment in this house. Obviously resale wasn't the object of this game. Whoever it was, my very own Unsub, was certainly putting the stolen photos to good use. Time would tell why they took the laptop. I fired up my desktop computer so I could check to see when my email was last accessed and see if the email of the foot was sent from my PC.

While I waited I opened the top drawer under my desk, where I'd had about a hundred photographs, loose. All gone. I shut the drawer and opened the next one. My spare weapon sat alone in the drawer. The next drawer had Mac's spare weapon and cuffs. The next contained a bunch of bills. I searched through them. Something was missing.

I sat back in my chair and chewed my lip. Leaned forward and searched again.

My notebooks were gone. Thoughts, notes, poetry, all written by hand. Someone took samples of my handwriting: a loud and clear message as to what might happen next.

When should I expect a letter or note? Maybe it would be my confession or something equally incriminating.

This was not good.

Lee and Sam were right; nothing else was missing from the drawers. The photographs from my walls were gone. The frames lay on the floor, empty. The ones on my desk were face down with the backs off.

The computer screen glowed in front of me. I pulled up the program I used to monitor activity on my PC. I'm such a trusting person. There was nothing to indicate my PC was used by anyone other than me, no usage showed up for the period I was away from home. I opened my email program and sure enough, in sent items was the email with the photo but the time stamp confirmed it was sent by someone else. I hadn't been home at all, and couldn't have sent the email. Whoever sent it must've known I monitored PC usage and circumvented the program. That sucked but made sense. The Unsub behind this wasn't a stupid person.

Something outside the window caught my attention. I listened but heard nothing. I flipped off the flashlight and crept back along the hallway to the living room. A twig snapped.

Without warning, glass shattering followed a thump. I pulled out my Glock and ran into the hallway. Another thump and more glass hit the floor.

Someone knew the gate code or someone had hacked the security system again. If they'd hacked the system then they would've been able to open the front door. Whoever it was wasn't clever enough to be the hacker.

I waited by the hinges of the interior laundry door. My breathing slowed as I listened. A click as a lock released. Crunching glass as the exterior door opened inward.

Steadying myself I swung into the doorway, aiming at the dark shape that filled the back door.

"Stop!" I said. "Hands where I can see them!"

The shape froze. I couldn't see the person. For all I knew it could've been one of Owen's minions. Familiar cologne wafted in on the soft breeze. My vision adjusted to the moon shadows cast across the room.

"Can I pick up my jacket?"

"What the hell are you doing here?" I said, holstering my gun. "Yes, pick up your jacket."

Rowan bent down to retrieve his jacket.

"Now what?" he said.

"Living room, you have some explaining to do."

The very last thing I needed was Rowan Grange involved in whatever the hell was going on here. Breaking and entering? Now that was different and I was sure he was jazzed to hell after that little confrontation.

I took a few deep breaths and counted to ten, then a few more deep breaths. He was lucky I didn't shoot him.

I followed Rowan into the room. He stood bathed in moonlight in the middle of the room pulling his jacket on.

"Are you okay? Not cut or anything?"

"I'm fine. I used my jacket to protect my arm when I opened the door."

"That ..." I waved an arm toward the laundry, "was not *opening* the door. That was smashing glass all over *my* floor."

He smiled. "The door is open."

"Nuh-uh, you don't get to use that smile on me right now."

His smile stayed.

"Quit it," I said with a scowl. "Why are you here?"

"I knew something was very wrong. I thought maybe I could help ..."

"By breaking into my house? How did you get through the gate? How did you know I was here?"

"What do you want me to answer first?

"How did you know I was here?"

"I was watching the house ..."

"You idiot! You were intent on breaking in whether I was here or not."

"I wouldn't have broken in but my code worked on the gate but not on the front door."

That'll be because I disabled it at the front door when we broke up. To prevent this sort of macho bullshit from a rock star from New Jersey. They're passionate people, especially the ones who are wannabe heroes.

"This is both stupid and dangerous," I said. Also sweet

166

in a misguided crazy way, and if he hadn't cheated on me, it just might have got him laid.

He took my hand. There was a long pause while he felt the ring on my finger with his fingers. He lifted my hand for a closer look in the dim light.

"That's not yours," he said.

"I don't have red hair either, remember. Undercover."

He nodded and I extracted my hand.

Something whooshed through the living room window, leaving a small hole and cracks spider-webbing across the night shrouded glass. I hit the floor, pulling Rowan down with me.

"Stay down," I whispered, covering his head with my arms.

Another pop. Another hole appeared. Another pop and the window pane gave way. Glass rained down.

Twinkling shards of moonlit glass littered the room. Something whizzed past my head. A thought hauled into my consciousness: I could stand up and hope they got a clean shot. Another thought shoved that one out of the way. Rowan didn't deserve to die. I was plenty mad at him but not mad enough to get him killed. That day may come but it wasn't here yet.

I grabbed Rowan by his jacket lapel and pulled. "Come on, we gotta get to the hallway."

We crawled over the thick carpet, through the open door into the hall. The bulk of the glass was under the window but shards had flown quite a way into the room. Glass cut and stabbed at us as bullets whizzed overhead.

I pushed Rowan ahead of me. "Go. Go. Go."

Wood splintered as bullets thudded into the paneling in the hall. I hooked my foot around the edge of the door and dragged it with me as I crawled through it. When it was near enough, I reached my hand around and pulled it shut. A bullet flew through the wood and lodged above my head as I sat in the hall.

Something screwy was going on. Bullets were flying into my house, close to us, and no one was getting hit. For a brief moment I wondered what would happen if I just stood up. A weird thought manifested: whoever was shooting didn't want to hit me?

"Now where?" Rowan asked.

"Down the hall to the office. Move!" He scrambled to his feet and took off. I ran with him. Bullets peppered my hallway seconds behind us. They were too close to be firing blind but not close enough to hit. Thermal imaging maybe, which would make sense if the shooter needed to know exactly where we were to avoid shooting us by mistake.

Chapter Fifteen
Army Of One

I shut every door I passed. In the office, I grabbed my other Glock, slid home a fresh magazine and racked the slide. We ducked as a shadow passed the window. I motioned to a closet door. "Open it."

Rowan did as asked. We stepped inside. I flicked the light on and watched surprise register on his face. He was standing at the top of stairs. "Basement?"

"Go down a few steps."

I went down one step and turned around, then hit the button next to the door we'd come through; a steel panel slid into place and sealed the closet entrance.

"Like a basement but not quite. Let's go." I passed him and led the way, hurrying down the stairs, lit only by dim emergency lighting. At the bottom, I pulled open a heavy door and ushered Rowan inside. The door shut behind us. On a small panel by the door two large buttons glowed. I pressed the "lock" button flashing red, which made the "unlock" button flash green.

Handy.

Idiot proof.

Rowan looked around. "You think this has something to do with you being undercover?" he asked.

There was a really good chance.

"No idea."

From the secure phone on the wall, I called comms and without even thinking said, "This is Supervisory Special Agent Conway requesting immediate assistance."

A calm reasonable voice said. "What services do you require, Agent?"

"SWAT."

Crap! My brain kicked in.

I hung up. I couldn't call the cavalry. What was I thinking? But I had and that can was now partially open and worms were escaping. I watched one slither down the side of the battered can and plop to the ground. They looked at lot like heavily armed SWAT worms to me.

"Why'd you hang up?" Panic tweaked his words.

"It's complicated and has a lot to do with me being a redhead and not wanting you in D.C. Hanging up doesn't matter. I made the call and SWAT will come."

I took the phone from my bag.

"Will that work from here?" Rowan asked.

"Yes, this is a safe room, not a cave at the bottom of the ocean." That wasn't nice of me. I tried again. "This room was designed to protect me, not cut me off from the world." I called Kurt. "I'm in trouble."

"Now there's a surprise. Where are you?"

I took a breath. "At home," I said, trying to make my voice sound nonchalant.

"Are you safe?"

"For now. I'm not alone. Rowan broke into my home about ten minutes ago."

"Jesus!"

"Tell me about it."

"What's happening?"

"Gimme a minute and I'll tell you."

I couldn't hear anything from the sealed underground room. I switched on the exterior and interior cameras. Screens on the wall sprang to life. I asked Rowan to watch for signs of life.

"Ellie?" Kurt whispered into my ear.

"You can't call me that, it's Laura now," I replied.

"What can you see?" Kurt said.

Rowan pointed out a male wearing tactical gear and full face balaclava running towards one of the cameras. It all went black.

"I had eyes on one wearing tactical gear and a full face balaclava, he just took out one of my cameras," I said.

"So, they know about the cameras. This could be whoever hacked into the system."

"Either that or they're FBI," I said. "Or they did damn good surveillance and are professionals."

"I hope not, that would not be good." Kurt's voice held a sharp edge. "Where exactly are you?"

"Panic room."

"Who knows about that room?"

"Delta and Dad."

"The hacker – is there anything that connects that room to the house grid?"

"No. Nothing. It's not alarmed and is self-controlled," I said.

"Anyone else in the FBI know about the room?"

"No."

"Were you followed?"

"No."

But Rowan might have been. Wouldn't be the first time he'd unwittingly caused me issues.

"I'll get the guys. We're coming to get you. Stay safe."

"If this is FBI—"

"We're coming to get you out," Kurt said with quiet determination and hung up.

Rowan watched me and the screens. "Don't you think it's time you quit this job before it kills you?"

I knew he'd say that.

"And do what? This is what I do. I am *this* chick."

"Take on The Butterfly Foundation full time, you've always said you'd like to have more time to devote to the kids," Rowan replied.

I shook my head. Not now. Wanting to spend time with teenage kids was not in my five-year plan anymore.

He was sitting in one of the two armchairs and had found the supply of bottled water, a bowl, and a first aid kit. He rinsed his hands over the bowl letting the water flush out the loose pieces of glass. Then with a pair of tweezers, he tried to pick out small pieces of glass from one palm. His hands shook. Beads of perspiration gathered on his forehead.

"Here, let me," I said. I took the tweezers and carefully removed the small shards from his palms. "You need to breathe, slowly."

"I'm okay."

He was shaky and breathing too fast.

"No, you're not but I need you to be. Breathe. Deep and slow." I watched him. "What you're feeling is the adrenaline in your system."

He slowed his breathing down.

I cleaned the cuts, checking for any more glass, and then applied Band-Aids.

"Thanks."

"Feel any better?"

"I think so."

I grabbed a bucket from the corner of the room and set it beside his chair. "In case you feel sick," I said with a smile. "Keep breathing."

For the first time I noticed a shiny piece of glass poking out of the back of my left hand. Funny how things don't matter until you see them.

I grasped the glass with my fingers and pulled the shard from my hand. It stung. I dropped the glass into the bowl and washed my hand.

"Impressive piece," Rowan commented.

It was about half an inch in diameter and three quarters of an inch long, tapering to a sharp point. Blood dripped from the wound.

"It'll be fine," I said. Using my good hand I searched the first-aid kit for some wound closures. Finding them I used both hands to rip open a packet of closures, flicking blood across the room in the effort, and stuck two of them across the back of my hand. Rowan picked out a sticky wound dressing and applied it for me.

"Better?"

"Yeah, much."

We settled in to wait for either the shooters to figure out where we were – and storm the house – or a hurriedly assembled mini SWAT team to come to our rescue – and storm the house. I had a feeling my house wasn't going to fare well. Nothing new in that. Houses and I never worked out.

I looked up in time to see another screen go black. Three cameras down.

My phone rang. Lee's name flashed on the small screen. "You never mentioned going out," Lee said, his voice reverberating in my ear. "We need to find out who you pissed off."

"No one, I swear," I replied. My fingers weren't even crossed.

"I find that very hard to believe."

Quite frankly, me too.

"It's not me this time. I'm losing my eyes out there. They've found three cameras now."

"You think this is some crazed stalker fan of Mike's with military weapons?"

"I wasn't followed."

But mister-I-wanna-be-a-hero probably was.

"We're on our way."

I smiled at Rowan and hung up. "Lee reckons it will be over soon."

Liar liar pants on fire.

"I hope so," he replied, dropping another piece of glass

into the bowl, this time from his hair.

"Comb it," I said. Inside the first aid kit, I found a fine-tooth comb. "I'll do it."

I combed his hair, carefully, making sure to get every tiny piece of glass from it. When I was done, I took off my wig and gave it good shake. Glass sparkled like glitter as it hit the floor. Satisfied there was no glass stuck in the curls I put the wig back on.

With only two cameras left it was easier watching the screen.

One camera tracked across the backyard. It moved in an arc from the birdhouse by the back fence to the house. The camera moved as if following someone but I couldn't see anyone. The other remaining camera, positioned above the front door in a bird's nest, covered the front of the house. I pulled the keyboard out from under the desk and moved the cameras myself using the arrow keys.

They'd taken out the cameras but only those connected to the main house system. My last two cameras were the only ones controlled by this room; they wouldn't know about these. I had a clear view from both cameras.

A shadowy figure ran past the front door. Another skulked under the broken window of the living room. They disappeared from view.

"There are at least two people out there."

Rowan nodded. "So someone hacked your computer system?"

"Yep." I saw where he was going. "They can't get in here. This room is not accessible from the household computers or the security system that is supposed to protect the house." I paid big money to have a state-of-the-art security system and for the protection/peace of mind that came with it.

But we weren't dealing with garden variety hackers. If they were inside my house, I might be able to find them and get some information. Typing my security password into a small box that appeared on one of the screens, a list of options followed. I read through the list and found the audio option. I had a nifty trick up my sleeve.

From my safe little room I could switch on microphones throughout the house, not only that, I could also switch on the stereo (entertainment system) in the living room and use the speakers to communicate with anyone in the house. This was a completely different system from the one controlled by my security company. This was the failsafe. No one knew about it apart from Sean O'Hare and he would never tell, not even if his sister, our beloved Director, asked.

Pretty sure no one wants to hear me in 5.1 surround sound. All I had to do was hold down the shift key to give the morons in my house an earful. I'm a Navy brat, I know how to curse. I've been known to make sailors blush.

I watched the screen display as noises came through our speakers. The screen changed to a floor plan containing red blips. Each blip was a person.

Three people.

"Look, Rowan," I said, pointing to the kitchen. "One in

the kitchen."

"And one upstairs in your bedroom, and in the hallway," he added.

A blip moved into the office. The blip smashed something into the closet door. I jumped. It was loud over the speakers.

"Where exactly are we?" Rowan asked, as another loud noise startled me.

"Under my office."

"How safe?"

"We're underground. Blastproof. Fireproof."

"Any other way in?"

"No."

"Gas?"

"Recycled air, no inlets. There are emergency air tanks, too."

Worry creased his brow. "Power?"

"Solar, which stores to large backup batteries. We have enough power for, well, as long as it takes really. The solar panels are well concealed on the roof. Even if they're found, we have the batteries down here."

"Who built it?"

"Sean O'Hare."

"I know him?"

"Yes, you met him in New Zealand."

"Ellie, could this have something to do with New Zealand?"

"You mean Hawk?"

He nodded.

"No, he's not coming back."

Rowan's expression changed. It went to the place that meant he didn't want to ask. Then a light flicked on behind his blue eyes. "That early morning, the men in black who came for you. You were different when they brought you back."

I smiled. Neither confirm nor deny.

Noises erupted from the speakers. I looked at the screen. "The blips are all in the office."

"Do they know where we are?"

"I think they've figured it out."

"Is this going to be bad?"

"Yes."

His eyebrows rose. "What no sugarcoated, 'we're okay'?"

"Nope. We're screwed, baby."

The microphones picked up knocking from within my office. Someone upstairs was knocking on the steel door.

"I'm tempted to open the doors, because they knocked so nicely." I checked my gun. They knocked again, louder this time. We heard a discussion about explosives via the microphone in my office.

"Does blastproof extend to the doors?" Rowan asked.

"Yes."

The noise up top continued. Knocking. Banging. Threatening. Demanding. In two distinctly different accents. The third person never spoke.

"What was that last thing?" Rowan asked.

"He said something about wanting my key chain."

"That's what I thought."

I put my hand in my bag and felt the heavy lump that was my keys. I pulled them out and scrutinized them. Front door. Back door. Work. Safety deposit box. Home safe. Car keys. Two key chain holders containing SD cards. One 8-gigabyte secure flash drive that contained current case files and photographs. "Would someone employ home invasion tactics to steal a key chain?" I was thinking aloud. "I think not, not my keys, anyway. It's not like I have access to anything important."

The banging and threats continued.

My thoughts continued aloud, "So not a key. Something I've photographed maybe, or information on my flash drive."

I pulled open another drawer, lifted out a laptop, and fired it up. I handed Rowan my cell phone.

"What's this for?"

"For you to answer if it rings," I replied. It seemed like he should have something to do. Rowan sat back down and watched me. I plugged the SD cards into my laptop and checked their contents one by one.

The banging continued. There were one or two large explosive noises.

It wasn't the first time someone had bashed on my door and threatened me, only this time the person wouldn't be smashing a window and gaining entry. That meant I wouldn't be escaping from the house into the woods and waiting for local police. Life has changed somewhat since those days in Mauryville.

I scanned through pictures from recent surveillance jobs. One set caught my attention. I stopped and went back over them. They were current. I'd taken them three days ago. Lee and I took the pictures on Thursday afternoon to be precise.

I zoomed in on the three men in the picture. They'd met at a park in Washington D.C. One I knew was a Consular officer from the United Kingdom embassy, another was my target who was an Irishman working as a consulate officer for the Irish embassy, I knew him as Gould. The third man was unknown. I thought he was western, even considered he could be American. But his face rang no bells and we hadn't yet run him through the facial recognition databases.

I closed my eyes and listened to the threats that emanated from my office via the speakers. American and Irish voices. I wondered if it was the same Irishman. I needed eyes on him.

"What's the matter?" Rowan asked.

"I don't know. The Irishman out there could be someone I have under surveillance but I don't know if it is."

Rowan handed me my cell phone. I grinned as I took it and called Lee.

"You all right?" he said.

"Yes."

"What is it?" As soon as he spoke another loud explosion burst through the speakers and the phone. "Jesus. You sure you're okay?"

"Yep. You can stop this anytime, though. Three people are in my office, trying to access the panic room."

"What is it you think is going on?"

"Maybe this is related to the surveillance job we did the other day – we followed Gould to that meeting. It's possible that Gould is one of the armed men. I could be wrong. I'm sure there are lots of Irishmen out to get me. We know I piss people off without even trying."

"You are talented at pissing people off."

"I'm grasping at straws."

"I know."

"It's probably nothing to do with our surveillance job."

He hung up. I chewed my lip. Someone wanted me strung up for something. It must be something big.

There was a weird warm feeling growing inside me. It came from knowing my team was ready to exact revenge should my life end suddenly.

Talk about conflicted. Did I really want my team exacting revenge when death seemed like such a welcome relief?

My phone rang. I glanced at the screen and saw Kurt's name. "Hey," I said with as much chirp as I could muster.

"Hey, yourself. You okay in there?"

"Just fine and dandy."

"Either of you hurt?"

"Superficial cuts from glass, nothing major."

"We'll have you out in a few minutes."

I could hear background noises via the microphones and over the phone. Yelling, rifle fire, orders being barked.

"Thanks for the update."

The call ended, I waited and listened. There was a lot of noise.

Most of the speaking comprised barked orders via Sam. There was a big part of me that did not want to climb those steps and leave the room: despite knowing Delta was out there, I wasn't a hundred percent sure they could contain the situation.

"Rowan, I need you to do something for me."

"Name it," he said.

"When we get the all clear, you go up."

"Why?"

"Because I don't know who is up there and how well the situation has been contained." I listened for a moment to the noises coming from the speakers. "And, you broke into my house."

He wasn't happy. "You haven't told me what's wrong."

"I can't tell you. Just remember I do not exist. The person you see in front of you is Laura Graham." A smile settled on my lips.

"What?" Rowan asked. "That's a borderline evil smile."

"I don't know what I'm worried about. I'm Laura Graham." I grinned at Rowan's confusion. "And you, baby, you're my reason for being here."

"How's that?"

"I'm a private investigator and you hired me—"

"I hired you to find out if Ellie is seeing anybody."

The speed with which he came up with that was

disconcerting. It seemed like one of those things Ellie should ignore. But Laura was curious.

I left the Glock I'd taken from my office on the desk in the room. I was wearing a holster and a Glock, and didn't need to surface with two.

My phone rang.

Sam said, "Laura, come on out."

Nothing in his tone indicated he knew me. Was that good or bad? I had no clue.

Chapter Sixteen

Keep The Faith

I heard the music before I got to the door and the big glowing green button. Didn't mean anyone else could though. A quick glance at Rowan told me he couldn't hear it.

"Go in front of me," I said. "Press the green button. If anyone asks ... you knew about the panic room and remembered the codes from when you were dating Ellie."

"Got it."

"Just don't over act. Be you."

"What does that even mean?"

"It means, *do not* over act. Be. You."

He shook his head. "Have a little faith, Laura."

For a split second I thought maybe he could hear the music. Bon Jovi's "Keep the Faith" filled my head.

Rowan hit the button and the door swung open. He hurried up the next set of stairs. I stayed behind, far enough that it would be hard to see me from the top. Rowan opened the next door. A dark shape filled the doorway and I saw a hand extend to Rowan and heard Sam's voice. They spoke briefly then Rowan was gone.

"Laura, come on out," Sam called.

My heart pounded as I climbed to the top of the stairs. From the doorway I could see Sam and Kurt. No one else.

"Everything okay?" I asked in a hushed tone.

"Yes, we have taken three men into custody and will move them to a secure facility soon," Sam said. "Your fiancé is waiting for you and you will have to answer some questions regarding your activities this evening."

Kurt took my arm. "Breaking and entering is illegal even for a private investigator. You and Mr. Grange have some explaining to do."

I said nothing.

Someone stood outside the door in the hallway. There was a moment when I almost prayed it was Owen. Kurt gave my arm a squeeze and walked me through the door.

Swallowing a sigh of relief I clapped eyes on Caine, Special Agent in Charge of Delta.

"Miss Graham, I would like a word," he growled. "Follow me please."

Kurt nodded and let my arm go. I followed Caine into my kitchen. There was no one else around that I could see but that did not mean there were no other agents on site.

"I'm sorry," I said, mustering contrition and using it to good effect.

"I'm sure you are, Miss Graham. Breaking into a federal agent's home with a rock star isn't what I would expect from a private investigator. Especially one of your caliber."

If I didn't know better, I'd think he didn't know who I was.

"There was a definite lapse of judgment on my part tonight."

"You're not going to try to explain this away then?"

"No, sir. I screwed up."

"Yes, you did," he growled. Caine leaned close to my ear so close his words vibrated as he spoke. "This could have gone very badly."

"Yes, sir," I whispered.

His phone buzzed. Caine checked the message. "Owen is on her way, you need to disappear now."

"And Mr. Grange?"

"Delta will deal with him. Go."

"Done."

I turned around, hurried along the hallway and out the front door to where Mike waited outside the gate. He hooked his arm around my shoulder. "I saw my car out on the street ..."

I fished the keys out of my bag and pressed them into his hand. "You drive."

He dropped them back into my hand. "Hell, no, I've been drinking."

We moved fairly quickly down the street, it was properly dark now. The street lights cast an eerie glow. We were in the car and on our way home when two FBI sedans passed us going the other way. Owen and her flunkies.

"You all right?" Mike asked.

"I'm fine." I adjusted the rearview mirror a little.

"The bandage on your hand says otherwise."

The white bandage was a little hard to miss with my hands on the steering wheel. "Little cut, it's nothing."

Silence fell upon the car. It was so complete I thought the world had disappeared. Until then I hadn't noticed the smell of alcohol on Mike.

"You drink scotch?" I asked as I parked the car in the same space as before.

"I do," he replied.

"Did you drink a lot of scotch?" I asked as we exited the car. I pressed the lock and alarm buttons on the key chain, and then walked away toward our hotel.

"A couple of glasses, why?" He caught up to me as I opened the side door to the hotel. His hand caught the door and closed it carefully behind us so it didn't bang.

"Just want to know if snoring will be a factor tonight," I said. I was already ahead of him walking to the laundry room. He couldn't see my smile.

Mike leaned on the vending machines and watched me unload the machine.

"I don't snore," he said as I placed the clothes into a dryer. Mike fed the machine eight quarters.

"Have you had that confirmed?" I checked my watch so I knew what time to come back for the laundry.

One glance at Mike's face and his barely suppressed amusement told me all I needed to know about snoring. We went up the stairs.

I stifled a small laugh. Why do men snore when they lie on their backs? Because their balls fall over their assholes and create a vapor-lock. I had to stop thinking before I found myself having to explain why I was laughing

Relieved to be back in our room, I wanted to make coffee but opted for hot chocolate. Coffee and sleep were not friends. Adrenaline and sleep were not friends. Neither adrenaline nor coffee needed to meet each other in my body at that point. I was conquering serious coffee addiction one hot chocolate at a time.

Chapter Seventeen
China Girl

My laptop called to me. Not literally of course, but I felt the pull to do some poking about and see what I could find out about tonight's little escapade, and there was something even more pressing. I had to know why someone took Carla's laptop and not my desktop computer, or even Mac's. His tower still sat on my office desk at home.

I fished about in the bottom of my bag, until I found the little pink pig flash drive I'd taken from Carla's room; I plugged it in and opened it up. In front of me, I saw the entire contents of her laptop. All her files, her picture folders, her school work. There was a lot of information on the pig. Unless I had some idea where to look, this would take all night.

What would be so important on a kid's laptop that some crazy hacker with a massive grudge took it? I slid the mouse pointer across the screen, pausing over each folder hoping to get a sense of where to start.

"What could you have had on here that was so important?" I whispered to the machine. "You were a fifteen-year-old high school student ... what could you have had?"

"Did you say something?" Mike asked.

"Talking to myself," I replied, refocusing on the screen

and the many folders. I steered away from the school folders and hovered over one labeled 'Torrents'. I hoped it wasn't downloaded movies.

The screen filled with various files. Fifty-seven files in all. Some in PDF form but mostly they were captured screen shots. I clicked on one screen shot. It opened in an image viewer. It was part of a dated Skype conversation between Carla and a person named Mr. RightGuy. All the files I looked at were dated and all in the week leading up to Carla's death.

Nausea flapped about in my stomach like a demented bat.

I opened about twenty images until I'd read several separate conversations between Carla and the Unsub. He was an Unsub because there was no way Mr. RightGuy was his real name. Some sick piece of shit had been grooming my kid.

I opened the PDFs. More conversations: this time not between Carla and the Unsub but between Joey and the Unsub.

I opened a Word document, the only one in the folder, revealing a detailed plan written by Carla and added to by Joey. They'd been trying to trap someone. A kid they knew had introduced them to this Unsub over Skype. I checked the top of the screen shots. His location showed as Montreal, Canada. I didn't believe that either.

Carla had documented everything.

I blew out a sigh. If only she'd told me what was happening and what they were trying to do. I pushed the laptop away, stood up and stared out the window. My mind worked fast, sifting everything from Carla's last week.

I kept coming back to my anger at what she'd done and my inability to understand why they would take pills to end their young lives. The new information in front of me made me doubt everything that surrounded their deaths.

With my hands on either side of the window, I pressed my forehead onto the cold glass. Was this the information the hacker wanted? Did he somehow know Carla had kept the conversations? How would anyone know that?

If there had been some kind of spyware on her laptop, then why wait so long to retrieve the information?

Why now? Something must have changed for this to become important now. I banged my forehead on the window. Each thump onto the cold surface reminded me she was dead and no amount of figuring it out would bring her back.

Fingers closed firmly around the top of my arms and prevented my head hitting the window for the fourth time.

"Windows make messes of faces," Mike said. I looked at his reflection in the window. He smiled. I didn't. "Is there anything I can do?"

I found that I couldn't use words to describe what was going on and how I felt, because I didn't know if the words existed. I could've directed him to the laptop and the screen full of conversations between my child and some sick bastard pedophile, but he didn't need to see that. I closed my eyes for a second or two and took a deep breath.

If the Unsub wanted the information on Carla's laptop then he or she had it already. So why chop up Eddie, aside from the fact that he was the single most annoying person on the planet's surface? Why frame me for it? For a split second, I saw something. Punishment. I am being punished by someone who is also being punished and blaming me for whatever is happening to them. Could there already be an investigation open on this Unsub? Was this all about destroying any possible evidence against them?

That was definitely worth looking at.

"I'm good. You can let me go," I said, making eye contact through the medium of the window.

"Promise you won't smack your head anymore?"

"I promise." I won't smack my head literally any more. Figuratively, well that's another story.

The pressure of his fingers relaxed and his hands dropped to his sides.

"Can I help?"

"No."

I could see the reflection of the laptop screen in the window. Time to deal with it. Mike went back to doing whatever he was doing before he staged the intervention. I copied the files from the flash drive to my hard drive then disconnected the flash drive and dropped it back into my bag. It seemed smart for me to make sure there were a few copies. Just in case.

Also, my gut told me the Unsub featured in the conversations had something to do with Carla and Joey's deaths. I intended to find out what. The Unsub could also be the person behind Eddie's death. Two birds, one stone.

I closed the screen so I didn't have to see the Torrents file any more.

David Bowie's "China Girl" filled all available space in the room. Mike didn't react. He was watching television. David Bowie wasn't on.

It made me want to call Sandra and find out if anyone had asked her to investigate China Caldwell but she didn't have a magic burn phone.

"Hey, Mike, what's Bowie's "China Girl" about?"

The television turned off.

"Play it ..." he said.

I opened the laptop and waited for it to fire back up then clicked on the YouTube icon in the browser window, reminding myself not to sign in and advertise my presence. After finding the clip, we listened to it twice.

"Could just be about a guy who falls in love with a Chinese woman but doesn't want to corrupt her," Mike said.

"Or it could be about drug addiction," I added. "China White rather than China Girl."

"You're Ellie again," Mike muttered. "Laura would have gone with the romance not the drug addiction."

I chose to ignore his comment.

"So, it could be a romantic thing or it could be drugs."

Mike smiled. "Just like Leonard Cohen's 'Suzanne.'"

Frown lines creased my forehead. "Really?"

"It's either about a woman who likes having sex by the river, or drugs."

"You talk some crap," I said. "Suzanne is about a woman he knew, a friend."

Mike laughed. "Doesn't take much to wind you up ..."

I shrugged. Nope, sometimes it really doesn't.

I went back to my research and ignored him. He turned the television back on. I could still hear "China Girl" in my head.

So where was China Caldwell?

Google provided quite a few answers. I found her Facebook page, Twitter, and something even more fun, she used Foursquare.

China Caldwell was at T.G.I. Friday on Fair Lakes Promenade Drive, just a few minutes' drive away. Or at least that's where she was half an hour ago.

"Road trip," I said jumping up from the table and grabbing the car keys from the counter top. "Leave the TV on."

Wouldn't hurt to let people think we were in the room watching television.

Mike grabbed his jacket. I pulled mine off the back of the chair and snatched up my bag.

"Where?"

"T.G.I. Fridays. It's four miles away."

"Why?"

I pulled the door shut behind us and pointed to the

stairs so we wouldn't be seen by anyone in reception exiting the elevator.

"China Caldwell is there."

Neither of us said another word until I pulled the car into the parking lot behind the bar.

Using the camera I had in my bag, I photographed the parking lot, getting as many tags from cars as I could without looking suspicious. Photos have a way of being handy later on. Ideally I would just ask the bar manager for a copy of the video surveillance of the parking lot. Ideally. Not possible as Laura and not carrying FBI identification.

I dropped the camera into my bag. My fingers lingered for a moment on the butt of my Glock – security.

Mike opened the door for me. I stayed very close to him. If the Caldwell woman was there and she was the stalker we were after, then having Mike walk into the bar would be a dream come true. Me, not so much. I hooked my left arm through Mike's right arm, that way my gun hand was free.

"Let's get a drink," I whispered. "Can you see her anywhere?"

"Not yet," he replied as we approached the bar. "What would you like?"

"Pinot Gris please, house is fine."

Mike ordered and we took our drinks to a booth, hoping Caldwell was in the bar and had seen us. It would make things so much easier if I could end the stalker issue and let Mike go back to his life, unencumbered by a

Glock-wearing undercover special agent on the run. Although, he proved a good accessory for Laura.

We chatted like a couple who knew each other well. I noted a few sidelong glances of recognition in Mike's direction from males and females alike.

While Mike told me about a movie he'd just finished filming overseas, I wondered how Delta was getting on with the vandals who'd trashed my home and how Rowan fared under the malevolent interrogation I knew would flow from The Evil Queen, Owen. I managed a few 'uh huhs' and a couple of light questions regarding the setting of the movie.

As if on cue my phone rang once and stopped. It rang again and stopped. On the third go-round it rang properly. Kurt.

"Everything okay?" I asked. I was watching people mill about, still no sign of Caldwell.

"Where are you?" his voice laden with suspicion.

"Hotel," I said, crossing my fingers.

Mike looked at me and smiled. "Hey, Laura, wanna watch this or that other movie?" he said.

"Noisy movie," Kurt commented.

I winked at Mike. "This is fine." I turned my attention back to the phone call. "Everything went okay?"

"Rowan may have a career in acting," Kurt said with a short laugh.

"That's a relief. Any mention of Laura?"

"No, he managed to convince Owen that he'd broken in himself and there was no one else in the house."

"Ah, his famous charm at work then. And what did he tell her he wanted?"

"A journal of his that he'd left in your room ... containing new songs he'd been working on."

"And she bought that?"

"He was convincing."

"She didn't want to know why he didn't just call me to have me mail it to him?"

"Not after his rendition of how awful the break-up was. She was putty in his hands."

I had a horrible feeling. "You let him into my room?" Please say no.

"She did," Kurt replied.

"Jesus."

Rowan in my room? Not brilliant. The journal he spoke of wasn't his, it was mine. Was that Rowan thinking on his feet or Rowan being fuc'n creepy and wanting to read my journal? It was a big red flag. He took advantage of the situation to gain access to my bedroom and my journal. He wasn't there for me. He was there for him. Worried what I'd said or thought about the break-up? Looking at covering his ass in case I decided to talk to the media?

Kurt's voice, in doctor mode, punched into my thoughts, "How's your hand? As soon as I get a chance I'll come check it and your shoulder."

"It's okay." My hand flexed without bidding. "I need more dressings, those clear waterproof op-site ones for my shoulder and hand."

"I'll bring some."

"Thanks."

The crowd parted at the bar. China Caldwell emerged from the center. She wasn't smiling when she looked at me. Her eyes flicked to Mike and a smile came from nowhere.

Crazy bitch alert.

"See you tomorrow. We're interrogating the prisoners tonight."

"Okay. I gotta go," I said. "Movie's getting interesting."

I hung up and dropped the phone in my bag. "Mike," I said. "Company."

Caldwell was six feet away.

Mike leaned across the table and whispered in my ear, "Now what?"

"Let's see what she does ..."

Caldwell was four feet from us. Her right hand moved upward. I rested mine on the grip of my Glock.

She made eye contact with Mike. Mike smiled. He's nice to everyone. Nut jobs included.

Caldwell took another step. I saw something glint in her hand. She smiled at Mike but she focused on me.

Ah crap.

I glanced quickly at Mike, watching the approaching woman.

Two feet from the table I saw the blade in her right hand. I jumped to my feet and thrust my hand out at her. "Hi, I'm Laura ... you are?"

Part of me hoped she'd drop the knife to shake my

hand, that I'd surprise her into a fluster.

She didn't.

Her hand and fingers tightened on the hilt of the knife. Instead of shaking her hand, I grabbed her wrist and spun her around. With her arm twisted up her back, I forced her into the seat I'd vacated. Carefully I removed the knife and slid it across the table to Mike.

What is it with crazy women and knives?

"You must be China Caldwell," Mike said, his voice as cold as his expression. I'd hate to be on the receiving end of that look. "Thanks for the pen."

"I love you," she whimpered. "You shouldn't be with that slut."

Slut? That's the best she could do? I shook my head at Mike, indicating he should not reply.

"Mike, can you call Lee, please. We'll need him."

Mike could call Lee's regular phone without raising any suspicion.

"Bro, need you to swing by TGI's on …"

"Fair Lakes Promenade," I said.

He repeated it to Lee. Judging by the expression on Mike's face, Lee was giving him all kinds of flak.

"Just come. Laura asked." Mike hung up and grinned at me. "Your name is like magic. Can no man resist it?"

I smiled. "Apparently not. But, baby, you're the only one that matters."

Choking sounds came from China Caldwell.

"I love him," she whined at me. "You don't know what love is."

I ignored her. My arm was tired holding her wrist. I took handcuffs from my bag and cuffed her hands behind her, hidden from view, jammed against the wall, whimpering between bouts of nastiness.

I saw Lee before he saw us. He was hard to miss, as was the reaction of most of the women in the bar. He was a chick magnet. Didn't matter that he kept his hair very short these days, he still looked like Tony Sharron from Grange. He still caused women everywhere to do a double take. Often a collective intake of breath accompanied his entrance – preferable to the mobbing and the shrieking.

Caldwell gasped as Lee nudged Mike to move over.

"Nice of you to join us," Mike said with a grin at his brother.

"You said Laura asked ..." Lee replied. He scanned the woman next to me with eyes that had seen damn near everything. "So, you are our little stalker."

She swallowed hard. "I'm not a stalker."

"That's what we call someone who behaves like you have been behaving," Lee said, his voice quiet and calm. "Now, you want to explain why there is a knife on the table?"

She shook her head. "Am I under arrest?"

"Not yet," Lee replied. "What did you hope to achieve here tonight?"

"They weren't supposed to be here," she hissed. "I improvised." Her eyes darted around the room then settled back on Lee.

Crap, this is a meeting place.

I kicked Lee's foot. "A word."

He did the eyebrow-lift-head-tilt thing that he and Sam adopted a few years back, then nudged Mike. "I need to talk to Laura. You okay?" I knew Lee had just slipped a Sig into Mike's hand under the table. "Bro, no second chances."

"Go ahead," Mike said. He seemed relaxed.

Lee and I moved a few feet away, just far enough to lose our conversation in the noise of the bar.

"What's up?"

"I think this was a meeting. We need the bar surveillance camera footage." I pointed to a dark dome on the ceiling mid-way between our booth and the bar. I'd counted six cameras just while we were sitting there.

"Meeting for?"

"My guess? Stalkers anonymous. The woman at the museum and now this one, all using knives, I'd be very surprised if they were working alone. I think there is some kind of collective stalking going on."

Women who like to cut up anyone who stands in their way, but none of them trained in the art of hand-to-hand combat. Luckily.

"I'll get their footage and take the woman back to the office."

"Thanks."

"Now go back to the hotel and stay there."

I stretched up to Lee's ear and whispered, "Did you just give me an order?"

"Go back to the hotel," he said with a smile.

"Okay."

"It's too dangerous out here. You need to stay with Mike in the hotel until his next engagement tomorrow."

I slipped into the seat next to Mike. "Shall we go?"

"Good idea."

Lee leaned over the back of the booth between us. "Stay for two minutes, I need to see the manager."

Caldwell alternated between a glare for me and doe eyes for Mike. I found it disturbing.

I was glad to get out of there when Lee came back.

Chapter Eighteen
The Way You Love Me.

The hotel beckoned – it felt so much safer than the world. But I wanted to be in on the interviews by Delta. Gunmen and two crazed knife-wielding women. Juicy stuff; more exciting than the usual interviews we did over a twenty-four-hour period and all of them would be extra interesting. Oh, to be a fly on the wall.

There was a time when not being able to sit in or otherwise participate would've driven me insane and I would've moved hell and high water to be there. Who was I kidding? I knew I was on the verge of doing just that, but couldn't quite get my exit or entrance plan together. Probably a good thing: there'd been enough rappelling over boundaries for one day.

Also, it was rather tiring being involved in such high-energy high adrenaline incidents in rapid succession. I had a feeling Mike could also do with some quiet time. I switched to domestic mode and stopped by the laundry room to retrieve our dry clothes.

Once in our room I conceded quiet would be good. It became apparent there was none coming my way. My highly entertaining brain was allowing Madonna to take center stage. "Mysterious Girl." Seriously? Right now?

The second song about a girl tonight. Two women were in custody and somehow I had the impression that

"Mysterious Girl" wasn't about any of them. It's a mysterious world.

"Laura?"

"Mike?"

"Everything all right?"

"Yeah."

"You don't seem overly sure. Feel like sharing?"

I chewed my lip. "Nuh-uh. I feel like sleeping, though." I picked up my pajamas and phone and shut myself in the bathroom. I removed the wig and put it on the counter.

A shower would help. A phone call would help more. I made a call, pleased I'd memorized Mitch's.

"Hey, it's me."

"Hey, you. Okay?"

"You heard anything?"

"Your dad called me. Should you be using a phone?"

"No. I shouldn't. Just wanted to hear your voice." I wanted to know for sure that he didn't believe the bullshit being touted about me.

"Glad you called," Mitch said. "How long can you talk?"

"We're about at the safe limit."

"Be careful."

"I will ..." and hung up.

Steamy water bounced off the shower wall. I took the contact lenses out of my eyes and stored them in their cases. My eyes were tired. I was tired.

I stood under the water so long the extractor fan struggled and the room steamed up. I shut off the shower, stepped out onto the thick bathmat, wrapped a big towel around me, and used a smaller one to dry my hair. The plaster on my hand flapped. I pulled it off and threw it in the trash basket. It would definitely leave a scar – another line in the road map that is my body. Pulling out a waterproof dressing from my toilet bag, I applied it to my hand. The dressing on my shoulder was still stuck, so it seemed smarter to leave it alone.

I put on my pajamas, and gave my hair a vigorous brushing. Should've cut it long ago. As the steamy mirror started to clear, familiar hazel eyes smiled from the reflective surface.

"You're back," I whispered.

"I never left."

"Don't start." And we were back to the haunting by the dead husband. I didn't know if I'd missed him or not but I was no longer angry, which was a good thing.

"You look nice," he said, pointing to my hair.

"Thanks."

"Sleep, Ellie. You need it."

"I know. I will."

Just as I wondered why Mac had come back after all this time, he said. "There's another woman ..."

"What?"

"Three women are actively stalking your charge, masterminded by someone else."

Mac pushed hair out of his eyes, where it immediately slipped back.

"You need a haircut," I said absently.

"Nothing much changes with me," he said with a smile.

I let my eyes focus on his. "Is Carla all right?"

He nodded. "She's sorry for all the pain she's caused you. She can't see you because of what she did."

As it should be: I was once a Catholic. Something's stuck.

Mac chewed his bottom lip and studied me from the mirror.

"Three knife-wielders? Someone is giving orders. Someone has a serious desire to end Mike's life," I said.

Mac nodded in agreement. "The other issue – my loving brother—"

"I did not chop up Eddie."

He smiled. "I know. It's personal. Someone wants you taken out of the equation and that person has resources."

"That much I figured out."

"There's more, babe. Carla and Joey were playing investigator."

"I know. I read her files."

"The person who has her laptop killed my brother."

Like I haven't already considered that? Once upon a time Mac's insights were insightful. I was disappointed. "If that's all you got, I'm going to bed."

He pressed his hand against the mirror. I placed mine over his palm. Heat radiated.

Weird.

A knock at the door startled me and Mac faded.

Mike called out, "You leave any hot water?"

I opened the door. "Did you miss me?"

"I heard voices. You talk to yourself much?"

"All the time." I moved past him into the room. "Helps me figure things out."

Something bugged me: Rowan had my journal. I picked the room phone from the nightstand and punched in Rowan's cell phone number.

"You took my journal!"

"We have to talk."

"No, we don't." I paced the room.

"We do, and we're going to. Now."

A large sigh escaped unchecked. My finger paused over the disconnect button. It would be so easy but he was right, we had to talk sometime. "Okay, so talk. Tell me why you did what you did."

It would make no difference to me.

"You shut down on me."

"You lied to me. You were never there for me – you were there to steal my journal."

"I wanted to know what was happening in your head."

I sighed again. He hadn't denied my theory.

"Don't sigh at me. We had a good thing and you shut down."

"I didn't shut down. My kid killed herself!" I paused. "Whether I shut down or not does not give you the right to break into my house and steal my journal."

"I needed to know what was happening in your head."

"That's bullshit. We were over months ago and whatever is happening or not in my head is nothing to do with you."

"I care."

"You're wasting your time."

"You don't have the monopoly on grief here, Ellie." There was an edge to his voice I didn't expect, sharp, pointy, and full of pain. "I was involved in her life, too. She was as much my kid and Delta's kid as yours. We were all there when you adopted Carla. We were there all the way through. You're not in that place by yourself."

The bathroom door opened. Mike stepped out: our eyes met and he disappeared back into the bathroom.

"It fucking feels like I am."

"Ellie, talk."

"No. You read my journal?"

"Some."

"Then why do I have to talk to you?"

"Because you are angry and you're angry at me."

"You say I shut down, but I was still fucking there ... you were off screwing some bimbo."

And there it was, the ugly part of this break-up.

"I cut you loose – it's what your management wanted." It's what was best for me. "What sort of fucktarded rock star cheats on an FBI agent?"

"Can we discuss this civilly?"

"No."

Way to be a thirty-something mega brat, Ellie.

"I'm sorry for what I did."

"Now tell me she didn't mean anything—"

"When you've calmed down and whatever case it is that has you all turned round in circles is done – call me."

"I won't call you, Rowan. I've moved on." I hung up and flicked off the light in the kitchenette.

I climbed into my bed and pulled up the covers. Mike emerged from the bathroom for the second time. I played possum in case he tried talking to me about the talking to myself thing, or the phone call he overheard.

The last thoughts that wandered across my inner screen before sleep took over were disturbing. The people doing these awful things have resources. The person doing this to Mike knows just how insane fans can be and is tapping into that. Where have I seen that before? The Unsub setting me up has resources and a massive ax to grind. Where have I seen that before?

Chapter Nineteen

Avalanche

A newspaper lay on the table where Lee dropped it. The large full-color picture of me and Mike was hard to miss. I was the stunning redhead wearing the Hope Diamond. It matched my real eye color but not Laura's. Some journalist had heard Mike say it matched my eyes and had surmised in print that my green eyes were enhanced. There was also a deal of speculation as to why no one had seen me before.

It was me with a mane of red hair, green eyes, and no scars.

It was me.

Even Owen on her dumbest day would have to admit Laura Graham needed further investigation. Time was not on our side.

The thing that niggled away at me all night popped out. "Rowan has the sort of resources required to fund a stalker gang."

"I can't believe he would be involved," Lee said, leaning on the countertop in the kitchenette.

"I don't think I believe it, either. I'm not even sure where the idea came from." Except that he used a situation to his advantage and tricked Owen into letting him take my journal.

Lee regarded me in time-honored fashion. "I know you

well enough to know we need to check this out."

We do. I don't want to, but we do.

"I don't think it's him but someone with the kind of resources he has, maybe someone with a big ax to grind."

"Giant chip on their shoulder."

"It's familiar, right?"

"Feels familiar," he agreed.

"To what?"

"You don't remember?"

By the look on Lee's face, I think I was supposed to know this. Maybe I'd just found a missing memory. There was no way to tell if I still had missing memories after a brush with death and amnesia.

"Nope."

"Rowan discovered a chat room for his fans during the Hawk case, someone posed as Rowan and the women believed it was him ... any of this sound familiar?"

I shook my head.

He continued.

"Those women would have done anything for him, anything. And we talked about this yesterday morning."

A lot has happened since yesterday morning. Jeez.

"So, we could be looking for a website? But why would someone pretending to be Mike get people to kill him? I know these women are nuts but even a nut job would see that logic was flawed." I laced my fingers together and stretched my arms until my knuckles cracked. "You sure we talked about this?"

"Really?" Lee sighed. "You don't remember?"

Okay, clearly I'm not funny today. Not funny at all by the concern that creased Lee's face. Half my brain scrambled to get myself out of the hole the other half was determined to drop me in.

"Hello, I was kidding." I smiled. Yeah, I forgot, sue me. "Obviously someone isn't posing as Mike to get crazy gullible women to kill Mike – that would be silly. But something is going on."

"Do you remember?"

"Of course ..."

John Lennon singing "Jealous guy," *sotto voce*, played in my head. Knowing how Lennon's life ended made the song that much more potent. I didn't want Mike's to end the same way.

And I thought a friend of Mike's was behind the attacks. The whole thing smacked of jealousy and envy. Lennon grew progressively louder. I had the impression he agreed with me.

"I have a message from Joe Harris in Los Angeles for you," Lee said, his voice broke into the song and cracked the lyrics wide open.

"What'd he have to say?"

Lee handed me a piece of paper, an email from Joe to Lee. He found a GPS tracker in the rear right wheel arch of Mike's car and also a listening device under the dash. Joe gained access to the house and found graffiti scrawled in red paint on the walls of the master bedroom, hallway, and living room: Asshole, Loser, Hack, Tease, Arrogant prick.

"Interesting?" Lee asked.

"Very. Gimme a minute." I walked over to the window and stared across the parking lot and over the roads into the distance. Sirens, traffic, more sirens, and John Lennon all mingled into nothing.

White noise.

In the midst of the drone, a word appeared on the window in front of me. It slid across the pane and stopped dead center. Envy.

Another followed. Jealous.

The words jumbled. Using my index finger I moved letters around until I made new words. When I knew I'd finished I had the words 'Joaunes Levy' in front of me. They flashed twice.

A name. I was relieved that it wasn't the name Mark David Chapman. After hearing Lennon I deemed anything to be possible.

I turned around and looked at the two expectant faces. "Joaunes Levy," I said. "Mean anything?"

Mike nodded. "Yes, we're friends."

Lee nodded. "It does."

"So why have I not heard this name until now?" I searched the faces in front of me for answers. They were looking at each other. I waved my hand. "I'm over here, answers would be helpful."

"I have a question," Mike said.

"Me, too, wanna answer it? Today?"

"We're friends, been friends since junior high," he said. "I didn't give you a list of close friends because they're friends. How did you do that with the name?"

"Just did." I studied him for a moment. "You never heard of Sun-Tzu a Chinese general and military strategist?"

Mike smiled. "Yes, I have. He said, 'keep your friends close and your enemies closer.'"

"He did. He also said—"

"'All warfare is deception. There is no place where espionage is not used. Offer the enemy bait to lure him in.'"

We were obviously on the same page. That was a very good thing.

I raised my hand and waved at Mike. "I am the bait therefore I need all available information."

"Understood."

"So tell me more about Joaunes Levy. Male or female?"

"Male," Mike said.

Interesting. I'd fully expected it to be a woman behind this until I heard John Lennon singing.

"Now what did you do to Joaunes that pissed him off so much that he went from friend to enemy? I take it you still kept him as close as possible?"

Mike thrust his hands in his pocket and rocked back on his heels. "I did and I honestly don't know what happened."

"Lee?"

"No clue. The guy was our friend, not just Mike's, and one day he lost it. Publically at that. He posted a nasty rant on Mike's Facebook page and unfriended him straight after doing so."

"Just like that? No warning?"

"None," Lee said.

"Then what?"

Mike grinned. "Guys tend to leave that shit alone. I never called him or challenged him on it. Didn't seem to be much point, he was angry and lashing out. You can't reason with angry people."

Sensible.

"And you ...?"

"I ignored his behavior and continued as normal. When I was in town I texted him, along with other friends, to catch up. He replied sometimes but never came out with us."

"Anything else?"

"Might have sent the occasional email telling everyone back home what I was doing, general updates and included his email address in the list."

A little bit of stirring. So guys do partake in that then.

"Was there ever any backlash following the emails or texts?"

Mike rocked on his heels again. He pulled his hands out of his pockets and sat on the edge of his bed. "Backlash? No ... no, wait ... yes, but I wouldn't call it backlash."

"Okay, so tell me what happened?"

"Not much, a couple of times there were some nasty comments left on things by the same person, a screen name I didn't recognize, but figured it was him. That's nothing unusual. People tell me if they don't like the character I'm playing, although some do get confused and think I am the character."

"So a few more nasty type comments on things publically?"

"Yeah." He shrugged. "Nothing worth worrying about, thought he was giving me shit, ya know?"

"What made you think it was him?"

"It sounded like him."

"Okay. Where were these comments?"

"YouTube and Twitter mostly. He can't see my Facebook page."

"It never worried you at all?"

"No." He looked confused. "He's a guy. If he was that pissed we would've settled it ..."

I grinned. "Oh, right, in time honored fashion?"

"Something like that."

"And you have no idea why he became hostile?"

He shrugged. "None."

"It looks to me like he's found another way to settle this and it's not face to face. He always been a coward?"

"You don't pull punches," Mike commented.

"Has he?"

"I never noticed if he was or wasn't. He's always been cautious. We'd get into it a bit as teenagers as boys do, he hung back, but I wouldn't have said he was cowardly."

I filed that in the folder marked Joaunes. It was time to throw another thought out there.

"Is he gay?"

Silence.

"Not as far as I know," Mike replied. "Does it make a difference?"

"Not to me. I'm looking for motive, for a reason for his behavior. Being ditched is an old favorite."

"I never ditched him. I'm not gay and I have no idea if he is or not. All I do know is that he never had a lot of girlfriends in high school." Mike stood up and paced the room before sitting down in front of me. "You seem very sure he's the one who has done this."

I do, don't I?

I gave Mike the paper I still had in my hand. "This is the report from your house. Tell me what you see?"

A long pause ensued as Mike read and digested the information.

"Someone doesn't like me very much."

"Yes. But this is personal, Mike. This isn't a stranger turned stalker, this is someone with a serious grudge."

Lee hooked his cell phone off his belt with one quick movement and called Sandra.

"Can you run a name for me? Joaunes Levy. We need current address and anything interesting you have."

I turned my attention back to the parking lot and watched cars moving around the much bigger one over at the mall. Joaunes Levy was out there somewhere. He'd spent a lot of time and gone to a lot of trouble to make Mike's life miserable. I didn't doubt he was enjoying every second. But ultimately everything seemed geared to ensure Mike's life came to a messy, abrupt end.

"This guy ... he's a planner of some sort, yes?"

Mike nodded. "He worked in manufacturing as a planner."

"Worked? Or works?"

"I don't know if he's still there, but he was a planner for about fifteen years."

"Anything else that you thought was irrelevant? Anyone else lurking in your past with a giant chip on their shoulder?"

"Don't think so."

He's a guy, would he even know?

"If you think of anyone, no matter how insignificant, tell me, okay?"

"Yes." Mike looked worried.

I smiled. "He's not going to succeed. I want you to know that."

Lee reached over and landed an affectionate pat on his brother on the back. "Yeah, Ellie is an expert at drawing fire and the attention of lunatics. You're perfectly safe."

Lee's phone rang. "I'm putting you on speaker," he said.

"I have the information on Joaunes Levy. His address is listed as New York. Currently unemployed."

I kept quiet and wrote a note to Lee. It wouldn't be a good idea for Sandra to hear my voice and say my name aloud in the office. Lee asked my question, "Where is he now?"

"His credit card was used in Los Angeles over the last

week and yesterday here in Washington."

My burn phone rang. I took it to the bathroom before answering it.

"Get out of the hotel and do it now."

"Sean?"

"Go, don't argue. Destroy the burn phones, take the laptop, but don't use it. Do not use it."

"Why?"

"I'll tell you when I find you. Do not contact the Bureau or anyone you know."

"Mike?"

"Take him and Lee, I know he's with you. No electronics."

"Lee's phone, Mike's phone?"

"Tell Lee to get rid of the burn phone remove the battery out of his own phone. Mike's fine. He's not involved."

I hung up, took my burn phone apart, smashed the parts into smaller pieces under my heel on the hard floor, then scooped up the bits and dropped them into the toilet. Two flushes later it was gone to parts unknown.

"We're leaving now. Lee, destroy the burn phone and take the battery out of your own phone. Zero contact with anyone we know as of now."

"What's going on?" Lee asked.

"I don't know. Sean called. Just flush that burn phone, do it now."

Lee took his phone into the bathroom. I heard the sound of breaking plastic.

"What about mine?" Mike said.

"Yours is okay. We're compromised, not you."

Mike said nothing else. He and I packed and packed fast.

Minutes after Sean's call we were in the lobby. Laura paid our bill. We left in Mike's rental car, leaving Lee's car in the parking lot. As we turned right onto Lee Highway I saw two black SUVs in the distance.

"We need a different car," I said. "There's a rental car place over at the mall, next entrance."

I opened Laura's wallet and found another license and a pre-paid credit card I had stashed over a year ago in the lining at the back. The license was for another redhead, this time she was a redhead with blue eyes called Sarah Philips. Sarah was from Kentucky.

Ten minutes later we drove away in a nondescript white Ford sedan with Pennsylvania plates, rented by Sarah Philips. I doubted anyone would figure out my latest identity change and they certainly wouldn't do it very quickly. I could change as many times as necessary to keep ahead of them.

If I learned anything in my time with the CIA it was be prepared. I never expected I'd need to use the things I learned but I was prepared and had several aliases of varying depths ready.

"Where to?" Lee asked.

"Antietam," I replied.

"You want to go sightseeing now?"

"I want to get the hell out of here and why not do

something fun at the same time?"

All right there is another reason. It's not a random urge to sightsee; it's a safe place that only my father and Sean O'Hare know about. I knew Sean would remember and come to find us with some kind of explanation as to what just happened. There was also a new identity waiting for me in Antietam.

I would've been an awesome scout.

"Okay, Antietam it is."

There was a lot of silence as Lee drove. If you could measure silence in decibels then this was deafening.

We stopped in a small town that seemed a lifetime away from the current situation. There was an open antique shop and a fabulous cemetery.

"I need a convenience store," I said. "Or a CVS."

"You all right?" Lee said.

"Yes, but I need wound dressings and so forth."

We found a CVS. I stocked up on wound dressings and a few other bits and pieces I might need. Our next stop was a gas station – one without surveillance cameras. We're not in Fairfax anymore, Toto.

"Anything either of you need while we're here?" I asked. "While we fill up."

"No," Mike replied.

"I'll live," Lee said. "I grabbed my go-bag out of my car. I got everything I need for now."

"Let's move then," I said. I opened the back passenger-side door and climbed into the car.

Lee drove, Mike rode shotgun.

"We still going to Antietam?" Lee asked as he pulled the car out of the gas station lot and onto the road.

"Yes."

My mind ran every possible scenario as to why Sean told us to leave the hotel. It didn't seem possible that the FBI could be that close, but I did see the black SUVs as we left the hotel. They certainly looked like FBI cars. It seemed incredible that Owen could find us so fast. It wasn't anything to do with the Joaunes Levy guy I believed wanted Mike dead or maimed. So what was it that caused Sean to make the call? Whoever hacked into my home security system? Whoever attacked the house while Rowan and I were inside? Someone was using some sophisticated software to track me and all other electronic signatures that could lead to me. If they weren't, then Sean wouldn't have had us ditch the burn phones.

We'd had those phones in the first-aid kits for at least six months and never activated them. Four were activated within a short space of time. How long would it take for someone looking to notice four burn phones all pop up on the same network at once and then see that they all communicated with one another and no one else? I'd notice. I'd have triangulated the positions of the phones using the nearest cell towers and be moving in. But our Unsub seemed to have more tools available than the norm. I felt the chances were high that the Unsub had managed to get tracking software onto the phones once the phone numbers popped up.

Sam and Kurt were in danger.

"Pull over at the next gas station," I said.

"Why?" Lee asked checking his mirror.

"Because if someone saw the burn phones fire up, then that person knows there are four of us."

"Sam and Kurt," Lee whispered under his breath. "You want me to turn around and go back to the gas station we were just at?"

"No," I replied.

"The car has GPS. That'll tell us where the next gas station is," Mike said, reaching forward to the Tom-Tom unit on the dash.

"Don't touch it," I said. "The longer we're off the grid the better." I scanned the fields and road as they flashed by. "There's a gas station about five klicks up this road, take the next right."

"Thanks," Lee said.

I'm not even sure the car came to complete stop before I jumped out and ran to the pay phone on the exterior wall. I searched my pockets for change. A hand opened in front of me. I took the proffered change and called Kurt.

"You okay?" I said when he answered.

"Yes," he said.

We had a contingency for this kind of emergency and it all hinged around our communal love of strong coffee.

"Coffee sounds good. The stronger the better," I said.

"You talking a quad-shot espresso?" His voice tensed.

"Yes. Meet you at the Firehook in twenty. Sean will join us," I told him then hung up.

Sam. didn't answer his cell so I called his desk. He answered on the sixth ring, just as I was starting to worry.

"Looks like you need a strong coffee."

"You talking quad-shot espresso?" The same tense tone I heard in Kurt's voice crept into Sam's.

"Yes. Meet you at the Firehook in twenty. Sean will join us," I said.

With a sigh of relief, I hung up and walked back to the car, followed by Lee and Mike. Dropping Sean's name into the conversation let them know whom to trust and who would know where we were going to be. We carried on our journey. Fifteen minutes later Lee asked where in Antietam I wanted to go.

"Bloody Lane."

Chapter Twenty

Love Is A Battle Field.

A tower rose from the end of the parking lot. I hurried over to it and climbed the steep stairs. The filtered light made seeing the edges of the stairs difficult. It seemed to take a long time to climb up to the covered viewing platform. From the top of the tower I saw civil war battlefields spread out below. A few tourists in the tower listened to a man in period costume tell them about the various battles fought there. Mike listened and watched where the man pointed as he spoke.

Lee wandered to the opposite side of the tower and peered over the side. He beckoned me over. "Is this yours?" he asked, pointing to a poem under a piece of Perspex on a section of wall.

I nodded. "It's mine."

His lips moved as he read the poem to himself. I knew it by heart and had no need to read it again.

One candle, one man, one life:
When I walked upon the field
Horses hooves, sweat, blood
Racing heart
Rifle cracks
Pounding guns
Burning, screams, acrid smoke
Flashes of colored chaos

Green runs red
Smells collide
Swallow hard and turn away
No escape.
They died that day upon the field.

Eventually the people finished with their questions and grew tired of the heat at the top of the tower. Swigging on water bottles, they made their way down the steep stairs.

"Did you want me to explain the history of the battlefield to you?" the man asked.

"What was the bridge called that the Union soldiers captured during the Battle of Sharpsburg?"

"Burnside's Bridge."

"Major General Ambrose Burnside got a bit of a surprise as he advanced on General Lee, didn't he?"

The man smiled. "Yes, A.P. Hill arrived from Harper's Ferry and launched a surprise counterattack. They drove Burnside back and ended the battle."

"Is there anywhere to get good sausages around here?"

The man's hand stretched out toward me. A grin spread across his craggy face. I shook his outstretched hand.

"Good to see you, kid. How's your father?"

"He's good, Uncle Jim."

"And apart from Martha's sausages, the best place for sausage is the Bavarian Inn over in Shepherdstown, West Virginia."

"Thank you. Is the family well?"

"Yes, drop by the house on your way out of town. Martha has something of yours. Your father left it for you last year."

"I will. Are you coming?"

"No, I have to stay here for a few more hours, but you go on and see Martha." He cast his eyes on the silent men with me. "Those two look like they could do with coffee. The pot's always on at the house."

We shook hands again before we left.

I'd grown accustomed to the silence, so when Lee spoke I jumped.

"Uncle Jim?"

"Not a blood uncle. He served with Dad in another lifetime. They kept in touch."

Dad said once that Jim was far enough removed from us, that no one would look there for me. He also said Jim's house would be a good place to stash a go-bag. My father is a smart man. By the time anyone made the connection, I'd be long gone.

Martha did have coffee on and she welcomed us with warmth. We left with the bag half an hour after arriving. By the time we got to West Virginia and the Bavarian Inn, I had a new wallet in my pocket complete with driver's license and credit cards. I was Anna Virginia Harley of Richmond, Virginia. My red wig safely stowed in the bag, I sported shoulder length straight black hair with bangs. My new look was guaranteed to give me a fright the first few times I caught sight of myself in a shiny surface.

The best way to hide is to hide in plain sight with a

new wig.

"One of you two needs to be my fiancé ... takers?" My plan was that we didn't slope into the hotel and keep a low profile, rather that we were loud and memorable. What better way to be loud and memorable than to have an engaged couple touring the area with the best man and groomsmen, looking at possible venues?

The following game of paper, rock, and scissors did nothing to boost my ego whatsoever.

"We do have one issue," Lee said as Mike beat him for the third time.

"Just one?" I replied.

"Mike here is supposedly engaged to Laura – so said his people, publically," Lee said.

"He's an actor. People get things wrong all the time," I countered.

Mike nodded. "You've seen some of the crap printed about me, you know how little of it is actually true. Plus, they said it so recently people will assume it was wrongly reported, or that we'd given misinformation to enable privacy."

"You'll be recognized and someone will tweet or Facebook a freaking picture ..." Lee said. "What's that other thing everyone's into now?"

"Instagram?" Mike asked. "Voxer? Vine?"

"Yeah, them. There will be pictures."

"It'll be cool," Mike said. "Trust me."

I smiled. It so would not be cool. But the potential for this to be vastly entertaining was high. Also, if the owners of the Inn thought we were considering their premises as a venue they wouldn't want word to get out. Celebrity weddings are worth a lot unless of course, the hoteliers can't be discreet and then they're worth nothing.

It's not in their best interest to let someone Instagram or in any other way document our visit. I hoped. Because it sure as hell wasn't in my best interest to have that happen.

We checked into the Inn without any fuss. I booked five rooms and let the front desk know that two more guests would arrive by the end of the day. Our five rooms were situated in a row. The first two rooms had an adjoining door. The porter automatically showed those rooms to Mike and me. There was a lot of nudging and winking going on between him and Mike.

Lee took the next room.

It was nice to be on my own for a minute. I dropped my bag on the settee and threw myself backwards onto the bed. All day it felt as though something was missing. I finally figured it out. No phone. No interruptions at all. No distractions either. I wasn't sure if I missed it because I enjoyed being part of the world, or if I missed it because it was something that was always there and now there was silence.

I wriggled my holster free of my belt and slid it onto the nightstand.

Silence at our end translated to chaotic activity for those hunting us. That realization made me smile.

I just wished I knew what the hell was going on. Then I

remembered Sean. I should've booked six rooms. I called down to the lobby and asked if they had another room, I intimated that I couldn't count and there were in fact four groomsmen. The woman on the other end of the phone assured me that was no problem and inquired as to how many bridesmaids there would be. Four of course. They wouldn't be arriving yet as this was turning into an impromptu stag event, organized at the last minute by my darling fiancé.

She kindly invited me to join her and several friends later in the evening in the bar so I didn't feel as though I was alone.

I liked this place. While I had her on the phone I booked a table in the restaurant for dinner then changed my mind and asked about eating on the terrace. She happily reserved us a terrace table.

Chapter Twenty One
Bird On A Wire

The sky was a shimmering blue when I opened my eyes and realized I'd been asleep.

Right away I noticed something was missing. Noise. No sounds of life at all. I rolled over and looked at the clock on the nightstand. I'd been asleep for nearly two hours. The silence was unusual.

Unusual because I'd been sharing a room with Mike since Owen started her crap and I hadn't been alone in days. The passing gleam of a notion hinted at trouble, as I wondered where everyone was. Joyous thoughts of a long hot shower overshadowed everything. Bliss.

I unpacked my bag and inspected the clothing available to me. Everything had short sleeves apart from my jacket and one long-sleeved shirt. I decided I'd save that for a later date. I would need Mike to work some corrective makeup magic for me after my shower.

The adjoining door was closed but not locked.

I shrugged.

At this point locked doors seemed unnecessary. Half an hour after waking, I stepped out of the shower onto a thick pale blue bathmat and dried off with a large pale blue towel. Dressed and with the black wig back on. I surveyed myself in the mirror, determining I did need Mike's help to conceal scars. They'd attract too much attention, attention I didn't want.

I knocked on the adjoining door before opening it.

"Mike?" I called, pushing the door all the way open. His bag lay open, his clothes strewn across the bed.

Thought he was tidier than that.

"Mike?"

He wasn't in the main room.

I knocked on the bathroom door. "Mike?"

No answer.

I ducked into my room and grabbed a jacket. I couldn't walk around the hotel in short sleeves. Creeping dread edged into my gut. I strapped on my belt, slid the handcuff case and holster into place then checked there were spare magazines in the pouches. I shut the adjoining door and went looking for Mike. Logical place to start was Lee's room. I knocked and waited.

Footsteps walked toward the door from the other side. Something felt wrong. The footsteps sounded wrong. They moved away from the door.

I knocked again. My hand right hand wrapped around the grip on my Glock, still holstered. Silence.

"Hey, Lee, open up," I called. "Is Mike with you?"

The footsteps returned to the door. I moved sideways away from the peephole. The handle turned all the way, the lock released.

I stepped into the center of the doorway and shoved the door hard. The noise told me it hit someone. Glock in hand I entered the room to see a male recovering his footing, his hand reaching behind him.

"Don't," I said. He froze. "Hands where I can see them."

He sneered. "You! You're making this too easy."

Not sure if he was alone, I kept my gun trained on him and glanced around the room. No other sign of life. And no sign of Lee or Mike. I figured he hadn't found them.

"And you are?"

He didn't answer my question. His eyes fixed on my gun. "Go ahead and shoot. You'll bring a world of hurt down on you. Police. FBI," he said. "That'll be fun."

I'd be long gone before they got here.

"And you'll never see a penny of whatever you're being paid to find me."

He shrugged. "Does it look like I care?"

No, it looked like he was sizing me up and getting ready to make a move. I was out of arm's reach and intended to stay that way.

"Hands on your head and turn around."

He did as I asked.

"On your knees."

He shook his head.

Wrong.

I stepped up behind him, took the gun from his back waistband, and nudged the back of his knees. "On your knees," I repeated as his legs bent and his knees hit the floor. I had my cuffs ready. I took his right hand off his head and pulled it behind him while snapping the cuffs on, then the other hand. Securely cuffed, I pulled him to his feet.

He seemed altogether too calm and obliging. Searching him netted nothing. No ID. No wallet. No car keys. Nothing.

"Walk," I said, shoving him toward the door and escorting him to my room. I pushed him into a chair at the small table. "Stay."

From my bag I took a handful of disposable restraints and used a couple to tie his ankles together then moved behind him. I holstered my gun. With a few more disposable restraints I made a nylon chain and secured his cuffed hands behind the chair. Dropping the chain I reached through to pull his feet under the chair. His legs kicked forward as he laughed.

Jumping to my feet I pulled my gun and smashed it into the side of his head. He groaned, his head rolled to the side and legs relaxed.

"Goodnight."

I kneeled down, grabbed the restraints around his ankles and attached the chain. Hog tied in a chair. The only thing left was to gag him, put a do not disturb sign on the door just in case housekeeping popped by, and go find Lee and Mike. I stuffed a washcloth from the bathroom into his mouth, secured it with another restraint chain, hung the DO NOT DISTURB sign and headed down to the front entrance of the restaurant. Making sure my jacket covered my belt and holster, with a deep breath, I sauntered through the door.

"Can I help you, ma'am?" a female voice asked from an alcove.

"I'm Anna Harley I need to find my fiancé ... Mike." I didn't even have to finish saying his name.

She went to smile then changed her mind. "He went for a walk with his best man. They were looking at the gardens."

"How do I find them?"

She took me back to the door. "Go down the driveway and turn left."

"Thanks." I took a breath. I hurried in the direction she'd pointed. Once out of sight of the main hotel I broke into a run. In the gardens, I slowed to a walk and started looking for Lee and Mike.

"Lee?" I whispered as loudly as I dared.

There was a gazebo ahead of me. I thought I saw blond hair.

"Hey, Anna!" Mike's voice came from behind me.

I spun around. "You're okay?" There was more emotion than I intended in my words.

He grinned. "Of course."

"Where's Lee?"

A voice came from the gazebo. "Over here, Chicky."

"No holes?"

"None but the ones I was born with," he replied, the smile he wore froze on his face. "Strange question."

"Anyone mind if I sit down for a second?" I headed into the gazebo and sat on one of the bench seats.

"What's up?" Lee asked.

"Oh, you know, just the usual. I went to your room because I couldn't find Mike and ended up handcuffing someone."

"Who?" Mike asked.

"No idea. He didn't want to say. No ID either."

"Not good," Lee muttered.

I felt it was a decent time to state the obvious. "We've been here three hours and someone shows up looking for me. This is not a coincidence."

"How?" Mike asked. "How did someone find us so fast?

"I don't know, yet," I replied.

It was time to phone a friend. We needed help and I knew exactly who to call.

"Where's the Unsub now?"

"Hog-tied and gagged in a chair in my room."

Lee grinned and high-fived me.

"Description?"

"White male, a little over six feet tall, short dark straight hair, brown eyes, a nose that's been broken a few times." I closed my eyes and dragged his image front and center. "Wearing a button-down cream shirt. Black trousers not jeans, well built, a little over six feet tall."

Lee nodded. "Doesn't sound familiar. We should go talk to your guest ..."

The three of us stood up and walked back toward the hotel. I listened for sounds of distress as we walked. The Unsub had been too calm by far. Maybe he wasn't alone?

"We should sweep the hotel in case he brought friends," I whispered as we closed in on the main building.

"I'll go in through the terrace, you take the front entrance to the actual hotel," Lee said.

"And me?" Mike asked.

Lee gave him a withering look. "I don't want you involved at all. This could be one of the loons out to get you."

Neither of us believed that.

"I'm here, where do you want me?"

"Go in the main restaurant entrance and remember you're not armed."

I grabbed Mike's arm. "Go into the restaurant, find people, and stay put. Observe. We'll come to you."

Chapter Twenty Two
Joan Of Arc

No one appeared out of place, or dressed so as to conceal a weapon, in the restaurant area or outside. We checked the entire hotel and found no signs of any other anomalies.

I walked into my room with Lee behind me. The Unsub had gone.

"This isn't good," Lee said inspecting the chair and the disposable restraints lying on the floor.

A faint scent, so dilute as to render it lost in the air, swirled about me. I may forget a face every now and then but I never forget a smell.

"Time to call a friend," I said in a half-whisper.

"Don't you mean phone a friend?"

"Don't need to phone him, he's already here."

Lee drew his weapon. I placed my hand over the slide and pressed downward.

"Put it away." I moved toward the bathroom. "Come on out, Iain."

The door handle moved. The door swung open. "How'd you know?" he said, stepping into the room. I was relieved to see him.

"Usher. I could smell Usher."

He smiled. "I'm not wearing cologne today."

"No, you're not, but I can still smell it. It's embedded

in the fibers of your shirt."

Iain grinned. "What else?"

"You wash your own shirts, don't dry clean. You used a detergent with jasmine in it."

"Yes."

Lee stepped forward and shook Iain's hand. "Iain Campbell. CIA is here, why?"

"SSA Davenport," Iain said returning the shake. "I was in the area, Tierney said you needed help."

My thoughts rallied around Jonathon Tierney. We go way back to when I was seconded to a joint CIA task force but more recently I saved his life when a rogue CIA officer wanted him dead. Unfortunately to save Jonathon I had to shoot his wife. Good to know he doesn't hold grudges.

"He's got watchers on me?"

Iain nodded. Lee had assumed his usual position, parade rest. It was his one tell that oozed military past and a special kind of confidence.

"How'd you get in here?" I asked.

"I'm very convincing."

No denying that.

"Who was the guy I hog-tied?" I asked.

"A very unfortunate independent contractor. Seems you have a price on your head," Iain replied. "This is not the best outcome but to be expected considering recent events."

What bothered me was that someone found us. Okay, my cover wasn't great but it should've slowed everyone down. Someone must've uploaded a photo of Mike to a location on the web. Instagram was my guess. Someone from the hotel. Could've even been a guest.

"And this person is where?"

"Better that you don't know."

"Who's offering up cash for me?"

"I don't know yet, but I will find out."

"And you just happened along at exactly the right moment?"

He smiled. "Not exactly. Tierney moved those gunmen who tore up your house to a secure location for you."

I smiled. "They're close?"

"Yes."

"And Owen?"

"Unfortunately we can't do much about Owen at the moment. But you can. You have the evidence required that can clear you?"

"Yes, no ... the original photos are stored on flash drives in the bank. I can prove the photo of me with Eddie's hand was faked, if I can get to the bank."

"Then let's do that. But first ... the men."

"What do you know?"

"They are Seamus Kennedy, ARW, Colin Holmes, SAS, and Timothy Jones, USAF pilot."

"Kennedy is an Irish Army Ranger? They're a premier hostage rescue unit. What do the SAS, ARW and USAF have in common?"

And it made no sense for them to be shooting up my home. That's one helluva group to be taking shots at me.

Something smelled rotten.

My brain ticked overtime. What was missing from this little group? Russia and the Israelis. I couldn't begin to explain how I knew that, but it felt right. So did the next thing that fell from my mouth.

"Where's Praskovya? He's your source, yes?"

Iain smiled. "Around."

"There is someone else missing. An Israeli?"

He smiled again. "Not here, as far as we can ascertain he's the missing component. It seems they have all assembled minus the Israeli."

They were the sort of specialist group that could be sent to clean up a mess or take out a high profile target. I couldn't think of any high-profile potential targets in the vicinity this week. My money was on clean-up.

"They're a clean-up crew," I said. The only thing I did know for sure was they weren't here to clean me. I'd be long dead if that was the case. But apparently, someone would like to see me dead.

Take a fucking number. I think I've proved I'm hard to kill. I smacked the Steven Seagal moment aside.

"To clean up what?" Lee asked.

"That we don't know. I think Praskovya knows, but he's not ready to share," Iain replied.

"Not ready to share, or you don't know where he is?" I said.

A wry grin took the place of his smile. He shrugged. "We moved the men. You could ask them yourself."

Lee waved a hand at Iain to get his attention. "She will

but she's not done with you yet."

Iain smiled.

"So you're telling me no one knows why they're all here and why the Israeli isn't with them, if indeed there is an Israeli involved – yet they plan an assault against my house trying to get our attention?" I pointed a finger from Lee to me. "Seems like a pretty stupid way to go about things especially if you're coming in for a covert cleaning operation."

"I think something went wrong."

"No kidding." I adjusted my tone. "Sorry. But really, something went wrong?"

"Would've been so much easier if they'd just emailed you and asked for whatever they wanted, right?" One corner of Iain's mouth turned up into a crooked smile.

I winked at Iain. "People shooting at me gets old."

"I remember," Iain said. "And I promised never to do that again."

Another time, another place.

"Just make sure you keep that promise."

My brain spun out in a way it hadn't done in a long time. I jumped back several years to sitting in the dark watching a huge screen in front of me. A live feed from Syria. A truck racing across a desert road. Dust billowing.

Six aircraft.

Three completed the mission. Israeli, American, and Russian. I knew where I'd heard the name Tim Jones before.

"The American pilot. Tim Jones. He flew Operation

Hoboken," I said with a sigh. Rowan mentioned Hawk while we were in the panic room and now this. This!

I lowered myself into the chair across the room.

"Praskovya was one of the pilots," I stated. "I never knew the name of the Israeli."

"Libowitz," Iain replied. "CIA intelligence was involved in Operation Hoboken. I think Libowitz is the missing man from this little gathering."

"How are Kennedy and Holmes involved?"

"I believe they were all part of an elite international hostage rescue-clean-up team. All the men here now were involved in some way with Hoboken – either on the ground providing Intel or ..." he paused for a moment, "... as you know, in the air."

"Who are they working for now?"

"That we don't know ... no one is claiming them but it's likely that they're not working for any particular government. They were definitely a joint taskforce at one point. But are they now? I don't know."

Mercenaries.

"And you don't know why they are in Washington, or why two of them were given cover stories by their embassies?"

"No."

Just to be very sure, I asked a direct question. "The CIA doesn't know?"

"We don't know."

"There has been no pressure from any of the governments to release them?" I asked.

"No one knows they're in custody. Tierney had them monitored, no flags went up. It led us to believe they refused phone calls or that they're working off the radar."

"Even the American?"

"Yes."

"I take it none of their information has been uploaded to databases or anything?"

Iain smiled. He was one of those men who could smile while killing you with his bare hands and no one nearby would be any the wiser.

"Tierney convinced Owen she didn't want to do that. He told her she was messing with a joint operation. And that we wanted to sit on these guys a while and see what else pops up."

Smart. If she'd uploaded their information, they ran the risk of losing the men to politics or another clean-up team.

"Curious that no one had anyone to call ..." I muttered.

"Not really," Lee replied. "They could be disavowed if caught. If they're working for a government."

The Mission Impossible theme pumped through my head.

"Mercenaries. They're not working for a government," I said. "They should have been smarter in their dealings with me."

I wasn't blown away by their magical super powers. They were caught. They launched a full-on assault of my home. Admittedly they could have killed me and Rowan, especially with the weapons they were using, but didn't.

Why didn't they?

"They wanted to get caught," I said and pushed the chair back until it hit the wall. "I need to get into a room with those men."

Iain smiled. "Thought you might."

"Where are they?"

"In a hotel nearby."

"You're using a hotel as a safe house?" I asked. It's not like we hadn't done that before but I thought maybe the CIA had safe houses sprinkled over every state like confetti.

"Easier than trying to rent a property at short notice."

"Is it secure enough?"

A small smile crossed Iain's lips. "Is anything these days?"

Fair comment.

Lee stood straighter. "Chicky, you getting into a room with those men is not a good idea. We need to wait for Kurt and Sam."

That made sense.

"Agreed," I said. "We also need to get Mike out of the restaurant, can you do that?"

I suspected it was too late and more Instagrams would've been sent out on the World Wide Web. Sometimes technology and smart phones are a pain in the ass.

Lee left to fetch Mike as Iain pulled the other chair over until it was in front of me and sat down.

"Meanwhile, we have another problem. Why does your

Assistant Director want your head on a pike?"

"We don't get along," I said.

"I'm perceptive enough to have understood that. Why?"

"Long story," I said hoping he'd let it go.

"I have time."

Damn.

"She tried to railroad my brother into her preconceived notion during a difficult case. She also told him our mother was dead during the interview."

"And you took exception?"

You could say that.

"A little bit."

He laughed. "I have a feeling it was more than a little bit. You've created a monster, you know that, right?"

"I didn't intend to." I chewed my lip. "She had no right to do what she did."

"She's your superior." There was no judgment in his voice, just stating a fact.

"Yes, she is."

And I don't know how, but she is.

"She's not going to stop until she gets you."

"I didn't kill my ex-brother-in-law, nor did I chop off his extremities. The chances of her finding me are slim. The whole of Delta is flashing on and off the grid to throw her off." I chewed my lip some more. "She's not the brightest crayon in the box."

"She's making all the right noises about wanting to find you and get to the bottom of the issue with Metro."

"She can sound very sincere when she tries."

Then the flying monkeys swoop in and do her evil bidding and her hands stay pristine.

"Where's your Director? Caitlin O'Hare, yes?"

"Yes. Hospital, as far as I know. My SAC is running interference to keep Owen occupied but there is only so much he can do."

Her hatred for me clouds her judgment. I tipped my head back and looked at Iain Campbell for a few moments. He said nothing when his phone rang. From his pocket he pulled the phone and handed it to me without looking at the screen display.

Tierney's name glowed in green letters when I looked at the phone in my hand.

"We can bring you back in," he said when I answered. I imagined his beady eyes darting all over the screen in front of him. I knew what he was doing without seeing him. He was checking satellite images. Bringing me in would imply I was still seconded to his special task forces, although I hadn't been for eight years.

"You've been watching over me?"

"You know I have. I sent Campbell. You seemed to like him." He cleared his throat. "Do you want to come in?"

"No."

"You and your team are the best the FBI have. Owen is trying to destroy that."

"If I come in, I've lost. I need to clear my name."

"You have Campbell as long as you need him, our resources are available. Tell me what you need."

"Thank you for the gunmen who shot up my home. I'll talk to you after I have spoken with them."

"Take care, Agent."

I hung up and gave Iain his phone.

"What now?" he asked.

"Now, you tell me those men are secure, and we can eat and get some sleep."

He nodded. "I'll go back to the hotel with our guests."

"Do you need help?"

"I wouldn't say no."

"Take Sam and Lee."

"You sure?"

"Actually no, take Sam and Kurt. Lee checked in with Mike and me – they'll think his brother abandoning him is odd. I'll send Sam and Kurt over to you as soon as they arrive."

"I wrote the hotel details on the notepad while you were talking to Tierney," Iain said, pointing across the room to the desk.

"Thanks."

"I'll see you in the morning, unless something comes up."

"Good luck," he said as he left.

I flopped back onto my bed. I was in deep deep shit but I wasn't overly worried. I had Delta, I had Iain Campbell, and I even had Jonathon Tierney in my corner. They were some big hitters.

At a knock on the internal door I called, "Come in."

Mike entered followed by Lee. "We saw your friend

leave," Mike said.

"We should have dinner," I replied, sitting up and rubbing my hands together. "Food. Let's eat."

There was no point thinking or talking about any of it now. Time to eat and hang out and pretend no one wants anyone dead or arrested. Back to our official story, I was Mike's fiancé and we were considering the hotel as a wedding venue. Time to act like that was our reality.

A heavy knock resounded at the main door to my room. Lee strode across the room and peered out the peephole. He grinned at me and opened the door. "Welcome to our new lives," he said with a flourish as Sam then Kurt entered.

"Everyone okay?' Kurt asked. His eyes landed on me then Mike.

"I'm okay, we're all okay. Is Sean with you?"

Kurt shook his head. "He told us where to find you and will be along as soon as he can."

"How was Washington?"

"Starting to feel decidedly unfriendly," Kurt said.

"Sam?"

"It's not comfortable being Delta at the moment, not in D.C. anyway."

"I have another job for you … did either of you see Iain Campbell as you arrived?"

Kurt shook his head. Sam furrowed his brow.

"Iain Campbell is here?" Sam asked.

"Campbell was here. Thanks to Jonathon Tierney, the CIA is helping us out. Tierney's doing, not mine." I stretched out my legs and swung them off the bed. "I would like you two to go help Campbell."

"Help him do what?" Kurt asked.

"Keep an eye on his prisoners ... I don't want them getting antsy."

A light went on in Sam's eyes. "The gunmen who attacked your house?"

"Yes."

I moved over to the writing desk and copied the hotel address and room numbers on the notepad to a clean piece of paper. I handed the paper to Kurt.

"We'll head over there after we've dropped our bags in our rooms here," Kurt said.

Good thinking. I'd booked them rooms; it made sense to make it look as though they were using them.

"Any news on that stalker, Joaunes Levy?" I really hated being out of the loop.

"I've a BOLO out for him but getting the information now may be difficult," Kurt replied.

"Any more photos?"

"A couple of real gems turned up before we left." Sam flicked up the gallery on his phone and handed it to me. "Scroll left to see the next two."

I studied the images. They were good. If I didn't know better I'd think that was me holding Eddie's severed feet and a hand.

"They were delivered to whom?"

"Metro, Sandra managed to copy the files for us."

"We must be about ready to run out of Eddie's body

parts."

I did a quick count. Last time I looked he only had two hands and two feet. I tried not to think about any part of Eddie because he ruined my appetite and there I was faced with two feet and another hand. These photos implied that Eddie was a freak with an extra foot. I'd already been photographed with one of his feet.

"Um, these parts can't all be Eddie, well not both those feet anyway," I said. "It's looking like I chopped up someone else here. Pretty sure even Owen will figure out that we've seen too many feet."

I flicked back and forth between the pictures. "Kurt have you seen these?"

"No, Sandra sent them to Sam."

"Have a look, because I think one of those feet belongs to someone else." I handed him the phone.

Two minutes later he was nodding in agreement. "One of those feet doesn't belong there."

"Wonderful. So now we have another person with missing bits," I said. I felt unwell. The thought of eating after seeing Eddie's feet made my stomach churn.

"The sooner you get the proof that these photos have been manufactured the better," Kurt said.

"I know." Easier said than done. Especially now none of us can be in Washington or on the grid.

"Maybe we should all eat together before Kurt and Sam head over to see Campbell. Make sure you're seen here, for appearances," Lee said.

"And appearances would be what?" Kurt asked.

Mike coughed. "You're part of our wedding party."

"Wedding what?" Sam asked. "Do I have to wear some kind of ugly suit?"

"Traditionally only bridesmaids get ugly clothes," I said. "And no suit necessary at this point."

"Dinner then," Lee said. "Some of us are hungry, let's do this thing."

"You all go ahead, I need to speak to Conway alone," Kurt said. He set his bag on the small table in my room.

Everyone left without a word.

"Let me have a look at your latest wounds," Kurt said. His bedside manner was decidedly lacking.

"Most guys buy me dinner before asking me to take off my shirt," I replied, pulling the shirt over my head and throwing it on the bed.

"Most women don't attract blades, glass, and bullets like you," Kurt replied and removed the dressing from my shoulder. He poked around the cut a little bit. "All right?"

"Yes."

"We can leave the dressing off, it's healing nicely."

"Good," I replied. "Can I put my shirt back on?"

"Go ahead."

I pulled my shirt over my head and as my head emerged, I caught a grin on Kurt's face.

"I saw that," I murmured.

"Hard not to smile. It's you, Conway." He held his hand out for my hand. "Let's see what damage you did here."

The sticky bandage pulled my skin as he ripped it off.

The Steri-Strips still held.

"Is it all right?"

"Yes. I'll put an op-site dressing on it. Because it's your hand it pays to keep it covered." He stuck a fresh dressing on my hand, mostly clear and very flexible, like another skin before wrapping the old dressings in a bag and sticking it in the bathroom trash.

"Come on, let's go eat. The others will be wondering where we are," he said, holding the door open for me.

We were shown to a table at the edge of the terrace. Good choice. It afforded us a little privacy. Although for appearance's sake we'd only be talking wedding and frivolousness, not work.

Mike played the ever-attentive fiancé to perfection, inquiring about my hand and shoulder in light whispers that to onlookers would appear to be loving words.

Kurt called a server over and asked for the wine list and for more water. She arrived with the list and a large pitcher of water.

"You're her, aren't you?" she asked, filling my glass and trying hard not to pour water on the tablecloth.

Questions that start like that never end well.

"Her?" My heart skipped a beat hoping she didn't say Ellie Conway and that she hadn't seen my picture on a post office wall. I calmed myself with the knowledge that I was not yet featured on the FBI's most wanted list and therefore the BOLO out for me was only available to law enforcement. I'm not electronic billboard material, yet.

"Laura Graham. I saw you in a magazine with your

fiancé." She cast her eyes to Mike then back to me. "You were wearing the Hope Diamond."

Thinking on my feet, "Yes."

What else could I say?

"You didn't check in as her and she has that gorgeous long red curly hair. When I saw your photograph I thought of Merida from Brave."

Oh good, a nosy yet complimentary server.

"I don't want people to know I'm here."

Too late for that now, what with the male I apprehended earlier and now the server. I leaned closer to her and adopted a tone that suggested she was now part of a conspiracy. "I'm supposed to be working, but wanted to slip away for a few days."

"Oh, I see. I'm sorry to intrude."

I smiled. "No problem. Suppose now that it's out, I may as well use my real name."

Her mental workings showed in her eyes. "Right, they said you were a private investigator. So that's why you've changed your hair, you're like undercover or something. Must be exciting."

"It sure is."

You have no freaking idea.

"Could I have your autograph?" the server asked Mike.

"Sure. Who do I make it out to?"

Mike asked for a pen. Lee fished one from his pocket and handed it over.

"Stella."

Mike wrote across the paper napkin then signed it with

a flourish. He passed the young woman the napkin and smiled as she thanked him profusely. He was a nice guy. I don't know that I could be as nice to annoying devotees and the constant intrusions into my life. I supposed he had to, just like Rowan had to. Public lives.

Kurt put down the wine list.

"Do we want to call her back and order wine or shall we make do with the water?"

"Water," Mike and I said in unison.

So he's not that nice then.

"Kurt?"

"Yes," he said making eye contact.

"How have you explained Delta A's absence from D.C?"

The team couldn't just disappear. I knew he would've put something in place to cover their asses.

"We're working a case out of state."

"What if the Evil Queen checks?"

"She can check all she likes. According to Sentinel, Delta flew to Colorado and is working on a possible serial killer case."

"I figured you'd think of something. But that was pretty quick thinking."

"Caine had been working on a contingency plan. He also signed off on the travel."

"Dangerous. He put his neck in a noose doing that."

"Yes, but he considers Delta, and you, worth it."

"Won't Owen notice if the case file isn't updated?"

"She would, but it is being updated – Caine is feeding

information from an old case into the system under a new case number, and using our authorization codes."

"And if Owen tries to contact any of you?"

"We're busy. Away messages. Out of cell-range. Working long hours. Take your pick," Kurt said with a smile. "It's okay, Conway, we've got this covered."

Before we left the restaurant I had a word with the manager and told her I was really Laura Graham and how I was working but had slipped away to spend time with Mike. I also mentioned keeping this whole thing as low-key as possible and how someone from the hotel had probably posted an Instagram photo of Mike and me.

Letting disappointment fill my voice, I explained how the possibility of people posting photos of us on the internet and acts like that threatened our nuptials. She was horrified and wanted to make sure nothing else interfered with our stay and impending wedding.

Nothing like disappointment to make people feel guilty and rush about hoping to fix things.

Chapter Twenty Three
Jealous Guy

I woke early. Instead of getting up right away I lay in the warm comfortable bed contemplating the day ahead, but the previous days encroached. My "disappearance", my father and brother knowing there was a warrant out for my arrest, missing Mitch, Mac's crazy mother making allegations. They were all things that didn't sit well with my gut.

I recapped the stalker situation. Kurt had put out a BOLO. That was something. Still we couldn't get any information from that because of our situation. Being on the run sucked, along with the fun of having an independent contractor turn up, hoping to cash in on the price on my head. So someone with resources must've put that up.

I surmised it could be the same someone who was behind the Eddie scenario. The extra foot was not a pleasant thing to think about. Bad enough having photos of me with Eddie's body parts but now someone else was involved or dead. For a brief moment I wondered who the other person was. It had to be someone close, someone they could easily pin on me. Apart from Eddie, who else did I openly dislike?

I rolled over and lifted the handset to the room phone. Then replaced it. I didn't know the number for the hotel where Kurt had booked in; I dragged myself out of bed and picked up the notepad from the desk. On my way back to bed I caught sight of my reflection. The difference in bed hair and just-had-sex hair is in the knowing. This was bed hair. It was also strange to see my own hair and not a wig.

I lifted the receiver and called Iain's room. He went and found Kurt for me.

"What do you need, Conway?" Kurt asked.

"Was the other foot female?"

"What foot?" He paused. His brain kicked in. "Oh, that foot. Possibly. Let me go get the phone and have another look."

I heard the receiver placed on a hard surface. A few moments later he was back.

"Yes. Female or a man who had spent a lot of time wearing women's shoes judging by the bunions."

"I suppose that's possible but I'm wondering if it could be Beatrice Connelly?"

"I can't tell from the photo, Conway. But it's an older woman, or the foot of an older cross-dressing male."

"Anyway, can you find out if Beatrice Connelly is missing?"

"Sure, I'll get Campbell to do some digging."

"Thanks."

I hung up. Everything I felt pointed to this being Beatrice Connelly. After all, she did say I was killing her family off one by one.

Her voice mail message to me said that was what she

thought was happening and that she'd told police her crazy theory. I wondered who else she'd told – someone who then had the perfect way to fuck me over.

I needed to talk to Bob Connelly. It was dangerous. Before I could talk myself out of it I called him from the hotel phone.

"Bob Connelly speaking."

"It's me. Are you all right?"

His breath rasped into the receiver before he spoke. "You shouldn't be calling here."

"I know. Are you all right?" If Eddie and Beatrice were dead, then Bob could be next.

"Yes."

"Where's Beatrice?"

"No one knows. She went to her sister's yesterday morning and never arrived," he said but didn't sound overly concerned. Couldn't say I blamed him. He didn't get a lot of peace with Beatrice in the house.

I just knew it was her foot.

"Bob, do something for me?"

"If I can," he replied.

"Go stay with my dad until I can get back to D.C. and get this mess sorted."

"That's not necessary, imposing on Simon like that."

"Please. I'll feel better knowing you're with Dad," I said. "This situation is not good and may get worse."

"All right. I'll go on over to Simon's."

"Thank you."

"Take care, Ellie." Bob hung up.

The whole mess was exactly that, a mess. I hit the shower. Hot water, lots of hot water. As I let the water wash over me, a song flowed from the showerhead. Bathed in David Gilmour's voice, I saw words splashing up from the bottom of the shower and sticking to the walls. They slipped down the white tiles, pooling in red, and running down the drain. More words flowed. Gilmour sang on.

Murder.

I turned off the shower and grabbed a towel. As I dried and dressed, Gilmour's words sloshed around in my head, taking on many voices.

Whoever was killing and trying to blame me was doing so to make their mark or maybe Gilmour had something when he talked of the voices in their head. Maybe it was both.

I made coffee and hoped the song would not come back. The internal door opened without a knock. I watched as the door swung all the way open and Mike appeared.

"Morning," he said. "Thought I smelled coffee."

"You don't knock now?"

He shrugged and grinned, a little lopsided, and a lot charming. "We're engaged."

"Sit down," I said with a smile. "For your information, that look you splashed across the room, it won't work on me."

"You sure? Because it very rarely fails."

"Trust me, I'm sure. Coffee?"

He nodded. "Any news?" he asked when we sat at the table.

"Not yet. I'm still on the run and your stalker is still at large."

"Why do you suppose he's doing what he's doing, this whole stalker trying to kill me thing?"

We've danced this dance before. He's looking for a different answer this time.

"Jealousy and a little revenge maybe."

A quizzical look shot through his eyes and landed on his facial muscles. One eyebrow shot upward.

"Still with the jealousy. Serious?"

"I can only offer possible motives from what I see and what I know."

Okay, maybe I'm working with gut instinct here but my gut knows a thing or two.

"The three most common motives for homicide are sex, property, and insults." I sipped my coffee for a moment. "Probably the most common motive for women is sex – someone cheating on someone. The most common murder for someone who is financially challenged, is property dispute. But by far the most common is death after a petty argument or perceived insult."

He considered my words. It was interesting to watch him think. Mike was not a blank canvas by any means.

"First off, he's a guy so sex isn't likely to be the motive here." He pointed at himself. "Secondly, there's never been a dispute of money or property – he has no claim on me at all in that regard. Thirdly, I don't believe I ever insulted him."

"But this isn't about what you believe or even what you know for sure, this is something that only he knows. Something in him."

"And you still think jealousy and revenge?"

"Uh huh. I still think he's acting like a jilted lover."

"This is extreme don't you think, even for that?"

"Absolutely."

Extreme and it was really pissing me off. If this idiot wanted to kill Mike, there are so many easier ways. I suspected he got off on the torment. Death was too easy. I had a really crazy idea, but it might just work.

"What?" Mike asked, leaning his elbows on the table. "You have an idea?"

He could read me? Now that was disturbing.

"We're getting married ... let's invite the crazy stalker to the wedding."

A grin broke free, dimples and all. "You're serious?"

"Oh yeah, you can invite him to our wedding, in two days' time. We know he's in D.C, it won't take him long to get out here."

"I just email him an invitation, short notice, won't he suspect something?"

"I doubt it, he has no idea we know about him." I studied Mike. He looked pretty calm considering what I'd just suggested. "And yes, email ... make damn sure it says something about this being a very private wedding with only your closest friends and family being invited and how we decided on a spur of the moment wedding, to keep it private."

"He could go to the media ..."

"He could and I think that would depend on how big a spectacle he wants to create for your final moments."

He'd been rather theatrical in his attempts thus far, so going to the media was definitely on the cards. We needed to factor in that possibility.

Mike rocked back in his chair.

"My final moments," he said, his voice filled with mortality.

"Has quite a ring to it, doesn't it?"

"What if ..."

"There are no 'what ifs,' you'll be fine. We can protect you. I can protect you." Look at me being all confident about something I had major doubts about. "This is my job."

"You ever studied acting?" he asked.

"Nope, though I've often thought it would come in handy."

He spent a few seconds in quiet contemplation. "If I say yes, what happens next?"

"I talk to Delta and then we talk to the hotel about having the wedding in two days' time."

Mike disappeared back to his room and returned carrying a tablet. He sat back at the table.

"I'm going to work on that invite," he said glancing up at me. "Lee's coming down in a few minutes."

I nodded. Talking to everyone together seemed a good

way to go.

I called Campbell on the room phone and arranged a meeting with him, Delta and me in my room within the hour. He didn't have a problem with that – I guess he had help with watching the prisoners, courtesy of Tierney. Probably the same team Tierney had watching me. Good to know that for the moment we weren't alone.

Lee and Mike started working on the invitation. The exercise generated a lot of amusement. Eventually they had a passable first draft.

"You've got time to tweak it. I don't want it sent until tomorrow morning."

"We're heading down for breakfast," Lee said. "You coming, Chicky?"

"I'll be along soon. Order me pancakes?"

"Sure."

The men left and I sat back, enjoying a few minutes of peace and deciding whether I would go back to being openly Laura with red hair or stay Anna with black hair.

As if he sensed my thoughts or honed in on my energy, Sean O'Hare swung open my hotel room door and strode in.

No one knocks any more. Security key cards should mean he can't just open my door.

"How'd you open the door and when did you arrive?" I asked without missing a beat.

"I lifted a master key from the concierge's desk when I checked in a few minutes ago."

That really didn't surprise me.

"What do we have?"

"A lot." Sean sat in the chair not long vacated by Mike and slid a manila folder across the bed to me. "Let's start at the very beginning." He flipped the folder open. Sean's index finger tapped the first page.

A report explaining the security breach at my home, and it included details on the installation of software on various government computer systems.

"This was planned," I commented, "because someone really wanted to get their hands on photographs of my family and a child's laptop?"

Sean flipped a page over. "I think that Carla's laptop is a bargaining chip. Someone wants something and needed leverage when they couldn't find it."

"That makes sense, except for the part about them wanting something."

"You sure?" Sean's steel grey eyes never left mine but he didn't have the same tractor beam gaze that Mike favored.

"Nope," I replied with a swift smile. "I just can't think what it is that caused this much interest and then an armed attack. If they had the laptop and that was leverage, why send armed men before attempting to extort whatever it is they want?"

"Speaking of which I heard the CIA took control of those men. It's pissed Owen off to the max."

"Really?"

"Yeah, she's making a lot of noise about this being within the United States and not CIA jurisdiction."

"And?"

He leaned in. "She was told this was a high level joint operation and she wasn't going to be read in."

That sounded like a line from Jonathon Tierney.

"What a shame."

"You know where the prisoners are I take it? Have you spoken to them yet?"

"Not yet."

He nodded sagely. "They were after something particular. Surveillance photographs taken recently."

"Well, that's quite the coincidence." I rolled my eyes. And also, I'd considered they weren't part of the hacking.

"Not really, Miss Smartass."

"All right then, fill me in. How is the break-in related to the armed invasion?"

"Your trio of doom piggybacked on the initial break-in. They knew what they were doing," Sean said.

Of course they did, they weren't chosen for this operation randomly.

"So, we're still waiting for a little bit more bullshit from the initial break-in and now whatever these idiots want? Good to know."

"You went home, so you know exactly what was taken?"

"I do. I also know someone sent an email containing a photo from my computer to Owen and Metro. Any idiot could run the email header code and figure out that it originated from my email account and that the ISP number is registered to me. I have a fixed number."

"Someone would have to request the address information from your provider," Sean said.

"It's not difficult, we do it all the time."

"What was taken, Ellie?"

"They took all the photographs from my office and also a notebook of mine. It contained handwritten poems and personal notes."

His eyebrows rose. "They have handwriting samples," he stated. "This will get interesting."

"Because we need more interesting things on our horizon," I muttered.

"Heads up ... you might want to go have a word with the mini United Nations team the CIA has stashed in those hotel rooms ... before there is an international incident and maybe hand over your surveillance."

"There won't be an international incident. These guys are off the radar."

"Mercenaries?"

"That would be my take on the situation. They're not here for the good of anyone's health and they're not working for a government." There was something else bothering me. "Also, your sister requested this surveillance. I'm supposed to hand it over to God-knows-who because they stormed my house to take it?"

"Something like that." Sean's fingertips tapped on his knee. "I spoke to Cait. She said to hand it over."

"I'm going to need more than that, Sean." A lot more. "What is it that they really want?"

"We don't know yet."

"And yet you know the Quasi-United Nations wants my surveillance photographs, which they somehow knew were on my keychain?"

"You had two cameras in your office – sitting on your desk, neither of which contained SD cards. Nothing was uploaded recently to your computer or laptop."

"How did they know I hadn't uploaded them at work and attached them to an evidence log?"

"They couldn't know that."

Or could they? I didn't go into work. I'd spent two days on surveillance with Lee and never went near our D.C. office. I went straight home and from home back to our surveillance area. Damn, was I tailed? I thought back over the last few days and tried to recall anything that stood out, or in fact didn't stand out. Nothing was jumping up waving. Apart from a couple of drive-by shootings, a few attempted stabbings, being three different people including Michael Fisher's fiancée, wearing the Hope Diamond, a gunman in the hotel ... really nothing stood out. I figured if I'd seen something, it would eventually make itself known.

"Right now we have three men who want my photographs?"

"That's where we stand right now, yes," Sean said.

"And you think this is the best option?"

"I'm involved but only as far as brokering a resolution," Sean replied.

It felt like he wanted to distance himself from the situation but couldn't and that interested me.

"You know who those men are, don't you?"

He nodded, possibly the smallest nod I'd ever witnessed.

"What the hell is really going on here?"

"The hotel is not secure enough for this conversation."

"The hell it isn't. I've already had a conversation with Iain Campbell about the men. We are having this conversation."

"Come with me." Sean stood and waited by the door.

"I can't leave this room looking like this. Wait." I hurried into the bathroom to emerge a few minutes later as Anna Harley again. Decision made.

"Waiting," Sean said tapping his fingers on the door handle.

"Patience," I replied and made a call to Iain and told him we were postponing the meeting, then left a note on the desk in my room stating I'd gone out with Sean O'Hare for an undetermined length of time and that it was directly related to our current predicaments.

Sean led the way through the building and out into the parking lot. He pointed to a silver sedan. "That car," he said. "Thought a rental would be smart considering the circumstances."

"Where are we going?" I asked as he unlocked the car.

"We need to see Cait."

"She's still in hospital?"

"Yes, and we're going to see her," he replied.

Chapter Twenty Four

God Save The Queen

I didn't feel much like talking as we drove back to Washington. I did consider that it was probably a good thing that I didn't tell anyone where we were going. No one would be happy with me going back to D.C, least of all me. But if Cait had answers then it might be worth it.

Sean left me in the car. I sat in the Grey parking lot of Fairfax Inova Hospital in Virginia thinking of another day I was in the same car park, different circumstances but just as much adrenaline.

I saw him running back to the car. He opened my door.

"Come on," Sean said.

"Clear?"

"Yes."

We walked quickly through the Emergency Department entrance to the elevators. At the seventh floor, we walked down a corridor and through several sets of glass doors.

"Wait here," he said and knocked on a door before opening it. He slipped inside the room, the door closed behind him.

Muffled talking followed.

The door opened. Sean O'Hare held the door. "Come on in."

Cait smiled at me from the hospital bed. I noted the drip next to the bed and tube in her arm. "How are you, Ellie?"

I returned the smile. "Well, thank you. How are you?"

"I'll be all right." Cait studied me for a beat.

Safely behind her closed door, we stood in front of her bed.

"Take a seat," she said waving a hand at two chairs.

I declined.

"We won't take up much of your time," Sean said. "There is a situation. It's getting messier by the minute."

Cait picked up the control for her bed and adjusted her position. "You better tell me what's going on."

"Where do you want to start?" I said.

"That bad?"

"Yes. It is."

"Then sit down and tell me everything."

So I sat and explained the whole messy situation with Owen and everything else that had happened; I even included the hit man at the hotel. And finished with, "Sean tells me the incident at my home was over my surveillance footage from the last few days."

"Are you talking about the surveillance I asked for?"

I nodded. "He also said you want me to hand over the surveillance."

"It seems the best way forward at the moment."

"Do you know who those men are?"

Cait smiled; she looked a little pained. "I think I do. Had a heads up from a friend of ours that something untoward has happened within our border and some cleaners were coming in. Clearly that was before I was admitted here."

"Cleaners." That was not news.

"If my source is correct there should be an Irishman, a Brit, and an American."

"And they are?"

I was interested to see if her names matched what Iain Campbell had told me.

"Seamus Kennedy, ARW. Colin Holmes, SAS. And Timothy Jones, USAF pilot."

"That's what my contact told me, I got the impression Praskovya was his source. So where is he? Because my contact didn't know ..."

Cait smiled. "I heard he was in town."

"Don't suppose you know where the Israeli is?"

She adjusted her position again and looked more uncomfortable than before. "Not here, he's the missing element. This has something to do with him."

"They are here to clean up what?"

"That I don't know. Praskovya wasn't ready to share."

"Awesome. So no one but Praskovya and the three gunmen know."

"Whatever is going on is probably not something we want to be involved in at this point. Who are you at the moment?" A small smile crossed her lips. "I like the new hair color."

"I'm Anna Harley. I will be going back to using Laura Graham. I was snapped at the hotel by a server. She recognized me as Laura Graham, Mike Fisher's fiancée, but thinks I'm undercover, hence the short black wig."

At least Laura can carry a concealed firearm.

"You've had a fun week so far?"

"Yeah, it's been a delight."

"How many identities have you used?"

"More than a person should ever need."

Sean spoke, "The Hoboken connection is disturbing."

"No kidding. I remember every second of the live feed when the three pilots took out the terrorist. How do you think Kennedy and Holmes became involved?"

They weren't pilots.

"I don't know."

"I don't suppose you know who they're working for now?" *Something told me she didn't, but I had to ask.*

"That I don't know ... no one is claiming them. But it's likely they're not working for any particular government. They definitely were a joint government taskforce at one point. But are they now? I do not know."

"And you don't know why they were in Washington, or why two of them were given cover stories by their embassies?"

My guess would be they came in separately and are still individually on government payrolls but this is some kind of private mission, maybe the call went out once they were on the ground.

"No. But I am going to ask you again to give them your surveillance."

"You are absolutely sure that is the only option here?"

Second-guessing my Director wasn't the best career move, but Cait's not Owen, she's intelligent and expects discussion, to a point.

"If they want it, give it to them. I've given this a lot of thought. Haven't had much else to do in here."

"Why give it to them?"

Because I was just told to by my Director – which didn't make sense, or sit well in my gut. That seemed to be the theme of the moment.

"I can see no good coming out of this situation. We don't need the surveillance now that we know who they are. Yes, it's interesting that two of them were provided with cover from their embassy but I don't see this as being a national security issue."

"Yes, ma'am." It seemed the right time to use a more formal reply.

Thoughts spiraled crazily regarding the quasi-UN; sure they might want the surveillance but why do what they did? Why get themselves detained? Unless it was their intention for some reason.

"They wanted to get caught," I said and pushed the chair back with my legs as I stood up. "I need to get back to the hotel."

Cait smiled. "I'll do what I can with regards to Owen and having this ridiculous warrant removed. Can you get me the original photos?"

"Yes ... Sean, can we detour via my bank?"

He nodded.

"Go, Ellie, email me the photographs and a complete

list of everything that was taken from your home."

Cait looked tired.

"Will you be all right?" There might have been a moment of panic edge in as I saw more color drain from Cait's face.

"Yes, I'm scheduled for surgery tomorrow – get me the information so I can act on it before then. Just in case."

Just in case.

Sean spoke, his voice full of reassurance. "She'll be fine, Ellie. It's Cait, nothing gets the better of her."

As we neared the elevator a man emerged from the stairs. Our eyes met. He seemed familiar. Recognition faltered as I looked back at the closed elevator doors. Urgency took over. I pressed the button again. I don't know why, it's not like it helps.

With a flash of clarity I placed the man. One of Owen's henchmen. It was hardly a fair description, but minion sounded too nice. I looked over my shoulder as the man started down the hallway toward Cait O'Hare's room. With a long exhale I focused again on the elevator.

Hospital elevators are so freaking slow.

"All right?" Sean asked.

"One of Owen's men is on the floor, heading for Cait."

The elevator pinged and the doors opened and I was face to face with Owen and another of her men.

She smiled at Sean. "Mr. O'Hare, I was just coming to visit the Director," she said, exiting the elevator. I stepped aside. For two seconds I considered averting my eyes but that would draw attention. Time to brazen it out and keep my mouth shut.

"Keep the visit short. I'm just going for coffee, so will be back up in a few minutes," Sean said. He managed to sound protective, almost threatening, and yet pleasant all at once. Such a talent.

I moved into the elevator. Sean followed me. I pressed the button. Owen turned back to say something else as the doors closed.

"We're sitting ducks, she's going to figure out who I am before we get out of the hospital," I muttered. My heart pounding as adrenaline surged.

"She wants to see Cait. Cait will cover for you, Anna."

A smile bounded across my face. Anna.

I'm wearing different clothes, have much shorter dark hair, the jacket covers my scars. I'm not Ellie. I'm Anna. Be Anna.

Walking out of the elevator and remaining poised when my whole body wanted to bolt for the nearest exit took a terrific act of will power. A man in a suit stood by the elevators. I picked him as one of Owen's. He didn't appear to be looking for anyone.

With huge relief, I slid into the car seat and Sean started the engine. Gallows Road never looked so good. I looked back as two suited men ran from the Emergency Department entrance and stopped.

"Bank?" Sean said with a grin.

"Yes. This needs to end."

Chapter Twenty Five
Right Side Of Wrong

Sean pulled into the parking lot adjacent to the bank and waited a few seconds. Watching traffic was my new occupation. No familiar black SUVs or sedans pulled into the lot behind us. To be honest, it was pretty hard to look for black SUVs and sedans within the beltway, every third vehicle fitted the description. With thirty-two policing agencies and an abundance of black town cars, trying to spot an FBI car wasn't the easiest task in the world. In some situations a little paranoia goes a long way.

Sean was sure we hadn't been followed or picked up a tail on the way. To be safe he was going to switch his rental car for another before we left for West Virginia again.

"Can I use your phone please?" I asked.

He handed it to me and watched me press in a number. As I finished, Dad's name popped up on the screen. Of course it did. Dad was the emergency contact on my security contract. Sean handled security at my home.

Dad answered quickly. "Sean?"

"Nope," I replied. "I need you to bring your safety deposit key and meet me at the bank. Now."

"It'll take me at least twenty-minutes. You'll be all right for that long?"

"I'm with Sean." That was a loud and clear "yes, I'd be fine," before disconnecting.

The waiting began. Somewhere deep in the stillness of my mind a dark cloud gathered sending lightning bolts across my synapses at infrequent intervals.

"You okay?" Sean asked.

"Sure, why?"

"You shudder every now and then."

I had no comment. The waiting continued. Traffic noises outside the car intensified as the afternoon drew on. Watching cars was my new hobby. Eventually I saw one I recognized. Dad. He did a circuit of the parking lot before pulling in beside us. He opened the back door to our car and climbed in.

"Sean, Ellie," Dad said. Our names were enough of a greeting.

"I need to access our safety deposit box," I said twisting in my seat to better see his face. "Which means I need you to access the box with the bank manager ... I can't be seen as me because of Owen and her flying monkeys."

"And you are?"

I wanted to say Laura Graham but I was wearing the Anna wig.

"Anna Harley, your niece."

Dad smiled. "Must be from my late wife's side of the family. Her sister's kid."

"That's me, Uncle Simon."

"Come on then, kiddo, let's go get whatever you need from the bank," Dad said, opening his door.

I paused and considered what was about to happen. "All right?" Sean asked, leaning his head back.

"Of course," I replied and removed the holster from my belt. I handed it to Sean. "I'm not carrying a badge."

"Good call."

I closed the door behind me and hoisted up my shoulder bag. Dad walked with me across the parking lot and into the bank. He chose a young teller and approached her.

"I need to get into my safety deposit box," Dad said. He held the key in his hand, visible on his key ring.

"Yes, sir. I'll get the manager for you." She smiled. "If you could wait by the door over there." She turned away then turned back. "Sir, your name?"

"Simon Conway."

We walked past the tellers to a door at the far end. A woman emerged and held out her hand. "I'm the manager, Estrella Rosenquist. You must be Mr. Conway."

"Correct."

She turned to me. Dad introduced me. "This is my niece, Anna."

"Just through the door behind you, Mr. Conway," Estrella said.

I followed my father and the bank manager through the door and down a short staircase. Behind another set of doors were the rows of safety deposit boxes. The bank manager entered a code into the panel by the door, changing the light above from red to green, and pushed open the door. Lights flickered on as the door closed behind us. Safety deposit boxes lined three walls.

"What number is the box, Mr. Conway?"

"Four-six-four."

Estrella went to my box and inserted her key into the bigger of the two locks and turned it. Dad fitted his key in the other lock. The box unlocked as soon as dad turned his key. He pulled the door open. Estrella removed her key.

"I'll leave you to it. The door will lock automatically when you close it. No need for the keys."

"Thank you," Dad replied. The woman left the room without looking back.

I looked at the gray plastic tray inside the open safety deposit box then slid it out into my hands. An inward breath shuddered through my ribs as I put the tray onto one of the tables in the middle of the room and lifted the lid.

Alternating between nausea and dizziness I stared into the almost empty box.

Chapter Twenty Six
Land Of Confusion

Where the hell were my things? There was an envelope. I looked around the room. No cameras.

"Anna?" Dad was at my side. "What's wrong?"

"Everything is gone," I said. "I didn't put that envelope in the box."

My eyes closed as I tried to picture the outside of the room. Two cameras. One on the door and one on the stairs.

I needed to check the envelope but didn't want to compromise any possible evidence. Why don't I carry a fingerprint kit? Really, situations like this would be a lot simpler if I did. Also, it would be easier if I had my smart phone and a fingerprint app.

Yes, there is an app for that.

"How could anyone get in here without the key?" Dad asked. "They can't," I replied as I scrabbled through the contents of my bag looking for something useful. A pencil, sticky tape, a large makeup brush, and my notebook.

That would do for a start. I searched for something to grind the pencil lead into dust. My hand came out of my bag holding a makeup compact of dark colored eye shadows. Never mind the pencil.

I poked at the eye shadow with the sharp end of the

pencil, turning it into a fine powder. I coated the brush with the deep blue eye color and swirled powder over the tray. Holding my breath as the powder fell delicately onto the hard surfaces and hoping I had enough control to keep it away from the envelope. Blowing away the excess powder, I held my joy in check: visible prints. I carefully covered the prints with sticky tape then lifted the prints with the tape and stuck them into my notebook. I repeated the process on all the prints and on the safety deposit box door.

"That's pretty clever, kid," Dad said watching me work.

I smiled and used one of his favorite phrases. "Up here for thinking." I tapped my head then pointed to my feet. "Down there for dancing."

It was a slow process but I had prints. Lots of prints. I also had no idea if the thief wore gloves. If I intended to steal something from a special agent, I'd wear gloves.

My next problem was the envelope. I couldn't pick it up without contaminating it.

I needed a bag. My mind stormed. Bags were the easiest part of this whole mess. In a cupboard near the door there would be paper bags. People used them to store things in the deposit boxes.

Lifting the envelope with the blunt end of the pencil enabled me to maneuver it into a bag. I sealed the top and shoved it in my bag then put everything away and blew any remaining eye shadow off the table.

Dad and I left the bank, and as I walked across the black top to Sean I thought about how to obtain the bank surveillance footage. Someone else needed to do it.

I couldn't send anyone from Delta and Sean was not an authorized federal agent. I could send Iain but he's CIA, not a law enforcement officer.

Dad gave me a hug and swung the car door open. "Stay strong. You will figure this out."

"I hope so."

How did anyone get into the box without a key? It's not possible. The locks have to be drilled out if the keys are lost.

"Dad, did you misplace your keys at any time over the last week or so?"

He supported himself against the car. A frown gathered, followed moments later by a slight nod. "A day or so ago, I put my keys in my desk drawer at The Foundation, went into Bob's office for a meeting then remembered I needed something out of the car. I went back for my keys and they weren't there."

"You're absolutely certain you put them in your drawer?"

"Yes." A worn smile edged across his face. "I'm old, kid, but I'm not losing my marbles yet."

"The keys turned up, how much later?"

"Not sure. I went back to the meeting, thinking I'd look for them when it was finished."

"And?"

"They were in my drawer when I got back."

"Were they there the whole time?" I had to ask.

"No. They were not." His tone said he was one-hundred per cent sure.

I sighed. "Did Bob authorize the installation of security cameras yet?"

"No."

"Ah, fuck."

"Go, Ellie. You've been here too long. I'll see what I can dig up at The Foundation. Someone might have seen something."

"Okay."

He gave me a big hug; all the times a hug from dad made everything all right came flooding back. I climbed into the car. Dad pressed the door closed, waved at Sean, got into his own car and drove away.

"Get it?" Sean asked.

"No," I replied. "No, someone emptied the box. Left me a letter, which I need your lab people to check for prints, please."

"It's all gone?"

"Yes, all of it."

"Things just got harder," Sean said, firing up the car engine. "Let's go to my lab now."

Chapter Twenty Seven
One Way Or Another

I checked my watch. We were running out of day and I needed to get back to Delta and the impending marriage plans. Also, the invitation would go out first thing in the morning. I needed to be back before the stalker arrived to finish his game.

"You wouldn't have any latex gloves in the car, would you?"

"Try the first aid kit in the glove compartment," Sean replied, negotiating traffic lanes.

I found the first aid kit and some latex gloves.

The process to make fingerprints visible on paper had the annoying side effect of potentially ruining any ink. Seemed smart to read the letter before we got to Sean's building and handed the envelope to the lab techs.

With the gloves on I removed the envelope from the paper bag. I felt it very carefully, it looked flat and weighed what I'd expect a single sheet of paper in an envelope to weigh but that didn't mean there wasn't some sort of explosive device in it. Satisfied there were no lumps or bumps or anything untoward, I opened the flap by slipping a finger into a gap and lifting with care.

I extracted the paper from the envelope. A single piece folded in three. I unfolded it, half expecting white powder to fall into my lap. Anthrax would not surprise me at this point.

Words jumped off the page and assaulted my eyes and brain. Words in what looked like my handwriting. The letter had yesterday's date.

I read it three times.

"Ellie?"

I looked up. We weren't moving.

"Where are we?"

"Under my building. You all right?"

I shook my head. "This is my confession ... the letter is my confession."

Sean's brow crumpled, he read the letter in my hands, aloud, "'I am Gabrielle Rylee Conway. Eddie Connelly has pissed me off for years with his constant harassment and by breathing. After the death of my daughter, his continued comments became unbearable. I chopped off his gross feet and hands with an ax. He was alive when I removed his left hand and right foot. He stayed alive for almost twenty-four hours. Whining constantly. With Eddie gone, it seemed prudent to turn my attention to Beatrice Connelly. I removed her right foot with the same ax I used on her son. More body parts to follow. What's left of Eddie's body is planted in my garden. Beatrice is planted in her garden.'"

Sean blew out air and looked at me. "That even looks like your signature."

"I know. If I didn't know better, I'd say I wrote the letter."

Sean took out his phone and photographed the letter.

"Put it back in the envelope," he said. "Let's get it to my techs."

I felt all kinds of sick. Next thing I knew I was in Sean's office sitting at his desk while he spoke to a tech and handed over the envelope. I heard him say they should examine the document inside the envelope and the envelope checked for fingerprints. The tech mentioned Ninhydrin. They'd paint that chemical onto the envelope. As it developed, fingerprints showed up in a deep blue or purple color. The tech left. Sean turned to me.

"Can I use your computer?" I asked.

"Go ahead," he said.

"Do you use proxy servers?"

He nodded.

I accessed my email account and watched as over a hundred emails downloaded. I scanned through the subject lines looking for one from Oakton high school. I spotted it and opened it and the attachments – the photos I'd asked for.

"Look," I said and beckoned to Sean. "This is the original of one of the photos the killer used. See, it's a microphone in my hand, not part of Eddie."

He grinned. "I knew you didn't do it. Move over."

I gave up the chair, perched on the desk, and watched Sean. He copied the photos to his secure drive, and then sent a copy to his sister with a note saying what I'd found at the bank.

Everything collided in my head and for the first time in a long time I felt hope abandon me. If Owen or Metro got hold of that letter, I was toast. Why would someone leave it in the bank? Why not just send it to Metro?

Had the Unsub expected me to take law enforcement to the bank to prove my innocence and have them find the letter then?

Would I do that or would I send it out?

I'd do both. I'd put the original in the bank and send out copies.

I swallowed hard. "Check to see what Metro are doing, Sean ... they may have that letter. If they have it, then Owen has it and that'll be why she was going to see Cait."

His email program beeped.

"Email from Cait," he said, then read the email to himself. I could tell by his clenched jaw that it wasn't good. "You were right. Owen has a copy. Cait said the photos I sent will help to prove that all the photographs were doctored and are not what they seem."

"But?"

"Until we can prove the letter is a forgery and the photos were forged, the warrant stands. She has no basis to recall it."

"Fuck."

I wanted to crawl into a hole and wait for the inevitable, which given the way things were going, was my arrest and the subsequent death penalty. Death I didn't mind, but I'd prefer it not to be at the hands of the state I love, for a crime I did not commit.

Options I didn't have taunted me.

"This isn't the end, Ellie. We'll fight this. We'll clear

you," his voice filled with determination.

"We need to backtrack and find out who has this much hate for me."

Meanwhile, I have an actor to protect, the quasi-UN to interrogate, and my family is hearing all this shit from the media, the FBI, and Metro without me being able to give my side of the story.

As much as it bothered me that my family was without my side of the story, I knew they wouldn't believe the bullshit. I'm a lot of things but I am not a cold-blooded calculating killer, no matter how hard I'm pushed. I could see a day coming when I might not be able to say those words with any kind of honesty, but they weren't here yet.

"Anything else you want to do while you have my computer at your disposal?" Sean asked, standing up.

I wracked my brain for things I needed to search while I could. "Yeah, there is," I replied and sat back in his chair.

Lee was right about warm chairs. Off-putting in the extreme.

"I'll get us coffee, organize us a clean car and be right back," Sean said. "I'm locking the door behind me."

"Thanks."

Lock me in. Lock me up. Keep me on the run. My freedom is a memory.

I logged into the website Aidan and I use to leave each other messages. He'd left fifteen for me. All saying almost the same thing. You have a warrant for your arrest. They think you killed Eddie. Dad says not to worry because you'll figure it out. Stay safe. Let me know you are okay. A few mentioned Mitch had been looking for me, and was concerned. Aidan told me Mitch missed his running buddy.

I missed him, too.

I replied to Aidan telling him I was okay and that it was all bullshit. I'd be home as soon as we figured out who was behind it and to let Mitch know I'd be in touch as soon as I could.

Dad had faith in me but I couldn't tell Aidan I'd seen him. I logged out.

Then I emailed Sandra from a secret email account. In the subject line I put "bacon." From memory, because I am that freaky, I wrote an email using the bacon cipher. It took me about twenty minutes to write one paragraph, but it would slow down anyone who happened to look over her shoulder as she opened it. I told her what had happened and asked her to dig into my old case files. I figured this had to be someone I'd arrested in the past, someone who was computer literate.

The door unlocked, the handle turned, coffee wafted in ahead of Sean.

"Hey, what was the program the hackers used?"

He smiled. "Something very sophisticated. Ever heard of SkyWiper?"

"No, explain it."

He set a coffee cup in front of me then pulled another chair up to the other side of his desk. "Scuttlebutt has it that the NSA, and the Israeli government, developed SkyWiper."

My blood froze. Israeli. Coincidence that there was an Israeli involved in another situation, a situation that piggybacked on the hacker? I think not.

"And is it a virus?"

"Not technically, no, it's a worm. It's not designed to destroy data, although it can be programed to do so. It's an espionage tool."

"Excuse me." My hand signaled him to stop speaking. "It's a what tool?"

"Espionage," Sean replied, as if it was an everyday thing.

"Its sole purpose it to spy on people?" By people, I meant governments and big business and I trusted that Sean knew that.

"Yes. Can I tell you more about it?"

"Sure."

"It infects machines running Windows 7, Vista and XP. SkyWiper buries itself deep in the Windows operating system. It runs upon computer startup. It also tailors itself to hide from specific brands of anti-virus software."

Sean took a sip of coffee before continuing. "And then it gets clever. SkyWiper turns on the computer's built-in microphone to record audio conversations, logs keyboard typing, changes the Bluetooth configuration to spy upon nearby cellphones, tablets and laptops, takes screenshots, monitors wired and wireless network activity and sends whatever information it's gathered to command-and-control servers. It's essentially an astounding spy tool."

I felt violated in a way I'd never felt before. It is one thing to have some low-life fucktard hide a GPS tracker in my mascara or a voice-activated audio bug in a pen. This was a new level of sinister; knowing a sophisticated piece of software monitored my every movement, keystroke, phone conversation, from every device I owned, scared me to the core.

The amount of work I did from home ... scattered my thoughts to the wind. How many cases could've been compromised by this evil piece of software?

"Can we backtrack, follow it?"

"I tried, believe me, I tried."

"So how did it get into my system and into the local government systems?"

"Most likely way was via a USB flash drive."

"It wasn't an accident? Doesn't it spread like a virus? I didn't click on some sneaky link inside an email?"

"Nope. This is a big program file, it's not something you could download yourself by accident. It also doesn't use the internet to spread like a virus does. This thing prefers to move along internal networks, it hitches rides on flash drives."

I thought about the flash drive I usually wore. I'd taken it off when I assumed Laura's identity. I used that all the time, but never for work, so had it ever been plugged into the FBI system? I scoured my memory to make sure I had never plugged that particular flash drive into any computers at work. The last thing I wanted was to have introduced something horrendous into Sentinel. I guess the downside of becoming totally digital is the vulnerability from attack.

I shuddered. Bad enough someone had access to any off-file work I did at home. Oh crap, it wasn't just work they had access to. It was my life and by default, Rowan's life too. Not to mention how Delta A may have been compromised.

Nausea twirled around my tonsils making me swallow hard and breathe deeply.

"All right?" Sean asked.

"Yeah. No. Had a moment, needed to make sure that SkyWiper had not come anywhere near Sentinel through my actions."

"Has it?"

"Absolutely not. The flash drive has been plugged into my personal computers and Carla's laptop." My stomach sank like a rock. The flash drive hadn't been near the work computers but my SD cards had. "SD cards."

"Breathe, Ellie. It's okay."

I took a breath.

"But the SD cards. I upload to the FBI computers all the time."

"Sentinel runs powerful and constantly updating virus and anti-malware software, even if you had plugged that drive into your computer at work, the system wouldn't have allowed anything like SkyWiper to upload."

I was somewhat reassured that our system was as safe from hackers and evildoers as possible.

My thoughts turned back to SkyWiper and how it got onto my computer.

"It had to be installed, that's what you're saying?"

"Yes," Sean said.

"Does it uninstall itself after a determined amount of time?"

"No. However, it does allow for a suicide module. It's possible that when the controllers have enough information, they can remotely activate a suicide command that deletes all of SkyWiper from the system."

"How do you know it is SkyWiper that was used?"

"Because nothing else fitted."

"Can we detect it and remove it?"

"Yes, usually. Most of the major anti-virus software vendors have upgraded their malware definitions to protect against SkyWiper."

"And yet it was still installed on my system ..."

"I think the version installed on your system and on the local government and Butterfly Foundation sites was modified to account for the updated malware protection."

"What if we get a copy of the program?"

"Then I'd know for sure if it was modified and maybe we could tell by the modification whose handiwork it is."

"There is a good chance it's on the yellow flash band I usually wear ... it hasn't been in another machine apart from my laptop so the program might still be there."

"And that is?"

"In the hotel."

"I think we should go back to West Virginia and see

what we can find on that flash drive. It'll take a while for the techs to pull prints. They'll send me the results."

"To be honest, the sooner we leave Washington the better." I had to say something about my home computers and the possibilities. "Do you have any idea how long that thing was in my machines?"

"No. Maybe a week, maybe two."

Chapter Twenty Eight
The Fighter

"Houston we have a problem."

"Spill it."

"Rowan's security has been compromised."

"Thought you broke up months ago ..."

"We did but ... it's complicated."

"And the truth is?"

I blew out air through my mouth and inhaled deeply though my nose. The nausea was not leaving in a hurry.

"We got married a few weeks after Carla ..." I took a breath. "A few weeks after Carla died. And then had the marriage annulled two weeks later."

When I sobered up.

"Whoa, hold up. You what?"

"Got married and then unmarried."

Mistakes happen. I'm sure we've all been known to have our judgment clouded by tequila, especially while in Las Vegas. Although that weekend, a combination of grief and tequila did the damage.

"Who knows about this?"

"No one."

Sean shook his head. A stunned silence fell over his office. I chewed my lip and waited. The pressure built.

He lowered himself into a chair and leaned forward on his elbows.

"Okay. What was on your computer that compromises Rowan?"

"Conversations. We Skyped a lot."

Once upon a time. Before it all turned to crap. He's too Rowan with all his "look at me, I'm a rock star" and I'm too Ellie with my "get out of my face with that freaking camera."

"Did you have copies of the marriage certificate and annulment, anything legal?"

"Yeah, there were. I copied them to flash drives and stored them in the bank."

Copied. That meant they still existed on the damn laptop. Why didn't I move them like I did with everything else that I deemed sensitive or important? I wanted to smack my head into the desk. Visions of smacking my head into a window popped up. I hadn't told anyone about what I found on Carla's flash drive. Time I did. Just had to figure out how.

"Photos?"

Of our insane tequila-powered Elvis wedding. They were real keepers.

"Again copies in the bank, but I left the original files on my laptop."

Lot of good it did putting anything in the bank. I considered how paranoid I'd become over the years, but it's not paranoia when they really are out to get me.

"I have Rowan's number," he said picking up the phone off the desk and scrolling through the menu. Moments later, he pressed two buttons and waited

"Rowan, it is Sean O'Hare. Can I have a word?"

I switched off. Listening to half a conversation was unappealing and I knew it would mostly involve Sean calming Rowan down before he asked to speak to Jed, who headed Rowan's security team.

Switching off.

Wouldn't it be great if we really could just turn off our brains for a set period? And there I was remembering the day that happened and I couldn't get parts of my brain back online. That was the beginning of the end for Rowan and I. As much as I had loved him at that time, I couldn't remember life with him at all for a few days. I forgot Rowan and I forgot Carla. Some days I'd give anything to go back to that moment and to feel no pain.

I re-engaged with the present when I realized Sean had finished speaking. He was packing up equipment and paperwork.

It was now or never. Elvis gyrated across my internal screen in his sparkly white jumpsuited tracks. It's been done. Get new material or leave and never come back. The door closed. Elvis had left my mind. There wasn't anything else for me to do but blurt it out and hope he had something insightful to say.

"Sean ..."

I had his full attention.

"Yes."

My hand delved into my bag and came out with the little pink pig. I held it out to him. "It contains the contents of Carla's laptop."

"The stolen laptop?"

"Yes."

He took it from my hand. "And?"

With care, I summoned the words that made me feel ill. "I found a file, Torrents, containing conversations on Skype between Carla and an unknown subject calling himself Mr. RightGuy. The unknown subject was grooming her."

Sean didn't say anything at that point. He pulled the head off the pig and stuck the USB connector into his laptop. Fifteen minutes of silence followed as Sean read every file in the folder. As he read he made notes in a notebook. When he finished he logged into Skype, I heard the noises of the program as it opened.

"Did you read them all?" he asked.

"No. Most, but not all."

"I think I found his account," Sean said. "Come sit over here." He indicated the couch where sat. "Easier if you can see, too."

I joined him and looked at the screen: Mr. RightGuy's profile. I read the name at the top of the screen. Eddie Connelly. The Skype name was still Mr. RightGuy.

"You've got to be kidding me."

"That's the name I found within the files in that folder. Carla had grabbed a few screen shots that contained conversations where the Unsub told her his name was Eddie Connelly and after that he appeared as Eddie Connelly in the conversations."

"Do you think it was Eddie?"

He shrugged. "Maybe, but why would someone want to steal evidence of Eddie being a pervert kiddie-fiddler now that he's dead?"

"If it was him then whoever killed him could use the evidence as justification for the death," I offered. "Eddie's death was a public service?" I actually believed his death was a public service but I didn't want to be railroaded on a service I didn't perform.

"Okay, that's a possibility," Sean agreed.

"It is, but that's not what's happening here. I think whoever the Unsub is, it's not Eddie, but someone who is already under investigation for something, maybe even to do with the corruption of minors and they want to stop this being used as evidence."

Sean typed fast, altering a profile on one of his many anonymous accounts to sound like a fourteen-year-old girl, then sent a request to add Mr. RightGuy to his contact list. "I hope this moron takes the bait." He closed the Skype program muttering about watched pots never boiling.

Sean stretched, being careful not to knock the laptop from his lap. "The stealing of Carla's laptop poses the question, how would anyone know a fifteen-year-old kid would keep conversations like this?"

"I don't know ..." I sat back on the couch. She was my kid. Did whoever it was target her accordingly?

Please don't make this about my job.

"Open the Word document," I suggested. "What did she say about the kid who introduced them to the

300

Unsub?"

We both read the document. Carla had named the kid and given a detailed account of what was said to her and to Joey. I didn't much care for what I was reading. What possessed them to do this alone?

The kid's name was Charlotte Campbell.

I reached for the laptop then changed my mind. I couldn't log into Sentinel, meaning I couldn't check if I'd ever come across Charlotte Campbell before.

"Do you know her?" Sean asked.

"No. I was going to check my old case files just in case."

"You can't, not yet anyway." Sean closed the files.

"I know." Signing into the FBI system would mark my location like big ol' flashing target. "We need to find Charlotte Campbell," I said, leaning forward and resting my elbows on my knees. "She's in some serious trouble."

"I don't think it'll be that easy," Sean said.

"Me neither. Can you check the National Center for Missing and Exploited Children? See if there is an Amber alert out for her."

"Logging into NCMEC now."

Up popped a parent's worst nightmare. An Amber alert issued a week after Carla's death for Charlotte Campbell.

"How did I not hear about it?" I muttered. "They went to the same school."

"You were locked in your house with a bottle of tequila."

That'll be why.

"That kid's gone. It's been months. She's probably dead."

"We'll get to the bottom of this." He logged off the laptop and set it back on his desk. Sean gave me back the pig's head. I stuck it back to its body and dropped it into my bag. We weren't much closer to finding out what was really going on but at least we had a starting point for the investigation. Carla was that point.

An uneasy mix of memories flew through the air and landed in a messy pile. At the bottom of the pile, I saw the dead body of Viktor Abbasi. Maybe Rowan was right about this being something to do with Hawk. Maybe Hawk was reaching out from the grave. Now there's a talent only a few possess.

From a cupboard, Sean took another laptop and carefully strapped it into a metal attaché case.

"We'll take this one with us, so I can isolate the malware if it's still on your flash band."

"Laptop? Won't the program find the suicide command if it gets onto a laptop?" I knew I meant it could connect to the internet. Luckily, so did Sean.

"Not with this laptop. It's a special one I use for isolating worms and viruses. It is not internet capable."

"Okay. Good to know."

Ten minutes after he started packing we lugged two heavy bags down to the parking garage. Sean opened the rental car and removed everything that showed we'd been in it.

Foot falls echoed across the garage as a man approached, intensifying my adrenaline cascade.

Level with the car he said, "Your new car is the fourth on the right, keys are in the ignition. I'll take this." He put a leather-gloved hand out for the keys. Sean dropped them into his palm.

"Thanks. I'll be in touch."

We carted our stuff to the new car. It was new. Brand new.

"Who is the registered owner?" I asked, making myself comfortable in the passenger seat and willing my hands to stop shaking. Easier said than done.

"My company. It's one of our new fleet cars."

A thought smashed into my consciousness. Nausea rose so fast I almost didn't get the door open. Vomit, mostly coffee, sprayed all over the ground.

"Ellie?" Sean handed me a tissue.

I wiped my mouth and closed the door. "Sorry."

"No problem. Are you ill?"

"No. The yellow flash band – I plugged it into my laptop at the hotel in Fairfax. I was looking for some emails." I swallowed hard to keep down the bile. "I talked to Lee about how I'd moved everything important to a bank deposit box."

"That's how someone knew about the bank."

"I don't think I mentioned which bank."

"You wouldn't have to. They could search the computer or even your phone for banking records."

What else did they know about me? What other

information was on my laptop or phone?

Chapter Twenty Nine
Under Pressure

It was dark when Sean drove out of the parking facility. I found it hard to relax in the car, even though I knew the likelihood of anyone spotting us was slim. Too many thoughts crowded my brain and none had satisfactory potential answers or conclusions. And the answers that I could attribute to the worm made me feel even more sick.

Every police car that went by sent chills up my spine.

I don't think I started to feel comfortable until we passed into West Virginia. It was crazy how pleased I was to see the hotel. Almost as crazy as the realization that David Bowie had been my constant companion since leaving Washington. I hadn't even noticed the music in my head until I walked up the hallway to my room. Bowie was right; I was under pressure and I wished I didn't know what the world was about. David Bowie was a smart man.

As the song ended, I wondered if this would be my last dance. When I opened the door to my room, I saw that Mike had the adjoining door open.

He called out, "That you, darling?"

At least I didn't have to worry about him getting names wrong. The actor was acting. He seemed comfortable with whatever was thrown at him. With all that was going on, his ability to improvise was a godsend.

"Yes, it's me," I replied. Sean waited at the door. I found the flash drive and gave it to him. "What about the SD cards?"

"Hang on to them for now. Let me get the flash drive situation clear first."

"Okay."

"I'll be in my room if you need me," he said.

The door closed and I was alone with Mike. He leaned on the wall by the door to his room regarding me with interest.

"The hotel manager was looking for you," he said. "Wedding plans, I think."

"Good to know." In truth, I'd almost forgotten about the wedding. "I'll be right back." I could still taste vomit so I hurried to the bathroom and brushed my teeth. Anna's dark hair had to go. Laura's red curls and green eyes from here on in. I took off the wig and ran my fingers through my hair. I could be me for a while.

Back in the bedroom, I flopped onto the bed. I really didn't want to get into wedding planning. A yawn escaped and made my jaw click.

"Tired?" he asked, hiding his yawn behind his hand.

"A little. Everything been okay here?"

"Yeah. Nothing much has been happening. I sent the invitation."

"Great. He replied yet?"

"Not yet."

I pushed myself about a foot across the bed to the edge, still lying on my back, and let my head tip back over the edge. Now I could see him better, except upside down. It probably would've been easier to sit up.

"You okay with this?"

"Sure, I'm okay with the wedding death thing." He smiled. Even upside down, it was a nice smile. My stomach rumbled.

"You hungry?"

"Apparently." That'll be because everything I ate was on the ground under Sean's building.

He was upside down but closer. I waved a hand to get him to move sideways and rolled backwards off the bed landing on my feet.

"Let's go eat," he said.

"Just us?"

"Why not?"

I supposed we should be seen together and without an entourage at some point.

"No reason at all, let me freshen up a bit," I said, looking at my disheveled shirt that bore traces of eye shadow.

"I'll be right here." A grin spread across his face. "Unless you need help ..."

"I got this," I replied, taking a clean shirt from my bag and hurrying into the bathroom before I changed my mind. I would have to be careful.

The crevices of my mind filled with 'Modern Love.' Bowie again. And again he had a point; I was looking at the power of charm, not a sign of life. The shower beckoned to me, tempting me with soothing hot water.

I stood under the streaming hot water and washed away the smells and feelings associated with being in Washington and Northern Virginia. Had to scrub extra hard to remove the horror of the letter in my bank deposit box and the missing memories I'd stored there.

Ten minutes later I was clean, dressed, with a fresh dusting of mineral powder on my face and black mascara on my lashes. The song had gone and I'd adopted Laura as my persona, complete with auburn curls. I fastened the buttons on the cuffs of my sleeves, the only long-sleeved shirt I had with me.

It's not easy being someone else all the time and a little bit of rebellion had crept in. A little bit of "why should I?" edged closer to the surface. Running because I was innocent went against everything I believed in: I was a stander and a fighter.

A knock on the bathroom door sent my crazy thoughts packing. I checked the mirror.

"Mirror mirror on the wall. Who is the most insane of them all?" A smile lit my eyes.

Yep, that was me.

My eyes. Blue. They needed to be green. With a sigh, I put the green contact lenses back in. Pleased that this time they didn't irritate as much.

The knock sounded again. I opened the door. Mike chewed his top lip, then smiled. "Dinner?" he asked, taking my hand. "You look great by the way." The power to charm.

"Thanks," I replied.

"Let's eat and be seen as a loving about-to-be-newlywed couple," he said as he closed the door.

A sense of nakedness swept over me at leaving my gun inside the room.

Dinner, not imminent death.

Mike enchanted the manager and delighted the servers. I looked on, amused and entertained. Clearly, he was very good at being him. Made me wish I was better at being me.

Made me wish I knew who I really was. Imagining Kurt hearing me say that sent a ripple of amusement through the pond that is my mind. The ripple became the Goo Goo Dolls singing 'Iris.' Without warning, the pond fell away. A waterfall cascaded taking me with it.

"I want you to know who I am."

Mike reached out and covered my hand with his. I felt the warmth of his skin, not cold water.

"I think I know who you are," he replied. "What's happening?"

I'd spoken aloud; so much for using my inner dialogue for crazy things.

My eyes flicked around the room. We were alone in a corner, about as secluded as it could get in the large open restaurant.

No waterfalls. No obvious running water.

"Nothing at all," I said with what I hoped was a happy smile on my lips.

"You said ..."

"I thought that was in my head." Dismissive, but with

an undercurrent of sweet. I didn't want to see the look I see on everyone else's faces when my thoughts go public. That special mix of concern and horror really wasn't cool.

"And everything's okay?"

"Of course," I said.

A trickle of water ran down the wall on my right. Another joined in. Then another. Before long, the trickles joined and became a torrent.

Water splashed onto the floor and lapped at the table legs, yet my feet stayed dry. The torrent of water coursed through the restaurant, upending tables, dislodging chairs, sweeping away patrons.

Mike slid his arms further onto the table. His hand tightened over mine. "What can you see?"

The more important question seemed to be, why couldn't he see it?

A torrent. What was I supposed to get from this? Bit torrent. Someone downloading information? Considering recent events, it was a reasonable conclusion. Someone had been downloading information, my information. My laptop had turned into an information superhighway for whoever installed that piece of malware, as did my phone, tablet, and desktop PC. But that wasn't it.

I held up my left index finger a few inches to signal Mike to wait.

He nodded.

Flowing, my thoughts centered on the word torrent. The very word I'd so recently seen as a file label among Carla's files. Interesting that it should pop up again. This time the context was different. It wasn't about grooming a child. Same word though and that fascinated me.

I gathered everything I knew about torrents and sifted through it. There was an answer somewhere. A torrent is data about a target file. It contains no information about the content of the file. The data that the torrent holds is information about the location of different pieces of the target file.

It's a location.

The waterfall poured down the wall. A torrent fell.

Torrent Falls.

"Does Torrent Falls mean anything to you?" My left hand flattened on the table.

"Torrent Falls, Kentucky. I've been there," Mike said. "What's going on?"

There was no way to explain what I saw and how it came to be. Well, not without eliciting an alarmed look; always a possibility when I opened my mouth and spouted my truths.

I stepped over the gushing water and found firm footing.

"Who were you with?"

"A group of friends." His eyes found mine and I knew he knew where I was going with my questions. "Joaunes was one of them."

"You wanna fill me in on that trip?"

He nodded. Our server approached carrying two plates.

Guess I missed the part where Mike ordered our

dinner. A plate slid into place in front of me.

"Steak, rare, ma'am."

"Looks delicious," I said with a smile.

The server turned her attention to Mike. We had the same meal. Clever man. Steak, rare, would've been my choice, too.

The young woman left saying she'd be back with the wine.

"Lee said you liked an Australian red wine. Brown Brothers Dolcetto and Syrah. They have it here."

Okay, he was good at this ordering dinner thing.

"Great. Now, start telling me about the trip to Torrent Falls."

"How did you even know?"

I can't explain it.

"The water told me, now talk."

He frowned and forked a piece of steak into his mouth. I watched him chew and think at the same time. Impressive multi-tasking for a man.

"A bunch of us from my home town ... I was the only one who climbed regularly ... someone said Torrent Falls had this climbing system that was good for newbies."

He put another chunk of steak in his mouth. The wine arrived. I took a sip of wine and chewed my mouthful of steak while I waited for the rest of the story.

"We had fun. We climbed. We ate. We drank."

"That's it?"

"What else could there be?"

"A reason for Joaunes to hate you like he does?"

"I don't think there is one."

"*Ding*. Wrong answer."

He ate more steak. I drank more wine; sweet with a hint of cherry and so good. Delicious. The meal continued with light banter and some good-natured ribbing. He was fun.

I waited to hear Mac's voice but it didn't come. The emptiness echoed my own, maybe.

"You been married before?" I asked, after checking we were completely alone in our little corner of the restaurant.

"Once," he replied.

"What happened?"

He shrugged. "Didn't get it right. I missed."

Obviously.

"Married for long?"

"A year, so not long."

"Kids?"

"No," he smiled. "Don't see kids in my future."

"But marriage is?"

"Yes, definitely," Mike replied. He winked. "The day after tomorrow I believe."

The day after the world began.

"How do you do that thing you did at the museum?"

"Thing?"

"Something with your eyes, I couldn't look away and no one else mattered. How'd you do it?"

Mike laughed. "That ... I learned it. That's an actor thing."

"It's intense."

"Yeah."

"And you gave me shit about being intense."

"It was expected. We were playing roles."

Fair enough.

"Let's go for a walk," I suggested. "I could do with some fresh air."

We left the restaurant through the side door and walked down the patio steps toward the gardens. Moonlight tumbled through the treetops making crazy patterns on the grass.

I linked my arm through Mike's as we walked across the expanse of dark lawn toward the gazebo and the rose gardens beyond. Garden lights glowed, marking the edges of various flowerbeds and the outline of the gazebo.

"Torrent Falls, Mike. Something happened there even if you aren't consciously aware of it. Something happened to Joaunes. It started the ball rolling."

"But if I can't remember?"

"You will. Trust me." I led him into the gazebo and pressed him to sit on a bench seat by the back wall. "Close your eyes."

There wasn't a better setting in all the world for a light interrogation. Moonlight spilled through the trellis above the walls. Checked patterns swam across the floor interrupted by the occasional cloud.

"You're in Torrent Falls with your friends. It's your first night. Where did you stay?"

"A nice hotel."

"Did you eat?"

"Yes, in the restaurant. We were noisy and probably disturbed the other patrons. Staff didn't mind."

"After the meal?"

"We went to a bar. Four of us. Played pool, drank beer." He frowned. "Two women joined us."

"Were they nice?"

"Fine, a little too eager, maybe. Not my type. Gerry and Joaunes were interested. I just wanted to play pool. We were climbing the next day so I didn't want a late night."

"And?"

"I ended up going back to the hotel with our other friend, John. He and I had a whisky in the hotel bar and went to our rooms."

"The other two?"

"I don't know when they got back."

"Next morning."

"Rock climbing. Joaunes struggled a bit. Some guys just aren't cut out for climbing. He was never sports oriented at school."

"You were?"

"Played a bit of football. I like to be outdoors."

"And you climb mountains?" I remembered Lee saying something about Mike climbing a mountain; until Mike mentioned climbing, I thought it was a euphemism. Turned out he actually climbed mountains.

"Yeah."

"Joaunes struggled. Wasn't having as much fun as the rest of you?"

"He didn't really like it."

"What happened to the women?"

"They were climbing too. One was with me, the other not far behind, all day." He opened his eyes. In the moonlight, they seemed silvery blue.

"Joaunes struggled with the climbing and was interested in the women, you didn't struggle and weren't interested ... did they know who you were?"

"Probably."

"What did the guys call you? Michael or Mike?"

"They didn't. They used my nickname."

"Sleepy?"

So it wasn't just a brother thing. It was more ingrained than that. So that meant Joaunes would've known that already without hearing the conversation.

He nodded.

"You never introduced yourself?"

He shook his head. "It was a guy weekend and I wasn't interested."

"How pissed was Joaunes about the women following you?"

"I didn't think he was. I was the better climber, he was still learning."

"What about ... John and Gerry was it?"

He nodded. "They were having fun."

"Everyone's having fun except Joaunes, would that be a fair assessment?"

"Probably."

"After the climbing ..."

"We went to the hotel bar, the women were there, too, and some other people joined us."

"People?"

"Women," he said. "Mostly women."

"And?"

"The guys and I chatted to everyone, had a few drinks, messed around. You know, fun."

Yeah, I remember fun.

"Where's Joaunes?"

"At the end of the bar," he replied.

"Who is he with?"

"He's close to us ..." Mike stopped and looked at me. His pale blue eyes reflected mine back at me. "He'd been hitting on the women and they thought he was kidding around. He started drinking pretty heavily and was heading to a dark place."

"Meanwhile?"

"Meanwhile, I was fending off advances."

I grinned. "You're very like your brother at times. You know that?"

"It's a good thing?"

"Yes, it is."

"So, are we any closer to finding his motive?"

"Oh, yeah. You out-sported him in front of women he was trying to impress. You were fending off advances from the women who'd laughed at him."

"I didn't do it on purpose."

"I know. He'd know that too, if he hadn't convinced himself that you were to blame for the mess his life had become."

"But we were still friends after that weekend ..."

"You were still his friend, Mike. He was festering hatred and every time anything good happened to you, his negativity came home to roost and bad things seemed to happen to him."

"How do you fight that?"

"You can't. People will do what they do regardless. You can't make someone see the truth if they don't want to see it. You can't make someone accept responsibility. All you can do is hope that they wake up one day and realize what they've done to themselves."

Whoa, intense. I was beginning to see Mike's point about the intensity levels I cultivated.

"So we know why. Now what?"

"Now we hope he takes the bait and shows up at the wedding."

My second wedding of the year and again it wouldn't last.

Mike stood in front of me. His hands held mine. "I need to find someone like you," he whispered and kissed my cheek.

"Someone like me would drive you insane."

"I doubt it," he replied.

Famous last words.

"You need to find someone who climbs mountains, loves life, and doesn't mind the attention," I said. "Someone like me is apt to shoot paparazzi, is way too intense, and has no time to climb mountains."

Mike dropped to one knee with a cheeky grin on his face he asked, "Marry me?"

"Sure, why not?"

He rose to his feet still holding my hands. "Spend the night with me ..."

My head shook just enough. "If I thought you were serious, I'd answer you," I said with a smile.

His eyes smoldered. "I am." He dipped his head to kiss me.

I ducked sideways. "Not happening."

"You're sure?"

"Very."

Chapter Thirty

Around And Around

Morning arrived with more clarity than I expected. I showered quickly and called Iain.

"I'll be over soon. You ready?"

"Yes. Everyone is having breakfast. Our guests seem in good spirits."

"See you soon." I hung up as I answered the knock on the connecting door.

"Morning," Mike said with a mischievous smile. "Sleep well?"

"Not really, you?"

He shook his head. "Not great. Bit wound up."

I laughed. "And I suppose that's my fault?"

"Yeah, it is. Nervous?"

"Nervous?"

"Day before the big event. Aren't brides supposed to be nervous?"

"Good point. Yes, I should probably be a little nervous." I added that to the list of things I should be.

"What's the plan?"

"We're going over to the other hotel. Some people there need to speak with me." They just don't know it yet.

"We?" he asked.

"Yes. I'm not leaving you here alone."

"Wedding is not until tomorrow. I'll be fine."

"Not a risk I'm willing to take. You are coming." I adopted a firm no-nonsense tone. "Think of it as research, who knows, one day you might need to draw on this for a role."

Time to cowboy up and get this done.

We arrived at Iain's hotel after breakfast. Kurt offered to keep Mike company and out of the way. After a quick word with Iain, I began my interviews.

I knocked once then walked into the first of the hotel rooms. A man sitting at a small table looked up. Lee stood beside him.

"I'm SSA Conway," I said, sliding into the chair across from the man at the table. "Who are you?"

"No one," he replied.

I had zero time for games and less patience. "Seamus Kennedy," I said. "You've got some explaining to do ... that was my house you lit up."

"I know that and I'm truly sorry."

"Great, that'll fix my shattered nerves and please my insurance company." I surveyed the man in front of me. "How many times did you shoot at me?"

"If I'd shot *at* you, Conway, we would not be having this conversation."

"So what the hell were you doing?"

"Playing ... with our toys ..."

"Let me help you out. You want my surveillance photos. Why?"

"It's best if no one knows we're here."

"Bit late for that. You saw the ruckus you caused. About fifteen agents plus SWAT and God knows how many police saw your arrest."

Let's not even mention the journalists and television crews. I can almost guarantee something was said over the scanners that some horrid journalist picked up on, and no matter what, I'd always be linked to Rowan and therefore newsworthy. It occurred to me that I may have to move again but then if I couldn't clear my name I wouldn't be going home, so moving was moot.

"No one saw our faces," he replied. "Not until we were in your building."

"You couldn't have known it would go down that way." My eyes narrowed. "Or could you?"

They were well informed. Misha Praskovya could have told them we wouldn't unmask anyone in public – my aversion to giving journalists anything usable. Let's say they've overstepped the line too many times for me to hand the vultures anything before I was good and ready.

Seamus's eyes lit with a suppressed smile. "Feck. We're not eejits."

Until then, he'd hardly seemed Irish at all. With difficulty, I kept my mind on the task at hand and resisted the temptation to ask him to say third.

"You didn't think new faces coming out of the embassies would go unnoticed? Really?"

"We had cover."

"Yes, you did. But it was my job to break the cover and find out why you're really here."

My job. Something darted across my consciousness, a fleeting thought combining my job and my home but it wouldn't cement.

"I need those photographs and any audio you might have."

"How about you get your embassy to put in a formal request to my Director—"

"I need your surveillance."

"And I need to know why you are here. I'm not buying the attaché status."

"An impasse ..."

"Not for me." I stood. "You are under arrest for the attempted murder of a federal agent. You will be detained until your arraignment."

"And so begins one hell of an international incident."

"I doubt it. You had your chance to call for help and none of you did. I'd say you were working under the radar." I shrugged. "Even if it does become an international incident it won't be my problem. You destroyed my home and tried to kill me. My government frowns upon such things, especially from outsiders."

"And again, Conway, if I'd tried to fecking kill you, we'd not be having this conversation."

He could take his sexy Irish accent and stick it where the sun don't shine.

The earlier thought that mixed home with hell surfaced.

"Have you ever heard the name Charlotte Campbell?"

To his credit, he looked like he was thinking about it.

"No."

"Mr. RightGuy?"

I saw it. He knew something.

"What did you say?"

"Mr. RightGuy."

"Where did you hear that name?"

"I saw it on a Skype conversation."

"He's not someone you should be having a conversation with."

"You know of him? What's his real name?"

Seamus shook his head. "We haven't got that far. He uses different aliases depending on the child he's targeting. Usually someone known to them, or a family member."

"Tell me more."

"From what we understand, he does his homework … if the kid starts to pull away or show signs of wanting out of the relationship he confesses he's Uncle Jimmy or lovely Mr. Brown from down the road to try to get them back."

"I need everything you have on this asshole."

"I'll make sure you get it."

I walked out the door, followed by Lee. We ducked into the corridor, where we could talk in private.

"I saw O'Hare and she suggested I give him our surveillance."

"Suggested?"

"Told me."

"Wow."

"I know. I want to know what's going on." I winked at Lee. "Next candidate, please. Where's the American?"

"In room seventeen."

I walked down the hallway and knocked on the door. Sam opened the door.

"Good to see you," I said.

"You too, SSA," Sam replied.

I smiled sweetly at the man sitting at the table.

"Talk to me, and make it fast," I said resting on the edge of the table by him.

"Nice weather, do you think it will rain tomorrow?"

"Good, a wise ass," I said sliding into the seat across from Timothy Jones. "Where's Praskovya?"

He dragged his eyes up from the table top. "I don't know anyone by that name."

"He flew with you during Operation Hoboken."

I watched the ignition in his eyes.

"I don't know anyone by that name. I do not know what Operation Hoboken is."

Man, that was feeble.

"Really? Stall tactics? What's the point?"

He didn't answer.

"Here's the thing, Tim. I know you know Misha Praskovya. He is a friend of mine. Hoboken was not just about two terrorists. It was about my husband." Still nothing. "The thing is ... I'm about a dozen sentences away from calling your commanding officer and calling you a terrorist."

He held my gaze. "I'm not a terrorist."

"You destroyed my home. That act caused terror, hence you are a terrorist – and that was two sentences, ten left."

"I don't know where Praskovya is."

"Where's Libowitz?"

Tim Jones's expression never changed. He stared straight ahead avoiding all eye contact. I walked around the table and sat opposite him. He adjusted his line of sight to avoid my eyes.

"Libowitz, where is he?" I said.

Jones's eyes flicked to mine. "I don't know any Libowitz."

"Yeah, you do, Tim. Yeah, you do." I paused. "Not to worry, if he's here we'll find him. Meanwhile, the display at my home, bit OTT wouldn't you say? You could've just asked for the photos."

"You'd give them up?"

"No, but you could've asked."

A smile raced across his lips and disappeared. "You don't want to be involved in this, Conway."

"Then you should've kept me out of it. Right now we have news crews crawling all over another of my destroyed homes, speculating wildly and loudly on all channels. I am involved. I am involved because one of you or all three of you wanted me involved and couldn't guarantee that without drastic means." The fleeting thought from earlier touched down. I didn't react fast enough to the surveillance footage, that's why the firestorm at my home; to get my attention, to make sure I couldn't sidestep it. I leaned forward and placed my hands on the table. "Am I close?"

"Close," he whispered. "Now what?"

"You need to talk to me. If there is something you need help with then you need to talk to me. There is no way this is about a few surveillance photos."

"I can't talk without the others."

"You ever heard the name Charlotte Campbell before?"

"No."

It was worth a shot. "Mr. RightGuy?"

He paled. "Where did you hear that name?"

Get a new line. I've already heard that one. "I was just talking to Seamus about him."

"Seems we have something in common, Agent Conway. The desire to find Mr. RightGuy."

"I'll be back." I didn't intend to give such an accurate impersonation of the terminator.

Tim Jones resumed sitting, motionless and expressionless, and I left the room.

Lee and Mike were outside the room. Mike held his iPhone in his hand. I glanced at the screen. He was watching the wireless feed from the interview camera in the hotel room I'd just left.

"Sound?" I asked him.

"No, just images."

Good.

"What's going on, Chicky?" Lee asked.

"I don't know exactly but it isn't good."

"And you said this wasn't television," Mike commented

with a wry grin. "It's riveting and entertaining, and I can't even hear what's being said, so I'm going solely on body language."

"And lethal, Mike. Don't forget lethal. These guys are here for something."

"Any ideas?" Lee asked.

"No, not yet." And I shouldn't be trying to figure it out, not after O'Hare told me to hand over the surveillance. Damn my curiosity. "Right now I need to talk to the last gunman and find our favorite FSB officer, Misha Praskovya."

"Misha is here?" Lee muttered. "Why doesn't that surprise me?"

"I'll be back," I said, leaving them and hurrying to the next hotel room and interview.

Chapter Thirty One
Sittin' On A Fence

Iain opened the hotel room door for me. I walked in and didn't bother introducing myself.

"Mr. Colin Holmes, what are you doing in D.C?"

"Visiting friends."

"Friends? Sounds nice. And you thought you'd shoot the shit out of my house for fun?"

"A misjudgment."

"That's what you call it? I have another word for it, one that begins with 'T' and ends in 'Guantanamo Bay.'"

Colin's mouth formed a thin straight line across his face.

"Where's Libowitz?"

"I don't know any Libowitz," Colin said.

"Where's Praskovya?" I asked.

"Who?"

I took a deep breath and stabbed into the dark. "Ever heard the name Charlotte Campbell?"

"No."

"How about Mr. RightGuy, know him?"

The thin line formed by his mouth, twisted into a sneer. "You don't want to be involved in that."

"But I am involved. Do you know who he really is?"

"No. Leave it, Agent Conway." Sounded almost like a warning.

"What are you doing in D.C?"

"Visiting friends."

"Names, addresses ..." I stood up. "Never mind I've reached my limit. We're done here."

Iain was outside the room waiting for me.

"Having fun?" he asked.

"Yes, I am."

Truly. I knew I'd be handing over the surveillance but no one said I couldn't enjoy myself first. And now I knew something about Mr. RightGuy. I knew they wanted him, too. It would be easier to let them find him and take him out. Just walk away and pretend I knew nothing about it. But I needed to know who he really was. I looked down the hall and beckoned to Sam, Lee, Kurt and Mike.

"Now what?" Iain asked.

"Get them all together in one room. I'll talk to them as a unit. Who do you think is in charge?"

"The Irishman," Sam replied. "Seamus Kennedy."

"Yeah, I don't. I think Libowitz is in charge."

"Libowitz?"

"They were all part of Operation Hoboken including Libowitz. He is not here and he is in charge or this is about him in some way," I said, leaning on the wall. "We'll use the first room to talk to everyone together."

Sam turned to walk away and gather his charge. I touched his arm and stopped him.

"Wait a minute, let's see if I can persuade Misha to join us."

I put my hand out to Iain and indicated I wanted his

330

phone. Misha's cell phone number was one of the few I'd committed to memory. I half-expected to hear it ringing from down the hall but I didn't. He answered after several rings.

"Hello?"

I slipped easily into Russian. "*Gde ty?*" Where are you?

"*Moĭ prekrasnyĭ drug. YA v Vashingtone, eto vse khorosho?*" My beautiful friend. I am in Washington. Is everything all right?

I changed my mind. I wasn't playing his "I only speak Russian" game today.

"Speak English," I said then carried on. "No, everything is not all right. I would like you to join me at a hotel for dinner."

"*Nyet, ya zanimayas' biznesom.*" No, I am attending to business.

"English! I have three friends of yours with me."

"*Daĭte im to, chto im nuzhno, i uĭti, Elli.*" Give them what they need and walk away, Ellie.

"*Nyet,* you meet with me."

"Ellie, this is not good."

"Enough, Misha. Where are you?"

"Washington," he replied.

"You sure?"

"Yes."

"Contact Jonathon Tierney for directions to the hotel."

I figured Tierney would make damn sure the information was delivered via a secure line.

"CIA?"

"Yeah, hurry up. You have two hours. Do not be late."

"I will be there as soon as I can," Misha replied. He could not disguise the amusement in his voice.

"Tell no one of this conversation."

"*Dosvidanija*." Goodbye.

I hung up and handed the phone back to Iain.

Sam was grinning ear to ear. "I take it he's coming in?"

"Oh, yeah."

Sam organized the movement of the men for two hours' time. Meanwhile they'd remain separated and watched. Closely.

"What's up?" Kurt asked, handing me a coffee. He and Mike were hanging out in Iain Campbell's room while we waited for Misha to show. I'd spent my time floating from room to room checking on everyone for the bulk of the previous two hours. The reality was I was trying not to think too much. The Charlotte Campbell thing preyed on my mind and made it difficult to concentrate on what was happening around us. They had more puzzle pieces than I did. I hoped Misha would cast some light on the Mr. RightGuy situation.

"I have Sam rounding up everyone and taking them to room seventeen."

"You have a plan?" Kurt asked.

"I'm going to give them the surveillance – but not until Misha tells me why they're here."

"You copied it," Kurt stated with a small smile.

"Of course."

Lucky for them I did, too, otherwise they could be

installing some particularly wicked malware along with the surveillance.

"Can they tell?" Mike asked.

"No, this isn't an episode from a television show. There is no way to tell whether the contents of the SD card have been copied." I resisted the temptation to roll my eyes. That technology may not be available right this minute but there were no guarantees that it wouldn't be someday.

"That makes it easy," Mike replied.

"Yes, it does."

"Where did you copy it to?" Kurt asked. "Not one of our laptops, I take it."

Yeah, I really want the surveillance to end up as a file sitting on Sentinel where any agent who wanted to have a look could access it. More importantly, where Owen could access it. Along with other information, like the time I uploaded it. It's better to keep me and all reference to me off Sentinel. And there was the little issue with SkyWiper. I did not want to be the one who let that loose on the FBI system. I'm sure Sean was right about the sophisticated anti-virus software that protects Sentinel but still, not a chance I was willing to take.

"Nope, copied to another SD via Sean's laptop."

"The files were never on his laptop?"

Nope just SkyWiper. It trundled off the SD card and happily installed itself. Don't think it liked being locked down though. There was no way out of Sean's laptop but by the time it had figured that out, we'd already copied the files we wanted to another SD card, with all hope of escape gone. I was starting to think of the program as if it could think: personifying software.

"No, I just used the laptop to copy directly from the SD card to a clean SD card."

"And the card is?"

I smiled and pointed to my pocket. "Safe."

Let's call it insurance.

Chapter Thirty Two
Rough Justice

The trio sat in silence in the room flanked by Lee, Iain, and Sam. Mike was in Iain's room, out of harm's way. When I left he was talking to Kurt and it sounded like he was researching a role. For a fleeting second I thought maybe he was, and just like that, I heard Nickelback's "Gotta be Somebody." The song ran its course and left me none the wiser. Niggling away was the feeling that the song would be back, bringing friends.

Time ticked on. Little pockets of general chit-chat broke the monotony. Several times I escaped the room and checked on Mike and Kurt. After making the third pot of coffee it became apparent that there is only so much coffee I can drink. Hurry-up-and-wait fueled by caffeine equaled boredom with the shakes.

Supported by the wall I absorbed the silence in front of me. As I was about to speak the door opened and Misha Praskovya breezed in. I shook my head at him. He smiled and pocketed a security keycard. Hotel rooms are only secure when people I know aren't thieving the master keys. Confusion raced across his face then evaporated.

"Ellie?"

The red hair and green eyes must've thrown him for a second.

I nodded. "Don't sit, you and I are going to talk in

private," I said, pointing to the door. I stood up and the trio stood too. "You three get to sit back down and think about what it is you're going to tell me when I come back."

I nodded at Lee, Iain, and Sam and left with Misha.

"It's good to see you, Ellie," he said as I closed the door.

We stood in the hallway and stared at each other.

"You might change your mind in a minute, follow me," I said. I led him back to Iain's room. I made eye contact with Kurt. He tapped Mike and they left the room. "Sit," I said, pointing to the small table and two chairs.

"You could never make me change my mind ... it's always good to see you, Ellie."

Smooth.

"What does Mr. RightGuy have to do with this situation you are in?"

A frown darted across his forehead. "Who?"

"Don't, Misha. I found his name in Carla's files."

Misha's eyes saddened. "He targets high profile children. We don't know who he really is, not yet. But we're close."

"Keep me informed, please." It wasn't a request.

"I will."

I turned my attention to the other matter.

"I can think of a million better ways to get the attention of the FBI. This assault on my home was extreme, even for you." I looked into his eyes, waiting for the telltale blink before he tried to deflect. "What is it you need that is inside the Hoover Building?"

Misha smiled quickly. He spoke with care and did not blink. "We have lost someone."

"Lost?"

"Several times now. A person, a person very important to our friends is missing. Every time we get close, this person disappears again."

"What has your inability to locate someone got to do with the Hoover building?"

"The person we lost is in protective custody, and someone within the building is selling information on her whereabouts and we think it might be the same person who is in charge of the case."

I took a deep breath. "Note how I'm not screaming about how that could never happen?" How could I forget Agent Chrissy McQueen and how living for several years with that particular traitor in our midst nearly destroyed the team? "You still could have come to me."

I knew there was more to it or he would have come to me.

"Kurt was working the case."

"Say what now?"

"Kurt was working the case."

Kurt had been assigned to Operation Joshua Tree, pulled in because there was an injured kid involved. An injured kid and now everyone admitting they know of Mr. RightGuy. An injured high-profile kid they're trying to make everyone keep quiet about.

"That's what I thought you said. That makes no sense

to me. You know Kurt. Hell, Misha, you could've called Kurt and set up a meeting yourself!"

Why is this a big deal?

"Not this time."

"What's so special about Operation Joshua Tree that meant you couldn't approach me or Kurt directly?" The way our new digital system worked meant that any agent could access case files and even flag case files so they were alerted to updates. Potentially that meant I could've checked out the case for Misha, if he'd asked. Checking out a case is one thing. Giving information to someone outside the FBI is frowned upon, in a career-ending way. I would have looked. I would not have handed over any information but he didn't know that.

Misha's eyes met mine. "Owen," he said.

Owen the Evil Queen was involved in the operation. Even with Owen overseeing the operation, I didn't see why my house needed shooting up.

Before Misha told me anything else, I knew I needed a witness. It was no secret how much I hated Owen and that could be misconstrued, or possibly taint what he was about to say.

"One minute." I stood up and cautioned Misha, "Say nothing about Mr. RightGuy." I poked my head out the door. "Kurt, can you and Mike come back in?"

Misha adopted a curious expression. "Kurt?"

"You said this is because of something he knows and has to do with Owen. I need a witness before you tell me anything about Owen, and you say Kurt is already involved."

Misha nodded. "I heard there was trouble. A warrant for you?"

"It will be cleared up shortly," I said with false confidence.

Kurt and Mike came back into the room, holding fresh coffees. I recapped the conversation so far. Mike remained silent and out of the way, an interested bystander and if needed, an impartial witness. Part of me considered that this whole mess might one day be a screenplay credited to Mike. So be it.

"I still don't get why you couldn't talk to Kurt or me," I said to Misha. "Or why one of you couldn't use an embassy liaison to get Owen to cooperate." And then I did. "Scratch that."

"Misha," Kurt said by way of a greeting and sat next to me. "What's going on?"

My mind rolled over the scenarios. Whoever they wanted was in protective custody; Kurt couldn't tell them where the person was, if he even knew, without risking his job. Owen must know, and she would cause a diplomatic incident if Misha asked, because that was how she was. A bitch. Plus she was after me, so she wouldn't help anyone who knew me. Again, because of how she was: bitchy.

"Why is Owen involved in Joshua Tree?"

She's an assistant director; that seemed a touch too invasive even for her. It struck me that she was suddenly very handsy. I did not appreciate her hands all over everything. She had a way of stinking things up.

"She muscled her way in when the identity of the missing person was revealed ..." Misha said. "The FBI became involved when the police found the missing high-profile child, and some details of her whereabouts until that point came to light."

"I still don't understand. Kurt, it's answer time."

He shook his head. "I don't know where the kid is."

I mulled his words over in my head. If Owen was handling the case herself, then it must mean the kid is important. As much as I hate to think it, she wouldn't be involved if it was a missing kid from Anacostia. No glory there. I really did have a low opinion of the woman.

"There was no other way to access the building?" I asked Misha. "Other than get themselves arrested by destroying my house?"

"Nyet."

"And you needed to be in there why?" I said.

"That is not important for you to know," Misha said, running his fingers through his hair.

Were they attempting access to our computer system? Not from an interview room. Laptops or tablets would never be in an interview room with suspects. So what was the attraction inside the Hoover Building?

"Who else went near those interview rooms when Seamus, Tim, and Colin were held in them?"

"It does not matter."

And then I had an aha! moment. "Owen. Why was Assistant Director Owen there?"

Misha smiled and touched his nose with his index finger. The pieces slipped into place. Owen would've been told three men attacked my house. She's jumpy because she can't find me to arrest me. So she'd want to get into those interview rooms to ask questions about why they attacked my home.

I doubt she would have made the connection between me and someone wanting to find the kid in FBI protection. That's why they shot up my house. They wanted her to enter one of the interview rooms. They wanted Owen.

I continued, "One of them bugged her. She knows where the kid you want is."

"I don't know what happened while she was in the interview room," Misha said carefully. "We believe she does know the whereabouts of the person we want. Kurt does not know where the person is. He has met her. He met her in a children's home after an incident there. They nearly lost her. Now she is somewhere only Owen knows."

I looked at Kurt and he confirmed Misha's account.

"So they don't really want the surveillance at all? They just wanted access to the Hoover building and to Owen?"

"The team wants the surveillance, too. No one can know they are all here in D.C. or who they are."

"It's all too cloak and dagger for me. I have no desire to get involved in this 'whatever it is.' Tell Libowitz I appreciate all he did in Operation Hoboken. See you later."

I left the room with Kurt and a stunned Mike.

"You buying any of this?" I said. Because I was buying it now I knew about Carla, Joey and Mr. RightGuy. I considered the kid protected by the FBI was a victim who escaped Mr. RightGuy and the parents of the missing child assembled the team to bring her home and remove the Unsub from the face of the earth. That meant the missing kid had a very influential parent. My gut told me she was related to Libowitz.

"If I didn't know Owen so well, I wouldn't be. But Misha's right, the only way to guarantee she'd put in an appearance was to light up an agent's home and the safest way to do that is make sure it's an agent Owen dislikes and is trying to discredit with her possible involvement in a murder," Kurt said.

We stared at each other, neither blinking as all we now knew fell into place. Except I knew more than my team and I wasn't in a very sharing place.

I held up an index finger. "Wait one," I said and went back into the room with Misha and closed the door behind me.

"How old is the Libowitz child?"

"She is nine-years-old."

And with that I had confirmation that Libowitz was involved.

"How did that pervert get to her?"

"Her father is working from the Israeli embassy. We think she was approached online."

"I'll be back," I said, rejoining Kurt and Mike, closing

the door behind me.

Mike spoke, "Did those men have anything to do with the hacker and the photographs?"

"Until now the opinion was that they had piggybacked on the initial hacker and break-in," Kurt said.

"And now?" Mike asked. "Because if this were a script, they would've been behind everything except maybe the crazy stalker thing."

It's not a script, but he had a point.

"We need to find out, because the malware used to spy on my computer is sophisticated and has military application, as in it's used to gather intelligence on various unfriendly governments. It's the sort of thing they may have access to."

Especially as the person pulling the strings here is Israeli.

"Now what?" Kurt asked.

"We let them go, with the surveillance. It's no good to us, we know who they are, and they need to get on with the job they have to do."

A little bit of me hoped that they'd take out Owen in the process, seemed like a handy conclusion to a tricky situation.

I opened the door and told Misha to come with me.

Misha, Mike, Kurt and I filed into the room containing the quasi-UN.

"You can go. Here's the surveillance." I dropped an SD card into Misha's hand. "Enjoy."

The Irishman grinned at me. "Anything you'd like us to

do?" he asked.

"Yes, but I can't say it. It would be the very last nail in my coffin."

Three little words that could send me to death row: take out Owen.

"We have Owen on our radar and that might help you."

"Considering you've been locked up for a few days and we've slowed your ability to do your jobs, you're being very obliging."

He smirked.

Duh. They were sidelined, but Misha wasn't. They already had everything they needed. Libowitz wasn't missing – he was just under the radar. The focus was on the three men who opened fire on my home, not on Misha and the invisible Israeli. The job is done. Owen would be spitting vitriol in all directions.

"Safe travels," I said.

"Can you access your email?" Tim asked.

I shook my head. Not without sending up smoke signals telling the Evil Queen where I am.

Tim looked around the room. "Campbell, you?"

"Yes."

"I need your email address. I'll forward you the link to the bug on Owen. You can monitor her movements."

"Audio?" Iain asked.

"Audio and GPS," Tim replied.

"Stop a minute," I said. "How the hell did you get a bug onto Owen? Curiosity will kill me if you don't tell me."

Grins spread across the three men's faces. The

Irishman laughed then said, "Anyone here have a badge?"

Kurt flipped his badge wallet across the room. Seamus snatched it from the air.

"You put it in the wallet." That was how Lee GPSd me. We always carry two things, our sidearm and our badge. He would've asked to see the badge in the interview room and slipped the tiny bug into the black leather case. Didn't matter if she changed her clothes or whatever, because the badge went with everything.

He nodded and threw Kurt's badge back to him. Kurt checked the wallet, just in case.

Iain opened a box on the floor by the window. He gave the three men back their mobile phones, handguns and other personal effects, and also gave Tim his email address.

"I don't want to ask where you three are going next, but where ever it is, be safe," I said.

Misha smiled. "You owe me dinner. When this is over."

"You can buy me my last meal," I said. Pretty sure death row inmates still get a last meal.

Misha held my shoulders and kissed both my cheeks. "You have an advantage now, you will soon be able to hear her conversations and know where she is and what she is planning."

"Thank you, my friend."

The large Irishman beckoned to me. "Conway, can I've a word?"

I nodded and we moved away from the group. The general chitchat behind us gave us cover.

"I will get everything I can from Mr. RightGuy before he meets his maker and forward the information to you. Misha can contact you, yes?"

"Always."

"Your kid, what happened to her, did he ... get his hands on her?"

"She killed herself. As far as I know, he never got physically near her."

"What was her name?"

"Carla Conway." I blinked, trying to stop a tear slipping through my lashes.

"For Carla, then." He crossed himself.

The room filled with silence as the men left. A hollow, deep silence that swallowed all sound. I pushed away the thoughts and the conversations. The roughest part of our day was over. Slowly, second by second, hope crept back into the walls of the room and oozed across the floor. I heard Iain's fingers tapping on the keys of his laptop.

Owen's voice, distorted, echoed through the crappy speakers and bounced off the furniture and walls in the room. We listened to her talking to two of her men. I recognized their voices. Tweedledumb and Tweedledumber. They were the ones who flew out the hospital doors as Sean and I drove off.

"Someone needs to monitor this feed all the time," I said. "In case she says something intelligent."

Sam waved a finger. "I'll do it."

"Thanks, we'll need to rotate, though. It'll drive you insane listening to the surveillance feed without a break."

"I'll take the first two hours, then Lee, Kurt, you ..." Sam looked at Iain. "You want in on this?"

"Yes."

"Good."

Mike coughed. "Can I?"

"You'll be busy being a blushing groom," I said with a grin. "Wedding remember?"

Chapter Thirty Three
In My Secret Life

We all trailed back to our hotel. Mentally I felt tired, but I knew that was mostly pent-up grief from talking about Carla, albeit briefly.

It seemed clever to get Mike into his room and safe without any messing around. Then find a recent photograph of Joaunes and use it to establish whether he was in the hotel or if he'd been seen anywhere. Kurt and Lee did a tour of the hotel and grounds looking for our suspect. Sean was on babysitting. Sam set himself up to monitor the Owen feed.

I went off in search of the hotel manager to make sure preparations for the ceremony were underway in the garden. A garden wedding, how lovely. The idea had come to me when I'd seen the beautiful gazebo.

We were putting together a very lopsided wedding party. It was almost tempting to have one of the men don a wig and be my maid-of-honor but the chances of people smelling a rat were high, as none of them looked good in a dress. Now there's a statement I wished I couldn't make, I also couldn't un-see it. The Butterfly Foundation Halloween party had a lot to answer for.

I needed a maid of honor. Sandra. Could I get Sandra out of D.C?

It's me. I can do anything. Laughter tumbled out. I

could do anything except call Sandra.

I went to Sam's room. "Hey, anything good from Owen?"

"Yeah, she thinks you're in New Jersey."

"Really?"

"Apparently someone saw Rowan Grange heading north with a blonde in the passenger seat of his car."

A big smile flooded my face; I didn't know or care who was in his car but I loved that Owen thought it was me.

"That's great. I take it she's concentrating on New Jersey and Rowan for now?"

"Sounds like it. She told someone she'll be interviewing him herself and is on her way to the Trenton satellite office."

"Good. Can you get hold of Sandra, and get her out here?"

With Owen out of the way it would be easier to get Sandra away from her desk.

"Sure, problem?"

"Sort of, I need a maid of honor for this wedding and it shouldn't be one of you in a wig and a dress."

Sam's left eyebrow shot up. "You're right. It should not be one of us."

"You'll contact Sandra?"

"Yes."

I went to find the hotel manager. Now I could tell her my maid of honor was on her way. A smile crossed my lips as I saw the gazebo ahead of me; it'd come very close to being a warming memory last night. What remained was a sense of slight frustration and a reminder that I am human.

The manager was in the gazebo with another woman who smelled like carnations and roses.

"Ms. Graham, just the lady we need. We're talking flowers for the ceremony. Do you have color and preference?"

So the other woman was a florist. Not pink flowers. Black might be too hard to pull off at such short notice. Red reminded me too much of blood. Good chance we'd be seeing some of that later if things did not go as planned. I hoped it wasn't Mike's blood.

"Yellow and white. Yellow roses and that white fluffy looking stuff."

That wasn't so hard after all.

"Sounds like baby's breath. It will be gorgeous," the manager cooed.

"Any thoughts on the form you'd like the floral arrangements to take?" the florist asked. "For the table arrangements, as well as for the gazebo."

Seemed like a lot of flowers and I had no thoughts on the subject at all.

"We haven't really had much time to think about much," I said with a hint of apology in my voice.

"Not to worry, I'll take care of it," she replied, her smile reassuring. Had I actually been a soon-to-be-bride I'd definitely have felt comforted by it.

"I'm sorry I don't remember your names," I said with my best confused facial expression. "I'm not very good with names."

"Entirely my fault," the manager said. "I'm Catalina Arcos. This is Juliana Sanchez. Juliana owns the florist in town."

I shook hands with Juliana.

"My maid of honor will arrive this evening. She'll need a bouquet."

"Formal or informal?"

Considering none of us have suitable formal wedding attire I decided on informal.

"Informal, lots of yellow."

"And your bouquet?"

"The same please."

"The men?"

"Yellow rose boutonnieres."

"How many?"

"Groom and best man, so two."

"You've trimmed your wedding party?" The manager asked.

"Yes, with the decision to marry now, we've decided on a much smaller wedding party. The rest of the party will be guests."

Catalina smiled. "We had another booking from a wedding guest late yesterday."

Only one invitation went out.

"Has the guest arrived?"

"No, he's not expected to arrive until this evening."

"Would you give me a call in my room when he does? I'm sure Mike would like to greet him early." I managed a casual tone.

"I'll leave a note for the receptionist," she said. "Any ideas for the flowers in here?" Catalina swept an arm around the gazebo.

I truly had no idea. Floundering, out of my depth, clueless. I thought I'd done pretty well so far.

From the corner of my eye, I spotted Mike. He stepped up beside me, and slid his arm around my waist, causing much fluster and bluster as the women introduced themselves.

Cool calm Mike stole the show. "My fiancée and I would like simple flower arrangements, here, here, and here," he said pointing at the back corners and then to the altar. "What color did you choose, baby?"

"Yellow."

His arm tightened around my waist and he gave me an affectionate squeeze.

"Your dress has arrived," he said.

"My dress?"

His lips brushed mine. "Your dress." Mike turned his charming smile toward the women. "Can we leave you to the arrangements?"

"Of course," Catalina said. She positively dripped with joy.

Mike and I walked arm in arm out of the gazebo and back up to the hotel. The whole way across the garden I felt the women watching and I didn't care, used to jealous glares, longing gazes, and vicious snipes.

I dated Rowan for long enough for those things to be

part of my everyday life.

Out of the corner of my eye I saw something move and tensed. My head turned toward the movement. A large black hen pecked at the grass. With a deep breath of relief and a small sigh, I let the tension go.

"All right?" Mike asked.

"Yes." I nodded toward the large hen. "I like chickens."

"Me, too," he replied.

"Really?"

"Absolutely. Roasted, deep fried or barbecued. I even like chicken sandwiches."

I laughed. "Well, aren't you hilarious?"

"Sometimes, but these days mostly frustrated."

Seemed smart to leave that alone.

"You said my dress arrived?"

"I did. You'll see."

As we made our way through the hotel, I kept an eye out for our only invited guest. No sign of him or anything that made my trigger finger itch.

Chapter Thirty Four
All The Mad Men

A large box sat on my bed. I'm sure a small child could've comfortably used the box as a bed. Next to that box was a smaller box, a shoe box.

Grinning like a Cheshire cat, Mike threw himself across the bed, landing propped on one elbow, facing the boxes and me.

"Cute. You're really are enjoying this, aren't you?"

"It's different from my usual days. Change is fun."

The glint in his eye told me more than his words. He was a closet adrenaline junkie; that's why this was fun for him, the ever-present element of danger.

"It's probably more fun when change isn't gunning for you."

"Open it," he urged.

My fingers ran along the full length of the biggest box. Instead of opening it, I lifted the box. It weighed about eight pounds. Heavy for a dress. I tipped the box gently from side to side. Nothing slid. The box didn't unbalance. I placed it back on the bed.

Mike watched me, his Cheshire cat grin gone. In its place, a look I could not immediately define. I'd never seen that particular expression on his face before. I inspected the box carefully while trying to place the expression. It was easiest to put the same expression on

Sam or Lee's face.

Horror.

I lifted the lid of the box with care. Moving the lid no more than half an inch at a time, I drew in a sharp breath and lifted the lid clean away from the base. All I could see in the box was white tissue paper. I dropped the lid onto the bed and smoothed the layers of tissue paper over the edges of the box, revealing white fabric.

White.

Oh my God.

I looked at Mike. His grin was back.

"A wedding dress." Nothing else came out of my mouth despite the myriad thoughts tumbling about my stunned brain. It never occurred to me that when he said my dress had arrived that it would be a wedding dress.

"Are you going to take it out of the box?"

"Um, sure, okay." Almost afraid to touch it in case I somehow marked the fabric, I rubbed my hands down my jeans then lifted the dress from the box.

Mike's mouth moved. About ten seconds later the words found my ears. "I went with an ivory taffeta, princess style with a scoop neck and chapel train."

I ran my hands over the intricate beading on the bodice and chewed my lip.

Ivory taffeta. Beading. A chapel train. If I were a bride, this would be my dress. A proper bride, not a tequila-fueled idiot marrying a rock star in an Elvis chapel. I can't even remember what I wore that night.

"How did you pull this off?"

"They have a wedding boutique in town. The hotel manager is very helpful."

I bet. It was my observation that most people Mike came across fell into the helpful camp. He brought out the good in people because he was a nice guy. A nice guy with a killer smile, and helluva body. His bio said strapping blond hunk. No disagreement here.

I pointed at the shoebox. "Shoes?"

"You might want to try them on, I guessed at your size ... and maybe the dress too?"

I nodded like a dummy. The fabric of the skirt and train spilled over my hands like froth. There was a full-length zip down the back of the dress. After studying the dress for several more minutes, I concluded that donning wedding dresses required help. I piled the dress back into the box.

Another thought popped into my head. Chewing my lip prevented a full-blown smile cementing on my lips but didn't stop it reaching my eyes.

"Something you want to share?" Mike asked.

What the hell, may as well throw it out there.

"I know I asked before, but you're sure you don't bat for the other team?"

"Excuse me?" He sat up.

"Flowers, dress, shoes ... I rest my case."

He smiled. "Would that make this easier for you?"

"Not at all."

"Because if you want gay, I can do gay."

"That wasn't where I was going with the question." The

jealousy aspect of this whole Joaunes Levy stalker situation was front and center. Maybe Joaunes thought he was gay, perhaps it wasn't about Mike stealing all the glory and the women at all. Just an idea. "You're Catholic, yes?"

He nodded. "And?"

"Just putting it out there with your flower arranging and fashion sense."

Mike laughed.

I lifted one of the ivory satin-finished pumps from the shoe box. "These are beautiful."

They'll look a helluva lot better than my black boots under a wedding dress.

Mike eyed me with what I think was interest. "You're questioning my sexual orientation because I'm a Catholic who knows shoes?"

As he said it, it sounded stupid.

"I had to ask."

"I suppose."

"For clarification ... you're hetero?"

"Yes."

Woman all over the world could continue to dream without restriction, he was straight.

Catholic. Common knowledge? How did I know? Because Lee is Catholic and it said Mike was Catholic on Wikipedia. In my defense, I did not know who Mike really was when I Google-stalked him after watching the first season of his new show. I would not have done it if I'd known he was Lee's little brother. Where would we be without Wikipedia? Lost, that's where.

"They ..." I tilted my head toward the main hotel. "They'll expect a Catholic ceremony."

"They won't be disappointed."

"While I was away?"

"Had to keep busy."

"I appreciate it. Dress, shoes, all of it. Thank you."

"Don't mention it."

Catholic wedding ceremony. Man, that was a straight road to hell if ever I saw one.

And there he was, right in front of me, Mr. Charming. Smiling, dimples, cool blue eyes that did more than just hint at wicked humor.

"What can I expect at our wedding?"

"A priest, traditional vows, a crazy stalker."

A moment of panic set in. Cold feet. It was my idea and I had the cold feet. Odd. Before I could stop it, the panic bubbled into words and spilled out of my mouth.

"I need family here. I wouldn't get married without Dad." That was a lie. He wasn't in Vegas. But Vegas wasn't proper. There was no priest. Elvis wasn't a priest. "No woman would get married without her family."

"Unless she was an orphan with no brothers or sisters. Is Laura Graham an orphan?" His answer stole my out. I couldn't grasp exactly why I needed an out. After all, it wasn't real. It was a staged wedding to catch a madman. "Tragic, but it happens."

"Does the priest know this is a fake wedding?"

Mike frowned. The lines disappeared as fast as they

came. "No. Is that a problem?"

"Won't he expect to see a marriage license?"

He shoved his hand into a pocket in his jeans and pulled out a folded piece of paper, opened it, smoothed the creases, and handed it to me. "He has already seen it," Mike said. "Let's hope Joaunes makes his move before we sign it."

"How?" I waved the paper at Mike. "It takes days to get a license."

"Lee organized it."

It looked real at first glance. I read it. According to this, Laura Graham was marrying Michael Fisher, two people who don't exist. Excellent. A smile sauntered across my face. "Thank God," I mumbled under my breath. "Still lying to a priest, but that I can do."

I gave Mike back the license. "Okay, stuff you need to know about your bride ..."

Mentally I picked up the file that belonged to Laura Graham and turned to the second page. "Laura's father died in 1999. Her mother passed away in 2010. No siblings. Raised Catholic."

"Anything else your fiancé should know?"

"She's an accountant turned private investigator."

"I really don't see her as an accountant, she made a wise choice to change professions."

"Really?"

"Too hot for a bean counter."

"Thanks."

"Anything else?"

Another page turned. He already knew Laura owned an agency in Washington and worked overseas.

Someone hammered on the door. I glanced at Mike. "Don't move."

Peering through the peephole, I saw Sam and swung the door open.

He barreled in. "Owen said she has a handwritten confession from you."

"I know," I said.

"That's the sort of information you could have shared, Chicky," Sam said. He shook his head. "It's need to know, we need to know."

He was right.

"Sorry." Seemed a good time to cultivate some contrition.

"She just used it to get a new warrant issued. No longer wanted for questioning, you are now wanted for murder."

"And?"

Being wanted for murder at this point was no worse than being wanted for questioning. An arrest was an arrest and had the potential to end in horror.

"And, we need to be more careful and keep you off the radar."

"Where is Owen?"

"Still in Jersey. She thinks Rowan is hiding you somewhere."

"Let me know if she moves on."

"Will do," Sam said as he left. I locked the door behind him.

"Where were we? Oh yeah, Laura's past. She wants three kids and to raise them in Virginia even though she spends most of her time in France."

"Damn. I need to be in Los Angeles and the kids? Not keen."

"That could be a deal breaker."

"I hope not," he said with a wink. "Anything else?"

"She's allergic to shellfish and penicillin," I said.

"That's important information," Mike replied.

"Yeah, but I'm not, so it's not real-life threatening. Got enough now?" I asked.

"Anything else that comes up, I'll improvise. You okay with that?"

"Sure." He could improvise the hell out of it. After all, he was the actor. "You ready to be a full focus target?"

"I trust you."

I hoped his trust wasn't misplaced. This was a crazy idea. May as well paint a bull's eye on his tux and be done with it. Time to change the subject.

"What are you and Lee wearing?"

"Black tuxedos, white shirts."

A smile soared. I really wanted to see him in a tux ... or out of a tux. There is something delicious about men in tuxedos. The whole thought was fabulous in a 007 kind of way. To be perfectly honest I wanted to see Kurt in a tuxedo, too. I had a feeling he'd be very hard to resist. That could be bad. The bride should probably focus on the groom and not a guest. I was all over the place like a mad woman's knitting.

"You need to wear a bulletproof vest under your shirt, did you get a roomy enough jacket?"

He nodded. "Lee was with me."

I picked the dress up by the shoulders and held it against my body.

"Help me into this dress?"

"Happy to. We need to find out if it fits. I had to guess the size." He cupped air with his hands.

My eye brows shot up. "You didn't do that in the store?"

He laughed. "Nah. I checked the labels in a couple of your shirts and your jeans."

Good to know.

There I stood with a wedding dress in my arms and no idea how to proceed. I couldn't put it over my clothes, so they'd have to go. Mike sitting on the bed smiling at me did not help.

"I'll be right back."

I took the dress to the bathroom and closed the door. There was nowhere to put the dress and I didn't want to drop it on the floor. I yelled for Mike to bring a chair. He appeared and held his arms out for the dress.

"I'll hold it."

"Um, no, just a chair would work fine."

"I'll turn around?"

Good try.

"The whole room is mirrored."

He grinned and fetched a chair.

"Wait right there," I said and closed the door.

A few minutes later I stood in the mirrored bathroom looking at myself in a wedding dress and willing tears back behind my lashes. The mirror in front of me shimmered and as it cleared and I saw Mac smiling at me.

"Beautiful," he said. "Takes me back."

"Me, too," I whispered. I didn't want Mike to hear my voice.

"Be careful, babe, misinformation is everywhere."

"Yeah, I know." I turned at the waist. The zip needed fastening. But the dress seemed to fit. "One day my prince will come."

Mac smiled at me from within his mirrored prison, and then ran his fingers through his hair. It still needed cutting.

"Open the door, Ellie," Mac whispered. "He's waiting."

The mirror shimmered and his image spiraled, then faded. Taking a deep breath, I opened the door. Kurt leaned with his back against the wall, where Mike had been.

His eyes followed the dress to the floor. He said nothing.

"Can you zip me, please?"

He nodded. Kurt pushed himself off the wall. I gathered the train and skirt into one hand, stepped out of the bathroom and turned around. There was a slight tug as the end of the zip freed and he ran the zipper all the way to the top. I could still breathe and the dress fitted perfectly.

"Turn around, Conway," Kurt said. I turned, dropped the train to the floor and swept it behind me.

"Passable?" I asked.

"Yes."

"Problem?"

"Did you look in the mirror?" His voice fractured, emotion crept along the fissures, softening his expression.

I opted for flippant, something to break the spell. "Yeah, me in a wedding dress. Been a few years since I've worn one."

His expression changed again, deepening, intensifying. I glanced at my bare arms and back at Kurt's smoldering eyes. Time to distract him with something else, flippant failed.

"Going to need Mike to use the magic makeup on these," I said, turning my right arm palm up. The scars on my inner forearm seemed to stand out in relief against the ivory dress.

I don't think he even heard me.

"Conway?" He stood close, his breathing stilted, a soft gleam grew in his eyes matching the dilation in his pupils. "You need me ... to ..." he made a zipping motion in the air, "unzip that now ..."

My cheeks felt warm. "Please."

He reached his left hand around my back and felt for the zipper and pulled slowly down. Kurt's eyes never left mine nor did I want them to. He was so close I could feel the heat from his body.

Chapter Thirty Five
Bad Romance

Something heavy fell with a sickening thud. I jumped, holding the dress to stop it sliding off. Kurt spun around. I saw the barrel of his pistol before he pushed me back inside the bathroom.

"Change," he said, all emotion gone from his voice.

I stepped out of the dress, pulled on my shirt and jeans, gathered the dress and plopped it on the chair in the bathroom.

I crept out the door and waited, back pressed against the wall. I peered around the corner. Kurt was gone. Reaching for my gun on the nightstand, I pulled it from the holster and chambered a round. I rolled over the bed and moved up next to the connecting door. I saw a figure move past the doorway. I took a breath and stepped into the doorway to get a better view.

Kurt knelt beside someone.

"Kurt?"

I searched the room: no one else and the window wide open. Footprints in the garden beneath the window pointed toward the driveway.

"Mike?" I asked, and joined Kurt by the fallen man.

"He's okay," Kurt replied, helping Mike into a sitting position.

He looked a little groggy. His hand touched the back of

his head. "What happened?" Mike asked.

"Someone hit you across the back of the head with this ..." Kurt said, showing him a book. "Did you see anyone?"

"No. I came in to answer the phone."

The phone was off the hook. I picked it up and listened – dial tone – and hung up. Kurt and I looked at each other and frowned. Neither of us heard a phone ring.

"The phone rang?" Kurt asked.

"Yes," Mike replied. "Wouldn't expect you two to hear it ... you were focused on each other."

I chewed my lip to stop the smile and avoided Kurt's eyes.

"A book hit me?" Mike said. He still appeared dazed.

"Hardback, no wonder it dropped you. Look at the dent in the spine."

Hard headed.

I took the book and looked at the cover. The cover had a photo of Mike climbing a mountain. *King of the Mountain* by M.T. Clark. "Did you know about this?"

"No."

I held up the book. It was a novel, not a biography. I flipped it over and read the blurb. Oh, man. It was an adventure romance and Michael Fisher was the main character. Fan fiction. Nice.

"No one talked to you about this book?"

"No, but someone hit me with it?" He sounded confused.

"I'm going out on a limb here and I'm going to say that

our only wedding guest has arrived and that he's none too impressed with you being the subject of a novel," I said. "Perhaps we should read this book."

"Perhaps I should talk to my manager and find out why I haven't heard about it until it hit me."

The author may have contacted his management as a courtesy at the very least. I did know his management wasn't good at passing on information. Maybe they withheld this, like they did the crazy letters.

"Yes, you should. Not just now though. You're in no condition to talk to management."

Had it been an electronic book I doubt he would've been knocked out. Although I guessed that would depend if the book-wielding nut hit him with an eReader or a laptop. Harder to wield a laptop than a hardback and who would want to break their eReader over someone's head? Electronic books were definitely a less dangerous option when it came to reading.

"Why didn't he just kill me?" Mike rubbed his head.

"Because this is more fun," I replied. "Guess the wedding death thing appeals to him."

I suspected he was delaying gratification and back in his room getting off on the adrenaline and the thought of what he'd do next.

Kurt stood up. "You can't be left alone at all until after we slap cuffs on this lunatic and also, you have a head injury. I'm staying close."

I smiled. Really, why not? It wasn't me this time.

Kurt glanced at me. His eyes spoke volumes. It wasn't

me this time. He reached down and helped Mike to his feet.

"Looks like we'll all be roommates until the crazy guy is caught," Kurt said. He seemed quite happy about it.

"Was the dress all right?" Mike asked. "You're not wearing it."

Good to know his eyesight wasn't affected.

"It's perfect. I didn't think it was appropriate to wear it now."

"How do you feel?" Kurt asked.

"Think I'm okay," Mike replied, his hand still on his head.

"Of course you are. Conway, I need to get my bag. Can you watch him? You know what to look for?" He grinned as he turned to the door. "Look who I'm talking to, I'll be right back."

Mike swayed. I took his arm and walked him to the bed. "Sit, before you fall."

"I won't fall." He sat down too heavily and toppled backwards. "Ouch. Damn, who knew books hurt so much."

"Okay?"

"Sure."

I pulled him back to a sitting position, slowly; sudden movement and a head injury were not compatible.

"Good. Just take it easy. Don't want to drag your unconscious ass up the aisle tomorrow."

"It's nothing."

"As the resident head injury champion, I can assure

you it's not nothing." I watched him. From experience, I knew how he felt and how his world was out of focus. A flash of Mike's life flew past my eyes: he knew, too. "How many head injuries?"

"A couple."

The perils of climbing.

"More than a couple, Mike. How many and when was the last one?"

"Six confirmed concussions. Two years ago, on set."

"On set? You do your own stunts?"

"Yeah, usually."

That didn't make me like him any less. I walked over to the phone and called Lee's room. "It's me, I'm in your brother's room. You need to be here."

"On my way."

I hung up.

"Why'd you do that?" Mike asked.

I detected a slur and willed Kurt to hurry up. "Because Lee should be here."

"I got h-hi-i-t ... with a book, its noth-thi-ing." Mike slurred. "A st-stu-upid book." His eyes rolled back in his head and he fell back onto the bed.

"Ah crap!"

I checked his pulse. He had one. He was also breathing. I rolled him over to the recovery position and rubbed his sternum. "Michael, wake up!"

I wanted my cell phone and my life back. I strode to the door of his room and opened it. My eyes checked the hallway. No Lee and no Kurt. No sign of anyone.

From the bedside phone, I called Kurt's room.

No answer.

I called Lee.

No answer.

I called Sam.

No answer.

An edge I didn't much like crept into my consciousness and it felt a lot like panic. Either Lee or Sam should've been monitoring the Owen feed and available via phone. If Lee was on his way here from two rooms down the hall, where was he?

I tried Sean's room.

He answered on the sixth ring. I counted. "Do you know where everyone is?"

"No." He paused. "Sam said earlier that they were going to plan a stag party for Mike. One of their rooms?"

"I tried. Mike is in no condition to party. He is currently unconscious."

"You need Kurt?"

"Yep. He went to get his bag from his room three doors away and has not returned. Meanwhile, I have an unconscious TV star."

"I'm coming."

I placed the phone back in its cradle. Mike still didn't respond. Not ideal.

"If your brain is mushed, your brother might not be very happy with me," I muttered as I sat next to him. "Especially with me supposedly protecting you. Clearly, I'm a bit shit at that today."

Usually I'm so good at keeping people safe from lunatics. My eyes rolled skyward, my focus scattered on the four winds, and I knew it. This was my fault.

Footsteps outside the door alerted me to potential company. I pulled my gun from my waistband and held it in my right hand. My hand and the gun rested next to my leg, hidden from view of the door. One knock. Three knocks. One knock again. Two knocks. An old code but an effective one. I jumped up and swung open the door.

"Come in. No one has turned up. What if the moron who hit Mike found them?"

"One man is going to take out Delta?" Sean said with a slight smile. "Don't see it."

"One man broke in here and waited. When Mike came through to answer the phone, he hit him with a book. Kurt and I were in my room, with the adjoining door open. This guy has balls."

Sean took a look at Mike. "He woken at all?"

"Nope," I replied. "Not since I called you."

"Hey, wake up!" Sean said rubbing on Mike's shoulder. "Up and at 'em."

Nothing.

"I'm sorry Mike has stepped out. He won't be joining us for the rest of the afternoon," I muttered. "Not going as well as I'd hoped."

"Good to know this wasn't in your pre-wedding plan," Sean replied. He pulled out his cell phone and called Kurt's cell.

"Don't usually need to knock men out to get them to

marry me," I muttered as Sean left a message on Kurt's voice mail. "A bottle of tequila and a few limes usually does the trick."

"We could have trouble," Sean said. "Lock the adjoining door. I'll call Campbell. Might need back up."

All soothing words that a girl like me loves to hear. They're right up there with, I'm out, meaning my magazine's empty, or agent down.

I disappeared into my room and checked I'd locked the outer door. From my bag, I took two spare magazines and made sure they were full. Back in Mike's room, I locked the internal door. Sean talked to Iain on the phone. Mike was still unconscious. He really wasn't a lot of fun like that.

"Hey, Mike, up and at 'em." I shook his shoulder.

Nothing.

"Come on, really, I have to marry you like this?"

Nothing.

"Cowboy, the hell up. It's just a head injury."

He groaned.

Proof of life, but not necessarily functioning brain cells.

"Come on, Mike. You're drooling on the bed, dude."

He groaned again but this time managed, "Not drooling."

"There's drool."

He moved his arm, his hand brushed across his mouth. "No drool."

I watched his eyes move behind his closed eyelids.

"You awake yet?" I said, giving his shoulder another gentle shake.

"Yeah," he replied.

"Open your eyes."

His left eyelid flickered, followed by his right. After a few more attempts, his eyes opened. Mike rolled onto his back and then gingerly sat up.

"Okay?" I asked, ready in case he fell back again.

"Bit rough," Mike said.

"No kidding. Can you focus?" I held my index finger in front of his face. "Follow my finger." His head moved. "Without moving your head."

He tried again, with more success.

"All right over there?" Sean said from a chair by the door.

"Getting there," I replied. "Iain?"

"On his way. He told me the contract on you is open to anyone, with no one in particular asked to fulfill it. The post is on a website accessible to anyone with a membership and password to the site."

"That's cheerful news. Could be a few more lunatics on the way then."

"That's a safe estimate of the situation."

"How do you think they're finding me?" If anyone knew how people like that worked, it was Sean.

Sean looked thoughtful for a moment. "Trolling social media sites, looking for recent pictures of Mike, would be my guess."

Not everyone knows that uploaded photographs can

contain location information.

"Time consuming?"

"Not really." Sean showed me the screen on his phone. He'd Google-searched a hashtag while we were talking, #MichaelFisher. "I found four recent images of Mike and you. The latest one was taken here in the hotel. And yes, it contains location information."

"Fuckadoodledo."

"They found you because of me," Mike said.

I smiled at him. "It's all good. It'll be fine. This isn't on you. It's just how these fucktards operate."

"Yeah," Sean agreed. "It's not on you, Mike."

The yellow flash band swung into view as I brushed hair off my face. "Don't suppose we could get a copy of that malware onto the site with the contract?" Now that would be an awesome use of an espionage tool.

Saving lives. Imagine that?

Sean stared at me for a beat. His eyes narrowed. "Yeah, I think I can do that."

"Good answer ... time to use their malware against them." We might even find out who is behind all this craziness and those bits of Eddie and what it had to do with my daughter. "How'd you get on with the program on this?" I held up my arm, letting the flash band dangle from it.

"It's been isolated, it's sitting on the laptop. No closer to uncovering a signature in the tweaked modules but I have disabled the suicide module. I also cleaned up and disabled the suicide module on the copy that was on the

SD card. I've kept them separate. I'll modify one to use on the contractor site and the other I'll keep working with to try to identify the signature."

"So we can use it?"

"Oh yeah, we can use it. I'll modify a few more modules and it'll be ours."

"Can you work on that once this situation is resolved?" I waved a hand around the room and let my gaze rest on Mike.

"I'm not a situation," Mike said doing his best to hold my gaze but unable to use his tractor beam. Proof that all was not well in his head.

"I'll make the program a priority as soon as we're good here," Sean said. "Feeling better, Mike?"

"Yeah, I'm good," he replied, doing his damnedest to be so. Mike rubbed his eyes and looked around the room. "I can see."

"Awesome," I said. He tried to stand but I held his arm to stop him. "Stay where you are. We're waiting for Kurt to come back."

Mike scratched his head.

"He was here before, I remember seeing him." His hand dropped to the bed and hit the book. He picked it up. "What the hell?"

"That's the book you were hit with," I said. "Have you seen it before?"

"No." He picked it up and stared at the cover for a few seconds.

"Can you see who's on it?" Had to ask, with head

injury, and obviously not his first, vision can be impaired. I knew that from experience.

"That's me." Mike sounded surprised and pointed to the man on the cover. "Climbing."

"Yep. Do you know where the picture was taken? Is it actually you climbing?" Just lately not too many pictures I'd seen were real.

He studied the cover. "I do and it is," he said and turned the book over. As he read the blurb, a crazy grin spread across his lips. "Who is M.T. Clark?"

"I don't know, we can find out. Where's your iPad, we'll ask the all-knowing Google."

Sean waved his phone. "Let's just ask Siri."

Siri told us the M stood for Maxine. Maxine Clark was a writer based in New York. She was agented and published by a small press. This was her second book.

Mike thumbed through a few pages in the middle. "Holy shit. Wow."

"Wow, good?" I asked, moving closer and reading over his shoulder. "Ohhh." Good grief it was almost pornographic. Never read over anyone's shoulder, no good can come of it.

Mike closed the book with care and set it next to him on the bed. His fingers tapped on the cover. "Just wow."

"Fan fiction equals porn, shoulda seen that coming ... *Shades of Grey* all over again," I mumbled.

"I hope not. I don't want to be portrayed as a manipulative selfish asshole."

That would be quite a stretch.

"You never saw an advance copy of this?"

"Not that I remember."

"Would you remember?"

"I'd remember. Never seen me as a character in a book before." His fingers still tapped on the cover. "That picture, it's from Torrent Falls."

"Interesting."

"Do you think one of those women was Maxine Clark?"

"The women you met down there? I would say so. Any idea who took the photo?"

He picked up the book again and studied the picture with care. "See that?" He pointed to something at the very top edge. "That's the sole of someone's shoe."

I thought back to what he'd told me about climbing at Torrent Falls. One woman was above him and one right behind.

"The woman below you ... could she have taken it?"

He studied the picture again. "The angle works."

Sean crossed the room and showed us a photo of Maxine Clark.

"That's her, that's the woman. She was really keen to talk to me."

I grinned. "No kidding, Einstein, Think we know why now, huh?" Boy, did he miss out that weekend. "Tell me, was she the one who turned Joaunes down first?"

"Maybe, wait, yes. She was the first one he hit on."

I took the book. "This isn't just a book. It's a freaking slap in the face for Joaunes."

Mike gave a reserved nod. "But I didn't do her or have

anything to do with the book. There wasn't any encouragement from me. I don't even think we spoke more than a few words to each other before the climb and maybe some chit-chat afterwards."

"That doesn't matter to lunatics and Joaunes is a big ol' nut job."

"There was a group of us and everyone was talking, I just don't recall spending any time talking to the women who joined in."

"It's okay, Mike. This is not your doing. You didn't bring this upon yourself. I've been looking for a motive, something to get me in his head and hopefully help us stop him. This is all on Joaunes Levy. He's the lunatic here."

Someone knocked on the door. Sean jumped to his feet and looked out the peephole. "Iain Campbell," he said and opened the door.

"They turned up yet?" Iain asked, walking in. Sean shut and locked the door behind him. Iain set a laptop down on the small table in the room.

"No."

"You doing okay, Mike?"

"I think so."

My smile beamed. "He just found out someone wrote a novel and he's the main character. It's damn near porn."

Iain laughed. "Do you get to play you in the movie?"

"I hope not. I can see it as the basis for some good stand-up," Mike said. "Take a look." He pitched the book at Iain.

Iain plucked the book from midair and admired the cover. "Nice shot. You climb much?"

"As much as I can. Heading to Ecuador next. You climb?"

"Yeah. Let me know before you go, I have a hankering to climb Cotopaxi."

"I'm hoping for Cotopaxi in January, I heard it's not as windy then but still dry enough to make it an enjoyable experience."

I coughed. "Vacation planning? Now? Can we find my missing team first, ya think, before heading up a volcano?"

Mike looked at me. "You should come."

Me, climb a volcano? Oh hell, yes! I'm all over that idea. A twinge of guilt began as a small seed. I gave his invitation due consideration while trying to find a way around the reaction I would get from Kurt. His displeasure at my enjoyment of so-called extreme sports had caused a few issues in the past. Sometimes he can be a real girl.

At first mention of any sort of fun, Kurt reactivated the old rhetoric about my having a death wish and acting out. Secretly, I enjoyed winding him up until he almost exploded.

Climbing a volcano was definitely on my bucket list. I looked at Mike and felt a sense of longing that came from the freedom of living on the edge.

"Yeah, I'll come." You only live once, may as well pack it all in while I still can. Before I end up a drooling wreck rocking in a padded cell. Mitch and I should go climb Cotopaxi. He'd enjoy it.

"What did you say to me the other night? That I should find someone who likes to climb ..."

"And won't shoot paparazzi. Don't forget that bit."

"You never said that."

"Yeah, I did. Let's keep this possible climbing trip between us and Iain."

Mike agreed. "At some stage I want to know why. Is that okay?"

"Totally."

Chapter Thirty Six
Someone To Save You

Sean showed me the screen on his phone. An incoming call from Sam.

"Speaker," I said to Sean.

"Where the fuck are you?" I said before Sam could open his mouth.

"I don't know."

"Wrong answer, Sam."

"Chicky, I don't know where I am." He didn't sound right. Sam was a big guy. A big guy who could handle himself and he sounded confused.

"Lee, Kurt?"

"Not with me."

"Describe what you see," Iain said.

"Table, chair, boarded-up window, mattress, door. Bottle of water on the floor."

"Don't drink anything," I said. "You hurt?"

"No."

That left drugs. The only way to subdue a guy like Sam was either with a debilitating injury or with drugs. I heard a muffled carillon.

"Sam, are they bells?"

"I don't know. It's something outside."

"Go closer to the window. I need to hear it."

The sound grew louder but not by much. Bells. Church

bells. The noise stopped.

"Bells," I said. "Iain, is there a church close by?"

I watched him thinking and it looked painful. "Yes, I passed one when I was trying alternate routes between here and my hotel."

"We're coming," I said.

"No, Chicky Babe, you're not. Why would someone take my gun and leave my phone?"

"So you'd call ... so I'd use your phone to track you."

Because someone wants me and with Delta around that's not going to happen. they also know i'd walk over hot coals to find my team. It's mutual. Our phones can send GPS coordinates to each other at the touch of an icon. It's an emergency thing. I didn't have my phone though.

"Sam, give me your coordinates."

I pointed at Iain's laptop. "Got Google earth on that?"

He nodded and fired up the machine.

"Stay where you are," Sam warned.

"That's not going to happen. I'm coming for you. We also gotta find Kurt and Lee."

"Coordinates, Sam, read them to me. We don't need our own software. I think we can get close enough with Google Earth."

Sam read the numbers out from his phone and Iain typed them into the laptop. "I'll see if there is a way out of this cruddy room," Sam said.

Iain turned the laptop to face me.

"We're coming for you, Sam. We know where you are."

"Be careful." He hung up.

"I have a feeling there will be two more calls like that from two more unknown locations, far enough away from each other that we can't get to them all at the same time without splitting up," I said.

But much worse than that, I had a feeling time was not on our side. No point separating the team if the person or persons behind this wasn't going to up the ante and make this really nerve-busting.

What would I do? I'd rig explosives and make each location a death trap. But that's just me. But just in case it wasn't just me, I called Sam back. "You smell anything?"

"Everything smells musty."

"What about by the door?"

Boards creaked as he walked across the floor and sniffed. "Bleach or some kind of cleanser."

That's not good.

"Keep away from the door. You got any cover at all?"

"The mattress."

"Bleach could be TATP."

"Mother of Satan."

"Exactly. We're coming."

I hung up. Iain was on his feet already.

Mike stood, swayed, but steadied. "What's TATP?" He looked suitably worried.

"Triacetone Triperoxide. An easy to make, highly unstable explosive. Suicide bombers like it. All you need is a willingness to explode, plus acetone, peroxide and hydrochloric acid. It also goes by the name, Mother of

Satan."

"Sounds like something MacGyver would make," Mike said.

It really did sound like a MacGyver do-it-yourself bomb, although I doubt he would've been dumb enough to make this stuff. It liked to explode for almost any reason. Which led me to believe that if indeed it was TATP, then whoever made it knew how to stabilize it.

Sean's phone rang again. It was Kurt.

"Hey, do you know where you are?" I asked.

"No, but I smell bleach and I don't think these retards are cleaning anything."

"Sam, too."

"What do you hear? We know Sam is near a church. Luckily he could give us his GPS coordinates from his phone so we can pick him up." I tried to make it sound like a casual drop-in-and-pick-him-up deal but we both knew it would be ugly.

"I think there is a railroad crossing close by. I heard a truck slow down and then judder a bit over something and a few minutes ago a long train went through."

I waited to see if Iain had any insight into where that might be. He was looking at a Google Earth view of the area.

"Kurt, can you access your phone's GPS coordinates?" I asked.

"I don't have my phone," he replied. "I have a burn phone. My regular phone is in my room."

"Never mind, I'll find you."

Iain pointed to the screen. "I see three crossings in a ten-mile radius, all different lines by the look of it."

I looked my watch. "A train went through a few minutes ago, Kurt said it was long. Call A&O find out if it's one of theirs and which line it's on."

Iain smiled. "I can do better." He brought up another program, typing quickly.

"What are you doing?"

"Using one of our satellites to find the train. If it's a long freight train it'll still be in view."

"How's Mike?" Kurt asked.

"Lost consciousness again, now up and talking. Don't worry, I'm watching him."

"Where's Lee?" Kurt asked.

"No idea. Hoping he'll call in next."

"I think I'm in a cellar. There's one light that's feeble at best. The place is dank."

"Are you hurt?"

"My head aches a bit. Think I was hit across the back of my head."

"Okay. What have you got with you?"

"A phone. No weapon. Can't remember if I had my bag with me."

Iain interrupted the conversation. "I backtracked from the train to the crossing. We've got an approximate location, Kurt. See you soon."

"Looking forward to it," Kurt replied. "Go slow, breathe, and stay safe."

"Don't die," I said and hung up. Something visceral

formed and I didn't much like it. It didn't bother me that someone wanted me. It bothered me that I may not be able to get to Kurt, Sam, and Lee in time.

I unlocked the adjoining room door and ran across my room to my bags. I took a jacket and a shoulder holster and ran back, locking the door behind me.

I put the holster on and shoved my Glock into it, the spare magazines snug in pouches opposite to my gun. I pulled on the jacket and zipped it up. I shoved my hand in my pocket and felt something cold, and withdrew it. I knew without looking at it what it was. I turned my hand over and let my fingers of my left hand slide over the gold design, feeling every ridge. My badge. My reason for being.

Fuck it.

I unzipped the jacket and clipped my badge to my belt then zipped the zipper again.

Iain checked his weapon. Sean did the same. Mike clutched the book in his hands. I smiled at him, hoping it was a reassuring smile. "When this is over, remind me to tell you about a story someone wrote about me."

"Porn?"

"Nah, bit of a national security threat to be honest."

"Sounds like a good story. Was it by a fan?"

"Sort of." I'm sure that's what he thought he was.

Without a phone I could safely use I felt lost. Without my team, I felt like both my arms were missing. I was walking willingly into a setup and all I could hope for was that we'd get to them before the explosives detonated and before whoever was after me won.

I'm a poor loser. Time they learned that.

"I wish Lee would call. We need to go get my team." I felt jittery. That was the best description I could come up with. My insides were liquefying and it was all I could do to stop myself running out the door and headlong into a trap.

Iain's fingers closed around my wrist as I reached for the door. "Rein that in, Conway, you'll get yourself killed."

"I'm fine. We have to go get them."

"This is not fine. Slow down."

"They're. My. Team."

"We'll get them back."

"Whoever is doing this wants me. If that's what it takes, that's what we do."

His hand stayed on my arm. "That's unacceptable. I can call the cavalry, just say the word," he whispered in my ear. "I've still got men on the ground here."

"How many?"

"Four."

I needed them. With his four men, that gave us enough people to do simultaneous extractions. No man left behind.

"Have them meet us out on the road. Half a mile south of here. I want them under my command. This is my team we're going after. There is no such thing as acceptable loss."

He pulled his phone from his pocket and made a call. I

listened as he gave direct orders. Now this was a joint CIA/FBI rescue operation. I hoped no select committee ever heard about it, because defending this would be an act of career suicide.

Sean alerted me to a phone call from Lee.

"Lee, where are you?"

"In the dark. Cellar, maybe. Can't hear anything. It's really quiet."

"You hurt?"

"Not really."

Not really. I'd heard him say "not really" before. Last time he said that he had a sucking chest wound and GSW to the abdomen.

"Smell anything?"

"Almonds and bleach when I go up the stairs to the door, which is locked by the way."

Everything just got worse. Almonds. Could be a compound similar to C4. Not everyone can detect the smell of almonds.

Iain tapped me on the forearm. "They'll be waiting. Did Lee say almonds?"

I nodded.

"Iain, I smell almonds," Lee said. "And bleach."

Clean almonds, awesome.

"Could be explosive 808."

"Or cyanide gas," I commented.

"Either way, it's shitty," Lee added.

"Is that your phone?"

"No, a burn phone."

That meant no GPS. We'd have to rely on tracking the signal via cell towers if there was no other way to find him. Even then, without our specialized software, we could only get an approximate triangulation.

"I'm in a quiet place, really quiet."

"I'll find you," I said. I didn't know how, but I knew I would. "Find some cover and preferably some fresh air."

I motioned to Sean to take Mike with him. I would go with Iain. Mike and I were both targets, so it made sense to separate.

I told the manager at the front we'd be out for a little while on pre-wedding business.

Kurt was west. Sam was east. We decided to go for them first, even though I suspected Lee was in more danger. He was in more danger and in an unknown location; my gut said close. We all went to meet Iain's colleagues. As Iain pulled in behind a black SUV on the shoulder of the road, I looked out over a field and heard Modern West. I listened for a minute, ignoring Iain who tried to speak. 'Angels came down' played, the volume increasing in my head.

If ever I needed a song it was then. A battlefield. Lee was near or on a battlefield. He was in a cellar. What was near a battlefield that could have a cellar?

I leaped out of the car and ran back to Sean. He zapped the window down.

"What?"

"Call Lee tell him we're coming. I think he's in Antietam. I think he's in a cellar near the Dunker church there. He could even be in the church."

"Proof?"

"Yeah, nah, gut."

"Good enough for me. Will call when we have him. I'm taking Mike." Sean turned over the engine. "Take care."

"Bring him home."

He nodded and pulled out.

Iain beckoned me over. I hurried to where he was standing, desperate to get moving on the next two addresses, in case I was wrong about Lee, and Sean needed backup.

"Where's he gone?" he asked, watching Sean disappear into the distance.

"Dunker Church to find Lee. We're going for Kurt and Sam."

"I'll take Sam. Have a feeling you want to bring Kurt back yourself."

"Can you send two of your guys after Sean? I want to make sure they get Lee."

Iain strode to the car in front. I had to take long strides to keep up. The door opened and the driver got out.

"A car left here heading to Antietam. He's going to the Dunker Church. Follow him. Sean O'Hare and Mike Fisher are in the car, they're going to bring back agent Lee Davenport. Make sure it happens."

"Yes, sir," he said. Then looked at me. "Agent Conway, I'm Cory Redfern." His hand stretched out to me.

I shook it. "Go bring my agent home," I said.

"Yes, ma'am."

The passenger waved as Redfern climbed back in the car. They were gone within seconds with nothing remaining but a cloud of dust billowing on the shoulder. As it cleared, the car we'd walked past came back into view. Two men sat waiting.

"I think you know Tim Cosgrove," Iain said as we walked back to the car. The driver lifted his fingers off the steering wheel to acknowledge me.

I gave an understated wave in reply. "Yeah, I do." Fucking small world.

"You ride with him. I'll take his partner, Graeme."

Iain opened the passenger door and stooped to speak. "Graeme, you're with me. Conway will ride with Cosgrove."

As soon as Graeme climbed out of the car, I slipped in and belted up. Iain signaled me to wind the window down. "I'll get Sam. You two be careful."

"Alert and safe, Iain," I replied and zapped up the window.

Chapter Thirty Seven

Right Now

"Where're we going, Conway?" Cosgrove asked, revving the engine.

I gave him directions to where I hoped to find Kurt. When I saw the railroad crossing ahead of us, I slowed my breathing. We drove up, crossed the railway line and then drove back to the first intersection. Cosgrove turned around and pulled over. We were quite a way back from the railroad crossing. We sat for a minute trying to determine if anything gave us a clue.

"Door to door?" Cosgrove said.

"I think we'll have to. We need a cover."

My mind went to a dark place. I fished out the eye shadow I carried in my bag: still enough purples and blues to create a good bruise. I flipped the visor down and opened the vanity mirror.

"Now I've seen everything," Cosgrove murmured. "Makeup now?"

"Watch," I said. I took the makeup brush and worked some magic across my cheekbone and under my left eye. Within about twenty seconds, I had a nasty looking bruise. I grinned at Cosgrove and ripped the pocket on my jacket, then messed up my pretty auburn curls. "Which houses look unoccupied?" I said, scanning the street.

"Three of them, the white Cape Cod over the road and the overgrown cottage two up from that, and the green bungalow." He pointed to farther up our side of the road.

"Okay, just go with whatever I do," I said.

"Wanna give me a clue?"

"You'll see."

I took a deep breath. He would not like the next bit of my cunning plan.

"Drive up the street, slow the car down to a crawl – make like we're arguing then stop, reach over and fling my door open. Tell me to get out. Make it good."

Tim Cosgrove shook his head and grumbled, "Great, let's make a scene, I want to be known as a complete ass."

It seemed prudent to ignore his complaining. "I need a few minutes, so park up somewhere close but not obvious when you've kicked me out the car. Keep me in sight. I'm going on my gut here. I'll try the Cape Cod first. I saw a curtain twitch over there."

The car slowed. Cosgrove and I yelled at each other, enough to make it look good. He stopped suddenly, reached over and flung my door open. "Fucking get out!" he hollered, giving me a light shove which I exaggerated with surprising theatrical flair.

"Asshole!" I shouted back at him while scrambling off the grass verge clutching my bag. Cosgrove took off in a cloud of molten rubber.

Surreptitiously I surveyed the area while hoping to appear as a distraught girlfriend looking for help. Sure that I'd created enough of a spectacle I made my way up the path of the Cape Cod house and bashed on the door. There were no answering footsteps. I waited a few seconds before bashing again, just in case the homeowner was otherwise occupied.

Nothing.

I knocked again and called out, "Please, I just need to use your telephone." I paused. Footsteps.

They drew nearer then stopped.

I hammered on the doorframe and called out, "Please!"

The footsteps started moving again. I stepped back, unzipped my jacket about halfway, ready to reach in and pull my gun from the holster.

The door handle turned then stopped.

A woman called out," Who is it?"

Cobbling together suitable emotion, I answered, "My name is Laura." I let my voice wobble a little. "My boyfriend threw me out of the car."

The handle turned all the way around and the door slowly opened. A woman in her late fifties greeted me then looked over my shoulder.

I turned expecting someone to be there. Nothing.

"Are you all right?" she asked. "That's a horrible bruise." Her eyes strayed from the bruise on my face to the street beyond then back.

"I was trying to find my brother. He's staying out here," I said, emotion rippled and cracked my words wide open. "I don't know where, just that he's near the railroad crossing."

"You poor dear. There was a car at the old Bradford

property yesterday."

"Where's that? I hope it's him," I said. "I need him."

The last three words sealed it for her. I could tell by the sympathy in her eyes she would help me all she could.

"Two houses up, closer to the crossing."

"You didn't see a tall sandy-haired man about an hour or two ago?"

"No, darlin'. A dark-haired man. He was unloading a truck."

Obviously a different dark-haired man from the one rifling through Lee's room at the hotel. Iain had removed him from the equation.

"Maybe he knows where Kurt is," I said.

"Come in and sit for a bit. I'll get some ice for that eye."

"I just need to find Kurt, and then everything will be okay." A rogue tear slipped over my lashes. I wiped it away carefully hoping I didn't dislodge the bruise. "Thank you."

"The dark-haired man went to the Collins's place, too. I think he could be a property manager or something. Heard those places were up for rent."

"Can you show me?"

She stepped out the door and pointed back to the green house.

"Thank you so much." I walked down the path to the sidewalk and hoped the Unsub wasn't watching but I also hoped that Kurt somehow knew I was close.

The green house felt right. The derelict tumbling down house was close to the railway line. Tears welled and took me by surprise. The horrible helpless feeling of not knowing for sure where he was, or where any of my team was, thumped with relentless desperation in my chest. This glimpse of what life is like for Delta on the few occasions when something happened to me and they've been in my position, sucked.

I crossed the road as Cosgrove cruised by and pulled up two houses back. Slowly I walked up the old and broken concrete path where weeds grew in the cracks, the front garden also overgrown with weeds, yet someone had mowed the lawn. There were no signs of life as I climbed three steps to the front porch; I knocked on the front door which had seen better days. Chipped and peeling dark green paint showed patches of pink primer.

I knocked. Waiting a sensible few seconds longer, I wondered about an alarm system but doubted anyone would bother alarming houses out here. Who would burgle them? Raccoons?

I knocked again and listened for signs of life. Nothing.

Glanced about, checking no one was watching, I pulled a small leather case from my purse and took two thin pieces of metal. Never leave home without lock-picking tools, gun, and clean underwear.

I tumbled the lock and let myself in, relieved there was no alarm. Four doors opened off the hallway, two on each side. Straight ahead was an archway. I glimpsed linoleum; kitchen maybe.

Barely breathing, I closed the door behind me. My gun in my right hand, I used my left hand to open the first door. Empty. I edged around the room to a large cupboard and flung open the doors. Empty.

Breathe.

I exhaled and drew in a long breath. I knew I was no good to Kurt if I did anything stupid now.

I cleared the next room. Still nothing.

From within the third room I heard footsteps outside. Ducking out of view I watched as best I could through the window. Dark brown hair. All I could see was the top of someone's head. I swallowed hard and moved to get a better view as the person moved toward the back of the house.

One more room to check before the kitchen. Moving with care, I cleared the last room and about to step into the hallway when I heard a door open and close, followed by heavy footsteps. The footfalls crossed the floor, stopped, turned around and retreated. The door opened and closed.

Why?

I breathed and listened, everything above the sound of my heart amplified. Small stones crunched underfoot as the man walked back along the outside of the house. Then nothing.

Sudden movement and the front steps creaked. Metal met metal. A key in the lock.

He must've forgotten something. I stepped into the kitchen where the smell of bleach swamped me as I cast around for somewhere to hide. I saw a door and figured it led to a cellar.

On the floor right in front of the door were two long rectangular containers, each about a foot long and six inches high; inside each were two smaller containers full of white crystals.

The outer container held rapidly melting ice. As the ice melted, the water escaped through two small holes and ran across the floor in a small river.

Footsteps sounded behind me in the hallway. I didn't hear the door shut. He must've left it open. I backed away from the cellar door and flattened myself against the wall by the archway at the entrance to the kitchen. The footsteps grew closer and closer.

He hesitated. A phone rang. The man answered the call and walked back toward the front door. I could hear his voice but not what he said. As long as his voice stayed where it was I had a chance to investigate the icy containers.

The inner containers held the explosive in its crystal form. The ice was almost all gone and it wouldn't be long before the crystals warmed up. Once they reached above fifty degrees Fahrenheit they'd explode without any help. I checked for anything that would remotely detonate the improvised bomb.

There was something not right about the outer containers. They were higher than they looked from the top. False bottoms, maybe.

My brain processed everything I'd seen. The TATP was the initiator and I suspected the odd-looking larger containers contained some kind of plastic explosive, C4 or something similar. Lee mentioned almonds. Could be Iain was right about the Unsub using Explosive 808 – preferable to thinking Lee would be exposed to cyanide gas. The ice had almost melted. The containers needed moving and fast

The talking stopped. A massive thud shook the floor. The last of the icy water ran from the containers, leaving only about five pieces of ice to melt. I shucked my bag from my shoulder, letting it slide silently down my arm and onto the floor.

A familiar voice yelled out, "Coming in, hold your fire!" followed by Cosgrove's boots thundering down the hallway.

"We have to move the bombs," I said. "I think the TATP is on top of plastic explosive." At that moment, I heard a knock from the inside of the cellar door. "Kurt?"

A muffled reply came, "Conway."

I stood close to the door and yelled, "Count to five then try to open the door."

Cosgrove and I looked around for a safe place for the explosives. Out the back door was the only option. I didn't even ask what happened to the Unsub as I tried to open the door. "Locked."

Cosgrove ran back down the hallway and returned with keys. He threw them at me. "One of those should fit."

One Mississippi.

I fumbled the keys, trying to find one that fitted.

Breathe.

Two Mississippi.

I slowed my breathing and heart rate. My hand stopped shaking. A key slid into the lock. The lock opened. I swung the door wide and slipped back into the kitchen as Cosgrove passed me carrying one bomb with the utmost care.

Three Mississippi.

I picked the remaining one up, gingerly carrying it, hoping I could get it to the backyard in time.

"Dump and run," Cosgrove yelled over his shoulder from the middle of the overgrown yard. He disappeared from view.

Four Mississippi.

I hoped I was far enough from the house to set mine down. I lowered it to the ground, turned and ran back to the house. I wanted to get Kurt out before the backyard became a crater. Cosgrove caught up with me.

Five Mississippi.

We plowed through the doorway.

Splinters of wood flew into the room as Kurt crashed through the cellar door. Tim grabbed his arm, turned him to the hallway and ran with him. I was right behind them as a massive explosion rocked the area. The concussion wave almost knocked me off my feet as dust, wood, and bricks flew through the air. A large chunk of something crashed down in front of me. I scrambled over it and fell out the front door, tumbling head over heels down the steps and onto the path.

I lay staring up at billowing dust clouds as silence

blanketed the whole area.

My name cut through the stunned quietness.

"Conway!" Kurt hollered.

"Over here," I called and pulled myself to my feet.

Kurt walked towards me. "Everyone okay?"

"Yeah," Cosgrove replied from about ten feet away from me. He had his phone in his hand. "I'm calling Iain. Let him know what they're dealing with."

In case they don't already know.

"Tell Iain this ... TATP is the initiator, sitting in a melting and free-draining ice bath above some kind of plastic explosive. How long they have depends on ambient temperature." The words tumbled from my mouth and all I could hope was they made sense. I stopped thinking about it to keep the "what ifs" at bay.

My attention turned to Kurt. "Kurt?"

"I'm fine," he said. "You?"

I dusted off my clothes and straightened up. Everything felt okay, little bit muffled but okay. "I'm okay," I replied. I remembered he'd said someone hit him. "Your head?"

"Nothing to worry about. Come on." Kurt reached out and took my hand. I couldn't help but smile.

"Cosgrove, any word from the others?" I asked.

"Sam's free. Same set up as here."

"And Lee?"

"Took longer to find him, he is under an outbuilding. They're getting him out."

They're running out of time.

The house was a wreck. Splintered wood, loose bricks. The dust settled, revealing more damage. Half the roof had gone, peeled back like a giant sardine can. No way would Kurt have survived if we hadn't taken the bombs outside. No one could've walked out of that if the bombs had detonated in the house.

"Where's the dark-haired guy?" I asked.

"Still inside," Cosgrove replied. "Didn't have time to move him."

"Is he useful?"

"I didn't kill him, but that's not to say he's still breathing now." Cosgrove pulled something from his pocket and threw it to me.

I caught it. A cell phone. "His?"

"Yeah, we need to find out who he talked to."

I looked at the phone and put it in my pocket, anything that phone contained required a clear head and mine wasn't. "Let's go see if he's still with us," I said. "Where was he?"

"Front room, left, inside the door."

Kurt's hand tightened around mine. "You're not going in there. Cosgrove?"

"On it."

"Cosgrove, get a photo of him," I said.

He picked a path through the scattered debris and into the house. We heard the floor creak as he stepped onto it.

"Carefully!" I called. Minutes dragged by. "Come on, Iain," I whispered.

Kurt let my hand go. "What's with your eye?"

"Nothing. It's makeup," I said, not taking my eyes off the front door. The more I looked, the more the door resembled a smashed face.

"Do I want to ask?"

"Later, I'll tell you all about it once everyone's safe."

Cosgrove called out from the house, "Kurt – there's a bag in the back of my car. Bring it to me."

"Stay here," Kurt said and ran toward car.

I wasn't going anywhere. The ground pulsated. The world was alive and thumping. Creaks and groans from the damaged house added to the ambience.

Chapter Thirty Eight

Welcome To The Jungle

"Hey, Conway." Kurt's voice wrapped around me. "Come on."

"What?" I must've missed his exit from the house.

"We're going to get Lee," Kurt said. "You all right?"

"Just great." I looked at the house. "Where's Cosgrove?"

"Taking care of something. He's coming."

Kurt opened a car door. "Get in," he said. "Buckle up."

Kurt closed the door after I climbed in. He opened the driver's door and climbed in. Tim Cosgrove ran toward us carrying my bag and another bag.

He clambered in the front passenger seat and slammed the door. "Go," he said.

Over the sound of the car engine, I heard sirens. Cosgrove reached his arm back and dropped my bag on the seat next to me.

We were almost at the intersection when another explosion rocked the area. I turned my head and looked out the back window. Bits of house crashed down onto the road.

"Did you do that?" I asked Cosgrove.

"Yes. A bit of house cleaning."

"Where's the dark-haired guy?" I said.

"He wasn't much help," Cosgrove replied.

"Did you get anything out of him?"

"He was hired to grab you." Cosgrove leaned his head back on the headrest. "The person who hired him used the name Mr. Green and conducted all business online."

Could've been through the website the other guy used.

"That's helpful," I mumbled. I knew things about Tim Cosgrove and one of the things I knew about him was that people didn't withhold information when he asked for it.

"I got a photo. I'll get Iain to run it through our databases ... he has access to yours as well."

"He didn't do this by himself. There is no way one guy subdued my team by himself. I doubt he could move a drugged Sam alone." Never mind trying to get Lee and Kurt into a truck or van.

"Hired muscle," Iain suggested. "We'll find them."

Two fire engines and an ambulance screamed past us.

"How much longer is this shit going to go on?" I rested my head on the cool glass and closed my eyes.

"Stay with us, Conway," Kurt said.

I opened an eye to see him glance at me in the rearview mirror. "I'm fine," I said. "Eyes on the road."

More sirens. The town must be out of fire engines and ambulances.

I'm not fine. I'm fucking awesome, just not right this second. My eyes closed again while I summoned the awesome back. The car stopped before it returned. Voices bounced around the car interior until some of them took shape and the words made sense.

"Hey, Chicky Babe, you all right?" Sam said.

"Fine, you?"

"Good to go. Let's go get Lee."

"You riding with us?"

"Yeah."

I racked my brain to recall who went for Sam. "Where's Iain?"

"He's behind us, in the other car."

No point saying anything else. My eyes closed but I heard Kurt tell Sam to watch me. Really, where was I going? Leap from a moving vehicle? Retreat into the happy place that is my mind? I struggled to suppress bubbling laughter. It worked for about two beats then laughter filled the car.

"Chicky?" Sam nudged me with his arm. "Chill."

That'll work. First, he's worried I'll somehow disappear from the moving vehicle and now he wants me to chill.

"This whole thing is ludicrous," I spluttered. "All of it. Eddie, Beatrice, some loon wanting to discredit and remove me from my life, the shit Carla and Joey pulled, everything that's happened to Mike ..." More laughter broke free. "It's fucking ridiculous and we can't do anything about it. I just want to go back to my life. I want to go home and see Mitch." The craziness grew into a massive ball of colored threads. "Colonel Mustard did it outside the rec room with an IED and Mr. Green did it in the kitchen with another IED. Would've been more fun if it was a lead pipe. IED has been done to death."

I knew the car had stopped.

"Chicky. Breathe."

"Sam, it's fucking nuts," I said, unable to stop more laughter. "It's like a game of Clue on steroids." Tears ran down my cheeks unchecked as I gulped air, hoping to curb my mirth. My door flew open. Kurt reached over me and undid the seat belt. He grabbed me by the shoulders and pulled me from the car. Laughter erupted with renewed vigor, mixed with anger. My right hand curled into a fist.

Standing in front of Kurt, I watched many emotions race across his face as he struggled to determine what was happening. His hands held my arms at my sides.

"Let me go," I spluttered, trying to pull free as more crazy laughter spiraled from within.

"Not until you're calm. I don't want you swinging at me." He dropped his voice and whispered continually in my ear, "It's going to be okay."

My life had become a series of badly thought-out plots in a soap opera and everything was going to be okay? Yeah right, that made a lot of sense. I struggled against his grip.

"Relax, Conway."

Concentrating, I reined in the anger coursing through me, leaving strangled giggles backed by choked amusement. Finally, nothing.

For several minutes, I reminded myself to breathe and worked to stop any more random laughter. When I was sure I had a handle on it, I took a deep breath. My fist opened and my fingers relaxed.

"We good?" Kurt asked. "You're not going to take a swing at me?"

"I'm good. Sorry."

Kurt let my arms go. "Don't be. You're right. This is ridiculous. The position we've been shunted into is almost unfathomable," Kurt said. His eyes studied mine with clinical interest. "We're going to discuss what any of this has to do with Carla and Joey in great detail very soon and we're going to talk about Mitch."

"What are you talking about?"

"At the beginning of that hysterical outburst you said something along the lines of 'the shit Carla and Joey pulled' and you mentioned going home to Mitch."

They were go-nowhere conversations. I'd certainly not meant to say anything about them. My safest option was to pretend I didn't. "Is Lee okay?"

"Ask him yourself." Kurt indicated for me to turn around.

Lee and Mike were standing with Sam, Sean, Iain, Tim Cosgrove and the three guys I didn't know. Lee grinned at me.

"We're all okay," he said. "And I just invited the boys here to your wedding."

My wedding. Oh crap. My wedding.

Sandra.

"You think Sandra is waiting at the hotel for us?"

"Probably," Lee replied. A strange solemnity descended. "You called it, Ellie ... we owe you."

"I did my job. You'd do the same for me."

After much congratulatory handshaking, everyone moved off to various vehicles. Except Mike. He stood in front of me, a grin on his face and his pale blue eyes glinting in the sun.

"What?"

"Standing in front of a real life FBI legend makes my heart race a bit," he said. Mike kissed my cheek. "Twice now I've owed you a debt of gratitude for my brother's life."

I shook my head. "I did my job."

It could've gone badly, we were lucky. I was lucky. But it was really nice to hear.

"We should be in the same car going back," Mike said. "Wedding."

"Yeah."

"I'm coming with you," Kurt said. He pointed to Sean's car. "Over there."

Iain took point and pulled out first, followed by us, then Tim Cosgrove, and finally the two guys I didn't know. Sirens filled the air. I saw the lights of a fire engine racing toward us.

The small convoy headed back to our hotel to face whatever was waiting for us there. We'd left our mark in West Virginia and Maryland, without a doubt.

My mother's voice echoed in my head, "Out of the frying pan into the fire."

A sigh escaped. She was right. And it would be a balancing act until all the issues were resolved. Always being thrown from the frying pan to fire and back again.

Chapter Thirty Nine
Everybody Knows

Catalina, the hotel manager, waited for us in the lobby. I didn't think I was in a fit state to make small talk.

"Mr. Fisher, can I confirm the final details before the ceremony?" She stopped when she saw me. "Do you need medical attention?"

Her question and facial expression took me by surprise. Okay, I was probably filthy but I wasn't bleeding. Was I? Someone would've told me. "No."

Mike stepped in and spun charm like a spider weaves silk, reeling the woman into his web. "We've been all over the battlefields at Antietam. We thought it would be fun to stage an impromptu reenactment."

"I'm sure it was fun," she replied, not taking her eyes off me.

"Much," Mike replied. "We'll meet you in the bar in five minutes to go over the final details." His hand rested on the small of my back and steered me toward the hallway. "We clearly need to clean up."

I whispered in his ear, "I could do with a drink."

"Me, too," he replied.

"I'll chill some champagne," Catalina called after us. Bionic ears. Damn, it was too late to squash the intro to the *Bionic Woman* that surged through my mind. I took a breath and waited for it to pass.

Iain and his men headed for the restaurant; I guess they were hungry. Would be good if I learned all their names.

I caught sight of myself in a mirror on the way back to our rooms. Jesus! Clothing filthy, smeared fake bruising halfway down my face, bits of twig and grass in my hair. Mike opened my door for me.

Kurt stopped us both before we could escape into the sanctuary of our rooms. "I'm getting my bag," he said.

I grinned. "I've heard that before."

"I'm coming right back."

"Heard that before, too," I said. "I'm going to stand right here in the doorway and make sure you do."

Mike slung his arm around my shoulder. "I'll be right here with her."

"You're both hilarious," Kurt muttered and hurried to his room. We watched as he opened the door. The door closed behind him.

We waited.

Moments later the door opened again and Kurt came out carrying his black backpack.

"See?" Kurt said, holding the pack by one strap. "In."

"We've gotta meet the manager in five minutes," I said. "And I really need to shower."

"No kidding. Go shower. I want to check out Mike's head."

I dropped my bag on the bed and pulled out the cell phone Cosgrove gave me from my pocket. I put the phone into my bag for later. The possibility of contaminating data or being accused of such if I examined the phone myself meant I had to wait until I could get it to the lab. I didn't expect the phone would hold clues to the identity of the person behind the mess.

Right now I trusted there were enough armed men in the hotel to prevent anything horrendous happening to me. Flushing out Mike's stalker – and hoping I was right about his identity – was the priority. Otherwise, we'd planned a wedding for nothing.

I gathered clean clothes and shut myself in the bathroom. The wedding dress still lay on the chair. My hands were dirty so I opened the bathroom door and using a clean towel, I wrapped the dress and carried it at arm's length from the bathroom. Kurt and Mike were not in my room.

A horrible feeling of déjà vu swamped me.

I folded the dress into its box on the floor by the bed. My heart thumped in an unnatural rhythm. Something in the next room dropped onto a hard surface. "Kurt!"

Kurt's head poked around the adjoining doorway. "You need me?"

"No, just didn't see you. What was that thump? Mike okay?"

"He dropped his shoe. He's fine. Shower," he said, tapping his watch.

The hot water felt so good, having a fast shower wasn't easy. I dressed, combed my wet hair and blasted it with the hair dryer. After giving my auburn wig a much needed shake and brush, and satisfied it was twig free, I tucked up my hair and pulled it on. Mineral powder and mascara made me look human again.

Kurt sat in a chair, waiting for me. He looked almost recovered from the day's excitement, apart from a small graze above his left eye. I heard the shower running in Mike's room.

"Mike in the shower?"

"Yes."

"How's your head?"

Kurt smiled and his eyes softened. "That's my line."

"Not today." I studied his face for a moment. "You okay?" I asked.

"Seem to be."

"Let me know if anything changes." I searched through the bags on the floor looking for a clean lightweight jacket I could wear over my short-sleeved tee shirt. I wasn't looking to cover a gun, just scars.

"That's my line too," he said.

"I kinda like dishing them out for a change," I replied. "Not so fond of having my team taken like that though."

"Not fun is it? Being on the other side?"

"Yeah, because it's such a barrel of laughs being abducted ..." I found a jacket and pulled it on.

"That's not what I meant."

I knew what he meant. I'd sooner be the one taken than the one left behind. Being on the outside looking in, now that's scary. Too many variables.

"We're all okay," I said and ducked back into the bathroom to get my shoulder holster and gun from where

I'd left them under a towel on the floor.

As I dropped the shoulder rig and Glock into a drawer in the nightstand, I smiled. It felt okay to leave them behind.

"What did you mean about Carla and Joey?"

Even though I knew it was coming, I wasn't prepared for the question. To be honest, I'd hoped Kurt had forgotten I'd said anything.

I sat on the edge of my bed and tried to keep all emotion from my voice. Just the facts, ma'am. "I found a folder of hers on her flash drive that suggests she and Joey were trying to trap a pedophile, by themselves."

Kurt leaped to his feet. "Christ!"

"Tell me about it."

"And?" He paced the room before coming to a standstill in front of me.

"Sean looked at the files. The name that the person used was Eddie Connelly."

"That doesn't seem like a coincidence," Kurt said as he sat next to me.

"No, it doesn't seem like a coincidence. They were introduced to the Unsub by someone from their class at school. A girl named Charlotte Campbell. There's an Amber Alert out on her," I said.

"Does her name ring any bells?"

"Not really, but I keep thinking it should. Not something I can check considering my situation." I knew I had to tell him the rest. "I threw Charlotte's name out to Seamus and the quasi-UN while I was interviewing them, just in case. They'd never heard her name but they did know the Skype name, Mr. RightGuy. He was the one Carla was talking to."

"They told you what?" Kurt asked.

"That he's someone who targets high-profile kids."

Carla was a high-profile kid even though I didn't want her to be; high profile because of my former relationship with Rowan, my job, and The Butterfly Foundation.

"Who's working this?" Kurt asked.

"I don't know if anyone is. I just found the files. I haven't opened a case." Hard to work a case like that on the run. "Someone must have a case open if there is an Amber Alert out on Charlotte Campbell but has anyone linked her disappearance to this Mr. RightGuy? I doubt it."

Kurt took a deep breath. "Do you think Seamus Kennedy, Charlotte, Carla, and Mr. RightGuy have anything to do with the case that has Owen so hot under the collar? The one she called me in on because she needed a doctor for the kid?"

"It's possible."

"Who is going to work this, Ellie? Because I know you and walking away is not how you operate."

"Not us. I can't. I'll fucking kill that Mr. RightGuy freak if I get near him. Much better to let trained professionals who aren't answerable to select committees deal with him."

The expression on Kurt's face told me I'd done the right thing by letting Misha's friends handle it. I chewed my lip as memories of my last week with Carla forced their way through my defenses.

"I'll give some thought to the Charlotte Campbell connection. Sam or Lee might have some ideas." Kurt ran his hand through his hair. "We thought the kids were hiding something ..."

"You guys all thought they were having sex and I thought they were doing drugs."

"We were wrong. So wrong." His hand touched my forearm. "This must be hard for you. You okay?"

"No, not really." I didn't mean to spill honesty like that. I'm always okay.

Kurt's expression changed in that split second, from unease to alarm. "What can I do?"

"Not look like that. I'll be okay, Kurt."

The dead feel no pain.

Our conversation stopped abruptly as Mike walked into the room, wearing a pale gray long-sleeved V-neck shirt, clean jeans and black dress shoes. He'd shaved. In his hand was a charcoal colored leather jacket. I wasn't unimpressed.

"Did I interrupt?" Mike asked. "I can come back."

"You didn't. We're done here."

Kurt nodded. "We're done." His hand moved from my arm.

"So you're ready?" Mike asked, plunging his arms into his jacket and shrugging it over his shoulders.

"Yes," I replied. "Can I let you take charge of the whole wedding detail thing?"

"Sure. Happy to do it," he replied. "But are you sure you'll be okay with that?"

"Yes."

I really didn't care. It was a fake marriage to trap a nut job with me as the bait. I wanted it over so I could find out what the hell my kid thought she was doing and what it had to do with her death. Intense had re-entered the building with friends. Intense brought along passionate, extreme, concentrated kick-fucking-ass and an urge to take my gun out of the drawer and wear it with my badge. That was not a good idea.

At a knock at the door, Kurt checked the peephole and opened the door. A smile bounced from his lips to the person at the door. I took a breath and wished hell away.

"Ready to get married?" Sandra said with her usual verve and bubble. "So typical of you, Laura, you always get the good men." She embraced me then moved onto Mike.

"We're just going to finalize the plans for tomorrow," I said. "Give us half an hour then come find us, we'll be in the bar. Bring Kurt with you. In fact, don't let him out of your sight."

"I heard there was a problem ... caught Lee before he dove in the shower," Sandra said.

"There was. Bring the whole gang when you come," I said. "Iain and his men are in the restaurant. Watch Kurt. Head injury."

Kurt shook his head, smiling. "You enjoying this?" he asked me.

"Hell, yes," I replied then turned back to Sandra. "Be aware there is fucktard loose in the hotel who wants to either kill me or Mike. Personally I don't think he'll make a move now until the wedding and then I think he'll try for me, to make Mike suffer for longer."

"I'll keep a watch out. Do we have a picture?"

"Ask Lee. And thanks."

Mike held the door. "Come on future Mrs. Fisher, let's go drink free champagne and make out."

I just wanted to go home.

Chapter Forty
Dance Me To The End

Four sips into the glass of champagne and I knew I needed food. I ordered stuffed potato skins and chicken dippers and enjoyed more champagne while I waited.

Mike and Catalina discussed how the day would go. When choice of music came up, I discovered I had a preference. "Not Elvis," I said. "I'd like Bon Jovi,"

"Which song, sweetheart?" Mike asked, topping up my glass.

"'Thank you for loving me.'"

"That's a beautiful song," Catalina said, typing on her tablet.

The bubbles tickled my nose and distracted me from thoughts of songs. To be honest, they distracted me from all thought. Bubbles and I have a history and it's not pretty. I discovered not caring was my theme for the evening. A wall of who-gives-a-fuck crashed over me, setting off the struggle to remain in the moment. "What is?"

Mike laughed. "Excuse my fiancée, we've had an entertaining but long day and I think the bubbles are going to her head."

"Think? I know," I said.

Catalina laughed. "You two are adorable."

This would end badly. Mike took me by surprise with a

warm kiss.

I whispered, "If you kiss me like that, you'd better follow through."

He kissed me again and lingered way too long. As he slowly pulled away, I resisted the temptation to grab his jacket lapels and yank him back. There were still enough active brain cells to prevent an act of no return. But for how long? My eyes stayed focused on Mike. As the images reached my engaged brain I wondered if he was acting for the benefit of Catalina and the room, or if the look in his eyes was real. Chancy thinking. Acting, I hoped.

The arrival of food interrupted the moment: saved by potato skins, chicken dippers and sour cream. Sandra arrived shortly after the food. She introduced herself to Catalina and promised to help with the remainder of the details. I ate, drank champagne and wondered about the kiss.

Champagne gave everything a soft focus, a dangerous soft focus. The little part of my brain untouched by the bubbles jumped up and down and screamed loudly that he was acting. The rest of me wondered how a person could act chemistry and dilated pupils.

"Laura, did you decide on music for the reception?" Sandra asked.

I shook my head. A wicked grin tweaked the corners of my mouth as a thought crystalized. "Grange, play their new album," I said and watched Sandra bite back a smirk as I added, "Pick the tracks co-written by his former girlfriend, they're way better than his stuff."

A poetry- and song-writing special agent, now that's what the world had been lacking until I came along.

"Good call."

I thought so. I'm sure Rowan would be delighted to know I'd chosen his music for my fake wedding. A flash of clarity told me the reason I was confused by Mike had something to do with breaking up with Rowan. Walking away from a guy like Rowan was never going to be smooth or easy. I really needed to go home.

"Shall we choose the menu?" Catalina asked. She produced the usual lunch menu. "Perhaps you'd like to select a few options from here?"

Mike took the menu. I lifted my glass and took another sip. Then another. Mike pointed out three entrees, three mains and four desserts. He reached for the bottle and filled my glass again.

I leaned close and murmured in his ear, "Are you trying to get me drunk?"

His arm slid around my shoulders, he pulled me close. His words ruffled my hair and tickled my ear, "What if I am?"

"You're playing with fire."

"You can stop lifting that glass any time."

He had me there with simple logic.

"I could ..."

But that wasn't going to happen. It'd been a day fraught with adrenaline and at times panic. I wanted to relax. It was more than that though. I wanted to cut loose, to forget for a few hours that I had a fucking great big price tag on my head and that Owen wanted me in cuffs, and that Joaunes wanted Mike to suffer.

Mike and Sandra took care of ironing out the rest of the details and sorted the timing. I drank more champagne and ate, safe in the knowledge that nine armed men weren't far away and tonight everything would be okay.

Faith in men with guns, that's how I roll.

Catalina left with her tablet, but not before assuring us the wedding would go without a hitch. I believed her assurances. Or rather, I believed that she believed them.

She also said she'd hired a local photographer to capture the event. Let's hope the photographer doesn't capture carnage and mayhem.

The wedding was set for ten in the morning. I wanted eight but apparently, that's a little early for a wedding. This made me wonder why the first meal after a wedding is referred to as a breakfast.

Sitting in the restaurant bar, in a booth, with Mike's arm around my shoulders wasn't a hardship. He smelled good. He tasted pretty good, too.

"I'll leave you two to discuss whatever you have on your minds," Sandra said with a smile. She waggled a finger in our direction. "I'll be with the gang, over yonder." She tipped her head toward the very back of the bar and stood up. "I see they've attracted a few stray women."

Hardly surprising.

"Have fun," I said.

"What's on your mind?" Mike asked, sipping his champagne.

"Champagne," I replied, lifting my glass. "Has a habit of ending badly."

"Yet you're still drinking ..."

"I was hoping there'd be a different ending this time."

"How would you like it to end?" he asked, his eyes locking on mine. Is it possible to feel heat through someone's eyeballs?

This was hazardous new ground. All it would take was a small shake to destroy it all. I swallowed another mouthful of champagne and gave his question more thought. Then changed the subject entirely. I knew where this could potentially go and how it might end. Fittingly I also remembered a Hans Christian Anderson quote, "Enjoy life. There is plenty of time to be dead." If I needed any encouragement, that was it.

"How's your head?"

His eyebrows rose. "It's fine. No lasting damage according to Kurt."

"You should still be under observation for twenty-four hours."

"You volunteering?"

"Nah," I lifted my glass. "Drinking."

Music filled the room drowning out the talking, laughing and jovial behavior from the corner.

"They're having fun," Mike commented. "Want to join them?"

I shook my head. "You can, but I'm fine here."

"I'd sooner stay with you, if that's okay?"

Sure, whatever. My shoulders refused to shrug. Traitors. I changed the subject. "Have you seen Joaunes?"

"No."

"He checked in though, right?"

"That's what I heard from Catalina."

"He in here anywhere?"

Mike cast his eyes around the room, lingering on groups of people. He shook his head and winced. "Don't see him."

"Head sore?"

"Yeah, a little bit."

You get that with head injuries.

"I expected Joaunes to make contact," I said. "Find out what room he's in and invite him down for a drink."

"Seriously?"

"Uh huh. I want him where I can see him." I finished my glass. He refilled it.

"Go call him. Get him in here in full view of everyone. I also want to see how he reacts toward you."

"Don't go anywhere."

"I'm right here."

I watched him walk toward the bar and how Lee threw an arm around him and man-hugged him.

At that moment, a surprising sense of joy welled and overpowered the relief that everyone was okay. Kurt looked in my direction. He mouthed, "Are you okay?"

I smiled and nodded in reply.

Sam slid across the floor and into the seat opposite me. "Chicky."

"Sam."

"Champagne. Celebrating?"

"Yeah. A little bit. We got you all back."

"We had faith." He bumped my fist.

"Kurt okay over there?"

"Yeah, Sandra and I are watching him," Sam said.

I knew Mike and I had to join the throng and wait for the man wreaking havoc on his life. I really had no proof it was him. Just me and my gut, or maybe me and my ability to tap into the universe, and pull information from the ether. Either way, we couldn't arrest him until he made his move, we had nothing on him.

"Did Kurt mention anything about Carla to you?"

"He asked if I knew a Charlotte Campbell. Said she had something to do with a situation Carla and Joey got themselves into. Turns out she's no relation to Iain, over there," Sam said.

That I knew already. "Ever heard the name before?"

"Wasn't there a Campbell killed during the Hudson Hawk case?" Sam said.

I took another sip of champagne and let the bubbles take me back to the beginning of that case. A list of the dead scrolled in my mind's eye – not a short list. A vile case, geographically spread across Virginia. As the names rolled on, I remembered details of the crime scenes.

"Christine Campbell, killed in her home in Alexandria.

Two kids who were with their father at the time. And she had a chicken, a pet in a cage in the house."

I remembered being surprised seeing a chicken in a cage in an apartment.

"We'll look into the case as soon as we can. I guarantee you we will find out if Charlotte is related to Christine and what she really had to do with Carla and Joey," Sam said. "We will, Chicky Babe."

"I know. There's an Amber alert out on the Campbell kid, Sam."

"I know that, too."

Another sip of champagne went a long way to removing the images of the crime scenes attached to Hawk.

I decided that when Mike came back we'd join everyone else and I would open a bar tab for the guys. Maybe I'd even check out the names of the guys who helped rescue Lee.

Chapter Forty One
I'm Your Man

Several couples entered the bar and settled at tables. The music grew louder. Iain, his men, and Delta took over some tables not far from the bar and looked as though they were enjoying themselves. Sandra floated between the booth where I sat and the tables. Mike hovered. I didn't want to join the others until our target arrived.

From the outside looking in, I witnessed relaxed happy patrons, laughing, talking, drinking, and eating. The longer I watched, the easier it was for me to spot the telltale signs of disquiet. Not even disquiet really, but everyone was waiting for something.

A man walked into the room and up to the bar. Propped against the bar, he glanced around the room. I watched without watching. His eyes paused on Lee then roamed until he found Mike.

Mike saw him and acknowledged his presence by tipping his chin upward. Lee followed suit, so tuned into his brother he seemed to sense what he was doing.

I rose from my seat and joined Mike. He looked at me as I slipped my hand into his.

"Is that him?" I asked, throwing a smile at the man by the bar. Mike followed my smile.

"Yes. Now what?"

"Let's go say 'hello' and let him congratulate you on

landing me." I grinned.

Mike hesitated. Houston, we have a problem. "You all right?"

"Not really. Is this safe?"

"Of course." I did have my fingers crossed, heading for drunk and about to meet someone I thought was a potential killer. "Come on, this is the plan, remember?"

"I remember, just after today, I don't ..." He turned to face me. "... I don't want anything to happen to you."

"It won't." Not tonight anyway. Where would the fun be in killing me before the wedding? "It's fine. Now make it look as though you are saying something sweet, he's watching."

Mike's expression softened. His eyes searched mine. "It would kill me if anything happened to you."

"And that is why you got an SAG and a Teen Choice Award this year."

He smiled. "How'd you know that?"

"Never mind." I might have noticed his name come up during award season. "Let's say 'hello.'"

We crossed the bar and Mike called out to Joaunes, "Hey, man, thanks for coming."

"Wouldn't miss your wedding," he replied. "And this is the soon-to-be Mrs. Mike Fisher I presume?" Joaunes extended his hand to me. "I'm Joe."

"Laura," I replied, shaking his hand. His fingers tightened around mine and squeezed a little too much. I flexed my hand to shake him loose, glad it wasn't my injured hand. I shoved my hand in my pocket to prevent him reattaching. One handshake and I already knew why the women in the bar at Torrent Falls wanted nothing to do with him. But it remained to be seen if he was the one who was carrying out the acts of terrorism against Mike.

I'd thought the magic word. Terrorism. Acts of terror. The Patriot Act swam before my eyes, the words parting to allow a glimpse of Joaunes locked in a cell. The camera pulled back until a sign was in full focus. Welcome to Guantanamo Bay.

I blinked and realized I'd missed some conversation. Mike slipped his arm around my waist. "We met in an alleyway," he said, letting humor rise in his voice.

"You're kidding?"

"He's really not," I replied. "Mike swooped to my rescue."

I knew I didn't have to worry about Mike losing the thread. He'd play off anything I said and I hoped he'd see what I wanted to achieve. Mike the hero. Mike the hunky actor. Mike the lucky bastard who has everything.

"I was the champion of the alleyway that day," Mike said with a grin. "It's not every day that a guy gets to play hero for a gorgeous woman."

"Sounds like a story that requires a toast," Joaunes said.

I didn't disagree. Hell, I had three glasses of champagne on board, I'd agree to almost anything. It was a miracle I was thinking and speaking with any sort of coherence. I wasn't a hundred percent sure I was thinking clearly but it was much too late to worry about that. I realized we'd sat down and I had no idea when that happened.

Champagne ... not such a smart choice.

"So tell me, Joe, how long have you known Mike?"

"Most of our lives," he said, ordering a drink. "I knew him before he was Michael Fisher. Back when he was just Mike. Do you all call him Fisher?"

I attempted a confused look.

"What do you mean?"

"His email said the wedding of Michael Fisher and Laura Graham."

"Oh, I see. It's just easier. It's what the world calls him."

"So you'll be Mrs. Fisher?"

"To the world, yes."

Look at me, the drunken diplomat who can quietly wind up Joaunes.

"I thought you'd go for a big wedding," Joe said to Mike. "Invite the world and make all the newspapers." He sounded a little disappointed.

"I'd sooner keep this a private moment," Mike replied. "So much of my life is conducted in the public eye, this ... this is our day."

He was good. I was impressed. Joe wasn't. I could tell by the sneer building on his lips.

"Excuse me a minute," I said and slipped away to see Lee.

I tapped Sam and he joined Mike and the lone wedding guest.

"Lee, did we ever get the video cam footage from that TGI?"

"We did, but then all hell broke loose."

"Can we access it from here?"

He frowned. "I think so."

"I want you to try, I want confirmation that Joaunes Levy was at that bar where we picked up that fanatic."

"Do you have doubts?"

"No, I don't. But I'd like to get our ducks in a row."

Lee spun around and grabbed Sandra affectionately by the arm. "Hey, Sandy, got a job for you."

"Right now?" Sandra asked with a grin.

"Please."

"How I can I resist that?" Sandra replied. "Be right back, boys."

Lee and Sandra slipped away to do my bidding.

Owen jumped into my thoughts. There was a good chance she'd be ready to give up on New Jersey as a location soon. If some dirtbags found me in an attempt to collect the price on my head, then she could find me too. Except she wasn't motivated by money; her judgment was clouded by her dislike for me. That fact alone was what had saved me thus far.

Mike called my name, dragging me out of my head and back to fun time in the bar. I smiled as I walked toward him, making sure I never lost eye contact. It was easy when he pulled me in with his tractor beam gaze.

"Hey," I said softly. "Did you want me?"

His arms circled me. He pulled me close and said,

"Always."

"Very funny," I whispered in his ear.

He let me go, adjusting his hold so we were side by side with his arm securely around my waist, squarely in front of Joe. "Joe was asking about our honeymoon."

"Did you tell him?" I asked.

"I did. I'm sure we'll have plenty of time for a honeymoon after you wrap up your current case and I finish this season's filming."

"You can't get away for a few days?" Joe seemed surprised.

"We have, we're here. We'll both be missed if we don't get back to our respective jobs in the next few days," I said. "As it is, Mike will be in trouble with management for ditching two public appearances in D.C. to come out here with me."

"They won't mind ... surely the golden boy can take a few days off?"

"Can you just up and take a few days off your job on a whim?" I asked him.

He looked uncomfortable as he formatted his reply. "I'm between jobs at the moment."

"Oh." I tried for a sorry expression, not sure how successful it was. "If that's the case we're lucky you could come down here for our wedding."

"I wasn't too far away. I had a job interview in Washington."

Job interview or meeting crazy chicks who want to kill me because that's how he gets his thrills.

"Fortuitous for us then." I decided to go for more information. "What field are you in?"

"I'm a production planner." He noticed my injured hand. "What happened to your hand?"

"Nothing much. Broken glass."

"Not as bad as her shoulder," Mike said. "Some nut with a knife attacked Laura in the Museum of Natural History."

A flicker crossed Joaunes eyes. "Sounds like a scary situation, why would anyone do that?"

"Something to do with me being with Mike and wearing The Hope Diamond," I said. "Washington was pretty crazy for a few days. I got attacked twice."

"And you're still going to marry him?" Joaunes said. The flicker of light in his eyes died.

Mike's smile radiated. "I'm a lucky man. Even the wacky fans can't deter my girl."

Lee came back into the room. He waved me over. Sandra walked toward us. I waited for her to draw near.

"Joe, this is my maid of honor, Sandra. I'll be right back. Seems my future brother-in-law has a question for me." I rolled my eyes. "Wedding plans."

With a quick kiss on Mike's cheek, I hurried to Lee. "And?"

"We've captured a still of him sitting at a table with the chick who tried to knife you at TGI Friday and another woman. We're running facial recognition on her. I'll have someone pick her up when we find out who she is."

"Thanks, Lee."

"You're welcome. Also, Sandra had some email alerts from Sentinel. Owen has tagged all your current files, Mike's case included."

"She's back in D.C. then … anything on Mike's files to suggest anyone knows where he is or who he's with?"

"She's added newspaper/gossip mag references that say he was seen with Laura Graham and the photos of you two at the museum."

"We're running out of time." I took a deep breath. "We need to find out who is behind the deaths of Eddie and possibly Beatrice Connelly before Owen finds me. Can you brief Sean, Kurt, Sam, Iain and Iain's men?"

I felt the Eddie situation had something to do with the theft of Carla's laptop not to mention her and Joey's harebrained scheme to trap a pedophile who apparently used the name Eddie Connelly. It was time to set my brain working on that problem while I concentrated on the issue at hand. I paused my thoughts and reminded myself that Seamus Kennedy and his crew were working on locating the pedophile. My focus had to be on not getting dead and not getting Mike dead.

"On it, Chicky."

"We need to trap this Joaunes idiot as he makes an attempt on me after the wedding tomorrow and then at least one thing will be over."

That was for my benefit, my little pep talk.

"It'll be okay. Owen has to go through Delta and the CIA to get you."

The look on Lee's face told me all I needed to know

about the loyalty of my team. I smiled and walked back to Mike just in time to hear him mention I was allergic to shellfish. He did it as casually as a person could mention certain death in a conversation.

"Honey, I just want to check the menu one last time," Mike said, kissing me on the cheek.

"I'm sure the manager is competent. You stressed the shellfish thing," I replied, giving his hand an affectionate squeeze.

"He's right, you can never be too careful," Joe said, siding with Mike.

Mike grinned. "There see?"

I threw up my hands in mock surrender. "Okay, go on."

Sandra smiled after Mike. "God, he's hot."

"Hellooo. My fiancé." I nudged her. "He's such a worrier."

"Because he loves you. You're his whole world."

Well played.

Joe's eyes gleamed and not in a nice way. "You should never take a shellfish allergy lightly. I hope you carry an EpiPen."

I rolled my eyes. "You too? C'mon, gimme a break. I'll be wearing a wedding dress, there's no hidden EpiPen pocket."

"Then that's why Mike is so concerned," Joe said. He patted my hand.

My skin crawled at his touch but the stage was set. Mike crossed the room to me, his eyes locked on mine, in his hand a fresh glass of champagne.

"For you," he said, handing me the glass and wrapping an arm around my waist. "We're all set for tomorrow."

"So, does that mean you'll calm down now?"

He nuzzled my neck and whispered, "This is taking my mind off it ..."

Joe cleared his throat. "I'll say goodnight and see you both tomorrow."

Mike shook his hand and thanked him again for coming. I saw Sam slip out the door behind Joe. Guess he was going to make sure he got safely to his room.

"How you doing?" I asked Mike. "Your head?"

"I'm fine."

My glass was empty. I took a step on the wobbly floor. It was like standing on a snake. "Whoops, the floor's a bit uneven," I mumbled, as Mike's arm tightened around my waist.

"Honey, it's not the floor," he said with a chuckle. "You're toasted."

"Champagne, I warned you. It's evil."

He laughed. "I'll take you to your room."

Sandra said something then Kurt appeared.

"Problem?" he asked.

"Nah," I replied, smiling. "Floor's a bit uneven, that's all."

He looked at Mike. Mike grinned. "Toasted."

"Accurate diagnosis. Have you got this? I'll be along soon. Sandra can go with you."

"I got her," Mike replied. "Come on Laura, let's get you

to bed."

"I bet you've been dying to say that," I said, leaning on him as we walked.

"You have no idea."

Chapter Forty Two
Unchain My Heart

Rain bucketed from the sky. An umbrella sprang open, shielding me from the worst of the deluge.

"Weather channel says it'll clear," Lee said.

"What does Siri say?"

"Bring an umbrella," Mike replied.

The ground underneath our feet soaked up water like a thirsty sponge. Before long, water sat on the surface and squelched underfoot as we walked down to the gazebo to check on the flowers.

I climbed the steps. It was dry inside and the air was so thick with rose perfumed humidity I felt I was breathing in scented cotton wool.

My head hurt and the overpowering smell didn't help.

Damned champagne.

"Very nice," Lee commented closing the umbrella and standing it in the corner. "How do you want to play this?"

"Low key but secure," I replied, surveying the tasteful flower arrangements. "We're supposed to be in the gazebo with the priest. You and Sandra standing on the top step. Everyone else on the grass below. Armed."

I looked out to the sodden grass and hoped the rain would stop in the next two hours.

"All right, I'll make sure everyone is in position. When do you expect him to make a move?"

"At the reception, he won't do it here. If he wants to utilize the shellfish thing we fed him, he'll try to poison the food. Maybe as we mingle about before the meal, eating and drinking, when everyone's relaxed or so he thinks. He may even try to poison the main meal."

"I hope he uses the fish thing," Mike said. "At least we know that won't hurt you."

"I'll be okay," I reassured him.

"We'll be vigilant. He's not the only problem. Two people have come hunting for you at this hotel."

"Two? Technically only one was after me ..."

"Chicky. Two. The guy you captured in the hotel and the person responsible for taking Delta, who wanted to explode you while you tried to free us."

"Hmm. Okay. Two."

"We're expecting more. The bounty went up during the night," Lee said.

Crap. When will these morons learn that I have nothing they want that's worth dying for?

"Sean put SkyWiper on that site, wasn't it supposed to take down the site?"

"He did install it. His modifications to the software took the site out about an hour after I got the bounty increase update."

"You got an update?"

"Sean modified the program to send information to us before it crashed the site and destroyed itself."

"So you know who picked up the contract?"

He shook his head. "We know how many people

viewed the contract. These people are using proxy servers, false identities, codes. You name it, they're using it to disguise their ISPs and themselves."

Technology: useful for the law abiding and criminal alike.

"How are they finding me?" I wanted confirmation that they were tracking me via social media as Sean thought.

"Iain told me the first guy was chatty. He tracked you by doing an internet search for relevant hashtags, then ran photos he found on Instagram and every other major social network site through facial recognition software to confirm your identity. Once he identified you, he accessed the location data attached to the image which lead him to this hotel," Lee said. "It's best to assume the bomb-loving independent contractor was similarly capable."

"Too easy."

"It gets worse, he confirmed the location of the image by comparing the background to other photos uploaded by the same user."

"Let me guess, the person tagged a photo with the name of the hotel?"

"That they did."

"Lock this place down. Seriously, lock it down – we can use the celebrity wedding as an excuse, but get management on side and get this entire complex tucked up tight. Also, do a room by room, I want photo ID of all guests checked in. No one who isn't staying or working here is to be allowed onto the premises." It was one thing to have some fucktards after me but putting Mike in more danger, putting hotel guests in danger, they were things I frowned upon.

"I'll get Sean and Iain, between them they can rustle up armed guards for the gate."

Yes, they could. One is ex-CIA running a security company and the other is active CIA with not only years as an intelligence officer but also, and now more importantly, with years as a protective agent. Jonathon Tierney had told Iain and his team to stay with me until this situation was over and Sean had left his business in the capable hands of his second in command.

Quiet, Mike seemed contemplative rather than worried, which was good. I didn't want him spooked. Cautious but not jumpy.

"We'd better go back to the hotel and start getting ready," I said. "While Iain and Sean are talking gate guards, get them to post a guard down here, too."

The thought of exploding while surrounded by yellow roses was colorful but I didn't want to be something others could never un-see. That's unfair.

The umbrella popped open as Lee stepped out of the gazebo. Mike followed him. I stepped up beside Mike under his umbrella.

"Let's do it," I said as we squelched across the sodden grass and prayed the rain would stop. By the time we reached the driveway, the sun had peeked through the clouds and steam rose from the ground.

Maybe there is a God. I was willing to believe in him. If he could just stop letting me down, we'd be all good.

Mike and I walked to our rooms together. Lee went off to find Sean and Iain and implement the security plan.

I checked Mike's room before he went in, and used the adjoining door to clear my room. Despite knowing how difficult it would be for Joaunes to try to jump the gun and take me out before the wedding, or how readily Delta would protect me from outside forces, I was jumpy instead of focused.

Mike stuck his hand around the doorframe and knocked on the wall.

"Okay to come in?"

"Sure."

"Not worried about me seeing you before the wedding?"

I smiled, hoping the smile would force its way to my eyes and blow away the doubts and apprehension.

"Coffee?" I asked, lifting the handset of the telephone.

"Sure."

I ordered a pot of coffee and a selection of sandwiches, still hungry, despite breakfast an hour earlier. I checked my watch. Ninety-minutes to lying to a priest

"They'll roll out special carpet-type stuff across the grass, so your dress won't get muddy," Mike said.

"Good." My stomach clenched and unclenched, the level of nervousness I felt, alarming. I didn't remember being so nervous, ever. Not even before I married Mac and that was a real wedding. I figured it was the bounty on my head mixed with lying to a priest.

Footsteps stopped outside the door. I heard the rattling of cups. Mike stayed where he was, used to our door-opening protocol. I peered through the peephole and saw one of the hotel staff members outside with a trolley. I opened the door, took the trolley, gave her a tip and relocked the door.

Mike poured the coffee and I ate a sandwich.

"After this, I'll get Sandra in here to help me get ready, and I won't see you until we meet at the altar." My stomach flipped over the sandwich and squished it into a little ball.

"Nervous?" Mike asked.

Maybe he sensed my discomfort or maybe he felt a little weird about the whole thing too.

"A little bit."

We didn't speak again until it was time to call Sandra and for Mike to leave.

"Lee will stay with you. Sam won't be far away. I have Sandra with me and Kurt close by. Let's get this wedding under way."

"See you soon."

I checked Mike's room again and called Lee before I let him go back, not prepared to take any chances.

Lee knocked on the outer door of Mike's room and called out, "Hey, Bro, open up."

I opened the door with a grin on my face.

"Ah, future brother-in-law, must say you're a huge improvement on my last one."

Lee laughed. "Thanks."

Of course, the last one was a fat troll who was now in a multitude of pieces.

"I'll see you two at the altar," I said and went back through the adjoining door. I shut the door firmly behind me.

Sandra was already at my door waiting for me to let her in. She entered the room with a pale blue dress over her arm and a makeup case in her other hand.

"Did you see the dress Mike bought me?" I asked as she draped her dress across the bed.

"No, not yet."

I lifted the large box off the floor and set it on the bed, whipped off the lid and revealed the masses of ivory fabric. Sandra lifted out the dress and spread it across the bed, shoving her dress aside as she did.

"Wow. Good taste."

"And it fits like a glove," I said, tracing a line of seed pearls down the bodice. It was a beautiful dress.

"Speaking of which, did you see what was under the dress?" Sandra asked holding up a pair of long white satin gloves. "He thought of everything." She smiled at me as she smoothed the gloves in her hands. "He wouldn't be a horrible husband."

He probably wouldn't. If I were in the market for a husband I could do a lot worse than Michael Fisher. My mind drifted home and I saw Mitch pulling into the driveway. If I were in the market for a husband, it wouldn't be Michael Fisher.

An hour later, I stood in the room in front of the full-length mirror. Most of my auburn curls were twisted up on top of my head and pinned, with thick strands left out from underneath, hanging in long curls. Sandra had asked the florist for buds, and clipped the small yellow roses in amongst my hair. I wore the dress, the shoes and the satin gloves, which came up past my elbows. The only scar that needed any corrective makeup was high on my upper arm.

I was a regular bride, not the bride of Frankenstein.

Sandra finished dressing and emerged from the bathroom looking stunning. Her golden locks adorned with rosebuds. Her dress now seemed more turquoise than blue.

"We look great," she said, standing next to me in front of the mirror.

"How much time have we got?" My stomach backflipped, I had sweaty palms and I fought the urge to wipe my gloved hands down the dress.

She checked her phone. "Five minutes to go before we should make our way down. Time for me to get the boys into position and our escort ready."

She made a few calls while I tried grounding myself and practiced breathing. It made no sense to me how nervous I was. Really? A fake wedding. Just another job.

I repeated it in my head. Just another job. It wasn't sticking as well as I'd hoped.

A knock at the door made me jump.

Sandra laughed and checked who it was.

"Kurt," she said, swinging the door open.

Kurt whistled through his teeth. "You look beautiful, Sandra."

"Thank you, you scrub up nice yourself."

The door closed. I hadn't turned to see Kurt, it was enough that I had to concentrate on breathing and not throwing up.

"Laura?" Kurt's voice bounced across the carpeted floor in my direction. "Ellie?"

"Yes."

"You all right?"

"Yes."

"You sure?" He was standing next to me. I looked into the mirror and saw Kurt in a tuxedo, wearing a yellow rose boutonniere, concern etched into his forehead.

"Yes."

"You're very monosyllabic this morning."

"Little bit nervous," I confessed. "Not used to nerves on this level."

"You'll be fine. We'll be right there."

A smile flickered across my lips. "I'm not nervous about having Joe the nut there, I'm nervous about lying to a priest and the wedding thing."

"It's a job like any other." His eyes searched mine from within the glass. "Sometimes lying is part of it."

Sometimes? Try always.

"Time," Sandra called from the door.

Kurt crooked his left arm at me. "Shall we?"

Chapter Forty Three

Marry You

I hooked my right arm around his left. It felt all wrong. That was my shooting hand.

Sandra got the door, she picked up the bouquets from the table and followed us out. She passed me mine, and then slipped by to walk in front. I glanced over my shoulder and saw Sean behind us.

It was the slowest walk ever. Painfully slow. Every step forward made me want to turn and run. Only the pressure of Kurt's hand over mine prevented me from running back to my room.

"Breathe, it's just another job," Kurt whispered, as the driveway dipped toward the rose garden.

Heads turned to us from the seats on the grass.

"Just another job," I repeated in a hushed whisper.

It took forever to reach the edge of the lawn. Mike was right, they did roll out a carpet, it ran down the middle of the chairs and up to the gazebo. From the end of the carpet, I could see Lee and Mike, and the priest.

A cold chill spread from my stomach.

Music started. Bon Jovi's 'Thank you for loving me' filled the garden as Kurt and I walked behind Sandra. I noted Joaunes sitting in the front row with Tim Cosgrove next to him. The chairs were full of hotel guests. As per instructions, everyone had surrendered their cell phones to the hotel manager.

My stomach bounced around inside me, trying to find a way out.

Please don't make me throw up.

Mike smiled down at me as we approached the steps. He took two steps forward and reached for my hand. I gave my bouquet to Sandra, who stood on the top step opposite Lee.

The priest smiled and introduced himself to me. "Laura, I am Father Keegan."

"Hello, Father," I said, hoping the tension I felt didn't flow into my voice.

He smiled reassuringly, patted me on the shoulder and began the ceremony.

"Laura and Michael, have you come here freely and without reservation to give yourselves to each other in marriage?"

Mike looked into my eyes. "I have."

"I have," I said. It was easier than I thought, with Mike right there in front of me.

"Will you honor each other as man and wife for the rest of your lives?" Father Keegan asked.

"I will," Mike said.

"I will."

"Will you accept children lovingly from God, and bring them up according to the law of Christ and his Church?"

Mike smiled. "I will."

"I will."

But thankfully, that won't be an issue. I corralled my

mind before it galloped away.

"Since it is your intention to enter into marriage, join your right hands, and declare your consent before God and his congregation."

We joined hands.

Father Keegan nodded at Mike.

"I, Michael Fisher, take you, Laura Graham, to be my wife. I promise to be true to you in good times and in bad, in sickness and in health. I will love you and honor you all the days of my life."

He'd memorized his lines. I struggled to remember everything he just said.

"I, Laura Graham, take you ... Michael Fisher, to be my husband ..." What was next? Mike mouthed some words at me. Thank God, I could lip read. "I promise to be true to you in good times and in bad, in sickness and in health. I will love you and honor you all the days of my life."

That won't be many days. The crazy guy who wants Mike to suffer will try to kill me soon, so I'll be lucky to last our wedding day. Best be a good one.

"Laura and Michael have declared their consent to be married."

Father Keegan asked for the rings. I hadn't considered rings. I looked around wondering if anyone had thought about rings. Lee stepped up and placed two rings on a small cushion held by Father Keegan. Question answered.

The priest spoke over the rings. Stunned that there

were rings, I had no idea what he said. My gloves. How would Mike put a ring on my finger?

Mike's hands squeezed mine. I looked into his eyes as he took my left hand and slipped a ring over my gloved finger. The man was magic. "Laura, take this ring as a sign of my love and fidelity. In the name of the Father, and of the Son, and of the Holy Spirit."

I took the remaining ring and pushed it onto Mike's ring finger; this time I managed to follow his words without help, grateful I'd heard the words and not just blah blah blah.

"Michael, take this ring as a sign of my love and fidelity. In the name of the Father, and of the Son, and of the Holy Spirit."

"Let us pray for God's blessing on this couple," Father Keegan said. After a minute's silence he declared, "What God has joined, men must not divide."

Mike dipped his head and kissed me. I expected gunfire or lightning. Neither happened.

Lee and Sandra joined us for the signing of the license.

As I sat at the small table to one side within the gazebo and signed Laura's signature, I glanced out and saw Joaunes stand up. I passed the pen to Mike and nudged Lee.

"Don't worry about it, Cosgrove is right there," Lee whispered and took the pen from Mike. Father Keegan showed him where to sign.

"Father, will you join us for our first meal?" Mike asked.

Clever. That would probably delay any action by Joaunes. Surely, no one wanted to commit a heinous crime in front of a priest. That would be worse than lying to one.

With the paperwork taken care of, Father Keegan congratulated us, and then announced, "I would like to introduce Mr. and Mrs. Michael Fisher."

Mike and I left the gazebo, followed by Lee and Sandra. We walked back up the middle of the chairs and off the lawn. Catalina met us with a photographer. We all made our way to a secluded rose garden for photos. Just like a newlywed couple.

We posed for photo after photo. Smiling, turning, holding bouquets, no bouquets, holding hands, photos of our hands. The whole time I wondered what would happen to the photos, certain they'd end up on the internet. There went Mike's chance of ever getting another date.

"Are we done yet?" I whispered to Mike. "I'd sooner get inside."

"Jumpy?" he asked.

"Little bit. Wedding's over. As far as Joe knows we're married, so anytime from now on would be a good time to take one of us out."

Mike looked at the photographer one last time. "Thank you, I think we're done out here," he said oozing charm. "My wife and I would like you to join us in the restaurant for a toast and a meal, and if you could get some candid shots throughout the reception we'd appreciate it."

My wife and I. I stifled a scoff. I don't recall Mac ever saying that. I probably would've smacked him upside the head had he tried. My wife and I. Hah.

Our small wedding party, plus hotel manager and photographer, entered the hotel through the main doors. The restaurant awaited us. It was beautifully decorated in yellow roses. Our table ran along the back and was raised slightly on a plinth to overlook the rest of the tables. The last supper sprang to mind.

Lee stayed close as we waited near the door to greet everyone who entered. Once the guests were all in, we mingled. Serving staff passed around glasses of champagne and trays of canapés. If I didn't know any better, I'd think someone got married.

Mike had double-checked the appetizers did not contain fish. I heard him mention it twice, once with Joe in earshot.

Sandra, at my side and ever watchful, whispered in my ear, "Joe is coming up on your left."

"Got him," I replied, turning slightly to greet him.

He tried for a kiss but got hair as I moved. I'm not fond of kissing strangers. His hand knocked my glass, causing me to adjust my grip on the stem.

"Congratulations, I'm sure you two will be very happy," Joe said. Something about his manner suggested he wasn't hoping that at all. Ah, well, stalkers are never satisfied.

"I'm sure we will. Did Mike tell you we are planning to start our family right away?"

Mike snaked his arm around my waist. "Don't you think we'll make beautiful babies?"

Joaunes pursed his lips. I hadn't seen a lemon-sucker face like that since Caine threw one at me years ago.

"Of course you will," Joaunes replied. He reached for a drink from a tray passing by. "To the happy couple." Joaunes raised his glass and clinked mine.

Sandra interrupted before I could take a sip. She took the glass from me in a theatrical display. "If you're planning on babies anytime soon, no drinking."

"That's unfair!" I complained and swiped a new glass from another server. Sandra shrugged and let me drink it.

She must've seen something when Joe came in for a kiss. Mike engaged Joe in conversation, distracting him from Sandra. I watched her carry the glass across the restaurant and hand it to Iain. Iain disappeared.

I caught a glimpse of annoyance on Joe's face and suspected he was trying for subtle but failed; sucked to be him. No doubt, he'd try something more in-my-face next time.

Mike swung me into his arms, my drink sloshed in the glass. "We should eat some of the delicious canapés I see doing the rounds," he said.

"Let me get a waiter," Joe offered.

"Server," I corrected as Joe trundled off after a man carrying a tray. I watched his hand dip into his pocket. He was holding something. Something small.

"All right?" Mike asked.

"Joe is going to add something to that tray of canapés. What do you bet it's something fish based?"

"You ready to feign anaphylaxis?"

"Tell me again how to do that, he's obviously not going to see any swelling. I'm not allergic to anything."

"Pretend to choke on your own tongue then faint. That should throw him off."

I nodded. I can do that.

"Make sure that photographer is around and catches this," I said. "You may get another date yet."

His eyes narrowed. "What do you mean?"

"Once the wedding photos hit the net, your days of dating are over, dude."

He oozed mischievousness. "You think? Nah ah, this ring makes me a babe magnet." He held up his ring finger and pointed to his wedding ring.

"To women of low morals."

He shrugged. "I'm a guy."

"Yeah, but you're not *that* guy."

His eyes sparkled. "You sure?"

"Yes, yes, I am. If the photographer gets shots of me dying, you'll get more action than you can cope with as a grieving widower."

"Heads up, honey, incoming." Mike snared me for a kiss.

Joe interrupted us with the server and canapés. "These are delicious," he said.

Mike and I took one each and placed them in our mouths at the same time. He frowned as he chewed.

Then he suddenly placed a napkin by my chin. "Laura, spit it out! It's got fish in it."

The server panicked and rushed away. Mike fussed. I swallowed half then spat the rest out. He was right. Fish.

Joe hovered and could barely disguise his delight. "Laura, you okay?"

I swilled back the champagne in my glass then let the glass fall from my hand. Joe caught it.

"My throat," I muttered. "Allergic."

Mike grabbed my arm as I stumbled backwards. His eyes held mine. He blocked Joe's view and mouthed words at me. "Look sick."

"Kurt!" Mike yelled lowering me to the ground. "Help!"

People milled about, generally getting in the way. Suddenly a clear space opened up and Kurt was next to me. He called an ambulance from his cell phone while making a show of asking someone to get his bag from his room. Joe still hovered.

"Lee!" Kurt yelled.

That was my cue. I rolled my eyes back in my head and took shallow breaths. Lee announced that everyone should leave the room and Iain's voice told me to hold on.

I wanted to reply. It was all I could do to keep a smile off my face. I figured the best thing to do was just go with the chaotic noises and wait until Kurt told me the coast was clear.

He spoke quietly to Mike. I couldn't hear what he said. A few minutes later Kurt said, "She's not going to make it."

He bent down and whispered in my ear, "It's almost clear. I just called off the ambulance … being a doctor has its advantages. I can sign the death certificate myself."

Mike's fingers tightened around my hand. I felt him lean over me. Water dripped onto my face. Water? Tears. He was crying.

Damn, no wonder he won industry awards.

Lee kneeled close to me. Kurt gave me the all clear.

"Thank God, that was hard," I said opening my eyes. Mike's distraught expression tugged at my heart. "You going to be okay?"

He wiped his eyes. "Not for a while, my wife just died in my arms."

"*Prêt pour participer à Opération* Torrent Falls, *part deux*?" Ready for Operation Torrent Falls, part two?

"*Oui.*"

"Let's do this thing. I want my body to stay in our room tonight," I said.

Kurt agreed, "Of course. Your grieving husband will insist on it."

I couldn't believe the next words were about to come out of my mouth but they did. "Get Father Keegan back in here to administer last rites."

Authenticity abounded.

"Okay, back to being dead for you."

"I need help, Kurt."

He moved things around in his bag. "I can help. I don't like this, but I can help."

"Just give me something good that will make me sleep.

Playing dead is too hard for a smartass like me."

He drew up a fluid into a syringe, pulled the glove on my left arm down until the inside of my elbow was exposed. "Goodnight. I'll wake you up when it's safe."

"What is it ...?"

I never heard his reply.

Silence and nothingness enveloped me.

Chapter Forty Four
Waiting For The Miracle

Noises in the background grew steadily louder. They overpowered my heartbeat and tapped on my sternum. I opened an eye. Kurt smiled down at me.

"Welcome back."

"What'd I miss?"

"A lot of tears."

"Really?"

"Don't sound so surprised." He took my pulse and checked my blood pressure. "No adverse effects."

"Good to know." I pushed myself up until I was sitting and looked down. "Still with the wedding dress."

"Your husband wants you buried in it," Kurt said with a grin. I looked around. There was no sign of the grieving widower. "He's next door for a minute, toilet break."

Yeah, I didn't need to know that but it was a good idea.

"I'd like to use the bathroom."

"Go easy, standing," Kurt said, helping me to my feet. He waited until I was steady before letting me go. "I'll be right here."

I walked as best I could to the bathroom. My appearance took me by surprise. I looked dead. I was a walking corpse. On closer inspection, it was makeup. Mike. It was good.

A few minutes later I emerged feeling relieved but not

for long. Kurt talked to someone on my room phone and Mike, red-eyed, sat on the bed. He smiled at me and held his finger to his lips.

I sat next to him on the bed while we waited for Kurt to finish.

"That was Joe. He'd like to give his condolences."

"Back to being dead for me then. But no drugs," I said. "We want a confession and I think I know how to extract one. Joe is an asshole but he thinks he's been so damn clever thus far ..."

"What are you going to do?"

"Revive suddenly."

Mike grinned. "Good, my eyes are raw from crying."

"One more time, Mike, then hopefully we'll have everything we need," Kurt said.

"We haven't already?" Mike asked.

"So far, we've tested Ellie's champagne and found that someone, Joe, dropped some fish oil into it."

"Sandra saw him put something in the glass, that's not enough?"

"Not really."

"Okay, more tears then ..."

"Now Ellie's awake, I can make myself scarce but we'll have Lee and Sam in here. Your brother and his best friend."

Mike nodded. "Assume the position, wifey."

I screwed up my nose at him and walked around the bed then lifted my skirt out of the way and climbed up. "You'll have to fix my dress."

Mike and Kurt spread the skirt out and made me look presentable.

"Where are Lee and Sam?" I asked.

"Chicky?"

Well, that answered my question. In Mike's room the whole time.

Kurt grinned and wished me luck.

Sam's phone rang. He answered and then looked at the door. "He'll knock on that door in ten seconds."

I closed my eyes and slowed my breathing. Then opened one eye and looked at Mike, "Don't let him touch me or stand close to me."

"I won't."

I closed my eyes and relaxed and heard the knock at the door.

Lee answered it and invited Joe in. I heard him ask how Mike was. The door closed. Mike sniffed and thanked Joe for coming. He steered him away from the bed and over to a couple of chairs by the window.

"So tragic," Joe said. "I'm sorry for your loss."

"I've never met anyone like Laura, you know." He sobbed. Through fresh tears he said, "She was my life."

Had I not been dead I would've cried.

"Do you know how the fish got in the canapés?" Joe inquired so innocently, I wanted to reach out and smack him.

"Someone did it on purpose. Lee thinks my stalker found us."

Lee muttered in agreement from near me.

461

"You have a stalker?"

"Yes. We never thought that Laura was in danger."

"What will you do now? Has this stalker been caught?"

Mike summoned more tears. "I don't know what I'll do." He shook his head. "They haven't caught the stalker. The FBI thinks it's a woman."

"A woman?" Joe asked. "How do they know that?"

"Poison, it's more a female crime," Lee replied. I was impressed with his ability to keep a straight face. "And we found a book written by a woman about Mike. She clearly had some unresolved feelings for him."

Keeping quiet while they wound up Joaunes by insinuating the stalker was female was not easy. I listened to the inflection in Joe's voice as he spoke again; he wasn't happy about the blame being given to a woman.

"It couldn't be a man?"

"We don't think so," Lee replied. "The whole situation is fraught with emotion. A man would be more likely to punch him in the head and move on. Plus Laura had run-ins with two other women who were intent on causing her harm and they were Mike Fisher fanatics."

Through fresh tears Mike said, "I don't know how I can go on without Laura."

I took a slow shallow breath. Lee took my hand. "I just can't believe she's gone," he said with more emotion than I'd ever heard in his voice.

They were killing me.

Fuck it.

I coughed and flicked my eyes open. Lee jumped. Mike

almost fell off his chair. Joe stood, his face registering horror.

In three strides Mike was by my side, he scooped me into his arms. Tears ran freely down his face.

"What happened?" Joe said. "This shouldn't be happening!"

"It's a miracle," Lee replied. "I've heard of this happening but never seen it."

"It can't happen!" Agitated, Joe paced the floor.

"It's a miracle," Mike said.

"You're the luckiest fucking bastard in the world!" Joe spat the words across the room. "Every woman you meet falls at your feet. Your fiancée dodges knives. What the fuck! You marry her, I find out she has a fish allergy. I give her fucking fish oil and she magically revives hours later. I bet your shit doesn't stink."

Mike took a breath. Lee stood up.

Sam stepped toward Joe. "You what?"

"N-nothing. Nothing."

Lee walked toward Joe. From behind his back, he produced a pair of handcuffs. Joe tried to duck out of the way but met with the wall that is Sam. He held him by the shoulders. Lee grabbed one wrist and pulled his arm roughly behind his back. He snapped the cuff on then cuffed his other wrist.

"You are under arrest for the attempted murder of a federal agent."

Joe flustered and blustered and denied everything.

Lee played back his confession. He'd captured the

whole thing on his phone.

"Goodbye, Joe," I said with a small wave. "It's been fun."

Sam spun Joe around and frog marched him from the room.

Kurt and Lee congratulated each other, then congratulated Mike and me on a game well played. I breathed a sigh of relief.

"Can someone pour me a drink and unzip this gown?" I asked, standing up. Too fast apparently. I tumbled forward into Mike's arms. "Good catch."

"Okay?"

"Yep, you can let me go."

"Turn around, I'll unzip you."

I did as he suggested. "Lee, are there pajamas in the blue bag over there?"

He bent down and poked about, seconds later he threw pajama pants and a tee shirt at me. "Catch."

"Yeah, nah," I replied, letting them fall onto the bed while holding up my dress.

Mike tucked the pajamas under my arm. I dragged myself into the bathroom.

The makeup was scary. I removed the wig, dropped the dress on the floor and stepped into a hot shower. It took several squirts of cleanser to remove the makeup. Scrubbed clean and feeling very much alive I dried off, pulled on pajamas, tripped over the dress and stumbled out of the bathroom and into the wall opposite the door.

"You okay?" Mike asked coming to my aid.

"Yeah, I tripped." I took his outstretched hand. "You look better."

"Had a shower, nice to have dry eyes."

We walked over to the bed and sat down. "You look human again. There was a bit of zombie going on when you woke up earlier."

"That was whatever Kurt gave me to make me sleep like the dead and your great makeup job."

"I'm glad you're okay."

"That was some impressive acting," I said.

"Thanks."

"You all right? Does all that emotion affect you?"

"I'm tired." He flopped back onto the bed, taking me with him. I rolled over and crawled up to the pillows. Mike followed.

He reached over and pulled me to him. Too tired to argue I let my head rest on his shoulder.

My eyes needed no encouragement to close.

Chapter Forty Five
Ashes To Ashes

The next time my eyes opened it was dark. Proper dark. No light coming in from outside and none in the room. I lay still and listened to Mike breathing next to me. He still had his arm around me. I lifted it gently and wriggled out of the way. Carefully I lowered his arm across his body. He sighed and rolled over.

I tiptoed across the floor, into the bathroom and closed the door. In deep darkness I felt the wall, searching for the light switch. My fingers clipped it, flicking the light switch up. Bright light blinded me for a second.

I blinked at myself in the mirror.

A shadow moved on my left. There was no time to wonder what it was. I saw the blade coming from the shower and jumped sideways. It missed me. The raised hand attached to the blade swung again.

With my vision in soft focus, everything felt like a hallucination. My brain kicked in and I stepped into the arc, reached into the shower, grabbed the person and heard a squawk. Like a radio squawk. I pulled hard, ducking sideways as the person toppled out of the shower and onto the floor. Something flew across the room and hit the door. Another squawk. A radio.

Focusing on the person on the floor, I realized it was a woman. She looked like the hotel manager.

Catalina? She rolled over and scrambled to her feet. My elbow connected with the side of her head. She fell. My fingers wound around the neck of her shirt.

I smashed the woman's head against the floor until her eyes rolled back in her head and she felt limp in my hands. I dropped her. Her head thudded to the floor.

The knife lay to one side of her and the radio near the door. Something dripped, leaving red drops on the white floor. I picked up the radio. It squawked again in my hand. My bare feet slipped on something slick. I grabbed the door handle and pulled. The door rushed at me. My feet went in two directions at once. Radio in one hand, handle in the other.

Harsh lights blinded me. I rolled sideways. Lying on the bathroom floor I tried to shield my eyes from the glare of the bathroom light so I could see. The woman lay unconscious in a pool of blood. Crawling was better than trying to stand. I reached her and felt for a pulse. Nothing.

On all fours, I escaped the bathroom. Once in the main room I stood up and found a light switch, guided by the bright pool of light flooding from the bathroom floor.

Mike was still sleeping.

That didn't seem right. Sure, we were both tired but to sleep through my crashing and banging, did not seem right.

"Mike!" My walking more like stumbling, I collided with the side of the bed.

Mike mumbled, "What time is it?"

"I dunno," I replied, trying to stand up straight.

"Come back to bed."

"In a minute."

"Can you turn out the light, please?" He rolled over the other way.

I didn't move. Things were a little foggy in my head. "Mike." I shook his shoulder. "Mike ..."

Mike rubbed his face and sat up. "What's up, apart from me?"

"I think I killed someone in the bathroom ..." I sat on the edge of the bed. "The hotel manager attacked me."

Mike jumped out of bed. He walked into the bathroom; two seconds later, the bathroom light went off and he came back out. "There is no one dead in the bathroom. There is no one in the bathroom."

Color me confused.

"There was a knife and a radio." I looked at my hand. No radio.

"A knife and a radio?" Mike repeated. "There is no sign of anything, no struggle, no knife, no dead body, no live body."

"I could've sworn ..."

Mike climbed back into bed. "Come here, but first turn off the light." He reached an arm out and flipped the bedside lamp on. A much softer glow than the main lights. I hit the switch on the wall and crawled into bed next to Mike.

"You sure there was nothing there?"

"Positive."

He lifted his arm and wrapped it around my shoulders. His fingers caressed my arm.

My left arm lay over his ribs. Mike kissed the top of my head.

"Sleep. No more dreams."

The bedside light dimmed. The room faded to black.

Chapter Forty Six

Hero

I woke to daylight streaming in through long gaps in the curtains. I rolled over trying to escape the light.

"Morning," Mike said, his voice husky from sleep.

"Morning."

"Any more dreams?"

"Nope." The light hurt and I closed my eyes again.

"How are we going to do this today, everyone thinks you're dead ..."

"They can't know I'm not. I have a horrible feeling that I'll be leaving the hotel in a wedding dress and a body bag."

"They wouldn't, would they?"

"Yep. It's best if everyone thinks we were married and I died, rather than trying to explain what really happened." I looked up at his face. He needed a shave. It was a good look on him. "Remember how I said this was going to make you a chick magnet ... it will you know, the tragic end to your short marriage."

His fingers moved against the cap sleeve of my tee shirt. "I don't want you to be dead. Can't Kurt find a miracle cure?"

"I doubt it." I didn't want me to be dead, either. It was nice being with him. "Prepare to be the grieving widower."

"How long do we have?"

"I don't know. What time is it?"

He twisted and reached for the phone on his nightstand. "Six."

"Maybe an hour, maybe a little longer."

"Wow, messages galore." He held the phone so I could see.

"Anything interesting?"

Mike scrolled with this thumb. "Looks like the wedding photographs have made it online already. I've pissed off my manager. Mostly they're tweets and Facebook messages congratulating us."

"Nice."

He put the phone back on the nightstand and rolled toward me.

"Everything okay?" I asked.

"Yes."

"Truth?"

"I've enjoyed hanging out with you."

I didn't know what to say. So I said nothing.

He continued, "We still on for Cotopaxi?"

"Death won't stop me climbing a mountain."

"About that, why did you want to keep the mountain quiet? Or it is that you're going with me that you want to keep quiet?" He reached over and pushed hair out of my eyes. "It's Kurt isn't it?"

"In a way, but not like you're thinking."

"You sure about that?"

"Yep. Very. Kurt and I were never destined to happen.

Too much history, not enough mystery. Plus, our timing always sucks, we work together, and he has a girlfriend."

He'd finally found someone who can cope with Delta. I wasn't about to mess that up.

"So what then?"

"He doesn't appreciate my choices in extracurricular activities. He likes to bandy words about like 'death wish' and 'PTSD.'"

"I'd have gone with 'sense of adventure.' What was it that sent him over the edge?"

"Skydiving I think, or maybe parkour."

His eyes lit up. "Skydiving?" The spark in his eye that told me he enjoyed the rush of jumping out of a perfectly good airplane. "I'd definitely go with sense of adventure."

"Me, too. You saw combat, yeah?"

"I did."

"Did you climb mountains and jump out of planes before you were in combat?"

"No, I was young. I couldn't afford to climb mountains back then. My first jump was while I was in the army though."

"Death wish or PTSD?"

"Neither, I like adventure, makes me feel alive."

Adrenaline junkie. I knew it. "We're not that different."

"Cotopaxi in January?"

"Yes," I said without hesitation. "You have my number."

"I do."

I closed my eyes and enjoyed the security of knowing

that for a few minutes more, everything was okay.

Cotopaxi in January, if I'm not in a federal prison by then. There was still a damn big issue to resolve. Murder charges and Owen. I figured the hacker was tied up with the murder charges because of the thefts.

Mike was safe, but I wasn't.

Laura was dead. I wasn't.

So much still had to be done to formalize the death of Laura Graham and bury her cover. The business had to be sold. Joe's story about Laura coming back to life had to be dismissed as a guilt fantasy or delusion.

And I needed to be Ellie again. We had to check out of this hotel and find another where I could go back to being me.

Mike needed to head back to LA and his life.

"If this were a soap, your evil twin would have tied you up somewhere and taken your place ..."

I flicked my eyes open to find Mike's pale blue eyes waiting. "... and you wouldn't know for months that you'd married the wrong sister. All that grief then one day I'd walk through your door and we'd ride off into the sunset together ..."

"...then a year or so later you'd find out I am a rapist."

I laughed. "But a charming one ..."

"That about sums it up."

"It's a shame we can't have a soap plot line and an evil twin."

"We could do this, you know. For real. You and me."

"We've had this discussion—"

"I haven't changed my mind."

"Nor have I." Time to change the subject. "Do you think your manager will forgive you?"

"Yeah. She will. Especially when she sees how much mileage she can squeeze out of the wedding/stalker/tragic death situation."

"You'll be tearing-up on talk shows all over the US." And I wouldn't be watching because it'd kill me just a little bit every time I saw him do that.

"I expect so." He smiled. "I'll also be able to disappear without repercussions because I'm the grieving widower."

"A mountain?"

"Maybe."

"Don't forget, you'll be the most eligible man in LA."

"Some definite positives coming out of this," he said, kissing the top of my head. "You're absolutely sure there won't be a miracle cure?"

"I am."

I needed Laura to die. Her death would buy me time. It wouldn't be long before news of the death escaped the hotel. My hope was that Laura's death would mean the end of hired killers hunting me. No sense having a contract out on a dead person. We knew the first contractor made the connection between me and Laura. Facial Recognition Software worked well for us and criminals alike.

Mike's phone rang. He picked it up and looked at the screen. "My manager." He didn't answer it. His phone buzzed in his hand. "Now text messages." He opened the first message. "It's out. You're dead."

He dropped the phone gently onto the floor. I dozed for a while until there was a knock at the door. Another knock; this time louder.

Mike stirred.

"Mr. Fisher?" It sounded like the hotel manager. Confirmation that I didn't kill her in the bathroom during the night. Neither of us moved. A few seconds later, I heard Lee's voice. It went quiet.

Chapter Forty Seven
Heartbreak Hotel

Mike called out from the bathroom, "Do you need these clips and flowers?"

Crap. The stuff from my hair. I could hear water running. Steam wafted into the room through the open bathroom door.

I knocked on the door. "Okay to come in?"

"Sure," he replied from within the shower cubicle.

I looked at all the clips and the baby roses littering the top of the vanity. There was no way I could put those back in my hair.

I stepped away from the counter top and said, "Let's leave my hair down. If anyone asks, you can say you like it like that."

"Can I tell them I like it blonde, too?"

His hand reached out and took mine; with a sharp tug he pulled me into the shower. Water poured over my pajamas.

"Really?" I said, splashing water at him. "You don't think showering with your dead wife is a bit odd?"

Mike pressed me against the wall. Water washed over him and flowed onto me.

"No."

I ducked under his arm and escaped.

Twenty minutes later, I stood in the bathroom in clean

dry underwear drying my hair before putting the auburn wig on for what I hoped was the last time. Mike had dressed and waited patiently with the wedding dress.

"What's the scar on your scapula from?" he asked.

He didn't miss much.

"Bomb," I said, running my fingers through my hair to see if it was dry yet. Satisfied, I put the hair dryer away, piled my hair on top of my head, put the wig on and turned around. The curls hung down my back and tickled.

"Bomb?"

I shrugged. "Yeah."

"That's why you were so careful opening the box this dress came in?"

Mike helped me step into the wedding dress and zipped the zipper.

"Sort of. The explosion I was in wasn't a parcel bomb. That was just my paranoia."

"I need to make you look dead again," Mike said. "You're looking way too good for a dead woman."

I looked at my reflection and viewed Mike from the mirror. "You need to stop grinning."

He smiled, dimples and all. "No problem. I'm a professional." He took me by the hand. "Let's get you back on the bed, and then I'll do the makeup thing."

"Bed?"

"Trust me, I'm a professional."

He smoothed the bedding before I lay down. Once I was lying comfortably, Mike arranged the skirt of the dress.

"Gloves and ring?" he said, searching the floor. He found one glove under the edge of the bed and another by my bags; I had no idea why they were scattered.

"Ring should be on the bathroom vanity with the hair pins." I had it in my hand when I took the pins out of my hair. "And bring the pins and rosebuds. Drop them by the bed or on the nightstand, like you've taken them out of my hair."

Mike disappeared then came back with the makeup, rosebuds, pins, and my ring. He pushed the ring onto my gloved finger.

He covered the visible scars on my upper left arm then did my facial makeup. Not too much, just enough dullness to make me look like a waxy corpse – he took a picture with his phone and showed me. I looked dead.

He scattered the rosebuds and hair pins on the nightstand.

Mike pulled up a chair and sat as close to me as he could, his hands holding my left hand.

There was a knock at the interior door. I closed my eyes. Time to be dead.

"Come in," Mike called. "It's not locked."

I heard Kurt's voice but didn't react until he was right next to me and assured me it was okay to speak.

"What's happening now?" I asked.

"Funeral director has arrived. We're going to put you in a body bag and wheel you out of the hotel on a gurney, and into a hearse."

A hearse. Not cool.

"Won't he notice I'm not dead?"

"No, Lee and I will do all the lifting and bagging in here, on our own because you should be in full rigor and once I've given you the sedative you won't be able to fake rigor. The funeral director will see you briefly before we bag you."

"I'm not dead. I don't want to suffocate in a body bag."

"I won't zip it all the way shut and we'll get you out down the road."

"Won't he think that's odd?"

"Nah, not when the grieving husband changes his mind and wants to take his bride home."

"He's going to drive my body to LA?"

Mike grinned. "I am?"

"No, but that's what the funeral director thinks you're going to do."

The legal ramifications spun inside my head. "He can't. There is no way a funeral director will release a body for transportation across state lines without a ton of paperwork." I did a quick calculation of the best route across the country. "We are in West Virginia there are another nine states to cross to get to LA. You have to contact them all and check their requirements and you can't drive a body around in a private car. This isn't the movies."

"Conway, relax. We have everything Mike needs."

Resourceful.

"Everything?"

"Everything," Kurt confirmed.

"What about the car thing?"

"We have paperwork saying that Mike has permission to carry you from every state you'll be driven through. Initially, that required embalming as the trip will take longer than twenty-four hours."

My eyes widened. That wouldn't work. "How did you get around that?" I asked, hoping he had found a way.

He shrugged and grinned. "Mike will convince the Funeral Director that he'll have you embalmed before leaving West Virginia when he hands over the paperwork to prove he has permission to transport your body."

"Why can't we just give him the paperwork now?"

"Because it's hard to come by and it needs to look like Mike got it just in time. You leaving with someone not involved means there is an impartial witness to your death."

"Whatever, just don't suffocate me or put me in a coffin. Small spaces. Not a fan."

"I'm giving you something, like yesterday."

Like yesterday. That stuff had me thinking I'd murdered the hotel manager in the bathroom.

"Don't leave me alone with the funeral director, I don't want to be accidentally embalmed."

Kurt smiled. "It won't happen. When you wake up remember you should be in full rigor. So when Mike and the funeral director move you from the hearse to Mike's car, you need to keep your body as stiff as possible."

"That's taking planking to the extreme," I mumbled. It

sounded a lot easier than the reality would be.

He had a syringe in his hand. "You ready?"

Panic coursed through me. Ready? No. "The car."

"The car?" Kurt queried.

"I'm too tall to fit across the backseat of a sedan in full rigor. Our rental is too small for me to lie down in."

"It's okay, Conway, no one is going to break your legs to make you fit in to that car," Kurt replied. "Sam has given Mike his Suburban to use."

I looked at Mike. "If you drop the backseat down and slide me into the cargo area through the rear door I'll fit quite comfortably in the back."

"You've done this before?" Mike asked.

"Not exactly. I've slept in a few cars over the years and it's a lot more comfortable in the back of a Suburban than the back of a sedan." Gear. Sam's car would have the Delta gear in the back. "Kurt, what about our gear?"

"Taken care of. Iain will transport anything we can't fit in a rental car." Kurt placed a hand on my shoulder. "Are you ready now?"

I nodded.

"See you on the other side," Mike whispered in my ear.

Chapter Forty Eight
I Walk The Line

It was dark and hot. Condensation dripped onto my face from the black above me. It was only about two inches off my face. I wiggled a finger into a small hole I spotted.

My finger worked the zip until it moved a few inches. Air. Air thick with the smell of carnations and flowers in general. I knew where I was but not why I was awake. Maybe Kurt hadn't given me as much of the drug as he had at the wedding. I was in a hearse. It was moving.

I'd always wondered what it would smell like in the back of a hearse. Flowers.

Someone was talking. I couldn't hear who or where the person was.

The car came to a stop. I waited. Water dripped onto my face. I tried to hold my breath as the car rocked. Someone got out. Footsteps on gravel. The backdoor opened. A rush of fresh air found its way through the gap in the body bag. I tried not to suck the fresh air greedily into my lungs.

Mike spoke, "Thank you for understanding."

"God be with you, young man."

I figured that was the funeral director. The gurney I was on shot backwards and bumped to the ground. I bit my lip preventing any noise from escaping my mouth.

A car door opened. The gurney bumped over the

ground, jiggling me unmercifully, as I fought to remain stiff. My teeth chomped into my lip. I tasted blood again. Dead people don't bleed. I hoped the funeral director didn't open the bag.

I forced my body to stiffen as I felt myself lifted, or at least I felt the body bag lift. My head bumped into something hard. Another door opened and the body bag moved along a smooth surface, hard but comfortable. Hands pulled the bag from near my head. I imagined it ripping and me tumbling out. Other hands pushed against my feet. It took concentration to remain still. Stiff. Two doors slammed. More talking, then the vehicle carrying me drove away.

I had no idea how far we'd traveled before I heard Mike calling my name and I finally bent my legs a little and relaxed.

"Ellie, you okay in there?"

I worked the zip down, until my head was free, and then worked it down some more until I could get my arms out. I could still taste blood and my lip had swollen.

"I am now. Fuck, it was hot in there."

"That's because you're breathing. I guess most people who travel in body bags don't."

I looked around. "Where are we?"

"On our way to a new hotel. We're going to Maryland."

"Can I get out of this thing?"

"Want help?"

"Think I can do it. And where is everyone?"

"Kurt, Lee and Sam are about half an hour behind us.

Iain and his crew are about an hour ahead."

Mike turned down a small country lane and pulled over. He stopped the engine and got out of the car. The back door opened. I unzipped the bag all the way and rolled out. Not the easiest thing to do in a wedding dress. Mike's hand reached for mine to help me down out of the Suburban.

I stood, free of the body bag, on the side of the lane in my wedding dress. I wiped my hand across my mouth. A cut fat lip: that was a good look. "Please tell me you have clothes for me."

Mike reached in and dragged a bag over to the door. I opened it to find new clothes and a folded sports bag.

"Who had time to do this?"

"Iain, I think," he replied, unzipping the dress without me asking.

I stepped out of the gown. Mike bundled it up with the body bag. I pulled off the wig and stuffed that into the body bag as well before he put it into the sports bag and zipped it shut. I pulled a long-sleeved tee shirt over my head, followed by a hoodie. I spotted my boots under a pair of jeans in the bag. Socks, jeans, boots. Dressed and comfortable.

I smiled at Mike. I could taste the blood from my lip.

His right eyebrow rose. "You still look hot, even in dead makeup, with a bloody lip and a hoodie."

Makeup.

Yeah, that's what I took from that.

"Makeup?"

"Check the side pocket of the bag."

Makeup removal wipes. I took the packet and climbed into the front passenger seat. I tipped the vanity mirror down and inspected the cut on my lip. It'd heal fast, it just felt weird. I started wiping off the makeup.

"What'd you do, bite your lip?" Mike asked as he fired up the engine.

"Yeah. Gurneys dropping out the back of a hearse are a bit bumpy."

Imagine that?

"Let's hit the road."

"I already did but technically I was on a gurney when I hit the road."

"Wiseass."

Scenery flashed past. It all looked the same. Fields, small towns, fields, small towns. Monotonous. I closed my eyes and let the motion carry me away.

When I woke up, I was sitting in the car alone outside a drugstore. One I didn't recognize. I swiveled in the seat and scanned the parking lot. Two pickups, an SUV, and Sam walking toward me from a car parked about fifteen yards away.

I opened my door. "Hey, where is everyone?"

"Around, Chicky. We're setting up a base. Sean is on his way back to D.C."

"And Mike?"

Sam shook his head. "He's supposed to leave once we switch you to our car and go to the nearest airport. They're waiting for him in LA."

"Supposed to?"

"Lee said Mike got hold of his management and told them due to the circumstances he was staying with his brother for another week."

"Did he now ..."

Sam did the eyebrow-chin-lift thing in affirmation.

"Damn." I didn't want to have to worry about his safety while we tried to find the hacker/killer/Unsub and clear my sullied name. I sucked my swollen lip because I couldn't chew it.

"Chicky, is there something we should know about you and Prince Charming?"

"No, Sam, not a thing."

His large hand patted my shoulder. "You sure about that?"

"Yes, I am."

Automatic doors slid open. Mike stepped out of the store and pushed a pair of sunglasses on. He was carrying a large paper grocery bag.

"Sam, everything okay?" Mike opened the driver's door, reached in and placed the bag on my knee. "Hey, sleepy head."

"Hey," I replied.

"We following you, Sam?" Mike asked.

"Yes."

"Okay, lead the way."

Sam winked at me and ran across the blacktop to the waiting car.

Mike turned the engine over. "Take a look in the bag,"

he said, while he waited for Kurt to pull out of the parking lot. "Thought you might be hungry. You missed a few meals."

I opened the bag and peered inside. Food. An assortment of sandwiches, some candy bars, and bottled water.

"Fantastic, thanks."

I settled the bag on the floor by my feet. Mike followed Kurt down a road. I watched him check his mirrors every few minutes and tap his fingers on the steering wheel in time to music on the radio. He looked relaxed and I felt relaxed. Experience told me I was relaxed, an unusual turn of events considering I was still wanted for murder and unarmed.

"Everything all right?" Mike asked without taking his eyes off the road.

"Why aren't you on your way back to Los Angeles?"

"My wife died, I'm taking time to give her a private burial and spend some time with my brother."

"And the real reason?"

"I don't want to go yet."

"I'm not the one for you." I leaned against the headrest. "If things were different, maybe, but they're not."

"We'll see."

An hour of silence passed. I blamed Kurt and his handy syringe of compliance medicine as my eyes closed again.

Chapter Forty Nine
Where Are We Now?

"Ellie, wake up," Mike said, leaning close to me. I felt his fingers stroke my face. "You awake?"

I opened an eye and looked at him. "I am now." Both eyes opened. "Are we here?"

"We are definitely here," he replied with a wry grin. "We were there, now we're here."

"Smartass."

I pulled up my hood and tucked my hair inside. We'd parked outside a motel room. Kurt's car was next to ours, beyond that I saw Iain's, and then Tim Cosgrove's. The motel was in luck, we must've just about booked out one whole wing.

Kurt tapped on my window. I zapped it down.

"Base is here?"

"Yep," he handed me a key attached to a large red tag. A real key, not a plastic card. Old school. "It goes, Iain, me and Sam, you, Lee and Mike, then Cosgrove."

"Thanks," I said checking the number on the key. "Internet?"

"Yes. There will be a card in the room somewhere with the instructions to access their wireless."

"Laptop?"

"Yes, I'll bring it over to you soon. Go get settled."

I zapped up the window, picked up the brown

shopping bag, clutched the key in my hand and eased out of the car. Mike reached over and pulled the door shut from the inside. He met me at the door to my unit and wrestled the key from my fingers.

Mike plugged the key into the lock then swung the door open. It wasn't as bad as I expected: dated décor, circa nineteen-eighty. I dropped the bag onto the table and inspected the bathroom. Large, clean, well lit. No problem. I bounced on the bed; comfortable. Bit of overkill with the television. A large flat-screen television adorned the wall, almost wider than the double bed.

"It's fine," I said. "Are my bags in the trunk?"

"Yes, I'll get them."

"I can do it."

"I'll get them, you eat something."

I let him go. Stunned by my lack of contrariness, I turned my attention to unpacking the drug store bag. I set the food out on the table and chose a turkey and salad sandwich.

The car door slammed and Mike reappeared with two bags in one hand, and one in the other. He dropped one by the door and set two bags on my bed. Then shoved the door shut.

Workwise there was no need for us to be together now his stalker was in custody, Laura was dead, and he was grieving.

"Taste okay?" he asked, motioning to the sandwich.

"Yep." I said and took another bite. I was hungry. Very hungry.

Perched on the end of the bed, I switched on the television and flicked through channels until I found a news channel.

Mike sat on the lone chair. "Looking for anything in particular?"

"Just want to get the lay of the land," I replied. Behind the news presenter's shoulder I saw a photo I recognized. Us, in the hotel garden in our wedding gear. "Look, it's us."

"We made a good couple," Mike commented.

I turned up the sound.

The presenter talked of our spur of the moment yet traditional wedding and then Laura's untimely death. She finished with confirmation that Mike would not return to Los Angeles until after a private funeral in Richmond, Virginia.

I smiled. No one was expecting to see him in Maryland. Good.

There was nothing on the news about me being wanted for murder or body parts being discovered anywhere in Washington. That was odd. I knew how persistent and rat-like reporters could be, so why wasn't someone reporting on that story?

We channel-surfed, pausing to watch partial programs. I ate two sandwiches and then went into the bathroom. I turned on the shower then closed the bathroom door.

Showered and dressed again, I gave myself a long hard look in the mirror. Didn't look too bad considering I was dead. Nice to be me again. Blonde with bangs. No more wigs.

"Ellie?" Mike tapped on the door.

"It's open," I said.

The handle turned and door swung in. "You're back," he said looking at my hair. "Blonde, blue-eyed, and lethal. I'm a lucky man."

I laughed. "Idiot."

He grinned.

I felt like me. It was a good feeling. So much so that I put my shoulder holster and gun back on over my long-sleeved tee shirt.

Kurt had brought a laptop and my phone over. The phone battery sat next to them on the table.

Lee and Mike were talking outside the motel door as Sam came in.

"That bug on Owen is still working. She is going to Richmond hoping to speak to Mike after your funeral."

I grinned. "Good, the farther away she stays the better."

"It won't take her long to realize there is no funeral, Chicky."

"Then let's organize one." I left the motel room, and tried to remember which room was Iain's. I turned right and walked back a room, knocking on the next door. As he opened the door, I said, "Can you organize a private funeral in Richmond? Owen wants to talk to Mike after Laura's funeral ... I'd like her out of the way."

Iain smiled and nodded. "It would be my pleasure. Let

me see what I can do from here." He opened his laptop and sat at the small table. He looked up at me. "This might be one of those times when a doppelgänger is a handy thing."

I knew where he was going: a Mike Fisher look-a-like and a private funeral. Owen could wait around with the paparazzi outside the chapel all she liked. The only person she'd be talking to really would know nothing about anything. Good for him and good for me.

"Two doppelgängers would be better, see if you can find someone who looks like Lee, too. Go for a Tony Sharron from Grange look-a-like and modify him to be less like a rocker."

"Was already thinking along those lines."

"Excellent. Make it so."

Iain laughed. "I'm glad you didn't say Number One."

I grinned and left him to it.

My next stop was Kurt's room. The door was open. I called out, "Kurt?"

"Come on in," he called back and emerged from the bathroom with wet hair, doing up his shirt. He glanced at me then finished with this buttons. "Everything all right?"

"Yes. Iain is setting up a fake funeral in Richmond. Sam told me Owen is expecting to talk to Mike after the funeral ... so we're making it look like he and Lee are there."

"Now what?"

"I need to find the Unsub and fast."

"Any clue where to look?"

"Not really." I rocked on my heels. "Anyone heard from Kennedy or Praskovya?"

"Not that I know of."

"So what do you want to do now?"

"I'd like to get the results from the fingerprints I took from the bank. Let's get onto Sean and get those. Find out if the other foot belongs to Beatrice Connelly. Get Sandra to snoop into the Metro case and see how many more parts have shown up. Also, get me a map and mark the locations of the body parts."

"You're back on deck?"

"Damn straight. While you're at it, get me the video surveillance of the bank. Whoever went into my safety deposit box had to go past several cameras."

"Anything else?"

"Yeah, when I give the word I want us all back on the grid."

"Okay."

Lee and Mike leaned against one of the cars, still talking. Instead of interrupting them, I gave a small wave as I passed. Back in my room I sat at the small table.

I opened the laptop, plugged in the power cord sitting on the table next to my phone and read the card explaining how to access the Wi-Fi.

In a few seconds, I was online again. As long as I didn't access Sentinel, I would be fairly invisible. I used a high anonymity proxy server to access my email account, then gave the server instructions to piggyback on an ISP from

Richmond, Virginia. Would be fun to let Owen think I was in Richmond.

Playing with the Evil Queen amused me.

Scrolling through over two hundred emails sitting in my inbox checking the subject line of each one was laborious, all the while hoping for something useful.

A subject line jumped out at me. "Connelly Family." Not my favorite subject but it definitely caught my attention.

I opened the email then opened a program that allowed me to capture headings from emails and trace their origin back to an ISP. Before reading the email, I copied the message source information into my handy little program and hit the search button. I didn't think for one minute that the hacker would have been stupid enough to allow me to find his real ISP but sooner or later, he would slip up.

The program dinged. I read the screen. It came up as a private address. I opened another program, this time one supplied to me by the CIA. I put the ISP address in.

Lee spoke from my open doorway. "What have you got?"

"An email from the Unsub, apparently he grew tired of trying to find me."

"Read it out."

"'Dear Agent Conway, You are starting to annoy me. I thought for sure the contract on you would end this cat-and-mouse game we are playing. Why don't you just turn yourself into the FBI? It's time to pay the piper, Conway.

Charlotte was not payment enough.'"

Time to pay the piper: when the Pied Piper wasn't paid he took the children. Thoughts in my brain sent sparks in all directions. Charlotte wasn't a high enough profile target. He wouldn't have gotten enough cash for her. Whoever he was selling to got off on who the kid was more than the fact that it was a kid. Sick bastards. I imagined the daughter of a well-known FBI agent would fetch a good price.

"Ellie?"

I held my hand. "Wait." The sparks continued flying and created fire. "He's been taking high-profile kids. He wanted Carla but didn't get her because she took her own life ... he somehow found out she had kept the conversations. Having those where I could accidentally access them would end his profitable business. So he breaks in and takes the laptop ... he's going to make me pay. He takes the photos and frames me for the death of Eddie. Guess that was fun for him. That wasn't enough. When I didn't immediately get arrested, he upped his game. He chopped up Beatrice, too. Then he used information he'd gathered from my devices to open my safety deposit box and leave my confession. But that wasn't enough. So he put out an open contract. But everyone who came after me was never heard from again."

"This is about kids?"

"It was. Then it became about revenge."

"And?"

495

"He probably wouldn't have bothered with any of it if it wasn't for Operation Jericho."

The fire burst forth into orange and yellow flames.

"Kurt was involved in Jericho. The hacker was monitoring me. He would've overheard conversations or seen emails, whatever, where Kurt and I mentioned Operation Jericho."

"Jericho?"

"Yeah. Can't explain, can explain ... we need Kennedy. I think I know where the Unsub is or at least was."

"Try explaining ..."

Words danced in the fire, then formed bizarre shapes as they contorted in flaming trees. Palm fronds made from words flowed like a torrent down the trunks and onto a beach. Torrent. Location.

"Operation Jericho is Owen's operation. She took over when a kid they had in protective custody was grabbed from a safe house or some so-called safe environment. The kid was hurt, and Kurt was brought in to tend to her. I don't have many details nor does Kurt. We do know the kid is Israeli. I suspect her father is high profile, which made her a target. The Unsub made two failed attempts at grabbing this kid. I guess in his eyes, I stood in the way of this kid and of Carla."

"Ellie, your mind ..."

Is a furnace of heated crazy?

"But wait, Jericho is also known as the City of Palm Trees." The program where I'd dumped the email header code pinged. I had a location for the private address. I love CIA programs. "Our Unsub is based in Palm Beach, Florida."

Flaming fronds threw jumbled letters on the white sand. The letters burned, turning the sand into molten glass. The shiny letters shuffled. Words appeared. Palm Florida. As I watched, the molten letters rearranged themselves and spelled out a name across the sand. Mal P I La Ford. I felt a smile etch into my face. It was like pulling Joaunes name out of the words I saw on the window of our hotel room in Fairfax. Seeing words inside words. Awesome. Wishing Lee could see inside my head I said, "The fiery letters in the sand wrote a name."

"Fiery what? Told you what now?"

"The name of the Unsub." I jumped to my feet and ran out the door to Iain Campbell's room. Without knocking I flung open the door. "Can you get hold of Seamus Kennedy?"

He nodded and gave me his phone.

I scrolled through his contacts until I found Kennedy. "This him?" I asked, showing Iain the entry.

"Yes."

I hit the call button on the screen and waited. As soon as he answered, I said, "It's SSA Conway. The Unsub, the guy you want. He's based in Palm Beach, Florida. His name could be Mal P I La Ford."

"Conway, you're a fecking charm. We'll let you know as soon as we find anything."

"Thanks." I hung up and threw the phone to Iain.

"You amaze me," he said, then went back to whatever

he was doing before my interruption.

I took off back to my room and the laptop, where Lee waited.

"Name? You shot out of here without saying the name."

"Mal P I La Ford," I said with a smile.

"Okay, let's do it, you need to check any more of these emails?" he asked, pointing to the screen.

"Nope, forward the one on screen to Owen, Sean and Cait O'Hare, will ya?"

"Proxy?"

"Of course. Let's make sure she won't get any location information from the email."

"Done."

He started a good old-fashioned search engine hunt on the name I'd pulled from the fire.

I paced up and down the room until Lee told me to go find something else to do. I saw Mike walk past the window. "I'll be back."

Lee waved without looking up.

Chapter Fifty
The Future

Mike spun around as I walked up behind him.

"Hot chick with a gun following me. I love my life." He smiled at me. "You look different. Happier."

"I'm closer to resuming my life."

"Damn, thought it was me."

"We need to talk."

"That doesn't sound good."

It really didn't. It sounded sensible. "Your room?"

"What about yours?" he asked.

"Your brother is in there working."

"Mine then."

He led the way, opened the door and stood aside. The room much the same as mine and smelled like man. Not unpleasant, just manly.

I chose the lone chair. Seemed a safer option than either of the double beds. Mike sat on a bed with his body angled toward me. His eyes barely blinked.

"You look nervous," he said.

I swallowed. My pulse raced. "Michael ..." I forgot about my previously cut lip and tried to chew it. That didn't work either. I wiped my sweaty palms on my thighs.

"Formal."

It felt like a formal situation. "Okay, the thing is ...

Michael."

"Still formal."

I sighed, more impatient with myself than his interruptions. "Just let me talk."

"You need help with this?"

"No ..." I closed my eyes for few a seconds and centered myself. When I opened my eyes, it all seemed so much clearer. "I like you. You're easy to be around ..." I searched for the words that would send him back to LA for good but nicely. "However, you married Laura and she died. So, we can't *be* because some clever dick will think I look familiar and compare my image with Laura's and figure it out."

"What if—"

"There are no 'what ifs.'"

His smile faltered but only for an instant. Mike lowered his voice, "You know what I want. I told you outright." His eyes shone as he supported his elbows on his knees, fingers entwined. "Tell me, Ellie, what do you want?"

I shook my head. "I want to go home. I want my name cleared and I want to go home."

"What's at home?"

"My life."

"Is there someone?"

I smiled. I couldn't help it. Technically, no, there wasn't but there could be. And the *could be* was worth everything.

"Go back to Los Angeles, Mike."

"What if I want to stay for a while?"

"We can never be seen together."

"Never?"

"People have long memories. Very long memories. Biometric databases never expire."

"But—"

"You're hard to dissuade aren't you?"

"When I know what I want."

"I'm sure that works great for you ninety-nine per cent of the time. Meanwhile, go back to LA."

He grinned. "Okay."

"Thank you. Now, if you'll excuse me, I'm hoping my running gear is in one of those bags." I could hear Kurt telling me not to run any marathons today and to take it easy. I wasn't planning on a marathon, just a light run to clear my head.

Chapter Fifty One
Should I Stay Or Should I Go?

Late afternoon turned into early evening.

We still hadn't heard from Kennedy. Lee had gathered a lot of information from search engines, so we knew more about La Ford.

A pillar of the community, old money and lots of it, which fitted with everything we'd surmised so far. He had some influential political friends in the form of several senators and a few Governors. He wasn't shy about contributing to campaigns. More digging revealed he also had connections to a company that held military contracts and developed software for covert application.

"Hey, Lee, the software thing ... SkyWiper, ya think?"

"Sean might know who really developed it. Open searches aren't going to find that information."

I picked up his phone and called Sean. "It's me."

"I was about to call you. One print came back as identifiable."

I held my breath.

"Malcolm Peter Ivan La Ford, last known address Palm Beach, Florida"

"What database?"

"I got hits back from several ... he has a string of traffic violations and is under investigation for the corruption of minors. He's doing his best to have the investigation squashed by pulling in favors."

My head spun. I was right. Jesus. "I came up with that name a few hours ago. Now, we have confirmation. Send me a photo. I want to match it to the surveillance from the bank."

"Will do. Emailing now."

I nudged Lee and whispered to him to check my email account, then said to Sean, "Can you find out if La Ford's connections with Crystal Tech mean he could've accessed SkyWiper?"

"If he paid enough, he could get it from anyone selling it. I can't confirm if Crystal Tech is the US company suspected of helping to create the malware."

"Is he techy or is someone working this angle for him?"

"From what I could tell, he's very much tech savvy. The guy went to MIT, so he's about as connected as it's possible to get."

MIT. Massachusetts Institute of Technology. That's one hell of a private research university. "Sean, how's Cait?"

"She's okay, waiting for you to get her information so she can call off the dogs."

"I'm working on it. We have a name. You have a print. Where was it?"

"On the letter."

Yes. The best possible place. "Keep me posted."

"Conway – keep your head down a little longer, okay? Let's all get the evidence before you charge at Owen, guns blazing."

Owen. Dammit. There was one other thing I needed to know.

"I need you to do something else for me, Sean." In my head it sounded possible but I knew the words I was about to say were game changers.

"Go ahead," Sean said.

"Dig into Owen and La Ford. I need to know if they've ever crossed paths and how."

"You serious?"

"Yes. Misha said something about the person in charge of Operation Jericho ... he suspected someone was leaking information."

"You think it was Owen? Your judgment isn't clouded at all?"

A smile settled on my lips. "My judgment is completely fucked when it comes to the Evil Queen. We still have to check."

"I'll look into it."

"Thanks."

"Meanwhile, Ellie, wait. Just wait. It's all coming together."

"I know. I just want to go home."

"You will, meanwhile go do Mike. I heard he won't leave."

"He is going home. Smart ass." I hung up.

Lee waited patiently for me to fill him in.

He grinned. "A clear print and an ID. Chicky, we're going home soon."

"Soon."

I gave him back his phone and headed out the door to find the rest of Delta A. Behind me the phone rang.

"Ellie, wait up, this could be important."

I turned to see Lee holding the phone in front of him. He pressed the speaker icon. I waited. "Lee Davenport," he said.

A familiar voice filled the room. "Agent Davenport, this is Deputy Director Thomas. I've been at my desk for the last four hours trying to ascertain what the hell is going on with Delta A."

"Yes, sir." Lee took a breath. "We're in a spot of trouble, sir."

"That's quite obvious, Agent. What are you going to do about it?"

"We're working on it, sir."

"How close are you to a solution?"

"Close. We've made good headway in the last day. Sir, SSA Conway did not kill or dismember Edward Connelly."

"I would be extremely surprised if she had, Agent. However, the entire Delta team is facing a disciplinary hearing. I have some very unflattering reports from Assistant Director Owen regarding your collective behavior over this situation," Thomas said with his customary southern drawl.

Lee pursed his lips.

I took a breath and said, "Deputy Director Thomas. We're coming home as soon as we have the last few things needed to prove I had nothing to do with my

505

former brother-in-law's death. Meanwhile, we have successfully completed the stalking case. We forwarded our reports to the office after the arrest of the perpetrator."

"I've already seen your reports, Agent Conway," he replied with a slow drawl. "Am I up to speed? Is there anything you need to tell me before you come in?"

"No, sir."

"How's your father?"

"I don't know, sir. I haven't been able to contact him."

"I do hope this nonsense hasn't overtaxed him. I believe he's had heart trouble in the past."

"I'm sure he's fine."

Nice tactic but that won't work on me. I have enough guilt.

"You are a lucky woman, Agent Conway."

"Sir?"

I feel real lucky. Being on the run seems real lucky.

"Not everyone has such a good friend in Director O'Hare."

"Yes, sir."

"Bring Delta A home, Agent Conway."

"Soon, sir." I ran my hand in the air under my chin. Lee disconnected the call.

He looked at me. "Ever noticed how a southern drawl can sound menacing despite the words?" he asked.

"Yep," I replied. "Let's dot our i's and cross our t's. We don't want anything to go wrong once we hit D.C."

If it did, a disciplinary action would be the least of our

worries.

Chapter Fifty Two
Going Home

At eight in the morning, we stood in a huddle behind our cars in the parking lot outside the motel.

Working as one, we reactivated our phones.

Everyone's phones lit up like Christmas trees and sang myriad tunes as messages downloaded at an alarming rate. We were back on the grid.

Several minutes disappeared in the cacophony of cell phone message beeps and ring tones. I had over seven hundred new messages. About six hundred were tweets from my Twitter account. It would be easier to delete them all and just send one tweet saying I was well and on my way home. I considered I should probably add the Butterflykids hashtag to the tweet, just to make sure all the kids from my Foundation got the message.

I paused over several messages from Mitch, reading them with care. Then I walked away a few feet and made a call. He answered on the fourth ring.

"Hey, fancy a run tomorrow?" Assuming I wouldn't be in jail by morning.

"Yes, I want to run tomorrow," he said. A smile evident in his voice. "You okay?"

"I am now. Meet you at the usual place. Seven a.m."

"Already looking forward to it. You going to tell me where you've been and what happened?"

"Yep, it's going to be a long run."

I smiled as I hung up and walked back to the group and continued reading some of the most recent text messages. One message in particular needed action. I walked away again watched by the group of men and made a call.

"It's Ellie Conway. What do you have?"

I listened to Seamus Kennedy's voice, concentrating on the content, not his lilting Irish brogue. "Using the information you shared with us, we found La Ford." He paused, I could hear noises in the background. A plane? Kennedy spoke again, "He didn't expect anyone to come for him. For all his clever shenanigans, he did not know about us."

"And?" The background noise grew louder.

"We got him. We also got his laptop. He is Mr. RightGuy. You are not to go near him, Conway. Don't. Not you and not Delta A. I will send the coordinates of the warehouse where he is but let another team bring him in."

My insides froze. He was right and I hated it. No way could Delta be involved in the arrest, not when La Ford was the man who'd tried to groom Carla.

"What sort of condition is he in?"

"Not great. We extracted his confession. He'll recant, saying it was under duress."

"Was it?" as soon as the question left my mouth I knew it was stupid to even ask.

"Not as far as we are concerned, Conway," Kennedy

said. "We're not bound by your rules."

A smile tweaked the edges of my mouth. "Would I have enjoyed it?"

"I believe so."

"Thank you." The Owen thing popped up again. "Did he mention Assistant Director Owen?"

"He said a lot of things. Her name came up. Watch the video."

"Thank you again."

"It's been a pleasure, Conway. Sorry about your house." The background grew in volume. The plane was about to take off. "We uploaded the confession to YouTube a few moments ago. Everything you need to prosecute La Ford is on its way to the Hoover Building via courier. I wish I could tell you why Carla took her own life, but I can't. I can tell you without any doubt that La Ford was the man she was talking to on Skype and that he targeted her because she'd fetch a high price."

It was all about me.

"Take care, Kennedy." I hung up and spent a few minutes thinking about what Seamus Kennedy had told me. I could feel everyone's eyes on me as I paced up and down the parking lot. With a sigh and a deep breath I settled the information and forced the sick feeling away. It was my fault Carla took her own life and nothing could be done about that. Dead is dead. The living have to find a way to go on.

With purpose in my stride I rejoined the throng. "We're going home," I said. "Kennedy assured me everything we need is with a courier heading for the Hoover Building. And just in case it's not, there is a copy of La Ford's confession uploaded to YouTube."

Lee had his phone out and found the YouTube link. We watched in silence. La Ford looked like he'd gone ten rounds with a gorilla.

"Pause, roll it back, hit play," I instructed after hearing Owen's name. Three times I listened to La Ford splutter about his relationship with Owen and how she'd help him and he'd never stand trial. "Family friends? Really?"

"Lee, forward that link to the reporter who helped us at the Museum of Natural History. Let her know I will make myself available for an interview as soon as I can."

"Doing it."

If all else failed, I trusted that one reporter to set the record straight.

Kennedy had obtained the real location for Eddie and Beatrice's bodies from La Ford. They were not buried in my garden. They were buried in a park near the Connelly family home. The exact coordinates were sent directly to Director O'Hare by Misha Praskovya.

"And La Ford is where?" Sam asked.

"Being held at a secure location within D.C., waiting for someone to arrest him, but not us." I checked the messages on my phone and found a new one from Kennedy containing the coordinates. That was the message I forwarded to Delta B and Caine Grafton with a note to pick him up and why.

Everyone smiled; even Iain Campbell wore a smile on

his usually serious face.

Tim Cosgrove walked around the circle and tapped on my shoulder. "I'm off, take care."

"Thank you for sticking around and for helping me get Delta back."

"Stay in touch."

"Definitely."

He shook my hand and walked away. Iain was next. He didn't shake my hand. He punched me lightly in the arm and wished me luck.

It was just us and Mike.

Mike hugged me. "It's been an adventure, Mrs. Fisher."

"That it has, Mr. Fisher."

I waved as he climbed into his rental car and drove away. Standing in front of my team I asked a question, "How are we going to handle the Owen-La Ford situation?"

My phone rang: a video call from Executive Assistant Director Owen.

"Speak of the devil," I muttered answering the call. "Executive Assistant Director Owen."

"SSA Conway."

I held the phone in front of me, so the team could all see and hear. "What can I do for you, ma'am?"

A little crucifixion?

"Time you came home," Owen said, as a small smile tweaked one corner of her mouth.

"Anything you want to say?" I was all about pushing

my luck and not tipping my hand.

"We'll talk about it when you get home—"

"Let's do it now."

"Don't push it, SSA Conway."

"I want to hear it now."

"You did not murder Edward Connelly or Beatrice Connelly."

"And?"

"Conway, this is not appropriate," she warned.

"Putting out a warrant for my arrest was not appropriate," I said, mustering calm.

She gave a minimalistic nod. "You were not in any way involved in their deaths. All charges relating to the Connellys have been dropped."

That wasn't enough, not after what she put Delta through. "Is that it?"

"What more do you want?"

"An admission that you were wrong."

Another minimalistic nod. "I was wrong and I should have handled the situation better."

"Thank you, ma'am."

"There will be a disciplinary hearing."

I already knew that. There was no way to avoid it, it didn't matter how many influential friends I had. I'd rappelled across too many lines and there were consequences. On the plus side, Owen's involvement would be in the spotlight and once everything came out about her connection to La Ford I doubted she'd keep her job. She could even end up in a federal prison. I found it hard not to smile at the thought of the Evil Queen behind bars. Less satisfactory was the fact that Misha Praskovya would take some heat for his part in the whole mess.

"We're coming home," I said, staring down the camera at Owen. "Hope you're ready."

Courage, it would seem, is nothing less than the power to overcome danger, misfortune, fear, injustice, while continuing to affirm inwardly that life with all its sorrows is good; that everything is meaningful even if in a sense beyond our understanding; and that there is always tomorrow.

Dorothy Thompson.

We hope you enjoyed Databyte by Cat Connor. Please turn the page for a preview of the next exciting book in the –byte series by Cat Connor:

Eraserbyte
Chapter One

Chasing Pavements

"Interesting?" Kurt asked.

"Email from a CI of mine. Suspicious activity at an abandoned factory. The CI thinks someone is being held there."

"Is this confidential informant reliable?"

"Usually. We'll go check it out." I picked up the phone on my desk and called Sam and Lee, "We got a job," and hung up.

Moments later they appeared in the doorway.

"Chicky," Lee said with a grin, "we're ready to roll."

Forty-five minutes later we stood in the rain across the road from the factory in question. There were no signs of life.

"Let's do it," I said. "Gear up."

Gloomy, cold, and draughty. Not a fan of abandoned old factories. Puddles lay on the floor. There were better places to be during a thunderstorm, especially when the structure leaked like a sieve. Another clap of thunder above shook the walls and vibrated under my feet. Water trickled down the wall on my left, feeding a large puddle in the broken concrete.

My LEDs on my flashlight lit up the area with white light. I scanned the walls. Lee was with me. Sam and Kurt were behind us.

"On your three o'clock," I called to Sam.

The flashlight illuminated a solid metal door. I kept moving forward but looked back quickly as he turned ninety degrees. With a reverberating clang, the door hit a wall. Kurt and Sam disappeared.

Moments later, I heard Sam's voice. "Clear."

Lee looked at me.

"Our nine," he said as his flashlight shone on a doorway and more puddles.

"Got it."

I followed Lee into the room. He went right. I went left. Nothing but decrepit machinery, rusted out hunks of metal, and more puddles.

"Clear," Lee said.

We moved on.

I wanted to move on completely and go home. It was a miserable afternoon. The dank corridor stretched in front of us with no end in sight.

A door banged. The echo bounced off the walls and slammed into us, directional information confused by the echo.

"Where was that?" I asked.

"Ahead?" Lee said, glancing over his shoulder at Sam for confirmation.

Sam nodded. "Ahead. The tip off might have been right. Someone is in here."

Or a big rat can close doors?

I felt Sam and Kurt close behind us. We had walked

two abreast earlier but in single file now. Lee had point, then me, then Kurt, then Sam in the rear.

Another door closed. This time it closed quietly.

"They know we're here," I whispered to Lee.

That was a given. We weren't exactly in stealth mode.

"Yeah, carefully does it," he replied. "They have the upper hand for now."

Counting paces helped me control my breathing and heart rate. It also meant I knew it was twenty-four feet before we saw another doorway and the closed door. Lee stopped. We listened for signs of life.

Barely breathing.

A tap or knock, so faint none of us would have heard it had we been moving at all. Could be our suspect inside. Lee nodded. We stood in pairs on either side of the door. I drew my weapon.

Lee leaned forward and twisted the doorknob. Locked.

I heard a distinctive metallic noise.

"Gun," I said. We stepped back as gunfire erupted. Bullets didn't penetrate the solid wooden door. "Hand gun, not a big-hole gun. Nine mil maybe," I muttered. "Or the door has a steel core?"

"We passed through fire doors at the beginning of this corridor. Looked like they separated the offices from the main factory area," Sam said, his voice low. "I think this door is just solid old wood."

He could be right. Old factory – fewer fire codes back in the day so probably no need for more fire doors?

Sam pumped the shotgun. We were about to find out if

the door had a steel core or not.

Breaching rounds. Not a time for being subtle.

He stepped up. I covered my ears and turned away.

"Knock knock!" Sam hollered as he fired two rounds at the hinges of the door and then one at the lock. Wood splintered. The smell of gunpowder filled the air. Sam gave the door a kick. It fell inward, crashing to the ground. Kurt and Lee were first across the smashed up door. In the corner of the room huddled under a blanket lay a human shape.

"Show me your hands?" I yelled at the quivering form.

Kurt and Sam followed sounds coming through a hole in the wall.

A hand came out from under the blanket, then the second. Small hands on small wrists. The blanket fell off her thin shoulders, exposing a short strappy top. The young woman remained huddled in the blanket.

"Are you hurt?" I asked, stepping closer. I let my flashlight beam rest on the woman and the blanket. She looked cold but the area she was in was dry.

"No," she said. "I am Sonya." An accent. Not American.

"What are you doing here?" I asked.

Lee moved up and lifted the blanket away, looking for weapons. He stood her up and searched her for weapons. She wore a small top with spaghetti straps and a very short skirt. Barefoot, in need of a shower, decent clothes, and a meal, by the look of her. I'd seen better dressed bag ladies with more meat on their bones.

"This is where I live," she replied with a strange slow

deliberation, like she was reading a script but the words had no meaning.

"And why are you in America?"

"I come from Croatia for better life." Again the same slow deliberation.

Learned responses?

"How's that working out for you?" I asked.

She didn't reply. Guess that question wasn't part of the script.

Lee signaled she was weapon-free and carried no identification.

She sank back to the cold ground, gathering the blanket around her. Lee moved to the other side of the room. His new position allowed him to watch me and the door.

A yell from Kurt spiraled out the dark hole in the wall. Footsteps pounded over wet ground moving toward us.

I turned to face the sound. Lee did the same.

Kurt's voice rang out, "Stop. FBI!"

A person erupted from the gloom. A gun, clearly visible.

The woman under the blanket squeaked and curled up smaller.

"Drop the weapon!" I aimed at the disheveled mess in front of me. "Drop it!"

The gun in the person's hand wobbled from side to side. I could feel Lee's muscles tense from across the room as he assessed the situation. Took me a moment to realize it was a woman in front of us with a gun. The gun in her hand steadied.

"Drop it," Lee said.

She squeezed off a round which flew over my head.

"Drop the weapon!" I said.

Her trigger finger moved again. I fired. The bullet slammed into her forehead. A fine spray erupted from the back of her head and hung in the damp air before drifting downward. She buckled then collapsed onto herself and sank into a dirty puddle.

"That went well," I muttered, holstering my weapon.

Kurt and Sam stepped into the room, dodging the body as they did so.

"No one else there. But it looks like several people were living back there," Sam said. "They're in the wind."

Kurt looked at the dead woman then at me. "Your handiwork?"

"Yeah, how'd you know?"

"Head shot ... you still worried about zombies?" He smiled up at me as he did the customary pulse check on the body.

"Zombies are no laughing matter," I replied. "One day you'll thank me for my head shots."

"She had a driver's license on her," Kurt said handing Sam a plastic card.

Sam looked at it then passed it to Lee. "Is this Russian?"

"Yes, and it's her."

I turned to the huddled woman. "Do you know her?"

"Yes. She keeps me."

"Are you a prisoner?"

She frowned.

"Can you leave?"

She shook her head.

I took out my phone and made a call. "It's me. My list for this afternoon. Crime scene techs, paramedics, coroner, scene guards and notify Homeland we found a woman I suspect is a victim of trafficking."

"Coroner?" Sandra repeated.

"She had a guard, too."

"Sending everything to your location." I heard her pause and take a breath. "Everyone okay?"

I smiled. "Delta A is okay."

I knew what that was about. She wanted to ask about Sam. Their not-so-secret relationship looked like a long haul thing to me. It'd been a year since I first noticed something was going on.

I hung up. "Wrap this up. Then we're off for the weekend," I said. "As soon as our people arrive I'll head back with Kurt and get the case file updated."

Sam and Lee nodded.

"Good result, Conway," Kurt said. "We got a live one."

It felt too easy. Or I felt uneasy. I wasn't sure which.

About the Author

Cat Connor is a prolific crime thriller author hailing from New Zealand. Her expertise in the genre is reflected in her engaging and suspenseful narratives, which have garnered a loyal following. Her work is known for its intricate plots, dynamic characters, and relentless pace, keeping readers on the edge of their seats until the very end. She has authored multiple books, including the popular "Byte" series, which follows the exploits of an FBI unit that investigates serial crime.

Cat's passion for crime and espionage is evident in her writing, as she strives to create a world that is both authentic and thrilling. Her meticulous attention to detail and extensive research have won her critical acclaim and accolades from readers and peers alike. In addition to writing, Cat enjoys speaking on topics related to writing and publishing. Her talks are known for their candidness, humour, and practical advice. With her unique blend of talent, expertise, and passion, Cat Connor has established herself as one of the most exciting and accomplished authors in the crime thriller genre.

Her other passions include music, reading, tequila, red wine, coffee, and chocolate. When she's not writing she can be found binge watching TV shows and spending time with her much adored animals; Diesel the mastador,

Patrick the tuxedo cat, Dallas the tortie Birman, and Jimmy the thug.

You can follow and contact Cat at the following places:

Website: www.catconnor.com
Twitter: @catconnor
Facebook: @cat.connor
Instagram: @catconnorauthor
Bluesky: @catconnor.bsky.social
Threads: @catconnorauthor

Also by Cat Connor:

The Kiwi set Veronica Tracey Spy/PI series:
[Nothing happens here] -2020
[Lure the lie] - 2021
[Leave a message] - 2022
[Whiskey Tango Foxtrot] - 2023
[Foxtrot Mike Lima] - 2024

The FBI based Byte Series:
Killerbyte - 2009
Terrorbyte - 2010
Exacerbyte - 2011
Flashbyte - 2012
Soundbyte - 2013
Snakebyte - 2013 (novella)
Databyte - 2014
Eraserbyte - 2015
Psychobyte - 2016
Metabyte - 2017
Qubyte - 2018
Cryptobyte - 2019
Vaporbyte - 2020 (red)
Vaporbyte -2020 (purple)
Raidbyte - 2021 (collection of short bytes)

Whispers in the water - the poetry of SSA Conway and SA Connelly
Torrent - a collection of short bytes